GF   Sept 15.

HELEN R. MYERS

LST

ISBN 0-7394-0855-0

LOST

Visit us at www.mirabooks.com

Printed in U.S.A.

Acknowledgments

With every book a writer's list of indebtedness grows. I would like to thank the following...

Ethan Ellenberg, not only for his input into this story, but for all the support, wisdom and perseverance from day one of our association.

Robert and Lacy Cooper, and Linda Varner Palmer for getting me through that ill-timed computer crash.

Betty and Cindy Meece for bunches, but most of all the Linda Vachon print. You did, indeed, inspire.

For answering questions and sharing anecdotes...

> Wayne Bryant
> Bobby Cole
> Carol and C. F. David
> Brad Taylor
> RCR

And to Burt, whose real "Precious" inspired Michaele into taking on that Cameo restoration in the first place. I can only hope that hers would have come out half as good as yours did.

Just in ratio as knowledge increases, faith diminishes.

—Thomas Carlyle

1

"Where's Faith?"

Her father's slurred question warned Michaele Ramey of two things: first, that despite her attempts to keep an eye on him, the son of a bugger had gotten hold of some hooch again; and second, that, as usual, her sister Faith's word wasn't worth squat.

Too annoyed to risk answering right away, she rolled out from under the '56 Chevy Cameo, and used her cleanest knuckle to carefully rub at the rust particles in her eyes. "There's a hole the size of an egg in her muffler," she told Pete Fite, the watchful owner of the old vehicle. "But I can't patch metal that's turning into confetti. You'll need a new one."

The chicken farmer bowed his head, which had Michaele thinking that the fifty-nine-year-old was beginning to bear a strong resemblance to the poultry he raised on the forty-acre farm on the south side of town. He had the same wide-spaced, blank eyes, the same sharp, beaklike nose, and damned if he wasn't scratching his boot at the concrete floor of the garage the way those razorial critters did when searching for food.

He slowly shook his head. "Can't afford that. Just wrap something around it to get me through inspection. I'll look into buying a new one as soon as I send off the next truck-load of hens."

This time Michaele used the back of her left wrist to wipe at the sweat trickling down her throat. "Why not the next egg shipment? I saw that batch of tired hens being hauled out of your place last week. You won't have another load for a while, and I'm not a magician. Make it the next egg check, Pete."

Shoving his hands deeper into the pockets of overalls that all but swallowed his skinny frame, he gaped. "You'd leave a man with nothing to live on!"

"Oh, stop." Michaele pulled off the baseball cap she'd been wearing backward while under the truck and slapped it against her jeans to shake off any lingering debris, replaced it, and tugged the bill low over her narrowed eyes. "Just sell me the damn thing, already. You'll only let it sit and rust until it's nothing more than a weed-covered snake den—"

"Where's my baby?"

The new whine from her father drew Pete's attention, but when Michaele continued to act as though she hadn't heard anything, he tugged at his earlobe and shrugged. "How much did you say you'd give me for her?"

They went through this every time he came in, which was becoming more frequent thanks to the increasing number of potholes on his lengthy, unpaved driveway. What's more, he knew what he had in the Cameo, as did Michaele. Chevrolet hadn't made over 5,000 of them in '55, and fewer than 1,500 in '56. Considering the growing love affair going on with the American pickup truck, this one would be worth a tidy bundle if sold for parts; a small fortune if restored properly, something Pete had neither the skill nor finances to do. Michaele wanted a chance to try.

''A thousand,'' she replied. ''Less the cost of a new muffler.''

Although that was a couple of hundred dollars more than she'd offered last time, he managed to look offended. ''Can't replace her for that!''

''You want to pay liability insurance and the registration fee on something that'll be illegal to drive in a few days, go ahead. I suppose once you get tired of collecting tickets, you can always use your '73 Ford.''

''Not likely. It's got two flats.''

''Mike!'' Buck snapped, his bloodshot eyes finally focusing on her. ''You hear me, girl? Where's Faithy?''

Michaele shot her father a cold look. Despite his grip on the door frame, he wobbled dangerously, and she found herself half wishing he would topple face first onto the garage floor and knock himself out.

''I'm with a customer,'' she said sharply.

Buck squinted. ''Well, shoot, that's just ol'—'' he hiccuped ''—Pete. Pete, you seen my little girl? Got a call for her inside. She's u-usually back from school by now.''

Yeah, right, Michaele thought sourly as she pushed herself to her feet. Only if the sneak couldn't find somewhere to hide until closing. More often than not, her younger sibling didn't show until Michaele was home putting dinner on the table.

Pete scratched at his thinning silver hair as he pondered Buck's question. ''Nope. Can't say I have.''

Exasperated with the whole situation, Michaele snapped, ''For heaven's sake, Buck, you know Pete lives south of here. Faith commutes to and from Mt. Pleasant, which is north. Tell whomever's on the phone that she hasn't arrived yet and hang up so someone with a real problem can get through!''

She turned back to the town's newest widower. She knew he was in no hurry to leave and would rather spend the rest of the afternoon shooting the breeze with her; but she had too many problems of her own to be swayed by compassion. ''Sorry,'' she said, rising, ''I have to finish servicing Chief Morgan's car, and I promised that it would be done by six. If you want to avoid getting a ticket in two weeks when this expires—'' she nodded to the sticker on the truck's windshield ''—you'll have to come to terms with what that means.''

She wiped her hands on the already filthy rag and shoved it into the back pocket of her jeans, then stepped over to the patrol car still in need of an oil change and lube job.

''Guess I could let her go for the thousand...if you threw in new tires for the '73 to sweeten the deal.''

Michaele almost let out a whoop. She'd been wanting to get her hands on ''Precious'' since she was seventeen, but wasn't about to admit anything of the kind to Pete. Instead she muttered, ''Jeez, Louise. All right, already! Bring the title tomorrow along with those flats, and I'll write you a check.''

''Cash.''

That would mean a trip to the bank, because she didn't keep that kind of money around; it presented too much of a temptation to Buck, who could easily finish drinking himself into a grave on a fraction of the amount. ''Okay, cash it is. I'll hop over to the bank as soon as it opens in the morning.''

''And I'll need a ride home.''

She shot Pete an irritated look. ''Why don't I just adopt you? Never mind,'' she added, as he began to grin. ''Okay,

I'll see that you get home. Now, please, go away and let me earn a nickel.''

Satisfied, Pete left, and Michaele went back to work. But no sooner did she start unscrewing the drain plug from the patrol car's oil pan than a vehicle pulled up to the gas pumps. She listened for the sound of Buck's shuffling steps. When he failed to budge, she called over her shoulder, "Customer!"

After several more seconds, she headed outside herself. "And people ask why I don't smile more," she grumbled under her breath.

Their customer was none other than Reverend George Dollar. Michaele's mood went from soured to curdled. Of the twelve-hundred-seventy-something people currently calling Split Creek home, why did *he* have to be the one driving up?

She circled around the back of the white Escort wagon that the church had inherited several years ago and went straight to the gas tank. "Fill it, Reverend?" she called up front.

He leaned out the driver's window and smiled into the sideview mirror. "Please, Michaele. I was beginning to wonder if anyone was around. You really do need to get that service bell repaired."

"Uh-huh."

The only thing wrong with it was that she'd disconnected the thing. Even when she manned the garage by herself, she would have to go blind and deaf before missing anyone pulling in.

Sliding the pump nozzle into the tank's mouth, she glanced over the car into the station's office-store area. As she'd suspected, her father was slumped on his *throne* again—whether asleep or unconscious, she couldn't tell.

What she could see, though, was that he hadn't put the phone's receiver back into the cradle.

She shook her head. And he insisted the crap he drank wasn't pickling his brain?

"The windshield needs cleaning, Michaele."

Sure it does.

Gritting her teeth, she latched the nozzle for automatic filling and reached for the squeegee soaking in the pail of cleaning liquid at the other end of the island. But she was burned. Damn it all, the old buzzard would have to be gumming the steering wheel to be bothered by the smudge or two on the otherwise sparkling windshield. No, he just wanted her stretched across his hood to get his cheap thrill for the day.

"I was sorry not to see you joining Faith at services Sunday."

She briefly considered enlightening him. The only reason her younger sister went to church was that there were few other excuses to dress up in Split Creek without looking like a lost tourist, and Faith did like to dress up. Not Michaele, though; nor did she have the stomach to sit through any hypocritical sermons, let alone the kissy-huggy stuff that followed those gatherings. However, the businesswoman in her stopped her from being all-out rude to a customer—even a tightwad like George Dollar.

"Well, Reverend, I had an emergency tow," she said, careful to keep her chest away from the windshield.

"I understand. Running a business is a mighty big responsibility on such a pair of small shoulders. Plus, you have sweet Faith counting on you to be both mother and—forgive me—father to her. But that's no excuse to turn your back on the Lord, child."

As he spoke, Michaele could feel his gaze moving over her. She was relieved when the pump suddenly shut off.

Then she glanced back and saw why it had stopped so soon.

Here we go again.

Michaele slammed the squeegee on top of the pump and with jerky movements replaced the nozzle in its holder. As she screwed the fuel cap back on, it was all she could do not to grind her teeth into powder.

"I haven't turned my back on God, Reverend," she said, finally stepping up to the driver's window. "It's just that it's been years since we had much to say to each other. That'll be three-fifty."

He made a great show of patting various pockets. "Dear me...I seem to have misplaced my wallet somewhere."

Was there no limit to the man's nerve?

"Try the glove compartment," she drawled.

"Ah! Of course." Without an iota of embarrassment, he reached into the compartment and soon presented her with a five-dollar bill. "You know, it grieves me to hear you speak with such cynicism, Michaele."

"Well, there's a cure for that, too." She stretched to her full five foot four to dig out change from the front right pocket of her jeans. "From now on, let your tank get closer to *E* before stopping by."

Accepting the money, he wagged a cadaver-white finger at her. "You're not getting off that easy. I'm a patient shepherd, and I will bring you back to God's flock sooner or later."

Michaele glared after him as he pulled away. "Do me and God both a favor," she muttered, "and hold your breath."

She didn't like that he brought out her worst side, but his arrogance irritated her as much as his sneaky sexual leers disgusted her. On the other hand, she allowed, for once maybe it wasn't such a bad thing that Buck was in-

ebriated. Had he been the one serving "the good reverend," he would have let the charity hog have the gas free,
thinking it would make him points Upstairs.

"Fruitcakes and freeloaders. It might as well be Christmas." She strode into the store and slammed the phone's
handset into the cradle. As expected, the resounding
clamor didn't win her so much as a muscle twitch from
her father. With his mouth wide open and the rest of his
alcohol-swollen body almost as slack, a thin stream of
drool was beginning to run down the side of his jaw.

Michaele kicked the sole of his booted foot with the toe
of her athletic shoes.

He jerked upright, the movement knocking his cap to
the cement floor. "Wh-what?"

"Where is it?"

"Huh?"

"The bottle."

He went from dazed to pit-bull mad. "I was sleepin'!
In case you ain't noticed, it's hotter 'n hell in here, and
I'm full wore out."

"Yeah, guzzling battery acid is exhausting work. Well,
I have news for you. It's hot out there, too—" she nodded
toward the garage "—and we're busy, which is the only
reason why I actually give a flying fig if you drink yourself
into a coma. Now we had a deal, old man. You promised
to carry your weight and not get soused during working
hours. So hand it over."

He stared at her outstretched hand and resumed his comfortable slouch. "Leave me alone, ya mouthy li'l bitch.
Nag, nag, nag. I shoulda drowned you back when I had
the chance and your ma wasn't looking."

The insults no longer stung as they once had. She'd
heard so many over the years, she'd grown numb to them.
"I'm sure it crossed your mind," she replied coldly.

"Aren't I lucky the liquor anesthetized any guts you had about the same time it leeched your mind of sense."

Casting a glance at the wall clock, she saw she had ten minutes before Jared was due. Leaving her father, who was already drifting off again, she hurried back to the garage.

There was still no sign of Faith.

2

5:03 p.m.

Jared Morgan dropped the previous day's reports on day clerk and dispatcher Norma Headly's desk. "Let Curtis handle them if you want. I'm out of here. See you in the morning."

"Just a second, Chief. I have Garth Powers on line one. He says there's something out at the high school that you'd better see."

Jared waited for more information, but Norma didn't elaborate. "Does he want me to play twenty questions? What's up?"

"I asked. He won't say. He's concerned someone will hear and start a scare 'again.' Those were his exact words," she added with emphasis.

Jared didn't like the sound of that. There weren't many things that would prompt the ex-jock-turned-administrator to call for outside help. It would have to be more than a hastily tossed-away reefer or a racial situation that had gone beyond the name-calling stage. A firearm brought to school? All possible these days, but none of those things would make Garth so secretive, and that had the hairs on the back of Jared's neck rising. He could have done without the inflection on *again.*

"Tell him I'm on my way to pick up my car. I'll be there in a few minutes." Slipping on his cowboy hat and sunglasses, he exited the white-brick building, resigned that the cold beer he was looking forward to at the house would have to wait a while longer.

Split Creek's police station was located on the northeast corner of Main and Dogwood, in a three-streetlight downtown. The community itself was one of the more resilient in Wood County, but that was hardly due to brilliance in city planning or any law enforcement. Situated between Dallas and Shreveport, Louisiana, and nestled in the heart of the photogenic Pineywoods, it also lay in the fork created by Big Blackberry Creek that eventually fed into the Red River on the east, and Little Blackberry that emptied into the Sabine River on the west. In other words, the town transformed itself into a virtual island during spring's and autumn's heavy rains. Hardly impressive strategy by anyone's standards, but the addition of bridges over the years had improved the situation somewhat.

It was the residents, however, who made the rustic, visually quaint community stand out. They were an odd assortment of old-fashioned eccentrics, economic progressives, religious conservatives and creative liberals. That strange brew could make things percolate during political elections, and passions didn't quiet down much during high school football or basketball season, either; nor when the competition was on for spring and autumn tourist traffic. But so far, the only blood shed was from the occasional bruised nose on the playing field...or when a picnic involved one beer or wine cooler too many.

Well, almost, Jared thought with a pang of sadness.

Overseeing this motley group had been his responsibility for almost five years. He'd been a member of the department for nine. Like many East Texans, his ancestors had emigrated here from the deep South—Georgia, in his case. For the first half of his life, he'd bounced around the Lone Star State as his father dealt with transfers with the Texas Department of Public Safety. Later there followed a stint in the marines and, finally, a last year down in Austin to finish getting his college degree, before returning here to move into the family home. The unexpected death of his parents had precipitated that. Now thirty-five, he was all that remained of his side of the Texas Morgans.

He often thought things should have turned out much differently, but it would be dangerous to dwell on that. It was Garth's call that had triggered the reminder, had triggered too many memories. He didn't need that.

Only as he crossed Main Street and approached Ramey's did it become easier to push away his gloomy thoughts, thanks to the sight of Michaele Ramey bending to pick up something from the concrete floor in the garage.

Damn, he thought. For a slip of a thing, she could snag his attention faster than a bored bull could pick up the scent of forbidden heifers in a distant pasture.

"Hold that pose, Ramey," he drawled as he drew nearer, "and you'll cause a traffic pileup out here the likes of which Split Creek's never seen before."

Michaele glanced over her shoulder, her expression showing she was anything but impressed with his humor. "Just once I'd like to see you come and go without making a sexual innuendo."

"It's a free country—I suppose you have a right to dream." He grinned to hide the more complicated emotions she stirred in him. "How's my car?"

"Not much better than your line of bull. I swear, Morgan, you're only across the street. Why can't you get this thing serviced on a regular basis? This old oil is thick enough to sculpt with!"

"Blame yourself. If you didn't turn me down every time I ask you out, I wouldn't need so long between visits to heal my wounded ego. Exactly how much rejection do you think a guy can take?"

She didn't waste so much as a blink on him. "Have Red or one of the others bring it over."

"You stay away from Samuels," Jared said, pointing at her. "He's a happily married man with two growing boys needing three big meals a day if they're going to bring home another division football title this fall."

"Idiot." Michaele punched the controls, and the lift began its slow descent.

The failure to get even a hint of a smile out of her told him that her day wasn't ending any better than his. He knew why; he'd seen the reason as he'd crossed the street. "I take it Buck's sleeping off another binge?"

"No, I fed him rat poison with his lunch, and I'm just waiting for dark to bury the body."

"And Faith's running late?" There was no sign of her red Trans Am.

"Who knows? And from now on, I refuse to care. She's about to graduate, she turns twenty-one in two months, and, so help me, the minute that happens, I'm washing my hands of her."

"Sure you are."

Blue eyes clearer than any dream and sharper than any laser sliced into him. "Watch me," she said.

"Caretakers don't know how to shut off, honey. Even the ones trapped in dysfunctional families."

She kicked the lift's power unit out of her way, and reached for the clipboard on the nearby workstation. "'Dysfunctional' doesn't begin to cover my zoo. Why don't you cheer me up and tell me you shot a bad guy today and saved us taxpayers a bunch of money on a trial?''

"My, you are in a bloodthirsty mood. Let's see...I wrote two speeding tickets this morning, spent lunch listening to the mayor worry about another store for rent on his block, moved a small mountain of paperwork off my desk. Nope, didn't empty so much as one chamber. Wait! I did run over a water moccasin, driving in this morning. Does that count?''

"Knowing you, it was probably an accident.''

He liked that she sometimes saw through him better than others did. Because of his military background and his hard line regarding certain types of legal infractions, some in town considered him a hard-ass. To be accurate, he had his calluses and edges, even an unhealed wound or two; but as long as people didn't probe those too much, he considered himself one heck of an amiable guy—and patient. Particularly where one diminutive career cynic was concerned.

As Michaele finished filling out the invoice for his car, he reached out to wipe at a streak of grease along her jaw. Like the rest of her, that chin was finely contoured, in total contrast to her personality and occupation. Barely tall enough to reach his Adam's apple, and easily a hundred pounds lighter than him, she made most people around her feel huge. But most knew she was as physically tough as she was psychologically resilient. Heaven help her, she had to be.

Not surprisingly, she stepped out of his reach, but kept writing. "Get it over with,'' she said, sighing.

"What?'' He waited for her to look up so he could feel the kick that always came when their gazes connected. To define her eyes as blue was as insulting as saying that short mop of hair, mostly hid under her cap, was black. The media could fuss all they wanted about Liz Taylor, but to him nothing struck the heart like Michaele's gem-clear eyes.

"Ask me out so I can say no, and you can be on your way."

"Not tonight."

As she handed him a copy of the bill, there was an instant when concern broke through her cool reserve. "What's wrong?"

"Did I say anything was wrong?"

"You don't have to. It's written all over your face. Come to think of it, you look as though you were served bad oysters at lunch."

"Maybe I'm worrying that nothing's ever going to change between us."

She quickly lowered her thick lashes. "Knock it off, Morgan. How many times do I have to tell you that you're wasting your time toying with me?"

"Until it sinks into that pretty but thick head of yours that I'm not playing a game."

"There is no *us*."

"Right. Keep trying to convince yourself of that." Fighting a stronger frustration than usual, Jared shoved the receipt into his shirt pocket.

Michaele slapped the clipboard back onto the work-bench. "What's gotten into you? We go through the same song-and-dance every time you come over, then you go on your merry way. Why get bent out of shape today?"

"Because, believe it or not, you're not the only one who's had a long day, and maybe I'm a little tired of you insisting this is all a joke, when you know damn well it's not."

Her laugh was brief, but confirmed her confusion and growing unease. "Of course it's a joke. That's why you

mess with me. You know I'm not interested in a relationship with anyone. And I sure as hell wouldn't start anything with someone who drinks!''

Jared knew that, all right, and thought her reasoning
reeked worse than their creeks' stagnant water during a
dry spell. ''Damn it, not everyone who has a beer once in
a while is going to turn into the alcoholic your old man
is!''

''Didn't say they were. But I'm not planning to test the
theory, either.''

He didn't want to analyze it, but something that
wouldn't stay contained got the best of him. ''Then start
dressing like you mean it.''

''*Excuse* me?'' Arms akimbo, she stared down at her
stained denim shirt and jeans.

''Getting as dirty as a man doesn't make you one. You
know full well that my office window faces here. In the
future, try wearing a bra once in a while and jeans that
don't look sprayed on, if you find my attention so offensive.''

As he headed for his patrol car, Michaele followed like
a rabid terrier on the heels of a postman. ''What I wear is
my business, *Chief* Morgan, have you got that?''

Jared didn't answer. Instead he all but threw himself into
the patrol car and slammed the door shut. Tight-lipped, he
gunned the engine and drove the hell out of there.

Son of a bitch. He groaned as he headed toward Split
Creek High School. Of all the stupid blunders...

He'd met Michaele Ramey when she'd been a runt of
sixteen, and she'd already known more about cars than
most men learned in a lifetime. Even then she was going
through seven kinds of hell with her family. Her inner
strength, that incredible determination not to crumble, had
quickly won his respect, just as her apparent disregard

for—or more accurately, her obliviousness to—her exotic beauty had won his admiration. But, of course, she'd only been a kid…and he had met Sandy. Sandy, who, after his parents' death, brought a calm and sweetness to his life—until that awful day six years ago when he'd kissed her good-night, not realizing it was goodbye.

Jared rubbed his stubble-rough jaw, disgusted with himself. This was the wrong time to think about that, just as he'd chosen the wrong moment to push Michaele. She still wasn't ready.

Fool, she probably never will be.

Damn Garth's phone call. Who needed old ghosts resurrected?

He owed Michaele an apology—and she would get it, right after he dealt with whatever was going on at the school. Watch that not be anywhere near as bad as Garth had insinuated, too, he thought grimacing. But then, nothing could be that bad again. Not ever.

Split Creek Jr.–Sr. High School was located right after the bridge over Big Blackberry Creek, a half-mile before the eastern perimeter of town. Jared pulled into the sprawling school's curved driveway, eyed the near-empty parking lot, and stopped before the canopied entryway. Hurrying inside, he found Garth Powers waiting for him in the main hallway.

At 42, the six-foot-seven-inch former basketball star had served as trail master to herds of high school kids for several years longer than Jared had been a cop, and had the trim build of a man several years younger. His open-minded sense of humor had helped him sustain a more youthful attitude than many his age, so he'd proven himself to be a big favorite among students, faculty and parents. Now Jared grew uneasy as he noted Garth's spooked countenance and the way the grim-faced man kept glancing nervously over his shoulder.

"Thanks for coming," Garth said. "By chance did you see anyone hanging around outside?"

"No. Are we waiting for someone else?"

"I'd say he's already been here and gone. The question is, for how long?" Garth pushed open the door to the men's rest room, and Jared entered.

He stopped only a step beyond the threshold.

Up on the tiled wall were scrawled large letters painted in a bright red that ran the entire length of the tiled urinal wall. Garth illuminated them even more by turning on the rest of the overhead fluorescent lights. That made the message look even more insane.

I'm back! 666

3

Although every instinct told him to turn around and walk out, to climb back into his car and keep going until he ran out of gas, Jared forced himself to stay put.

"Tell me it's not blood," Garth said, his voice barely more than a hoarse whisper.

"It sure as hell looks it."

"But surely not...?"

"Human? Considering the amount this would have taken, let's guess against it for the moment, and hope to heaven somebody doesn't show up missing within the next day or so."

"Jesus, Jared."

"If you don't want the truth, don't ask the questions."

The harsh reprimand had the older man backing away a step. "Just tell me what kind of sick bastard decided to resurrect this part of our past."

Someone who remembered what horror they'd lived through that terrible day six springs ago tomorrow. Someone who knew what it had done to the town and wanted another taste of that craziness. But he knew Garth didn't want to hear that any more than Jared wanted to believe such a thing possible.

"It's almost graduation," he said, grasping for a credible alternative. "You of all people know how revved kids get at this time of year."

"This isn't something to joke about. Not in Split Creek."

Amen, thought Jared, because the last time they'd been exposed to anything like this—the first time—the price had been a life, one very dear to them both, a life that had cost the town its innocence. Anyone who thought it amusing to stir up any of that was sick, pure and simple, and needed to be found.

"Who else has seen this?" he asked, unable to take his eyes off the numbers.

"Just me. I noticed the light under the door, but knew Brady had finished in here over an hour ago."

"Brady Watts? Where is he?"

"Over in the science lab. Should I get him?"

The school's janitor was a gentle-natured old black man, who kept to himself and wasn't the kind to repeat gossip, let alone encourage it. But first and foremost he was a Southern Baptist. Seeing this message would shake him enough to seek out spiritual guidance, which would mean Reverend Isaac Mooney entering the picture, someone who *did* like to talk. Jared neither needed nor wanted that.

"No. But if you can find a couple of mops and pails, then lock that door, I'll help you clean up this mess. Or paint over it, if we need to."

"Don't you want to take a picture, get a sample, or dust for—"

"It's kids!" Jared snapped. "Yeah, it's six years tomorrow, but that's no secret. You've heard the talk around town. People always remember what they should forget and forget what they should remember." He turned back to the wall. "No, this is a juvenile prank meant to shock us, and why should we be surprised? Local gossip reflects what's on TV and in the movies these days. People are being desensitized right and left, and the kids are the first to be affected. Apparently, one or two of them thought it would be fun to spook you. Don't give him, or them, the satisfaction. We'll wash it off and forget it. When they see this didn't get a rise out of you, they'll lose interest and move on to using keys to scratch car paint or something equally lamebrained.''

''She was my sister-in-law, Jared. How can I forget?''

''Damn you, Garth. She was my fiancée! I say, let her rest in peace.''

Garth looked as though he wanted to continue arguing the point, but after several seconds, although red-faced, he stormed out of the rest room. As soon as the door shut behind him, Jared reached for his pocketknife and pulled a paper towel from the wall dispenser. The procedure wasn't as pure as using the collection gear in his trunk, but he couldn't afford to take the time to get it. If Garth got so much as an inkling of how deeply troubled Jared was by this, the guy would need a tranquilizer to get any sleep tonight, and that would mean bringing Jessica into the picture. Sandy's older sister didn't deserve this, either.

Acutely aware of the risks he was taking, he used the knife to scrape at the driest corner of the first letter.

4

Michaele didn't bother trying to rouse her father after locking up. It wasn't the first time she'd left him snoring in his chair, and she doubted it would be the last. In any case, she didn't have the energy to put up with the wrestling match and verbal abuse it would take just to get him into the truck; what would she do with him at home? Besides, with the police station directly across the street, he was perfectly safe, and she would have the time alone that she needed with Faith…once her sister showed up.

Preoccupied, Michaele drove badly through the intersection, and the wrecker shuddered in protest to her delay in downshifting. But she finally got the 454 big-block engine smoothened out and continued north on Dogwood, then turned west on Cypress and across Little Blackberry Creek.

Convinced she would find her sister at the house soaking in the tub, as Faith was apt to do on afternoons when she was feeling particularly lazy, Michaele was disappointed to reach their place and find only the family's aging pickup truck in the dirt driveway. The irony of her reaction didn't escape her. How often had she pulled in here hoping there would be no one at the two-story frame house?

So be it, she decided. If this was to be her moment, she would celebrate. There was more to be grateful for than peace and quiet; there was also the acquisition of the Cameo. This called for a pan-fried steak, and later maybe one of Faith's luxurious, long baths. She couldn't recall the last time she'd taken the time to pamper herself.

But once inside the house—dark and stuffy from being shut up all day—she felt like a stranger. It was the unusual quiet, she supposed, so unnatural considering her volatile family. The mess was the same, though. There were dishes in the sink, newspapers and magazines everywhere, laundry waiting for someone to shove it into the washing machine or dryer.

"Gross," she muttered.

She supposed she could keep the house in better shape if she did everything herself; however, working herself into an early grave the way her mother had wasn't on Michaele's list of goals. Bad enough her father and sister let her support them.

She loaded the washing machine, adding the shirt and jeans she'd been wearing. Then, stripped down to her cotton panties, she ran upstairs for a shower.

It was a rather quick shower. Thanks to her line of work, she could scrub herself raw daily and still fail to get off every last trace of the day's grime. That was also part of why Jared had upset her so.

It had been unfair of him to accuse her of being a tease. She had never tried to be anything but what she was—a damn good mechanic, who would never have clean nails or Faith's flawless skin. Michaele dug around in too many engine manifolds, had wrestled with too many stubborn nuts and bolts to win those kinds of compliments. So where did that big lug get off thinking she was interested in provoking him? She needed a man about as much as she needed an earring pierced through her tongue.

When she returned downstairs, there was still no sign of Faith.

Determined to wait up for her no matter what, Michaele fried the steak and nuked a potato in the microwave, then ate the simple meal, balancing the plate on her knees as she sat outside on the stoop to escape the stale house smells.

For as long as she could remember, they'd lived on this wooded dead-end street in the middle of a cleared pasture that a tornado hadn't yet found. Thirteen acres of sandy loam that liked yucca cactus, nut grass and every other variety of weed, but resisted her sporadic attempts to grow vegetables without pesticides or heavy doses of chemical nutrients. The garden had been her mother's idea, as had been the *E* tacked on to Michaele, after Buck—disappointed that he wasn't getting the son he'd wanted—insisted on keeping the male name, anyway.

By the time she returned inside, it was nearly dusk. After cleaning up in the kitchen, she threw the washed clothes into the dryer and added another load to the washing machine. Then she stretched out on the couch with a mystery novel she'd been meaning to get to since buying it for herself as a Christmas present.

By ten o'clock she gave up trying to pretend she was concentrating and accepted that something was seriously wrong. Faith had never been this late, not from classes; and if she'd had plans, she would have stopped at the house first to change.

Michaele's concern grew after she called her sister's closest friends. All of them—with the exception of Harold, whose mother had answered and informed her he wasn't home yet, either—said they hadn't heard from her today.

Could Faith be with Harold Bean? They hadn't dated in some time, but both attended Northeast Texas Community College and remained friends.

Frowning at the clock, Michaele decided to give her sister until midnight, simply because she dreaded the thought of calling the police station. It didn't matter that Jared wouldn't be there; he would be told, and she didn't want to be accused of playing another game. Surely Faith would wander in before then.

Michaele returned to the front room, turned off the lights and settled in the rocker by the picture window. It looked so much darker out there tonight. The driveway seemed longer, and the woods across the street appeared downright ominous. For the first time since those early days after her mother's death, she regretted that their neighbors were acres away, hidden by trees and thick brush.

She closed her eyes against the view and tried to think pleasant thoughts. What came was an ugly scene this morning with Faith, the way her sister had stormed out of the house...the taunting image of her lying bloody and crying for help in a crushed car somewhere...her father telling the police, "It's Mike's fault! She drove my poor baby to her grave!"

The ringing phone made her jerk upright. Disoriented, in her rush to get to it she almost knocked the whole thing to the floor before successfully bringing the handset to her ear.

"Hello?"

"Is Faith there?"

She didn't recognize the voice, wasn't even alert enough to know if it was a man or a woman calling. "Um...no. Who's this, please?"

"You mean she didn't call to say goodbye? She wanted to."

Michaele's confusion turned instantly to lung-freezing dread. She gripped the phone more tightly. "What did you say? Who is this?"

There was no reply…only a soft *click* as someone hung up.

5

Thursday, May 14
12:01 a.m.

Michaele stood there in shocked disbelief. Even after the buzzing reminded her to hang up, she remained rooted in place, trying to reassure herself that she'd heard incorrectly.

Suddenly, reacting as though the phone's handset was a venomous thing, she dropped it back into the cradle, then stared out the picture window at the empty road. Beyond. Into the opaqueness of the dense woods.

As understanding grew into fear, she reached for the phone again, only to draw back.

Who are you going to call? Calm down. What if you're wrong? What if this is somebody's idea of a joke?

That was it. Michaele rushed into the kitchen and jerked open the door. "So help me," she muttered under her breath, "if you borrowed someone's car phone or got someone else to call me, thinking you would pay me back for—"

The Firebird she had expected to see in the driveway, with her sister laughing behind the wheel, wasn't there.

Michaele's stomach grew queasy. Quickly locking the door, she snatched up the phone book next to the refrigerator and, with trembling fingers, flipped through the white pages. Her dialing was equally haphazard, and she exhaled with relief when she finally heard the ringing that told her she hadn't botched that last attempt. The stove clock read 12:03. The ghoulish time didn't slip past her, nor did the belated realization that she must have dozed off, after all.

On the fourth ring, he answered. "Yeah?"

"Jared, thank God." His strong, though irritated, voice had her instantly forgiving him his earlier behavior. "I know I should've called the station, but I—"

"Michaele?" There was a muffled sound as though he were sitting up. "What's wrong?"

"I think Faith is missing."

He was silent for several seconds. "Come again?"

"She never got home, and I just got this awful call. He said—"

"Are you and Buck at the house?"

"Yes. No! Buck's at the garage."

"You're there *alone? * Stay put," he snapped. "I mean it. Don't go outside. Do nothing until I get there."

"But I haven't told you—"

He hung up.

She couldn't believe it. Instead of listening to what she had to say, instead of assuring her that he would immediately have his men on the night shift look for Faith, he was coming here because *she* was alone? Heaven save her from the entire male race! Calling him instead of the station had been a mistake, after all.

But her frustration didn't last long. As soon as she hung up and looked out the parted kitchen door curtains, out beyond the moths circling dizzily in the porch light to the indecipherable darkness beyond, the skin along her arms and at the back of her neck began tingling. Someone could be standing just beyond, maybe hiding as close as behind the wrecker, watching her. The thought made her feel exposed even though the oversize NASCAR T-shirt she liked to wear to bed almost reached her knees.

Her heart pounding, she rushed over to tug the curtains closed and to recheck the lock. The lock was one of those flimsy twist jobs in a door that was half glass, which made her think about the other doors. Not once since she'd come home had she bothered checking them to see if they were locked or not.

With a new dread, she hurried from the back door to the front, testing each one. Everything was as it should be, but her heart continued its wild beating, anyway, and so when done, she stopped in the hallway, her back pressed to the wall, the one spot where she knew she couldn't be seen from any window.

Get a grip, Ramey. This isn't like you.

Nevertheless, a flash of lights on the living room wall made her catch her breath. In the next instant she recognized them as car lights. Jared? He lived north on Dogwood, more than a half-mile away. Could he have dressed and gotten here this fast?

Faith!

Anger blossomed anew as Michaele ran to the kitchen. Once again she flung open the door.

With mixed feelings, she heard the white patrol car's engine shut down just before Jared climbed out and rushed up the steps. It looked as if he'd pulled on the short-sleeved blue shirt he'd been wearing earlier because one of the buttons was undone, and his jeans were zipped but not fastened. Although his face was shadowed by the straw cowboy hat, she saw that his eyes were bloodshot and that the always pronounced shadow of whiskers was darker than ever. The scent of beer that drifted in with him confirmed the hunch that he hadn't gotten as far as bed yet when she'd called.

"Should you be driving in your condition?" she asked as he entered.

"If that's an invitation for coffee, I won't turn it down."

With a lift of her eyebrows, she took the saucepan they kept on the stove and filled it with what she estimated was enough water to fill a large mug. They didn't bother with coffee machines in the Ramey household; Faith refused to drink anything but store-bought *latte,* and Buck doctored anything put before him with so much sugar and milk, Michaele figured instant was good enough.

As she went to the pantry for the jar, she said, "Maybe you should call one of your men to handle this."

"I'm not drunk."

She refused to be intimidated by his terse reply. If anyone had the right to be out of sorts, it was her. "I call you and tell you that I think my sister is missing, and not only don't you ask me any questions about her, but you waste valuable time driving over here when you should be out looking for her."

"My first priority was to make sure you were all right."

"Of course I'm all right. I'm here!"

Jared took off his hat and ran his other hand over his hair. "Michaele, you don't know what's—" He signaled her to give him a moment, then replaced the hat. "It's not going to help anything to get sarcastic."

Although not ready to admit she was out of line, she did back off by getting a mug from an open cabinet. "Faith never got home from school," she told him. "And there's been a phone call."

She repeated everything the caller had said. When she finished, she glanced over her shoulder. Jared just stood there, his eyes closed.

"You're thinking someone's pulling one over on me, that I'm being melodramatic. I hope I am. But the more I think about it, the more I feel— He was smiling when he spoke, I could tell. That's what unnerved me. He was *enjoying* himself."

Once Jared met her gaze again, not only did his expression tell her that he didn't think she was overreacting, but he looked sick to his stomach. "Did you recognize the guy's voice?"

"No." She suffered a new pang of guilt. "To be honest, I'm not even sure it was a man."

"You just said—"

"I'd fallen asleep and was disoriented. The call lasted only a few seconds." As she replayed the awful conversation in her mind, she tried to portion out a spoonful of coffee granules. Most spilled onto the counter.

Jared took over and completed the task. "Could the caller have altered his or her voice?"

"I guess. I don't know. No, it had to have been a man."

"Because…?"

"Because."

"Harold Bean, maybe?"

One of the less appealing things about small towns was that everyone knew everyone else's business, including who was or had been paired with whom. Michaele shook her head. "Jeez, no. He's still nuts about her, sure, and as far as I know they've remained friends, but…no. Faith's moved on."

"That's not what I asked."

"Harold's voice cracks like a thirteen-year-old's when he's the slightest bit emotional."

"You sound more like a protective parent than a worried sister."

"Damn it, Morgan, I'm not protecting him. I'm simply not going to say what I don't believe, so back off!"

Jared held her angry stare. "When did you receive the call?"

"At midnight. I phoned you right afterward. Maybe I should have called the station or 9-1-1."

"You did the right thing."

Then why did he look as though she'd become his worst nightmare, as though he were about to excuse himself and charge for the bathroom?

Before she could say as much, he stepped around her, turned off the flame under the pot and poured the boiling water. "Have you searched the house thoroughly? There's no sign that she might have been here while you were at work? Maybe she packed a bag or something, planned to stay with friends for a few days?"

"No, I didn't notice anything when I was going around opening windows, and she didn't say—"

The pot clattered as he slammed it back onto the burner. "You had the windows open?"

"Hello! This is Split Creek, not L.A. What's more, two of the three people living here think we have round-the-clock maid service. Maybe you can tolerate that kind of stench, but not me."

"Okay, okay. Go lock up. Then check the closets, under the beds... *Do it,*" he intoned when she didn't budge. He started for the door. "And yell like hell if you find anything. I'm going outside to have a look around."

"For what?"

The glance he cast her over his shoulder left her feeling like a slow five-year-old. As the screen door shut behind him, she muttered, "It's my house, buster. I have a right to at least ask."

What did he think he was going to find out there, anyway? She'd told him Faith wasn't here. And what did he think she'd run into upstairs?

Somewhere above her a board creaked. It was the same sound Faith used to make when she tried to sneak out of the house for a date on a school night. Of course, this time, Michaele thought, it was the house cooling, a board expanding—

Another creak sounded.

"So I'll placate him." She might as well, she decided. Otherwise he would do it for her and know once and for all what slobs the Rameys were. The heavy flashlight she snatched up along the way was for her own peace of mind.

Five minutes later they were both back in the kitchen.

Jared reached for the still steaming mug of coffee. "I've radioed the station and told them to keep an eye out for Faith, and to check on Buck. You know we can't initiate an official missing persons search for twenty-four hours, but I'll set in motion what I can. If you could give me a recent photo of her, that would help."

For what? Everyone in the area knew what Faith looked like. She was one of those people who never met a stranger and talked to everyone.

"We'll need it if we have to broaden our search," Jared said gently. "Also, come morning, if…well, you'll have to come into the station to fill out some forms."

As he spoke he made less and less eye contact. That, more than anything, triggered a new dread in Michaele. "You don't think she's going to show up, do you."

"I'm merely explaining procedure." He put down the mug. "Could you get me that photo?"

The one she chose was from the top of the TV in the living room—a Glamour Shots creation, yet another indulgence the girl couldn't afford. At the time it was taken, Michaele had been too angry to admit her sister looked gorgeous, more stunning than most of the empty-eyed skeletons in the countless fashion magazines the kid bought. It wasn't just the filtered lens, the way Faith's long black hair was brushed in uncharacteristic but sexy disarray, or the artful makeup that gave her eyes an almost Far Eastern tilt, her mouth a pouty just-kissed look. Faith simply had...something.

Returning to the kitchen, Michaele handed the picture to Jared. "All I was trying to say before was that if you know something, I think I have a right to be told what it is."

Jared slipped the photo into his shirt pocket without looking at it. "I'll be in touch."

That was it? "Fine!" she snapped, as he headed for the door. "Then hear this—as soon as I change, I'm going to start searching for her, too."

"The hell you will."

Before she could move he'd spun around and grabbed her upper arms, almost lifting her off her feet to bring her face-to-face with him. It wasn't hard to do. He might not be the tallest guy in town, but he had to be one of the strongest, and if he wanted, he was capable of making a larger man feel like a Chihuahua confronting a rottweiler.

"You stay put," he growled. "And don't think I won't be checking in to make sure you're here."

"I can't sit and do nothing."

"Then pray."

Jared Long Morgan talking about prayer? Next to her, he had the worst church attendance record in town. "Now you're frightening me."

"It's about time." But he frowned once he noticed his grip on her, and abruptly let her go. "Stay here. If she shows up, you'll be able to let me know all the sooner."

He started to leave again.

"Jared." When he looked back, Michaele chewed on her lower lip. "You might as well know something. We fought before she went off to school this morning."

"So what else is new?"

Despite his wry, even kind tone, she didn't allow herself off the hook. "This time I threatened to shut her off financially if she didn't start helping out more. She left crying and cussing." Remembering the awful scene, Michaele felt her own throat ache. "What am I going to do if…?"

Jared swore under his breath and this time drew her completely into his arms. "Don't go there, honey."

Holding Jared was like trying to wrap her arms around the single, ancient oak in the middle of their pasture; but for once Michaele let herself need his size and strength. She almost believed that if she held him hard enough, if she shut her eyes tight enough, she could stop what felt like a free fall into the worst nightmare ever imagined.

Jared's breath teased the top of her head. "Ah, Mike. Everyone knows the burden you've been carrying for years, just as they know it's a fact of life that siblings fight. There's nothing to beat yourself up about. Now listen." He eased her to arm's length. "Lock up tight behind me. Don't open up for anyone except me, Faith or Buck. If there are any more calls, let me know immediately." He nodded to the card on the counter. "I've left you my cellular phone number."

She hadn't noticed, and gave the card only a brief glance; all she was focusing on was him. He was about to leave, and she didn't want him to. She didn't want to be alone.

"I'll get back to you as soon as I can."

"I'll try to be patient."

"Don't hurt yourself straining."

Although the words were warmly spoken, there was

something close to despair in his eyes, and suddenly she had the strongest urge to be in his arms again, to smooth away the grim lines that were deepening around his mouth. The need was as frightening as it was compelling.

"About this afternoon...I'm sorry," she heard herself say. "I hated that we fought."

"Me, too."

"I mean *really* hated it. Your—" she didn't know what word to use "—your respect means a lot to me."

"We'll talk about that someday."

His thumb's caress at the corner of her mouth had a surprisingly debilitating effect on her ability to remember all the reasons for believing romantic entanglements weren't for her. Nuts, she thought, finally succeeding in putting more space between them.

Sighing, Jared reached for the doorknob. "Remember what I said. Keep everything locked up."

"Yes."

And she did...only to find it didn't quite work, in that she wasn't alone. Jared's presence lingered long after his car was out of sight. That disturbed her almost as much as everything else going on.

6

12:30 a.m.

"Where've you been?"

Harold Bean froze in the doorway, blinded by the glare of the kitchen's fluorescent lights flashing on, and though he instinctively squeezed his eyes shut, he decided it was just as well that he couldn't see. Looking at his mother at any time was a grim chore; it became downright painful at twelve-thirty in the morning when she wore only a nightgown and still had to stand sideways to fit through the hall doorway.

"Jeez, Mama." He squinted, then blinked hard to get used to the brutal glare. As his vision cleared, he stepped inside the double-wide trailer, shutting the door behind him. It was all about buying time, and when he turned back to face her again, he saw that at least this gown was made of a dark, opaque material, less transparent than some. Unfortunately, the huge orange-and-yellow flowers on it reminded him of gaping mouths screaming for freedom. He figured he and those flowers had a lot in common.

"I asked you a question, young man. Where've you been?"

"The usual."

He headed straight for the refrigerator. He hoped this

would be one of those nights when she gave up quickly and went back to bed.

"Don't give me that. You should've been home hours ago. Ain't nothing open this time of night."

No shit, he thought. That was another reason why he intended to get the hell out of Split Creek as soon as he graduated next year. This was a do-nothing town full of know-nothing people going nowhere. He might not be brain surgeon material, but he was smart enough to know he could make a good life for himself in the military— and not as a bottom-of-the-shitcan grunt, either. He was going to be an officer. Recruiters down in Tyler had convinced him of that. One more year, he fantasized as he took out the plastic gallon jug of skim milk from the top shelf, then it would be "Anchors aweigh!" for him.

"Don't drink all of that!" his mother cried. "I need some for my cereal in the morning."

Keeping his back to her, Harold rolled his eyes at the whiny demand. The sow drank no-fat milk and diet soda all day, bought everything and anything guaranteeing lower calories on the label, yet he was the one losing weight around here. *Because I'm not scarfing down cookies and chips as a chaser to everything.*

In fact, he had trouble trying to keep a hundred sixty-seven pounds on his six-foot frame, while he regularly had to replace the extra boards under his mother's bed to keep it from crashing through the floor of the trailer.

As thirsty as he was hungry, but unwilling to listen to more of her yammering, he poured himself a mere half glass of the cold liquid, then returned the container to the refrigerator.

"You were out sniffing after *her* again, weren't you?" his mother demanded.

"No."

"How many times do I have to say it before it sinks into that thick skull of yours? The girl's done with you, stop chasing her. Ain't you got no pride?"

"I wasn't anywhere near Faith Ramey."

"Well, her sister must've believed otherwise. Why else did she call here looking for her?"

That got his attention. He stopped the glass inches from his mouth. "She didn't."

"You calling your ma a liar?"

"All I'm saying is that Mike knows Faith and I don't drive up to school together anymore."

"Probably 'cause she got tired of you laying out and goofing off. So where were you? At some club drinking? I won't have a drunk in my house! I got rid of your no-good father, and I'll get rid of you if'n you're turning that way."

"This is a trailer. *Ouch!*" She'd leaned into the kitchen just enough to slap him across the back of his head. White bursts of light exploded before his eyes and his eardrums ached. "Fuck it," he groaned.

She swung at him again. "No cussing under my roof, and don't be correcting your superiors! Guess you figure you're too old to answer to me, but let me tell you, Harold Bean, you're nothing until I say you're something. Got that?"

Shaking from humiliation as much as fury, he almost spilled his milk as he stretched to set the glass on the counter. Somehow he resisted the temptation to commit violence, rubbed the back of his head and simply replied, "You're gonna wake Wendy, Mama."

"Don't you worry about her. Unlike you, she knows it's a school night and went to bed at a decent hour. She'll get her rest. Now I asked you a question."

A question he wasn't about to answer, not truthfully,

anyway. But he had a lie practiced and memorized. "I was at the school library until they closed. Did you forget that I told you I had a paper due as part of one of my finals and needed more footnotes?" He hadn't said anything of the kind, but while his mother had the memory of a whole herd of elephants when it came to what happened on each and every TV soap opera, she couldn't recall diddly about anything he told her regarding school. To keep it that way, he exaggerated shamelessly. "Remember, I explained all the instructors care about is footnotes, footnotes and foot-notes?"

"Oh…yeah." Her eyes, thin slits in a moon-pie face, scanned the length of him. "Then where is it? You bad-mouth your teachers, but don't bring in so much as one sheet of paper to prove you've been working? How dumb do you think I am, boy? You think I don't remember that the library closes at nine, and that it only takes you forty minutes to get home from up there?"

That voice. Sometimes Harold fantasized about wrap-ping his hands around his mother's fat neck and squeezing, squeezing until her head popped like a ripe zit. His loath-ing for her incessant nagging was that strong. But this was hardly the time for her to know his darkest thoughts.

"It's late, Mama." He reached for the milk again. "I left everything in the car so I wouldn't have to tote it all out again, come morning. If you don't believe me, take my keys out of my pocket and look for yourself. As for the rest of the time, if you'd given me a chance, I would have explained I had car trouble."

His mother snorted. "A likely story."

"If I'm lying, I'm dying." To pledge himself, he held up his hand the same way she did hers at church. "Car battery went on me. It was deader than—" he barely stopped in time to save himself from earning another smack "—I had to wait until somebody came by who was willing to drive me all the way to the Wal-Mart in Mineola and back, which was the only place open at this hour."

She looked doubtful. "Who would go way out of their way to do something like that for you?"

"Jack Fenton." It had taken some thinking, but Harold had remembered his former high school classmate who lived on the far side of town. "Fenton" was a name his mother had heard before, since the guy had been the class valedictorian and had impressed everyone by doubling up on his college courses to graduate a year early. But most important, Fenton was someone his mother would probably, hopefully, never meet. "He happened to pass me on his way home from Texarkana after checking on some cattle for his folks." It wasn't a lie that the Fentons were among the more successful ranchers in the area.

His mother brushed her stringy, chin-length hair from her face. "Well, I hope you paid him for his trouble, or at least reimbursed him gas money."

"He wouldn't take any." Slinging back the last of the milk, Harold rinsed out the glass and put it in the dish drainer, fully aware of what would happen if he didn't. "He said he hoped somebody'd do as much for him sometime if he got into trouble."

"Now that's what I call a Christian gesture." The trailer groaned as his mother rocked back and forth to get enough momentum to turn around and make room for him to precede her down the hall. "You be sure to add him in your prayers, and thank the good Lord for sending you an angel in your time of need. In this day and age, there's no telling what kind of evil could have been out there."

The only thing Harold prayed for was that Rose Bean's Lord "took her home" via natural causes before he was driven to murdering her himself. "Ow!" he cried, as she pinched the back of his arm. "What was that for?" Hell, was the old witch capable of reading minds now?

"You could have called from the store so I wouldn't have lost sleep worrying. I'll bet Jack called home. I'll bet his parents don't hear any lip from him, either."

Instead of answering, Harold escaped into his room, quickly shutting and locking the door behind him before she could ask another question. He'd had enough. Besides, the key to lying well was knowing when to shut up.

As he hoped, his mother's heavy steps moved on down the hall to the other bedroom that she shared with Wendy—"Sow Jr.," as he called his younger sister in the safety of his mind. What a relief that she hadn't taken him up on his challenge to check his car to make sure he'd been telling the truth. He'd been counting on that, and if he'd been wrong…he didn't want to think about the consequences.

Not at all hampered by the darkness of his room, he twisted around and dropped onto the middle of his twin-size cot, then fisted his hands over his head like a boxing champion before an audience of thousands of cheering fans.

He'd done it! Once again he'd made it home without anyone being the wiser about where he'd been and what he'd been doing. And that's how he planned to keep things.

7

1:15 a.m.

Patrolling Split Creek by day was about as exciting as watching a cow chew her cud; things rarely got more lively at night. Until that message in the high school rest room and Michaele's call, Jared had begun to believe, as did most of the rest of the community, that they were overprotected. Two cops patrolling the area at night, while Curtis Jarvis manned the station, should have been enough manpower for a town twice their size. Now, who knew? And yet despite his concern, he had to fight against another yawn. He would never make a good vampire. His internal clock was better suited for day work, and his butt and mind were starting to protest this extended time behind the wheel—especially since it was getting him nowhere.

With a deep sigh, he radioed the station for a status report, but Curtis informed him that Eagan and Griggs weren't having any more success than he was. Next he called the sheriff's office over in Quitman to get an update and to determine what else they were willing to do at this stage. By the time he once again had both hands on the wheel, he'd reached the southwest perimeters of the community. It was the least likely area for Faith to be—mostly farms, woods and marsh—however, it also had the main access road to Tyler, and Faith was a city girl at heart. Maybe she'd decided to go down there and had had car trouble.

There had been a full moon on Monday, and three-quarters of it was still high in the night sky, but an increase of low clouds kept the terrain pretty much dark. His car's headlights picked up another pair of eyes in the tall grass on the side of the road, and he warned, ''Don't make my day,'' to what he suspected was either a raccoon, small dog or cat. The last thing he wanted was to add to the roadkill count.

The woods abruptly ended to expose two chicken-coop-size houses, neither of which was lit by security lights. Old Mrs. Fahey lived in the shack teetering on cinder blocks, and her widowed daughter Pearl Wascom resided in the one with the screened porch, set farther back from the road. Jared often thought that the two women should move in together and rent the second house to supplement their meager income, but they squabbled too much to stay under the same roof for any length of time. Only their shared commitment to keep Ezekiel Baptist Church across the street polished and ready for any service, as well as the cemetery beside it groomed like a public park, assured any civility between them. What bothered Jared was knowing he could walk up to either house and find the doors and windows unlocked. These were the same two ladies who'd been among the most spooked when Sandy was murdered in her own home. It amazed him how quickly they'd forgotten that, or, more accurately, how they preferred the comfort of living in denial—as had so many in their community.

Continuing, he drove past a few dozen equally isolated residences. With every mile he covered, he willed the radio to relieve him of his growing tension. It didn't happen, though, and when at last he'd come full circle, he drove past the gas station again.

Buck seemed content to spend the night where he was. Just as well, Jared decided. As much as he didn't like Michaele being alone at her place, her father would only add to her stress.

Once inside the police station, he headed straight for the coffee machine. He'd barely begun pouring himself a mug full of the potent brew, when Bruce Griggs and Buddy Eagan shuffled in. Bruce, who looked more like a lifeguard than a doting father of two little girls, reported that all he'd come up with was a small domestic disturbance in the trailer park where the Mexicans who worked at area commercial nurseries lived. Buddy, divorced and always a bit edgy, grumbled how his trip hadn't even yielded that much.

"Bet she's holed up with one of her instructors getting...tutored." Smirking, Buddy poured himself a mug of coffee.

"Knock it off," Bruce replied. "Faith's a sweet kid. She used to baby-sit our girls, and she was the most responsible sitter we ever had."

"Hey, my ex's kid sister went to college down in Austin, and is only a couple years younger than Faith. Some of the stories she told about when she sat kids—"

"That's enough." Whatever Faith was or wasn't, Jared didn't want anyone discounting the possible seriousness of the situation. He carried his coffee to the city map and studied it again before checking his watch. It was after two o'clock.

Where are you, kid?

"Bruce," he said to the younger cop, "you take the section I just covered. Buddy, you repeat Bruce's route, and I'll go through yours again. Everybody, look a little harder. Pause to check out remote properties. If you see anything suspicious, call for backup, pronto.''

Bruce looked the least thrilled; however, he accepted the assignment as he usually did. He simply finished his coffee, rinsed out the mug and headed for the bathroom. Buddy went to shoot the breeze with Curtis for a moment. Confident the men would be back on the street in minutes, Jared refilled his mug and carried it out to his car.

His was the only vehicle on the road as he worked his way through town. At the corner of Magnolia, he noticed Reverend Dollar's study light just going off. It wasn't the first time he'd noticed how late the minister worked, but others were up late, too. At the other end of the street, he found Dillon Hancock still at it. Hancock lived in the attic of Last Writes, the bookstore taking up the lower two floors of the sprawling Victorian. Jared's mood soured somewhat as he passed; the town's number one rebel and most notorious bachelor had befriended Michaele with ease, and although Jared was fairly confident that it was only a platonic relationship, he was jealous nonetheless.

The last street in the immediate part of downtown was Cedar, and there, at the elegant, contemporary-styled house on the corner, he saw the shadow of Garth Powers moving around in his home office. Jared couldn't blame the guy for pacing, but hoped he was keeping his mouth shut and hadn't upset his wife, Jessica.

Once again he turned onto Dogwood. This was the road Faith would have taken to and from school. Soon after driving by his own home, commercial zoning replaced residential property, followed by mini-farms, tracts of five to twenty acres owned by the more successful retailers in town and some commuting professionals out of Tyler. By the time he reached the City Limits sign, the only lights around were from larger farms and ranches. He kept hoping to come across a disabled Firebird around each bend...but it didn't happen.

A mile beyond the sign, surrounded by solid woods, he had no choice but to cut a sharp *U*-turn and head back. There was still Big Blackberry Drive and the northeast side of town to check out beyond the Powers place, he told himself, although he knew finding anything there was a long shot. With deepening concern, he reached for his cellular and punched in Michaele's number.

She answered before the first ring ended. "Yes?"

"I was hoping you'd be napping some."

"How can I sleep?" she replied. "That call keeps playing over and over in my mind. Have you found anything?"

"I'm afraid not. We're on our second pass through the area. The sheriff's office reports things have been quiet for them, too, but in a way that's good news. They're able to spare the manpower to pick up wherever we're leaving off."

"He has her."

"You don't know that. All you know is that someone wants you to think that. They may only be out to play with your mind."

"They're doing a good job of it."

Jared heard the fatigue and the strain in her voice and wished he could go to her, even though he knew she wouldn't welcome the comfort he wanted to offer. "I checked on Buck. He's fine."

"I don't want to think what he'll be like when he finds out."

Jared sympathized. For all the trouble the guy gave Michaele, he'd treated Faith more like an adored puppy.

Past tense? Listen to yourself, Morgan.

"Don't assume the worst," he forced himself to say.

"For all we know, she met up with some friends and decided to spend the night there."

"I'll kill her. I swear, if that's what happened, I'll shake her until she's bald or—"

"Chief! Come in, please."

Curtis's usually calm drawl was edged with anxiety, which immediately made Jared cut short his conversation with Michaele. "I'll get back to you," he told her, and disconnected before she could ask what was going on. Something told him that she didn't need to hear what his dispatcher had to say.

He reached for the radio mike. "What've you got?"

"A call's come in from the Fite farm. Old Pete's found something out there. Sounds like Faith Ramey's car."

So a jaunt to Tyler wasn't out of the picture. "Just the car? No sign of her?"

"Pete didn't say anything about seeing anyone. All he said was that his dogs went crazy and woke him. When they wouldn't settle down, he went outside to check around, and as soon as he saw that a strange vehicle was on his property, he ran inside to call it in."

"Well, did he recognize it?" If it wasn't too dark, he should have. Like most everyone else, Pete knew Faith.

"I don't get that impression from what he's said so far, and I sensed he was too scared to get a closer look."

"All right, that's good, too. It'll keep him from contaminating anything. Have you notified Griggs and Eagan?"

"Yeah, did that first since they're closer. Eagan's just arriving, and Griggs is about two minutes behind him."

"I'll be there in ten."

8

2:40 a.m.

Reverend George Dollar shut off the lamp and sat in the darkness of his office wanting the absolution, temporary though it was. He had yet to stop shaking, but it was slightly better than when he'd first come in and had almost knocked over the umbrella stand at the back door. Just the thought of the attention that noise could have brought from upstairs triggered a more violent shudder. No, Miriam could not know that he was the biggest sinner in his congregation. Disgusting. Doomed.

How could he have let it happen? He'd been making such progress. Had he grown complacent? Surely not.

He was being tested, he decided with a flash of revelation. Satan had sent a demon, not unlike the two that had taunted Jesus upon entering Gadara. His demon had been informed of his progress, and, like a maggot, had infested his mind and contaminated it until he'd succumbed to a fever. He'd never noticed it coming on because it was natural to feel warm at this time of year. Especially this year.

Tears welled anew behind his closed lids, and this time they weren't only tears of remorse, but of self-pity. Why had the Lord taken so long to share this insight? For almost two hours he'd been praying and paging through his Bible, while asking for forgiveness. He'd read Psalms 130 and 139; then, when there'd been no sign from above, Psalm 143. He'd even fallen to his knees and raised his palms in supplication, and in the loudest whisper he dared—ever conscious that Miriam had the ears of a safecracker—had invited the Almighty to strike him dead if that was His will. Unfortunately, his knees gave out before getting a response, and now, sitting here in the darkness, it had come.

A test…no doubt because I've proven myself a worthy soldier.

The thought made him bite at his knuckles the way he had when, as a schoolboy, he'd sit outside the principal's office awaiting a thrashing for a childish infraction. Oh, but for a return to those innocent days.

''Give me a sign to know I have Your forgiveness,'' he declared in a low vibrato. Impassioned, he raised his right fist to the ceiling and pointed at it with his left hand. ''Say the word, and I'll smite this wicked limb here and now that it might never again act in weakness!''

With growing zeal, he reached for the carved-bone letter opener a member of his congregation had made for him several Christmases ago. The blade had as sharp an edge as anything in Miriam's kitchen, and he'd already had a close encounter with it. The last time he'd invited the Lord to smite him, he'd slipped and cut himself so badly, the wound had required seven stitches—not to mention a lot of explaining to his wife.

Now, as then, the room remained silent.

The reverend smiled knowingly. ''You don't think I would do it, except by accident. And You're right, of course. I'm as big a coward as I am a weakling.''

He replaced the letter opener in its wooden tray and

covered his face with his hands. Despite having scrubbed them in the kitchen sink, they still carried the smell of sex and the earth he'd dug in.

As visions of his earlier behavior flashed again in his mind's eye, he flung himself to the carpet and began sobbing. ''Help me. Stop me. End this, damn it. End it!''

9

2:40 a.m.

The scene before him was at once typical of investigations, and yet eerie; however, Jared wasted no time climbing out of his car. "What do you know?" he asked Buddy, who was the first to come over to him. He'd parked next to the patrolman's unit, making his the fifth vehicle in the semicircle.

About a dozen yards in front of them stood the red Firebird. A few of the cars were idling, their headlights being used to illuminate the Trans Am that was parked slightly off Pete Fite's driveway on the grassy, sloped embankment. The driver's door was wide open, the interior light on. There was no sign of Faith.

"Is that how you found things?"

"Exactly this way—the engine and headlights off, but the door wide open. Pete swears he didn't touch a thing. Doesn't look good, Chief. She's not here."

"Well, somebody was." He could tell that it was Faith's car from the license plate. But what had him placing his hands on his hips was the man who rounded the thing and leaned into the vehicle. "Who the hell is that?"

"Deputy DeFreese Adams. Sheriff Cudahy's newest boy."

"Where the hell did he train? Hollywood? Get him away from there before he touches anything. As it is, he's probably contaminated the surroundings. Look where he's standing—right where there would have been the only footprints of the driver." He had to all but yell over the baying hounds, and he scowled at Pete's dogs leaping and cavorting around the visibly upset man. "Why hasn't someone told Fite to lock up those mutts?"

"I was on my way to do that when you pulled in."

Chagrined, Buddy didn't wait for Jared to comment further; he took off. Halfway there, he yelled something at Deputy Adams that Jared didn't catch, but it made the lanky cop pull out of the Firebird so fast, he hit his head on the frame. His sharp curse and subsequent shuffling made Jared half tempted to reach for his gun.

"Shooting the son of a bitch wouldn't make half the mess."

Turning away from the pitiful scene, he came face-to-face with Deputy Roy Russell. The shorter man's dark, somber eyes and gray, thin hair testified that he had as many years in law enforcement as Jared, and was as disturbed by Reese's actions.

"Sorry, Chief. He's new."

"So I heard." Sometimes new was good, because then people did everything by the book as though each page was tattooed on the inside of their eyeballs. Why hadn't they been blessed with one of those? "Well, this sure is starting off bad."

"I've only been here a minute, but it feels worse."

"Yeah, Eagan tells me there's no sign of her."

"That's not all." At Jared's questioning look, Russell lifted both eyebrows, as well. "He didn't tell you?"

"Can't say I gave him time to." Actually, he'd expected

his man to share anything pertinent immediately. It seemed the new guy wasn't the only one screwing up tonight.

"Her purse is in there. At least, I'm assuming it's hers. That's why I was in my car. I've called the sheriff, told him we're going to need John. Hope you don't mind me making that decision before talking to you."

"I would have done the same thing." John Box was the new detective for the Sheriff's Department. A transplant from the Dallas PD with fifteen years in Homicide, he'd moved his family to the Pineywoods after hearing his teen-age son and daughter respond to him once too often in mall-speak. Wood County was fortunate to have him, and because Pete's property was only partially in Split Creek, the sheriff's people had as much jurisdiction here as Jared did. "Tell me about the purse. What makes you think it's hers?"

"It looks like something my teenage niece would carry. You know—less than half the size of what older women carry, and the seams splitting from being crammed with brushes and cassettes and makeup. It's on the passenger floorboard."

"Tipped over as though the car had been stopped sharply, or as though thrown back in for…whatever reason?"

"Neither. It's pretty much upright, kinda leaning toward the console. Looks intentionally placed there, as though that's where she kept it. My wife keeps hers that way, too, since I told her how at city corners thieves like to bust in windows and steal purses they see on the seat."

"Are there any signs of a struggle? Blood? Spilled liquids?"

"I wish. It's such a stagnant scene, it gives me the creeps. But listen, I only had a quick glance around. Once

I guessed what we were dealing with, I got the hell away from there.''

''Wish you'd given your cohort the same advice,'' Jared replied with a nod toward Adams, who was still standing too close to the vehicle to suit him.

Roy sucked air between his front teeth. ''That's an ambitious boy, Chief. Made it clear after his second day that he wants to be the department's second detective.''

It wouldn't happen because of his performance on this case. ''Ignore me if I'm insulting your intelligence,'' Jared replied. ''But if I don't get to him first, remind Box to take print samples from Mr. Up-and-Coming so we don't waste time on false leads.''

''I hear you.'' The deputy glanced over toward the house, where Pete was penning his dogs, then back at the street, and finally the woods. ''Where do you think she is?''

''Until a few minutes ago, I'd hoped at a friend's having a good pout.''

''Spoiled type?''

''A little. More accurately, part of a struggling family. Anyone related to Buck Ramey has her work cut out for her.''

Roy's eyes widened. ''She's *that* Ramey?''

''There aren't any others in these parts that I know of.''

''I'd never seen her at the garage.''

''It's not exactly her idea of a fun place to hang out.''

''Mike's little sister…damn.'' He eyed the Firebird with new dread. ''It's gonna be tough on Mike to see this.''

''She isn't going to.''

That, too, won him a look of surprise. ''Who else is going to tow it and keep it locked away from vandals and the curious? You know she has the contract for Split

Fork—half the county for that matter. Even Cuddy would call her, seeing how close we are to town.''

True. And considering the hour, Bendix up in Winnsboro would cuss him until Sunday for hauling his butt out of bed at this hour if it meant crossing into Mike's territory. Besides, he did want the Firebird close. But, heaven help her, Mike didn't need this.

Once more Jared peered into the darkness toward the farm-to-market road. There wasn't so much as a security light at the entrance to Pete's farm. What would make Faith turn in here of all places?

''You sure you didn't see anything or anyone while driving over here?'' he asked Roy.

''Not a soul. Folks don't frequent rural clubs the way they used to, and even less so on a weekday. It's also too early for the milk trucks to start making the rounds to the dairy farms. I know you're hoping the girl had car trouble and decided to walk home, but I reckon if that was the case, she'd have been more likely to grab her purse and head up to the house and ask the old guy for help.''

''Could be Pete's dogs scared her.''

''So why not honk the horn until he came out?'' He gestured toward the abandoned car. ''Her keys are still in the ignition. Who leaves a vehicle like that?''

Someone who was in a hurry, or hurt...or who didn't have a choice. Before he faced Michaele, he had to have a clue as to which it was, because one thing was for sure—Mike would demand answers.

''We have to search the woods,'' he said.

With a fatalistic sigh, Roy glanced down at his shiny new boots. ''Thought you'd say that. I'd hoped that since Pete's hounds hadn't picked up any scent, we could pretty much cancel out worrying about that.''

''With the chicken stink around here, it's a wonder those

noses can lead them to their food bowls.'' He grew more sober. ''Plus, we don't know that if something is out there, it's above ground.''

Roy stopped tucking his pants legs into his boots. Straightening, he met Jared's unblinking stare. ''I'll keep Adams close by me,'' he said quietly. ''Hopefully, that way I'll be able to stop him if he's about to make another mistake. But I'll tell you up front—I'd be cool if this turns out to be a waste of time.''

''Me, too,'' Jared murmured as he headed to take a closer look at the car himself. ''Me, too.''

10

2:40 a.m.

Garth Powers stared at the massive Southwest-style desk his wife had given him for their first Christmas in this house. It gleamed from a recent dose of lemon oil, testament to the faithful attention Jessica awarded everything in their home. He ran his fingers over and over the light pine surface, as he had been doing for some time now, when he wasn't lifting the near-empty tumbler of scotch to his mouth. No housekeeper or cleaning woman for them, no sir. No matter how often he suggested it to her when she occasionally broke down and complained about a touch of arthritis or her overscheduled life, Jess didn't believe anyone could care for their possessions the way she did, and he knew better than to argue when she made up her mind about something.

But they definitely would end up arguing if he didn't get his ass up to bed. It was—he did a double take as he noticed the time—late. For that matter, where was *she?* It was well past time for her to be home. Had he forgotten some special thingamajig again? With all he had on his mind tonight, it wouldn't surprise him.

He tried to remember her schedule. *Wednesdays...* It had been Republican Ladies night. Except that once a month she missed that session to attend Split Creek Gardeners. No, the gardening club met just a few days ago…didn't it? Either way, no social gathering lasted this long.

Moaning, he rubbed his face. He should call her on her cellular, but how could he in his condition? She would know something was wrong straight off. He hoped to hell she hadn't had car trouble and needed a lift. After polishing off his fifth scotch, the last thing he needed was a summons to collect her.

He was reaching for the switch on his amber-screened desk lamp when he heard a sound in the hall. Damn, he thought, self-consciously touching his sore right hand. He hadn't even heard the garage door open.

Seconds later, Jessica tall, slim and elegant even in designer sweats, leaned in to his study. Her intelligent brown eyes immediately settled on the crystal tumbler before shifting back to him. "What's this? You should be fast asleep by now."

"On my way. I was just…making some notes for Commencement exercises."

This time her gaze dropped to the cleared blotter, but her smile was sympathetic. "You always do a marvelous job, Mr. Perfectionist. I don't know why you drive yourself crazy worrying so much."

She waited for him to come to her, then offered her cheek. Jessica was an attractive woman at any time—forty, with vibrant hair every bit as rich as the lustrous walnut door, perfectly coiffed into a smooth swept-back style that framed a strong forehead and high cheekbones. Her somber eyes embraced him, but he didn't miss their canniness. Jess loved hard and long—but not carelessly. Most of the time her dedication to him and his career left him beyond grateful, almost humbled. Sometimes, however, he struggled with a feeling of suffocation.

What he felt tonight, though, wasn't her fault. No, not tonight. Not in a while. It was his doing. All him.

"How'd it go?" he asked, suddenly noticing her clothes were paint-stained. "What did you do, start early on the Christmas parade float and lose track of time?"

She lifted precisely tweezed eyebrows. "I figured you would forget—and after I only told you three times!"

"Sorry."

"How many of those scotches did you have?"

Her Dallas-bred, SMU-educated drawl showed up most when she was ready to fuck or fight, and he gestured helplessly, wanting neither. "You threw me, that's all. That's not what you usually wear to a meeting of any kind."

"I wasn't at a meeting."

Shit. What did I miss? "Well, Deirdre Collingwood phoned to ask about the University Women thing." He wasn't about to admit that he couldn't remember squat about that one, either.

Jessica slipped her hand inside the open *V* of his dress shirt. "She's been out of town. I'll call her in the morning. What's wrong, Garth?"

"Nothing." But when she tugged lightly at his chest hairs, he knew evasiveness wasn't going to work. He decided on a portion of the truth. One truth. "Waylan Ivens."

"That's old news. You matched that other school's offer to Coach Ivens. Don't tell me he's trying to blackmail you to up the ante."

She was his biggest fan, proud to have brought him to what had been her grandparents' property, although they'd leveled the house and rebuilt; proud to parade her celebrated "super-jock" husband around town, and claim the prestige that won them in the community. For the past twelve years she'd made sure they built on that celebrity status, to the point where he only half joked when saying that after he died, he would be lucky if she didn't bronze his balls to display at parades and during town elections.

With his left hand, he lifted her fingers to his lips. ''I don't deserve you.''

''Agreed. Now answer the question. Is he?''

Since it wasn't the primary concern preying on his mind, Garth had to think a moment. ''Not him. Them. The other school has made a counteroffer. No way am I going to be able to go that high. We'll lose the bastard—and after he gave me his word that he'd stay at least five years!''

Jessica freed herself to touch his cheek. ''What will you do?''

''Try to be a good sport and wish him the best.'' Growing comfortable with the story, Garth shrugged and allowed some embellishment. ''It ticks me off that he's doing this to us now, though. How am I supposed to find somebody equal to his talent and reputation at the end of the school year? Hell, football practice starts again in seven weeks!''

''Something will come up. Everyone loves to work for you.''

''Obviously not.''

At his droll reply, Jessica began to mimic his earlier caress. It was then that she noticed his bruised hand. ''What have you done to yourself?''

''It's nothing.''

''Every knuckle is bloody and bruised. Your fingers will be swollen to twice their size by morning. Please tell me you didn't do something foolish to Ivens.''

''Ah...no. Actually, it was something more asinine. When he left my office, I punched the wall.''

"You poor idiot." She slipped her arm around his waist and directed him toward the stairs. "You need a warm shower, and then I'll put some medicated cream on it."

"Sounds tempting, but it's already so late."

"You're tight enough to snap. You won't sleep unless we get you relaxed."

Despite his preoccupation and fatigue, he experienced a twinge in his groin, helped, of course, by her hand sliding down over his ass. Amazing, he thought. "What did you have in mind?"

They'd reached the top of the stairs. She directed him through the white-on-white bedroom, which in the glow of the bathroom night-light looked far more inviting than on bright summer mornings when the sun drilled him awake. The king-size bed called to him—but not as clearly as did Jess's eyes.

"What's my lover's favorite thing?" she murmured, stopping him in front of the double-sink vanity in the bathroom. Not waiting for an answer, she reached for his belt.

Garth watched, bemused. Before she had his zipper opened, he was erect. "I don't deserve you," he said again. But he also urged her to her knees.

It was better this way, he thought. No explanations, no burdening her with his messes. Of course, he was only buying time. In the back of his mind, he'd always understood and accepted that. But as her mouth closed on him, he shut his eyes and blocked that out for one more night—blocked out everything but the pleasure.

11

4:12 a.m.

Michaele couldn't sit for more than a minute or two at a time. Ever since Jared had left, she'd been moving from room to room, window to window, stopping every few minutes, tempted to reach for the phone to call and ask for an update. Surely it had been long enough to do that now?

She glanced at the kitchen clock and uttered a deep-throated groan. No wonder she ached all over; she'd been awake for almost twenty-four hours. But no way did she dare lie down at this stage; even if she could fall asleep—which she doubted—she would never be able to rouse herself again in time to reopen the garage.

"This has to end," she muttered. "It has to."

She wondered again at why Jared had cut short their conversation. Sure, she'd heard Curtis on the radio, but that didn't mean it had been about Faith. But what other reason could he have, not to have called her back by now?

That's it, Ramey. You're overdosing on self-impor-tance—

At the sound of a vehicle, she immediately dashed to the kitchen door. Yanking it open, she saw that it was indeed Jared's patrol car. For one instant her heart lifted with hope—only to plunge when she saw the empty passenger seat. She felt a strange sense of disconnection, until he started up the stairs; then she noted his expression was as ominous as she'd ever seen it. Except the time...

"What is it?" she demanded.

He didn't reply, not until he was inside. How she held on to her temper, she didn't know; probably because of his appearance. He looked as though he'd been rolled in mud and again in weeds.

"We haven't found her," he finally announced.

"Then why do you look as though you did, but can't find the stomach to tell me?"

"Because we do have...something. Her car."

Once, when she was thirteen, Buck had punched her in the belly. After she lost her lunch, Michaele had knocked him cold with the empty bottle at his feet, and when he'd come to, she'd vowed that if he ever touched her again, she'd have him arrested, and she and Faith would take their chances with foster care. Jared's announcement brought that sickening pain back. Only, this time she couldn't afford to lose it, not in front of him.

"We had a call from Pete Fite," he continued. "His dogs woke him. When they refused to calm down, he figured he had another coyote or worse after his stock."

"That doesn't make sense. Her car at Pete's place?"

"The tags and VIN number check out. Also... Hell," he muttered, looking as though he'd prefer to be anywhere but here. "There's no other way to do this, but say it straight out. Her purse was in there, too."

Her mind refused to register what he was saying. She heard the words, but their meaning somehow would not pass through the icy morass that had shut down her brain.

"Maybe you'd better sit down," Jared told her.

"You've been searching the woods out there, haven't

you?'' she said with dawning realization. ''Looking for her body.''

''There's every reason to assume she's alive.''

''You searched the woods!''

''We had to!'' His equally testy reply reverberated through the house. That seemed to shake him as much as it did her, and although he placed his hands on his hips, he said more calmly, ''What you need to take comfort in is knowing we found nothing. There's no evidence of violence—not in the car, not anywhere.''

That wasn't comforting at all. ''So she was forced. Taken away at gunpoint.''

''Damn it, don't make this harder on yourself than necessary.''

''You took fingerprints and—what do you call them? Trace samples?''

''We brought in John Box. He got a few prints. As good as they are, I suspect they're Faith's—and yours.''

The slight delay in adding her name made Michaele lift her chin. ''So now I'm a suspect in my own sister's disappearance?''

''Of course not. The point is aside from those prints and a little red ore on the driver's floor mat, it's as spotless as if she had just washed the thing.''

''She did. Yesterday. She's very proud of that car. Should be, considering what it cost.'' The crass comment made her grimace. ''What about the steering wheel?''

''Clean.''

''You mean, except for her prints and mine again, right?''

''No, it's been wiped down.'' That revelation triggered her queasiness again. ''The caller.''

''Maybe.''

''What now?''

"I need you."

They weren't new words to her. He'd said them before; in fact, they were his usual "call to duty" whenever he phoned to say he had a vehicle in need of a tow. But tonight they sounded different, somehow…and stirred emotions too complex to deal with.

"Good," he said, when she didn't respond. His gaze moved over her face. "I was afraid I was going to have to fight you about this. I'm glad you don't want to go out there. I'll call Cuddy and tell him to get Bendix. It'll go over better if he phones—"

She clamped her hand over his on the phone's receiver, and held him still. "Don't even think it!" Of course, it was merely a token gesture, but she had to try.

"It's the best way to go in this case," he told her.

"That clumsy ox isn't putting his paws on my sister's car."

"Could you please let me save you from having to do this?"

"You didn't let anyone hide anything from you when you lost Sandy." His warm breath on her face made her release him and take a step back, but she didn't yield on her argument. "This is my job."

"You've got the wrong wrecker. You'll need the roll-back for the Firebird."

Seeing that he knew he'd lost this round, she grew calmer. "Which is at the garage and directly on the way."

"You'll wake Buck."

"Fat chance."

"I'll talk to Bendix and watch him like he was on the Ten Most Wanted list. He'll have to be careful, and under the circumstances I'll bet he'd have no problem with dropping off the car at your place. C'mon, Mike. For once, don't turn this into a twelve-round championship fight."

Is that how he saw this? To her, it wasn't about stubbornness, it was about being a professional—dependable and efficient. But as she rubbed her sweating hands against her hips, she was reminded of what she was wearing.

"From what I heard today on the police scanner, Bendix's already had a pretty full day. Give me a minute to change, and I'll be ready to go."

As she started for the stairs, he blocked her way with his arm across the doorway.

"No matter how hard you try to prepare yourself, this isn't going to be like a normal call."

"I thought you said there's nothing there?"

"There isn't. That doesn't mean it's an easy scene to look at. Everything reverberates with more questions than answers, as though someone stood there and set a scene."

"Premeditation."

"No, sweetheart. Psychological fucking. I don't care how long you've been in the business, a situation like this preys on your mind, starts eating at you from the inside out."

"Right now, I'm more concerned that Buck might wake up as Bendix drops off the Firebird, and instead of asking questions, take a crowbar to him."

"Bendix is three times your size—he can take care of himself. Don't you get it? One Ramey is already missing— I'd rather not go for two."

It was then that she felt his fear, almost tasted it. "You do think she's dead," she whispered.

"Don't start putting words in my mouth."

"Don't treat me like some just-hatched chick. It's even in your eyes. You're thinking the worst."

"No."

"Why give up so soon? You said yourself that all you

have is an abandoned car. Or is it? If there's something you haven't told me, I want to know. Now.''

''Will you give it a rest! Somebody is playing a nasty trick. You know it. I know it. But until I understand why and find Faith, I want you safe.''

They were logical words, but as insistent as he sounded, there was something in his expression that kept her from believing him.

''I'm not ready to explain more, Mike.''

She continued just standing there.

''It's for your own good.''

How she hated that line. ''In case you haven't noticed, I already have one *daddy* more than I need.''

''If you think that's how I think of you, you're in deeper denial than I thought.''

She felt a muscle twitch under her right eye. Embarrassed, she bowed her head. ''Not now.''

''You brought it up, not me. Either way, I'm not going to pretend your safety isn't as important to me as finding Faith.'' Before she could interrupt, he removed the arm blocking her. ''All right, all right. Go do what you have to do. I'll be outside. Just understand this—I'm not letting you out of my sight until you're back here and locked up tight again.''

Afraid he might change his mind, she hurried upstairs.

Once she'd exchanged wreckers as quietly as possible and was driving toward the Fite farm, Michaele's adrenaline really kicked in. It was one thing to want to save face in what was a male-dominated profession; it was quite another to act the classic masochist-martyr. But how much worse would it be to be stuck at the house with her overactive imagination? No, she needed to see everything Jared had seen before facing her father, let alone everyone else who was bound to stop by, once word got around, asking innumerable questions.

Jared's car lights remained close behind her. She wasn't used to such mother-henning. This had to be triggering something about Sandy long buried in him; in any case, she hoped he would snap out of it. Although she wanted and needed friendships—more than was comfortable to admit—if this search stretched out, she was going to shelve the whole concept and focus on protecting herself. That would mean not allowing anyone to know just how vulnerable she was feeling.

Less than a mile down the road, she turned into Pete's driveway. Considering the hour, the number of vehicles and people that were subsequently illuminated by her headlights was as touching as it was disconcerting. She was comfortable around cops and enjoyed shooting the breeze as much as anyone, but this was overwhelming. There hadn't been this kind of turnout of law enforcement personnel since young Doc Arnold's ten-year-old suffered a fatal jet ski accident out on the town lake.

She maneuvered around and between people and vehicles to turn the wrecker on the narrow driveway, since the Firebird was parked sloping toward the woods and would first have to be pulled back onto the roadway. A simple *J*-hook would be the least intrusive method.

Bruce Griggs, her personal favorite aside from Jared, helped her navigate and get people out of her way. By the time she had the thing set to load, her nerves were back in control.

She jumped down from the cab, aware of the numerous eyes on her.

She'd already greeted a few of the guys, but had made it clear that she wasn't interested in small talk tonight— or any consoling. As promised, Jared was watching, too, and she didn't want to jeopardize her right to be there, or anywhere else down the road if the occasion arose.

If it hadn't been for the license plates and the familiar crystal star dangling from the rearview mirror, Michaele might have tried to convince herself that this vehicle wasn't her sister's.

"How you holding up, Little Bit?"

The voice spawning images of mangling gears belonged to Chester "Cuddy" Cudahy, the sheriff of Wood County. As usual the six-and-a-half-foot beef-loving, bourbon-worshipping man had an unsmoked cigar clamped between his stained teeth, and his red face was half hidden by a huge straw Stetson. Stereotypical as he looked, one glimpse of those compassionate, rheumy eyes made her own suddenly burn as though she'd rubbed them after harvesting a field of jalapeños.

"Hey, Sheriff. Sorry you had to be called out tonight."

The East Texas icon, whose motto was "Keeping the department lean and the county clean," tugged her close with a gruff gentleness for a brief hug. "Would have come regardless, once I heard this involves your kin, honey."

"I appreciate that." Michaele drew a deep breath. "I've already asked the chief his opinion of this. Would you mind giving me yours? What do you think is going on?"

Cuddy rolled his cigar between his tobacco-browned fingers. "Be easier to teach a three-legged dog to scratch."

Jared joined them. "She thinks I'm keeping something from her."

Michaele shot him a frustrated look. "I said no such thing. Did you tell him about the call?"

"He knows."

"So she's been kidnapped, right?" she said to Sheriff Cudahy.

"Possibly."

''Well, what else could it be?''

''We're trying to figure that out, Mike. Unfortunately, no one left us a note.''

His gentle chiding forced her to check her impatience. But as she made a complete circle to inspect their surroundings, the sight of the woods on either side of the driveway intensified her convictions. Even on a clear night with a full moon and the floodlights on, Michaele couldn't get Faith to toss out a bag of trash for fear something might slither across her toes. The idea that she would willingly have come here, let alone walked away, was more than unacceptable. There was no way—not if a wild boar were snorting up her skirt.

''She's been kidnapped,'' Michaele said. ''And with every hour the kidnapper is carrying her farther away.''

''Everyone in my department was called in as of a half-hour ago,'' Cuddy replied. ''Chief, you've called your day-shift people in, too, haven't you?''

''Right.''

Cuddy gave her a ''You see?'' look. ''I've also notified the Texas DPS, and all the counties around us have been called, too. Have a little confidence in us, Mike.''

She would love to; the problem was, nothing this close to home had happened to her before. Embarrassed, she nodded to the car. ''Are you ready for me to take it?''

The two men exchanged glances, before Cuddy said, ''It's all yours...but you know the drill.''

A vehicle brought in as evidence was to be secured until released by legal authority. That meant she had to keep it locked in the fenced yard behind the garage so that it would be out of reach of anyone and everyone, in case it needed another going over.

''Tattooed on the brain,'' she replied.

Michaele went back to work, anxious to get out of there.

The place felt…evil. It was probably her imagination; nevertheless, she couldn't help thinking something bad had happened in or around this car. The aftermath lingered, fouled the air, and sent images of inexplicable things flashing through her mind.

"What?"

Startled that Jared had managed to get so close without her hearing him, she dropped the leather gloves she'd just tugged off, now that the car was secured on the bed of the wrecker. Swearing under her breath, she swept them up off the ground.

"Michaele, something's going on in that busy head of yours. I want to know what it is. If you've seen or heard something—"

"It's just a feeling." She noted his blank expression. "Disappointed, huh? What did you think—I spotted something under the chassis? Maybe a message stuck there by bubble gum. Or how about the kidnapper's wallet, complete with address and photo so you can head straight over to his house and arrest him?"

He did what she'd done to him: he remained silent and just waited.

"Nothing about what went on here was her idea," she said quietly. "And what I said about kidnapping? Forget it. Anyone who knows us, knows it would break us to pay the most modest of ransoms."

"I'm thinking more of some kid wanting the Firebird. Maybe he dropped her off a few miles away, then lost his nerve and dumped the car, too."

"You mean someone connected with a chop shop?"

"I hope not. Those folks can be rougher on the driver than on a vehicle. It's almost graduation, Mike. You know how the kids are at this stage. They gulp a few beers, they start to get stupid."

"The purse I saw John take from the car—it's hers. Can I check it? Maybe I'll see something noteworthy."

"Sorry. It's been bagged."

Just in case, that's what it all boiled down to. They would even keep things from her if it suited them—just in case.

"This is crap," she muttered, and, slapping the gloves against her thigh, she climbed into the cab of the tow truck.

12

Checks and balances on a small-town level resulted in a longer wait than Michaele expected before she could actually leave with the Firebird, and it wasn't all that much earlier than usual that morning when she finally unlocked the gated back lot at the garage and unloaded Faith's car. Once that was done, she parked the roll-back up front beside the other tow truck. By then, Jared, who had been observing her from across the street, yielded his post to Jim Sutter, the other day-shift officer, and went inside. As she crossed the street to go to the café behind the station, she waved Jim inside, too.

"I'm just going to get myself a cup of coffee," she told the youngest of Jared's officers. "Everything's taken care of."

"Chief said to watch you until Buck's up and behaving himself, Ms. Mike."

"You let me worry about Buck—and Chief Morgan."

"You bet. Then I'll just enjoy the quiet out here a bit longer. Don't pay me any mind."

Resigned that the recent academy graduate feared Jared's ire more than hers, she went to the café. On her way back, she thrust a bag with coffee and a breakfast burrito at the always-hungry cop, before crossing the street and unlocking the front door of the family business.

Not surprisingly, her father barely stirred as she entered. He'd always been a deep sleeper, and the drinking only made that worse. It was the fluorescent lights that finally did it. Once he spotted her, he launched himself straight into the bathroom.

When he reappeared, she had two coffees and his favorite breakfast—biscuits and sausage—on the counter ready for him.

"Come eat," she said.

Instead, he reached for his hat where it had fallen behind the chair sometime during the night. Slapping it onto his head, he shot her a look steeped in animosity. Even from that distance, Michaele could tell he hadn't bothered with mouthwash or the toothpaste she kept in there. The lack of air-conditioning intensified the odor.

"My back is killing me," he snarled. "I should whip your ass for leaving me here all night."

"You just need to put something in your stomach."

"What is it?" Circling the counter, he lowered himself onto a stool with the caution of someone respectful of hemorrhoids. "My gut feels like it's been scrubbed with steel wool. Can't eat nothing spicy."

Considering what he regularly primed his insides with, she didn't doubt it. The only nonliquid she'd seen him ingest in the past twenty-four hours was a package of salty peanuts from the vending machine by the front door. "It's mild sausage with just a little sage."

"I hate sage."

"*I* hate sage. You love it."

He leaned closer and peered down at the biscuit and well-done pork patty, a perfect replica of what he liked to eat—when he did eat breakfast. "Looks like shit. I'll go find something myself. Better yet, I'm going over to Eugene's. A little hair of the dog'll fix me right up.''

"No way." Eugene Folsom ran the body shop directly behind them on Pine Street. He was also Buck's source for liquor when he couldn't get it anywhere else, but Eugene's brew was homemade and lethal. "Forget it."

Michaele grabbed a handful of Buck's overalls as he started for the door. The force of his wrenching free sent her flying back into the soda vending machine.

Stifling a moan for the pain in her shoulder, she righted herself and tried again. "We need to talk, Buck."

"Not in the mood. Jeez, the lights're still on out there. Why'd you wake me so early?"

"It's only fifteen minutes earlier than we usually get here—and there's a reason. Will you please listen?"

Something in her expression must have gotten through to what was left of his functioning brain. With a groan he rubbed at his whiskered jowls. "Got a helluva headache."

"Aspirin are in the bathroom. Take three, and then if you won't brush, at least rinse your mouth with mouthwash. Please. Whether it's a good idea or not, I'm afraid you're going to be doing a lot of talking today, and that breath of yours could crack steel."

"You shut your trap or I'll—"

"Buck!"

Michaele hadn't heard Jared approach, but there he was in the open doorway glaring at her father.

Buck dropped the arm raised to backhand her. "Hey, Chief. Whatcha know?"

"Michaele's only trying to sober you up so you don't make a bigger ass out of yourself than need be."

"What did I—? Why're y'all picking on me?"

Stepping closer, only to grimace as he got within reach

of Buck's breath, Jared replied, "I take it she hasn't had a chance to tell you yet?"

"Tell me what?"

"Go pull yourself together. Rinse out your mouth, too. It's time to start acting like the head of your family."

More confused than offended, Buck shuffled toward the bathroom again. "Ain't one of you making any sense. Wish y'all would just leave me be."

As he shut the door, Michaele rubbed her sore shoulder, then started rewrapping the food. She knew better than to expect Buck to eat once he was told the news.

"It wouldn't hurt if you took a bite of something," Jared told her.

She didn't want to argue about food. "Did you learn anything new at the station?"

"No. I was in the midst of debriefing everyone and setting up a new game plan for the day, when Buddy yelled that Buck was getting temperamental."

"That wasn't temperamental, that was plain old sour. What's the new game plan?"

"Among other things, I'm putting a call in to the college as soon as they're open, to notify them about Faith. I've also got a call in for the sheriff up in Camp County. Before I talk to him, I need names from you."

"Whose?"

"Faith's friends."

"You know them almost as well as I do."

"Not only the people around here—those up there. Also teachers she was close to."

That was rich. "Ever since Faith graduated from high school, I've barely been able to keep track of where she's going, let alone who she's going with. I did well to pin down her class schedule and get a glimpse of her grades at the end of each semester, and I only managed that because I was writing her tuition checks.''

"I understand. All I'm saying is that the more you can give us, the more thorough we can be. If the Department of Public Safety has to be called in, they'll want that and more.''

At midnight, she'd wanted the state law enforcement people—shoot, she'd wanted the National Guard; but now the thought of bringing them in meant accepting that Faith might be lost to them. Not quite ready to take that psychological step, she was almost relieved when Buck reappeared.

"Ain't you got somebody else to harass?'' he muttered to Jared.

"Stop it,'' Michaele replied. "There's been bad news. It's about Faith.''

Immediately her father's sullen attitude vanished. He looked from her to Jared. "What about her? What's wrong?''

"She's missing,'' Michaele said. "She never came home yesterday.''

A myriad of emotions played over her father's face— incomprehension, denial, anger—but the sudden slump of his shoulders told her that he understood. "There's gotta be…''

When he didn't finish the statement, Michaele shook her head. "We don't know the reason. And to complicate things, her car's been found. It was in Pete's driveway.''

Buck frowned, though his bloodshot eyes focused on nothing. "Pete Fite? Why would she be staying with him?''

"She's not. That's the point. She had no reason to be there.''

"Why, that dirty slug. I'll tear him in two if he—''

"Pete is incidental in this, Buck."

"As far as anything or anyone can be ruled out so far," Jared added.

Michaele shot him a thanks-for-nothing look. "Pete was as upset as I was," she told her father. "The car was just abandoned there."

Heaven knew what was going on in her father's mind. His facial muscles twitched and spasmed.

"Must be with a friend."

"I don't think so. I had a call. He made it clear that she wouldn't be coming back."

Dazed, Buck stared at her. "Where's she going?"

"Nowhere that I know of. At least, not willingly. We think someone's kidnapped her."

At that troubling pronouncement, he began fidgeting. He dug deep into the pocket of his overalls and came up with a single crumpled bill and several coins. Michaele understood he was checking to see if he had enough to buy a pint of whatever rotgut he could find.

"Don't even think it," she intoned. "I need you here. We haven't managed it in years, and maybe we'll never do it well, but for once we have to stand together like a real family."

"Sure. You're right. But I have to…I'll be back in a few minutes. Just need a sip of something to wash away the cobwebs."

"For crying out loud, are you planning on staying comatose so you can't be asked to identify a body?"

He brushed past her and lurched into the garage. Michaele followed, but it was a waste of time. When he escaped out the back door, she swore. "Don't you dare touch that Firebird! It's evidence!"

The car might as well have been coated with Anthrax, the way he kept his distance. But he proved amazingly adept at unlocking the back gate connecting their property to Eugene's.

''Buck!'' she yelled, as he threw open the gate and ran off. ''Buck!''

Seething, she followed and locked up after him. Jared was waiting for her in the doorway when she returned. Even as she accepted that her father wasn't Jared's problem, she was ticked that he hadn't helped to stop him.

''You okay?''

''Considering that it's been this way since I was ten?'' She shrugged. ''Even before my mother died, it was no picnic. Why am I ever surprised that he's inept at being a parent? All he cares about is that his clothes get washed, there's money to swipe to buy booze, and he has a bed to fall into—provided he's sober enough to find it.''

None of this was news to Jared, but then, she didn't see why he was asking if she was okay, either. That was the most useless question to ask a person at a hospital, in the company of the police, or dealing with a funeral.

''I need to open,'' she muttered, leaving him by the Firebird to return up front.

As she raised the garage's overhead doors, she saw the sky was beginning to resemble the lavender shade of Faith's favorite nail polish. The unwelcome analogy made her grateful to see a customer immediately pull in, although the late-model Cadillac wouldn't have been her choice.

He sure is early, Michaele thought, as Garth Powers shut off his vehicle. Although she liked him well enough, he wasn't one of her favorite customers and she'd never felt the impulse to drool over him the way some females in town did. But all in all, who could say anything really negative about Mr. Clean?

The ex-sports star offered a warm, if tired, smile as she

rounded the car, and once again she was reminded of how men almost always aged more gracefully than women.

"Morning, Michaele. Would you fill her up for me, please?"

A tight-lipped nod was the best she could do, and she quickly had the hose set, the pump running. "Need any checking under the hood?"

"No need. Just had her serviced at the dealer in Tyler. Is that Jared in there? He's up and at 'em early."

"So are you." Because that sounded too curt, she added, "He's been up all night working a case." What the heck, she thought. He was going to hear the news within the next hour or so, anyway.

Garth did a double take. "Trouble?"

"Faith's missing."

"What?"

She repeated the spare few bits of information she'd shared with her father only minutes before.

"Has Fite been arrested?"

The question reminded her that even after all these years, he didn't know the community—aside from the students—the way Jessica did. "If there's one thing I do know, it's that Pete Fite can barely bring himself to put down one of his dogs when they get old or sick. He'd never hurt anyone."

That only made Garth more upset. "My God," he uttered. "It *is* happening again."

13

Jared lingered by the Firebird only long enough to satisfy himself that it hadn't been tampered with, but when he followed Michaele and saw Garth's Cadillac, he knew he'd made a tactical mistake.

"Why didn't you call me?" Garth demanded the instant he joined them. "Didn't you think I had a right to know?"

Mindful of Michaele's sharp gaze, Jared replied, "I would have checked in with you soon enough."

"What did you mean 'again'?" Michaele asked Garth.

Ignoring her, Garth snapped, "I have priorities, too. Exactly 703 of them. How do I protect those kids when you're keeping me in the dark?"

"Try not making irresponsible intellectual leaps."

"How can you say that? He left his message in my school!"

Jared narrowed his eyes. "Stow it!"

"You still think it's a prank," Garth said, incredulous. "But what if you're wrong? What if that sicko's got Faith, and next targets one of those kids?"

The pump clicked off; however, Michaele stayed put. "What message?"

"Damn it, Garth," Jared growled, "you're out of line here. There's no evidence of a connection."

"And there won't be, because you refused to take it seriously! You should have taken samples, Jared."

"That's enough!"

"Hey!" Michaele shouted, smacking the roof of the sedan with her fist. "The next guy who treats me as though I'm this oil spot on the concrete gets a close encounter with this fist. Now one of you tell me what's going on!"

For several seconds her demand hung heavily in the air. It was Garth who broke the silence. "I'm sorry, Jared. By remaining silent, I become an accomplice. Michaele, someone left a message at the school yesterday evening. Jared's convinced that the message was merely a prank in bad taste about Sandy, because of the timing and all. But if the message is true and Faith ran into this guy, you deserve to know what you're up against."

Linking Sandy to her sister had the obvious effect on Michaele. Jared watched her face turn gray; her demeanor resembled something caving in on itself.

"Sandy was murdered in her own home...her own bed," she murmured. "Butchered. Oh, God..."

"Don't go there," Jared said, automatically reaching out to steady her. "The only connection is the timing."

She brushed him off. "Six years today. Who could forget something so horrible happening here in our town? That poor girl stabbed...her throat cut...and the killer was never caught!"

"Michaele, listen to me. It's a prank."

"There was something written above Sandy's bed. Is that what was at the school? 'Welcome to Hell'?"

"The numbers were there again," Garth replied. "But this time he simply wrote 'I'm back.'"

"All right, that's enough," Jared snapped. "She doesn't need this."

"*I'll* decide what I can and can't handle!"

Seething, Michaele jerked the nozzle free and slammed it back on the pump. Then she refastened the cap. "I can't believe this. You had a clue, a warning of trouble, and you kept it from us?''

''While you're busy working yourself into a knot, try remembering that crap written at the scene of the crime was published in every paper in Texas, and picked up by the media in half the country,'' Jared said coldly. ''Perfect fodder for every halfwit copycat in the mood to get some attention.''

''But you don't know for sure, and now Faith could be lying out there with *her* throat cut!''

Hearing his worst fears voiced, Jared struck back—at the messenger. ''Pay her and get the fuck out of here,'' he ordered Garth.

''I need answers,'' Garth argued.

''Get in line.''

''Those kids are my responsibility. Do you know what their parents are going to say when this gets out? You'll be lucky not to wind up with a town-wide panic on your hands.''

Thanks to you. Jared wished he'd gotten that sample he'd taken secretly sent out last night. But because he'd gone home and buried his own bitterness and bad memories in a few beers, the sample hadn't left until a while ago.

His delay in replying won a bitter smile from Garth. He began handing Michaele the money for the gas, saying, ''You have my sympathies.''

She waved off payment. ''We're even. If it weren't for you, I guess I'd still be in the dark—about a lot of things. Just tell me one more thing. Exactly when did you find that message?''

''About an hour after the last club and practice session let out.''

She closed her eyes. When she opened them again, she

looked straight at Jared. "You knew. Something was terribly wrong, and you said nothing. It never crossed your mind that a warning, some kind of outreach to the public might have been in order?"

Jared felt as though he were standing in a huge vacuum, where everything sane and reassuring was being sucked away. "Listen to yourself. To protect whom? Faith? At the time she was miles from here. How would that have helped her?"

"You don't know that. You don't know anything!"

As she stormed off, Jared fought the strong urge to hit something.

"Sorry," Garth said. "But you deserved that."

"I think I told you to take a hike."

"You owe me an answer, and I can't give you much time."

Jared knew that, and knew what he was up against. He was a small-town cop, used to settling drunken brawls and officiating over fender benders. His department hadn't even been able to resolve most of the burglaries that had been on the increase in the past year. This situation with Faith was fast rising out of his league, and Cuddy's, as well. "Give me another twenty-four hours before you make any announcements. People are going to be upset enough about Faith to make everyone cautious, which is what you want, anyway."

"Except for one technicality, namely, the *who* in the fear quotient. No." Garth shook his head. "If you don't have news by noon, or, better yet, have Faith back safe and sound, I'm going to hold an assembly and make an appropriate announcement. We owe them that. There needs to be time to notify parents and assume safeguards."

Jared stepped back from the car. He'd lost ground and had to accept it. "Do what you can."

"Noon, then. And that's only if nothing else happens. If we're contacted again, or—" Garth started the engine and shifted into gear "—well, I don't suppose I need to tell you that's when choice will be out of my hands, too."

"You're perfectly clear, all right," Jared muttered after the departing car.

Despite Garth's having complicated things for him, Jared wasn't totally lacking in sympathy for his friend. It was the situation and the stress that was making him overlook so much—like asking about Garth's bandaged hand. Hell, had things turned out differently, Garth would be his brother-in-law.

After the death of Jessica and Sandy's parents, Garth had been almost a foster father to Jess's kid sister. Later, once she'd earned her business degree, he'd given her a job at the school despite some minor flack about nepotism. Fortunately, Sandy had proven herself capable, running the entire administrative office, as well as coaching the girl's twirling team. When the team brought home their first state championship trophy during a dry year when the boys couldn't win anything for the town, Sandy had been a local heroine. And that was why Faith's disappearance was going to be so hard on the community: the ex-high school cheerleader inspired the same affection from people.

Drawing a deep breath, he went in search of Michaele, and found her hunched over her workstation preparing a service form. Jared noted the pronounced shaking of her hands, and the way she kept clenching her teeth as though fighting some emotional onslaught.

He wanted to hold her, as he had last night, to offer her comfort and maybe take a little for himself. But he knew that trying would set her off. "I'm sorry," he said instead.

"I had a right to know."

No, she wasn't going to beat around the bush, he

thought. She'd never been that way about anything, except when it came to him. That was one of the many things he admired about her...when it wasn't driving him nuts.

''I know. Why do you think I'm here instead of back at the office like I should have been ten minutes ago?''

''Don't let me keep you.''

''What you heard me say to Garth, I meant. I don't believe there's a connection. Equally critical for you to understand is that no matter why I do what I do, hurting you isn't on the agenda.''

She made a mistake and ruthlessly scratched it out. Then, because that made an even uglier mess, she ripped up the form and tossed it away. Her rigid stance told him that only pride was holding her together.

''Look at me, Mike.''

She ignored him.

''Then do me a favor—go home. I'll have someone collect Buck and bring him to the house, too. You've been up all night. You can't—''

''Don't!'' she ground out. ''Just find my sister. That's all I want from you. Find Faith, and then leave me the hell alone—!''

''Chief? *Chief!*''

14

Norma Headly's urgent call from across the street canceled any hope Jared had of trying to reason with Mike. He loped over to see what was up.

"Sorry to interrupt." Norma gestured toward the station. "Loyal's on the phone. I'm not surprised that the town Clearing House for Information heard the news, but it's been some time since I've heard him this upset—and he hasn't even left home yet."

Loyal, the mayor of Split Creek and owner of the local barber shop, also owned one of the six city blocks in town, so it wasn't a surprise that he'd heard something. He knew everybody and their pet cat-dog-gerbil and, since the death last year of his wife, he had lots of free time to indulge in his second passion—listening for hours to his short wave and police radios.

"He probably picked us up when we said we were calling in the sheriff earlier this morning." Jared walked with her to the station and held the door open for her. "What specifically did he say?"

"Let's put it this way considering what he filled my ear with, it's a wonder he didn't show up hours ago." As they stepped inside, Norma patted her hair in place, although it was permed and sprayed to the degree where it would have taken an F-3 tornado to disrupt the short, dense mass.

"Don't be surprised if he asks why you haven't asked for the National Guard to come in."

Jared grunted. "If we don't find the kid soon, that may be on the table."

He cut a left behind her desk and strode into his office. Snatching up the phone, he began, "Loyal. I should warn you, every light on my phone is blinking. Make it short."

"Why the devil haven't you made an announcement, called for reinforcements, put up blockades yet to monitor who's coming in and out of town?" the mayor retorted, equally testy.

"Are we talking about Faith Ramey's disappearance?"

"You have more missing people I don't know about?"

Jared massaged the bridge of his nose. "No, sir. I'm just making sure I know which conversation you eavesdropped on."

That had the intended effect, and Oliver Klemper Loyal, who'd survived the childhood nickname "Liver Klump," sputtered for several seconds before regaining control. "My radios are legal, and you know it. Besides, I'm the mayor. Are you suggesting I don't have a right to know what's going on in my own town?"

"Absolutely not. That's why I was planning on calling you as soon as I got back into the office."

"You were?"

"We're at the point where we can conclude with some conviction that we have more going on here than some ill-timed hoax." Jared then filled him in on some of the details of the situation—at least, those pertaining to Faith Ramey.

The mayor exhaled heavily. "I can't believe this, and I don't have to tell you how bad the timing of this is."

"No, you don't," Jared said, all but holding his own breath.

"What do you suppose has happened to her?"

"The sooner I get off the phone, the sooner I can get back to finding out."

"Not so fast," Loyal replied. "People will be asking me questions when they can't reach you. I want to be able to respond and reassure. What's the plan, son?"

"Grunge work," drawled Jared. "We don't have shit, Loyal, but that's off the record. We're still trying to figure out what happened, and the last thing we want to do is to provide a media sound-bite that'll start a town-wide panic."

"You forget I'm as responsible for the people in this community as you are!"

Great, Jared thought, another one. "Not quite. Not yet. Only my head's on the block right now, and what I want you to understand is that from my perspective, offering information, even with the best intentions, might end up aiding a perpetrator."

Loyal's silence spoke fathoms. "You think I would intentionally endanger a member of our community?"

"I'm saying I don't want to put you in a position that you might do it without realizing you are."

As the mayor mulled that over, Jared accepted the coffee Norma brought him in the Darth Vader mug she'd given him two Christmases ago and only brought to him when she felt he was being unfairly criticized by someone. He winked his thanks and took a greedy sip, although the brew was piping hot.

"Am I hearing that you think one of our own could be involved with whatever is going on here?" Loyal said at last.

That made a helluva lot more sense than the theory that a serial killer had returned to the scene of a six-year-old crime, though the very idea sickened Jared to his soul. ''No comment.''

''Well, what's Cuddy's opinion?''

It annoyed Jared that Loyal's faith in him should suddenly show itself to be so visibly thin after he'd spent three years heading the department and enjoying an all-in-all harmonious relationship with the man. ''We're in agreement there. But, hey, don't take my word for it. Call him. He's had thirty minutes' more sleep than I have—he might not mind one more interruption.''

''Aw, don't go getting bent out of shape. I'll do what I can to rein in gossip, but will you please keep me as informed as you can, so I can avoid looking like an ass without a head and keep the piranhas off my hide?''

Jared barely heard him. He was looking out his office window as a black van pulled into Ramey's. He didn't need to see the tombstone painted on the door with the writing *Last Writes* to recognize who that was. ''Great,'' he muttered. ''Just what I need.''

''What?''

Checking himself, Jared muttered, ''I'll call you as soon as I know something,'' and hung up the phone.

But his narrow-eyed glare was all for the man who climbed out of the van and hugged Michaele. ''And what are you doing out of your tomb at this hour, you son of a bitch?''

15

Dillon Hancock was instinctively sensitive to how avidly Michaele avoided intimacy, but he hugged her, anyway, and was impressed that she endured his touch as long as she did. It spoke of the strain she was under—the same strain that had compelled him to get out of his van and not make this as quick a stop as he would have preferred.

"I'm okay, really." As expected, she soon put some space between them.

"How can you be? I'd be nuts. Spit, damn it. Cry. Threaten to turn that nozzle on the whole town and light a match until someone tells you where she is. Stop being so in control. You're giving me the creeps."

He knew that was exactly the response she wanted, why she liked him while others wanted him run out of town. As the owner of Last Writes, and consequently the "outsider" businesspeople loved to hate, he saw himself as the uncompromising voice of honesty. Others saw him as the bad influence nudging their kids toward juvenile delinquency or worse.

"Calm doesn't begin to cover what I am, Dillon. But what would be the point in turning into Buck Jr.?"

That had him smiling, if ruefully. "Jesus. There's a thought. By the way, where is he? Already off looking for the liquid equalizer?"

"You guessed it."

"And you really don't have a clue as to where Faith is?"

"No. We've been up all night searching for her." She glanced toward the road in the direction he'd come from. "But if you've been out of town again, how did you hear?"

His smile wavered. "What?"

She nodded to indicate his night's growth of beard. "You haven't shaved, either. What did you do—drive all the way to Houston and back for one of those book fairs or estate sales to fill a special order?"

He'd once explained that if he didn't do that, he couldn't afford to appease his less faithful, but equally interesting, sporadic customers. Used books, mass market releases and computer games in the darker or adventuristic medias were the real source of his revenue; but he also went out of his way for a student or a homebound senior citizen interested in a first-edition classic. Michaele took advantage of his goodwill herself on occasion, having him order manuals for cars she was asked to work on. He liked to think himself instrumental in nudging her toward spreading her professional wings.

He pretended confusion and rubbed his eyes. "Feels like I've been to another planet and back. As for the news—I overheard a conversation at the coffee shop in Mineola. It blew me away, and I left without ordering anything."

Visibly touched, she gestured inside. "There's coffee and some food, if you're interested."

Not only was Dillon eager to get back to the sanctuary of his own place, but he didn't like the strong feeling that his back was being drilled full of holes as he stood here. Driving in, he'd glanced across the street and noted the mini-blinds at the police station were drawn. Nevertheless, he had a hunch one special someone was there watching, and he had no intention of encouraging Jared Long Morgan's curiosity or ire.

"Sounds marvelous, but you're right, I'm a wreck. Tell me what I can do to help after I clean up."

As expected, Michaele replied with a sad smile. "You're great to offer, but everything that can be done is—unless you happened to see anything unusual or suspicious on the road as you were driving back here."

"Wish I could say otherwise, but it was an exceptionally quiet trip this time. There must be some reasonable explanation, though."

"Like?"

"She's with someone."

"There's no one right now, Dillon. I covered that with the chief."

"Uh-oh. It's 'the chief' again."

"Please don't start teasing me about him. This is hardly the time."

"Just remember who you're talking to. I know he practically salivates at the mere sight of you."

"Dillon."

"I know, I know, you're destined for more cerebral pleasures, like sabotaging Detroit's plans to turn us into even greater consumers. A mere red-blooded male is of no interest to you."

"If you're not going to talk to me like someone with an IQ over your age, I'm going to shut off this machine and send you up to the convenience store to pump your own gas."

"You want common sense? Here it is—don't give yourself an ulcer worrying about Faith. She's twenty going on twelve compared to your twenty-seven going on forty. You'll never understand her, but the young tend to be resilient. You know yourself, she's probably thought up some stupid, wild scheme to punish you for heaven knows what latest infraction. Sure, I know that despite acting like a tough guy, you want that girl to have opportunities not available to you, and that whatever crap she's pulling, it hurts. Don't let it.''

''What if she's not behind this? Her *car* has been found, Dillon.''

''I didn't know that. Where?''

She told him about some chicken farmer down the road a bit. He used the time to admire her eyes; he'd always thought their keen intelligence every bit as appetizing as their beauty. She really was a doll, and under different circumstances...

''A chicken farm? That's almost laughable,'' he drawled. ''Right up Faith's type of humor.''

By her expression, he could tell Michaele wavered. He decided to push a little harder. ''Does she know this Pete guy?''

''Sure. He's not only been a long-time customer here, he's provided the feathers to repair the high school's mascot every year because she asked him. So what?''

''So aside from being a generous old buzzard, he's what? A sweet old dork. Faith knew that—that's why she tucked her car there. She knew she didn't have to worry about anything being stolen. She probably figured she would pick up the car later whenever she was through doing whatever she was doing, or got tired of scaring you out of ten years of your life.''

Michaele frowned. ''She left the door open. If it hadn't roused the dogs, it would have run down the battery.''

''You don't think she figured that out?''

''Maybe. Then again... Let me tell you what else happened.''

He listened. It was his biggest talent aside from pinpointing a person's weakness. She told him about a phone call she received suggesting that Faith had been kidnapped and about the purse being found in the Trans Am. He noted that the pump shut off while she spoke, but she didn't pay much attention. That told him more than what she said.

"What would you do if she eloped?"

"Be thrilled to death."

"No, you'd be thrilled to know she was safe and sound. About ten seconds later you'd shake her silly for throwing her opportunities to the wind for what would probably result in a baby seven or eight months from now."

"You know me too well."

He tapped the brim of her hat. "You're a dreamer, despite your crusty exterior. So, let's go down this hypothetical highway another stretch. Who would be the worst person you could imagine her hooking up with?"

"I hate when you start getting logical on me."

"You're a logical person yourself. It's our curse. We're too sober for our own good. Talk."

She looked up at the metal roof of the overhang. "Harold Bean, I guess. You remember Harold?"

"Vaguely. He wanted me to buy his textbooks and couldn't understand why I wouldn't give him the cover price for them, especially since he had barely bent, the spine on half of them. Good grief, hitching up to him would be a swan dive into obscurity. Isn't there anyone else? Maybe you're missing someone," he whispered, leaning close to hypnotize with his gaze as much as his voice.

Michaele crossed her arms, but she didn't budge. "If I am, someone else is going to have to figure it out. I told Jared as much when he asked for a list."

"Good. Let 'the chief' dig. That's his job." Dillon

calmly disengaged the nozzle and shut off the gas pump. ''But there's something else, isn't there?''

''How did you know?''

''Michaele, love, the disruption of molecular momentum around you is…riveting.''

''You remember what today is? You were fairly new compared to some, but you were here.''

''Was I? Ah. Jeez…that.''

''Well, Garth Powers found a message scrawled across the boys' room at the school yesterday evening, just as Faith should have been arriving home, that was reminiscent of that day.''

''Talk about coincidences.''

''You want to know what it said? 'I'm back. 666.' ''

Dillon didn't reply. His thoughts were far away, years away.

''Dillon?''

''Hmm?''

''What do you think? It was Garth Powers who told me. Jared sure didn't plan to.''

''I think—'' Dillon slipped his arm around her shoulders and eased her to the driver's door of his van, where he reached inside for his billfold ''—that she's in Houston, or San Antonio or, better yet, Guadalajara having a damn better time than you are.''

''I almost hope you're right,'' she replied, as he handed her what he owed her.

''Call me if you need an ear. I'll make you some chicken soup and massage those knots out of your shoulders.''

He climbed back into his seat and in his sideview mirror watched her smile. It was a wistful smile at best and wouldn't last long. He could only hope his secret did.

16

Michaele returned to her workstation, brooding over Dillon's comments. It wasn't that she was wholly disappointed in what he'd said; he'd been as supportive as his personality allowed, considering that being a hand-holder wasn't any more in his genes than it was in hers. She just wished he'd had a more helpful reaction to the news about what happened at the school. But then, she reminded herself, he'd been up all night, too.

Her own growing fatigue had her stifling a yawn, and she drew out another work order for the white Taurus left here last night. It belonged to Misty Monroe of Cut 'n' Curl, and she saw by the note Misty had left on the seat that she wanted a full service, including the tires rotated. "'P.S.,'" she read aloud. "'That is, if you can't turn this into a Lexus.'"

Michaele appreciated the humor, and the work. The job would keep her busy for an hour or two, especially since Buck wasn't here to take care of the customers who stopped by for a fill-up. It didn't, however, keep her from thinking.

What to do about Garth's news? Did she go talk to a lawyer? It seemed too soon for that. Just because she was upset with Jared didn't mean he was wrong in his judgment. What Dillon said made sense, too.

At the rumble and stutter of another vehicle approaching, she stepped out of the garage. Pete Fite pulled in with his Cameo.

"Pete." Not only had she forgotten their arrangement, but he was early.

"I know it," he said as he climbed out and approached her. "Should've called first. Reckon you'll wanna put this off for a bit?"

He stood there, his head bowed, looking as forlorn as one of his floppy-eared hounds.

"No, no. A deal is a deal. But not even the drive-thru window at the bank is open yet." It wouldn't be for another hour yet.

He brightened. "That's okay. Truth is, I wanted to get away for a spell. Got to feeling kinda strange again, being out there by my lonesome and all."

As overwhelmed as she was starting to feel herself, Michaele was hard-pressed to ignore the tug of compassion his words triggered. She knew that knee-jerk impulse to run away from unpleasantness and responsibility.

"Have you had anything to eat?" As she had with Dillon, she motioned him inside. "Buck didn't touch his breakfast. Go help yourself before everything gets too cold to be edible."

"Guess I could eat something. Where's Buck?"

"In search of some hair-of-the-dog."

Visibly cheered by the news, Pete launched himself inside with long-legged strides. When he returned, he was chewing with enthusiasm and waving what remained of the biscuit-and-sausage at her. The coffee was in his other hand. "Good," he mouthed. "Sure appreciate this."

"Glad it's not going to waste." Forgetting about the Taurus for a while, she started checking through her inventory of repaired tires to see what she could use to fulfill the rest of her deal with him. "Did you get any sleep after everyone finally left?"

"Naw, didn't even try. Sat picking ticks off the dogs and listening to the farm reports on the radio. Guess you just stayed here, huh?"

"That's right. Did you remember to bring all of Precious's paperwork?"

"You betcha. I don't aim to cause you no more work than I have to. That one of my tires?" he added, as she started rolling one to the back of the pickup truck. "Let me help."

He loaded, while she hunted another. "I sure do appreciate this, Mike. Don't know how you're holding up as well as you are. I was feeling limp as my chickens in this heat wave, until you offered me your food."

She murmured something unintelligible, her attention captured by Jared coming out of the station and quickly getting into his unit to drive east down Main. To the high school? Harold Bean's? Where?

For an instant he looked straight at her, then he was gone. Neither of them had waved, smiled, anything, and the tension in that brief connection upset her.

"I'd be proud to stick around."

At the unexpected remark, Michaele spun around to find Pete standing just behind her. He nodded to the old twelve-gauge shotgun in the Cameo's gun rack.

"It ain't pretty, but it carries the right message. Considering how worried the chief is looking, I figure it might ease his mind to know you got somebody else here while Buck's away."

Michaele indicated the station. "It's not as though I'm not being monitored, but thanks. To be honest, with Buck gone, I sure could use the help with the pumps."

The arrangement worked out well, especially since aside

from being a full-service station, Ramey's was an authorized state inspection location, and two people came by to renew their window stickers.

But at exactly seven-thirty, Michaele stood at the drive-thru window of the bank. She'd even beat the teller Louise Green, who lifted the mini-blinds and gave a little shriek in surprise at the sight of her.

"Michaele!" Sapling thin and as pale as a bleached bone, the young teller pressed a hand to her flat chest. "You scared me to— Oh! I'm sorry."

"You can say it, Louise. 'To death.' See? No lightning." She sighed, though, realizing how fast the story was getting around town. "How'd you hear?"

"Mama lives next to Mayor Loyal. She was outside cutting roses for the nursing home as he was leaving the house, and he told her." The young woman leaned closer to the window that separated them. "Any news?"

"Not yet." As the drawer extended toward her, Michaele slipped her check into the scooped belly and waited for Louise to pull it back. "I need to cash that, please."

Louise picked up the check made out to "Cash" for one thousand dollars. Her expression went from sympathetic to aghast. "Michaele, tell me this isn't what I think it is. If you're fixing to pay a ransom, I'd be obligated to call the police."

"What self-respecting kidnapper would ask for a lousy thousand?"

"Who would expect Split Creek to become the crime capital of East Texas?"

Anyone who was around when Sandy was murdered. But Michaele kept that to herself, as well as the explanation for the money. People would be bound to think her cold-blooded for buying a truck right now.

Simply nodding to the check, she said, "Hundreds will

be fine. I left Pete Fite watching the garage for me. I need to get back.''

''Guess poor Buck's just not up to working today, is he?''

The more apt question would be whether Buck would ever be close to sober again, Michaele thought.

''Michaele?''

''Make it hundreds.''

Her expression sympathetic, Louise indicated that she already had the drawer with the money slid out again. Embarrassed, Michaele quickly grabbed the cash envelope.

''Should I have Mr. Rushing go out front to watch and make sure you make it back okay?''

The thought of the bank's cashier, who'd been opening and closing this financial institution for a decade longer than she'd been alive, standing guard for her was almost humorous, if it didn't reflect so well how ill-prepared this small community was for trouble related to violence. That's all she needed—another life on her conscience.

''Thanks, Louise, but it's not necessary.''

''Then you take care, hear? I mean that in all respects.''

''Thanks.''

''And if there's anything I can do...''

Michaele let the offer serve as their goodbye and hurried back to the garage. Pete was filling the tank of one of those new little VWs, and reported that while she'd been gone there had been two other customers; however, as yet, still no sign of Buck. She accepted the money he'd collected and let him finish the job, using the time to mull over her next dilemma.

How was she to get Pete home? Yesterday, she'd planned to send him with Buck, thinking Buck could spend the morning putting the new tires on Pete's other truck. But at this stage, if Buck even returned, he would be in no shape to pump gas, let alone drive a truck. Nor could she afford to leave until the morning rush was over.

"Don't worry about it," Pete said, after they did their transaction for the Cameo and she explained things to him. "I can wait."

"You sure? I know with the weather getting hotter every day, you have to keep an eye on those chickens."

"They'll be all right for a while yet. Want me to take care of that customer, too?"

She glanced over her shoulder and saw the turquoise '87 Monte Carlo pull up to the pumps. Her insides did a sickly churn. "Damn. No, this one is mine."

17

7:48 a.m.

"Uh-oh." As he spotted Michaele leave some gaunt-cheeked farmer-type to cross over to him, Harold Bean swore under his breath. So much for hoping that Buck would be attending the pumps. Buck was easy to blow off, but not Mike the Mouth. He wouldn't have come here if he wasn't low on fuel and hadn't pushed his credit limit at the Fill 'n' Save. But if he didn't give the Monte Carlo a drink, she wouldn't get him out of town, let alone up to school.

"Morning," he said, flashing her his brightest, I'm-a-harmless-good-ol'-boy-too grin. "Fill it, please? I'm bone dry."

"And running late."

"Tell me about it." He laughed, uncomfortable not only because of the odd expression on her face, but because she knew his schedule almost as well as his old lady did. "Guess Faith's way ahead of me, huh?" he called out the window, as she moved to the back of his car.

Michaele set the pump and returned to continue studying him with that where-should-I-stick-the-straight-pin look. "What the hell is going on, Harold?"

"What?"

"Don't pretend you don't know. Your mother must've told you about my calling your place last night."

"Oh, shoot. Yeah, she did. Y'know, I had car trouble and got in late, so I didn't think it right to call back. She get home okay?"

"No."

He paused in the middle of pulling his wallet from the back pocket of his jeans. "Pardon?"

"You heard me. Faith's missing."

"Shit."

"This is a surprise to you?"

No, he did not care for her attitude at all. "Hell, yes, it's a surprise! You can't think I— Oh, no. No, ma'am, I do not know what's going on here, but it has nothing to do with me."

"But you weren't home, either, and your mother was pretty upset because she didn't know where you were."

"I told you, I had car trouble."

"What time did you finally get in?"

"What difference does it make? Jeez, you're as bad as—" Recognizing that he was about to make a tactical mistake, he grimaced. "Sorry. I'm just tired, and— Damn, Mike, I'm really blown away by this."

"Harold, I've always been sympathetic to the way things worked out between you and Faith. But I need answers, and I don't think there's much time to get them. I thought maybe Chief Morgan had just gone to see you, but I suppose I guessed wrong."

"I haven't seen him. Listen, anything I can do…damn." He covered his face with his hands. "Faith." He allowed his voice to break. It was easy, just as it was easy to imagine her face. She'd been his first love. His only. "What can I do to help?"

"As you said, you have to get to school."

''So I'll explain to the dean and make up what I have to, later.'' Scowling, he glanced around her toward the police station. ''It's so quiet, so normal…have they organized a search yet?''

''The local and county police have been out all night. They found her car at Pete's.'' Michaele indicated the old guy behind her. ''No, don't ask me what it was doing there, Harold, I have no idea. I was hoping you might. Did you see her at all yesterday?''

''Uh-uh.''

''But she'd told me that you two almost always follow each other up there.''

· ''Not yesterday. Our exams are at different times. Maybe she didn't have to be in when I did.''

''She left the house at the usual time.'' Michaele bit at her lower lip, which was pretty raw already. ''You didn't by chance call the house late last night?''

''I told you, by the time I got home, I thought it too late to bother y'all.''

The pump shut off, but Michaele was preoccupied with looking over his car. ''What was the problem? She seems to be okay now.''

''Yeah, sure. It was the battery. I'd stopped to grab something to eat on the way home and left my lights on. Guess that was just enough to wear it down the rest of the way.''

''You should have called me. I would have been happy to help.''

''Thanks but, um, luckily, an old high school pal stopped at the same restaurant and gave me a lift to Wal-Mart.''

Nodding, Michaele removed the nozzle and replaced the fuel cap. When she turned back to him, Harold handed her a twenty-dollar bill. As she dug into her jeans for change, she asked, "I'm sorry if I came down hard on you."

"Forget it. I'm surprised you're not climbing the walls."

"Will you keep an eye out on your way up there?"

"You know I will."

"And ask around. I know Chief Morgan's going to be notifying people up there, but you know her habits and schedule better."

"Absolutely." He accepted his change. "You can count on me. I'll be in touch again as soon as I get out."

Eager to get away, he accelerated too fast, and not only did the car stall, but there was a loud *thump* in his trunk. He saw Michaele's startled reaction and swore silently.

"What do you have back there, a tree stump?"

He shot her a weak smile and restarted the car. Holding his breath, this time he pulled away without incident.

"That wasn't good," he said to himself. And neither was his excessive explaining. Better than all that yakking with his mother, but still too much. "Start praying she's too overwhelmed to remember much of what you said, pal...or your ass is a goner."

18

Within hours Michaele had firsthand knowledge of how fast news could travel. By mid-morning, there was a veritable traffic jam at their intersection as the town power brokers, business owners, residents, and those simply caught up by the growing congestion, stopped by to confirm what they'd heard and to offer their sympathy and support, or to just stare. Even the first member of the press had arrived—a reporter from the local newspaper. Though mostly well-meaning, the invasion was fast changing her mind about staying open.

Buck had not returned, and the thought that he might, and the subsequent scene he was likely to cause, added another shadow to the one already hanging over her. She also hadn't gotten Pete home yet. He didn't appear to mind, but his eagerness to recite his part in the mystery started to get on her nerves by the fourth telling of his part in the tale. That annoyance was soon replaced by a different agitation as Reverend Dollar climbed onto the display of tires she had stacked out front. Within minutes of starting a group prayer, there was a three-car accident in the middle of the intersection.

"Okay, that's it," Michaele called above the cacophony. ''Everyone? Y'all can't stay here. I appreciate your support, but this is getting out of hand, and someone's going to get seriously hurt. Hello?'' she yelled louder. ''Please, everybody? Go home!''

The entreaty won her several sympathetic looks and the support of Ellie Ashley, owner of Flowers by Ellie on the west side of Dogwood, who also took up the cry. But while everyone made sympathetic comments, few people seemed in a hurry to go anywhere.

''What are they expecting, refreshments?'' Ellie muttered.

The accident did bring Jim Sutter out of the police station again. He'd been out earlier, but no sooner had he gotten one small group to move on than his efforts were undermined by another group arriving. Looking exasperated, he reached for his radio. Minutes later a siren sounded; then Jared eased his patrol car through the crowd.

He pulled into Ramey's and parked by the tire display. Michaele couldn't deny she was glad to see him, or how impressive and in control he looked. He leaned on the roof of the car and slipped his sunglasses down his nose to eye George Dollar.

''Reverend, what do you think you're doing?''

''Encouraging the great flow of love being generated here, that it may assist us in finding our lost lamb.'' The preacher beamed down from his makeshift pulpit. ''Join us, brother. We're having an effect. I sense it.''

''Has your antenna also happened to pick up that you've helped create a traffic hazard? This pep rally needs to be moved somewhere else.''

''Surely you're not going to deny us the right to be with our sister in faith?'' Dollar spread his arms in a gesture that at once embraced those who surrounded him, as well as asked for their support.

There was a mild murmur of agreement and an "Amen," but Jared remained unfazed.

"Wouldn't think of it. But I will remind you that you don't have a right to block access to all these businesses that are trying to accept deliveries and care for customers. What's more, I see at least two folks smoking, and this area is clearly marked a hazardous area. Now, every minute I have to stand here pointing these things out to you— all of you people," he added to the crowd, "there's a missing girl somewhere out there who's not getting the attention that she deserves from us. Do you think that's fair?"

"What can we do to help, Chief?" someone called from the crowd.

"The mayor has agreed to open the Civic Center in fifteen minutes to organize search parties. You want to help, head there. These groups are going to be worked hard. There's a lot of ground to cover, and it's going to get into the high eighties today. So they'll need refreshments. Those of you who can't join the search groups might want to set up tables and provide cold drinks, coffee, sandwiches, whatever. Please. Go over there and talk it over."

Michaele was heartened by the group's display of goodwill. Their organized exodus allowed Jared to make his way into the intersection to check on things there. Unfortunately, that left Michaele alone, as Reverend Dollar sought her out.

"Would you like me to stay behind for a private prayer with you and your father, Michaele?"

There was a thought. "He's not here."

"Ah. I understand the crushed spirit and the natural craving for solitude in times of crisis."

Somehow she doubted he understood anything of the

sort. She'd lived under the same roof with Buck all her life and *she* didn't understand what his problem was, except perhaps that some people had never wanted to be born to begin with and enjoyed making the rest of humanity pay for the error.

"I have to get back to work, Reverend."

"I could come by the house later."

She could feel her control slipping away, and she had to dig her short nails into her palms to avoid telling this pompous fraud what she really thought of him. "If I can get Buck home, he's going to need rest. Thanks, anyway."

"Well, if there's anything else I can do... I'll be with the others at the center."

The farther from here the better, Michaele thought, as he left.

Jared passed him midway. It looked as though Dollar wanted to be seen chatting with him, too, but Jared kept going right past him. His expression remained unreadable when it was fixed in that granite lawman mask, and her emotions ricocheted among relief, annoyance and guilt.

"Have you had enough?" he asked as he stopped before her.

"I had enough at midnight. But if you're asking if I'm ready to shut down, the answer is the same. I can't."

"Not until there's a six-car pileup out front and someone's seriously injured, is that it? Because that's what's going to happen if you stay here."

"So much for wondering how long it would take for you to pay me back for what I said earlier. Thanks for the extra guilt trip, Morgan."

He closed his eyes briefly. "Why insist on misunderstanding everything I do, particularly when the intent is to help you? What do I have to say to get you to listen?"

"I'm listening."

"No, the sound of my voice triggers your Red Wall of China. Or maybe I'm being too hard on myself—maybe it's any man's voice."

She wasn't like that, was she? Well, at any rate she didn't hate men. She hated—God, who had time for lists?

A discreet cough from the garage reminded her that Pete was still around and didn't know if he should give them more space or venture nearer. She glanced over her shoulder. "Could you do me a favor and restock the soda machine? That crowd really wore it out, didn't they?"

"Key's in the register. I remember."

Thanking him, she turned back to Jared. "This isn't easy."

"Tell me something I don't know."

Yes, he knew, and he was forcing the issue, anyway. They were building to something that terrified even as it tempted her. She couldn't see its having a happy ending.

"You've been gone for hours," she said quietly.

"And yet there's nothing to report. Oh, there've been a few calls now that the news is getting around. One alleged sighting."

Her hopes soared. "Who? Where?"

"It turned out this was Tuesday or even Monday morning, Mike. Way up on Dogwood. The old guy reporting it is in the early stages of dementia. His daughter had already picked him up and brought him to her place on the east side of town. That's why I went that way. She apologized for his bothering us."

The drop back into disappointment was fast. "Nothing since then?"

"I was on my way to talk to Harold Bean when I heard about the commotion here."

"Harold's up at school by now. He stopped here on his way."

"Because he knew?"

Michaele shook her head. "He was as blown away as everyone else."

"When did he last see her?"

"Well, it wasn't yesterday. They usually follow each other up there, but he said that he'd missed her. And remember what I told you about calling there last night? He confirmed not being home. He had car trouble and was late getting out of Mt. Pleasant."

"He better be able to back that up with witnesses."

"That should be no problem. He said a friend helped."

"Did he mention a name?"

"No."

"How did he act about Faith?"

"Concerned."

"That's it? The guy's supposed to still be nuts about her."

"He is."

"Is that how you'd want someone who's nuts about you to act if you'd suddenly vanished into thin air?"

"This isn't about me. Stop making it into a damn—what do you call it?—Rorschach test! Would it have made you happier if he'd ripped his shirt and sobbed?"

"Frankly, yes."

"Excuse me if I'm not exactly an expert on how men react to something like that."

"Then let me give you a clue—it's rather like having your lungs ripped out."

The passion beneath his softly spoken statement told Michaele that he might not have recovered yet. "Was that the way it was for you?" she whispered.

Instead of answering, he went into the store and looked around. "Don't tell me that Buck's still gone?" he called over his shoulder.

"Yes."

Grim-faced, he turned to Pete. "What are you doing here?"

"Sold Precious there to Ms. Mike. She was gonna give me a lift home, but ain't nobody to watch the station."

"I'll take you. I want to have another look out there anyway."

"Why?" Michaele asked, following him inside. "Do you think you missed something earlier?"

"No. But we aren't doing squat anywhere else, and since it's daylight...who knows? I might get lucky."

"Well, Pete still needs tires put on his other truck. It's part of our deal."

Not looking at all happy, Jared asked, "Have you been across the street to sign the forms I told you we'd have to process?"

"No."

"Do it. I'll find Buck, follow you over to the farm, then home, in case the press start harassing you."

"I told you, I'm needed here. More than ever if they're starting search parties."

"There's always the Fill 'n' Save up the street."

No, the convenience store already had won enough of their business. "If I close, I'll search for Faith myself."

Jared took hold of her arm and urged her back into the garage. "Within the hour, maybe sooner, Garth Powers is going to spill the news about what happened there. When he does, that scene you had here is nothing compared to the circus that'll follow. Then, even if you want to sell someone gas, they won't be able to get in here. And that one reporter will be joined by a swarm, who'll follow you like deerflies sniffing a fawn. What if one of those blood-suckers corners Buck?"

The thought of him on the five o'clock news decided her. "Okay, you win."

"Thank you."

"One thing... Could you be a little easier on Pete?" She glanced around Jared to see the farmer shuffling around, trying to pretend he wasn't uncomfortable about being left out. "He's scared," she whispered.

"I wish you'd be a little more of that yourself."

"As soon as I have time."

He sighed and nodded toward the police station. "Go ask Norma to give you those papers, and I'll meet you back here in a few minutes."

19

11:15 a.m.

Although she took her time showering and getting dressed, Jessica Powers skipped breakfast, and because of her late start settled for a few sips of a diet soda before heading for the garage. She had plans, but she needed to fill up her BMW, so she made the circle down Cedar to Dogwood, then Main, where she discovered that no one was at Ramey's and everything was locked up tight.

Transfixed by the scene across the street, she almost sat through a green light, her sunglasses sliding to the tip of her nose and her freshly painted lips pursed. Only someone's gentle tap of their horn roused her.

"Well," she murmured, accelerating. "How do you like that?"

Dealing with the self-serve pumps was a pet peeve of Jessica's—the stench of fuel, not having anyone to clean your windshield...and the cashiers! She was almost glad many locations were switching over to wholly computer-operated pumps. At least they could do math and said "Thank you" after processing your credit card. But she would never forgive the gas companies, not to mention Wall Street, for the greed that had made a full-service station a veritable dinosaur.

"Misogynist bastards. But they all want a trophy wife."

She fumed the whole time that she fumbled with the various buttons and levers at the station. Not only did she not know what anything was called, but she never planned to learn. Bad enough the power brokers had figured out a way to force her to pump her own gas while dressed in a Victor Costa silk.

Careful not to break another nail—she'd stayed up until three to repair it and touch up the rest—she put away her receipt and then used the rest room inside to wash the offensive smells off her hands. Adding another spritz of her perfume, she beamed into the rest room mirror, then set off once again, riding the serene plane she had been on since she first rose from bed.

Three pairs of eyes looked up as she entered the administration office, and the mixture of respect and wariness her impromptu arrival garnered more than made up for the previous unpleasantness.

With a brief nod to the blond student-aide at the reception desk, Jessica beamed at the plump woman sitting outside Garth's office. "Bea. I love the new look. Garth told me you had changed hairstyles, and how flattering it is." In truth, there wasn't much the old girl could do with what amounted to frog hair, but the short, fringe style was better than the rigid helmet she had worn for the last ten years. At the same time, Jessica had to wonder—why go to all the trouble if it was the color of what you plucked out of a drain trap? "Inez, how's the grandmother-to-be?"

Behind her glasses, the records secretary blushed, but her smile was one of quiet pride. "Counting the days. How *are* you, Mrs. Powers?"

"On a mission to save my husband's sanity. Is he in?" Before either woman could answer, she was at his office door. "Don't warn him," she told Bea, who'd reached for the phone.

"But he's due at a meeting in—"

"Then I'll do you all a favor and make sure he's in a good frame of mind."

She opened the door. "Hello, darling." She slipped inside and closed up behind her.

Garth swung his feet off his desk and sat up. "Jess. What the hell—?"

"Ah-ah-ah. Remember where you are, Principal Powers."

"I wasn't expecting you."

"That was the plan. I thought I'd surprise you, and we'd have lunch."

"I'd love to, but—"

"Nothing doing. I'm not going to let you go into any meeting with that gloomy expression on your face. One look at that sour mug and your teachers will demand a twenty-percent-across-the-board raise just to come back in the fall." She crossed to his desk and leaned her hip against it. "Besides, I need pampering. Do you know Ramey's is closed? I had to pump my own gas at that dreadful do-it-yourself place down the road. I swear, I don't know what's happening to this country. What's next? If I want a filet mignon, will I have to butcher my own cow?"

"Jessica, we need to talk."

It wasn't a particularly strong request, but she fell silent, since this was what she'd been waiting for since coming home yesterday and sensing something was off and that he was keeping something from her. But with customary patience she'd waited until she knew he was ready to share what was bothering him.

She dropped her gaze to his hand, gauging how to make it easier for him. "How's the hand?"

"Fine. Listen, darling, about Ramey's being closed…"

He pushed himself out of his chair. He always stood when he was going to break bad news, try to talk her out of something, or lecture. It was as though he thought his added height might intimidate her as much as it reassured him. If only he knew: as much as she loved his body, he couldn't intimidate her, even if she'd caught him holding an Uzi in each magnificent hand.

"Two things happened yesterday that on the surface may seem to have no correlation whatsoever," he began, cupping his bandaged hand and circling around her to pace.

Jessica knew he liked, *needed,* to pace; it helped him think. But so did a drink. "Garth, can't we talk over lunch? I haven't had a bite yet and I'm hungry enough to chew on these sandals. Better yet, come home with me. I'll make us a salad and open that bottle of Chardonnay you found on our last trip to Dallas."

"Faith Ramey's gone."

"What?"

"Lost. Missing. That's got to be why Ramey's is closed. I'm sure Jared finally put his foot down and talked Michaele into locking up. I doubt anyone else could get her to do it, unless someone cornered Buck and stuck him in front of a camera. Imagine that idea scared the town elders enough to want to arrest the poor sop, and to compromise, she hauled him home."

"I can't believe it. Was she on a trip or something?"

"No. Supposedly just going to school."

"When? This morning?"

"Yesterday afternoon, I suppose. At least, that's when Michaele started worrying."

"Michaele Ramey's levelheaded. She wouldn't be prone to overreacting."

"That's not the only reason this feels legitimate, Jess. There's more. Something that may change things between us and Jared. Permanently, this time."

Jessica set her woven shoulder bag on one of the chairs facing his desk.

"Now you are scaring me. Tell me everything."

It was an unsettling story, but not a wholly believable one.

"Maybe Faith spent the night with a friend—or more likely a lover," Jessica said at last. "This may sound unsympathetic, darling, but I've always thought Faith not quite what she seems. A tease, if the impression must have a label. All girlish innocence on the outside, but...well, these are the '90s, and haven't you ever noticed there's a faint *slyness* beneath her veneer?"

Garth rubbed his uninjured knuckles against his lips. "You always offer a perspective to things I've either missed or want to deny. Maybe there was—excuse me, *is* that side to her, but she's so young."

"She may have been involved in something over her head."

"Unfortunately, there's more."

Jessica arched an eyebrow.

"I found something after classes yesterday."

"Now I really am confused. What would you have to do with Faith Ramey?"

"God, Jess, will you just hear me out! Do you know how tough this is for me, today of all days!"

Jessica's eyes filled. "Please. Not this year. I don't want to discuss that this year."

Garth immediately put his arms around her. "I know. But we have no choice."

"You're in trouble. I knew something was wrong when I saw your hand. You didn't hurt yourself the way you said, did you?"

"No, but it was an equally stupid move. It's about the past, Jess." He searched her face. "Can you be strong?"

"Haven't I proved that I am?"

He bowed his head. "Ridiculous question. Forgive me. It's just that yesterday after school someone left a message in the rest room down the hall that triggered all of our worst nightmares. Jess...it said 'I'm back. 666.'"

"Dear God," she whispered, pressing closer to him.

"From what I can gather, not long after that Faith must have disappeared."

"That poor child. But wait...the authorities determined Sandy was a victim of a random serial killing. People who do things like that may hang around, but they eventually get caught, don't they? I mean, they don't leave and come back...do they?"

"Then where is she? She's vanished, Jess. On top of that, Michaele had a call last night that sounds as though the writing on the bathroom wall meant business. Yet Jared's on my ass to keep quiet about it."

"He can't do that. Your responsibility is to these children."

"That's what I said." Garth pressed his lips to her forehead. "Thanks, darling. You don't know how much I needed to hear that—someone confirming my own beliefs."

"I'm not just someone, Garth, I'm your wife." Jessica leaned back to gaze deeply into his eyes. "I'm the one who's always on your side. Because I happen to love you," she said, taking his injured hand and brushing her cheek against the bandage. "And this? It wasn't frustration with your coach, was it."

"More like disgust with myself for giving in to Jared. The result was the same."

He kissed the tip of her nose as though she were a child, a gesture usually saved for public moments, or when he was emotionally at his most vulnerable. She thought it endearing, a boyish quality. But when she leaned back, her focus was pragmatic.

"What are you going to do?"

"Hold an assembly just before lunch and inform everyone. Believe me, it's not a scenario I relish, but I want the kids who are on the work-study program to be warned before leaving the premises, and also give the latchkey kids who go home to an empty house time to notify their parents. Everyone deserves time to make arrangements, or at least warn some authority figure."

"Very smart. That protects you legally."

"I'm not thinking about that."

"No, you're too noble, so I will because it's in the mix, whether you want to see it or not. Jared is opening himself to tremendous criticism if he doesn't handle this properly, and you don't need to get pulled down by him. What exactly is he willing to do?"

"Who knows? He sure doesn't seem to think there's anything to worry about here. To him, that message was only a nasty prank by one of the seniors."

"Poor wretch. He's still in denial about Sandy. But that's no excuse for not respecting you or the burden you carry. No, I'm sorry, Garth, that's how I feel."

"C'mon, Jess, losing Sandy was as rough on him as it was on us."

"We came to terms with what happened. Maybe I don't want to talk about it on every anniversary, but that's because we're trying to let her rest in peace and remember her for more than the way we last saw her. What's he doing? Has he tried to get on with his life the way we have? Six years, and has he formed another relationship with anyone?''

''Nothing serious that I know of.''

''Don't you wonder why? I've thought a lot about it, and do you know what I think? Something must have happened the last time he and Sandy were together. Maybe they quarreled, maybe they even broke off the engagement—remember, she wasn't wearing her ring when she was found.''

''Sheriff Cudahy explained that, Jess. He said it might have been taken as a souvenir—that killers sometimes do that to remember their victims.''

''That may be the case. All I'm saying is that his behavior isn't normal as far as I'm concerned. For a man to have virtually given up on his personal life like that? I think he's eaten with guilt.''

Garth sighed heavily. ''Whatever. But I can't let that get in the way of my obligations.''

''No, indeed.'' She thought of something. ''At least tell me that Jared took samples to send to a lab?''

''He didn't want to waste his time.''

''That's outrageous! Loyal needs to know about this. So does the Board of Education. If they hear the news from a student or teacher... Call the mayor.''

''I've been trying. He's not at the barbershop.''

''Yes, half the town did look shut down. Now that I know what's going on, my hunch is that he's in the middle of organizing something. Tell you what...I'll go look for him, and you hold that assembly.''

''Jess, I can't dump this on you.''

''Hey.'' She gently wiped her lipstick off his mouth. ''We're a team, remember?''

20

12:00 p.m.

Leaving Buck inebriated and dozing in the cab, Michaele unloaded the second tire from the back of the Cameo and, following Pete, rolled it to the flatbed. As she headed back to get the third, she watched Jared farther down the driveway where Faith's car had been found. He would take a few steps, crouch down and study the ground, then repeat the process. She didn't see him actually pick anything up, and couldn't decide whether to see that as good or bad news.

"Y'know, I been thinking," Pete said, returning from unlocking the farmhouse. "You don't have to put on them tires. Ain't fair, all things considered. You got Buck to look after…and the rest. I can do it myself."

She knew that and shrugged. "A deal's a deal. Besides, Buck's not having a problem with this."

Sure enough, he'd stretched out now that he had the bench seat to himself, and had begun to snore loudly. While Jared had not had any problem maneuvering his considerable bulk into the truck, Michaele suspected Buck might be sleeping there tonight if she couldn't rouse him once they got home.

"You go do what you have to do," she told Pete. She

nodded toward the baying hounds that hadn't calmed down since they had pulled in. "I'll handle this. It won't take me any time at all."

The job did go faster when she was left alone to keep her own pace. She'd changed so many tires in her time that between her experience and the improved lifts on the market these days, she was able to replace all four tires by the time he returned from replenishing his dogs' water supply and checking the fans on the hen sheds.

"You're set for now," she told him. "But come back into town in the next few days, and I'll make sure they're aligned so they'll wear properly."

"Reckon the chief won't want you opening tomorrow, unless things sort themselves out, huh?"

Michaele glanced down the road, but Jared was out of sight. "He doesn't run the garage. Tomorrow will be fine. Are you going to be okay?" she heard herself asking. Inwardly, however, she cringed at the question. As though she didn't have enough two-legged headaches.

With a halfhearted nod, the old-timer reached into the open driver's window and lifted out his shotgun. "Suppose I will be with the old equalizer here."

But he didn't sound convinced. "Maybe you should let your dogs out after we leave. They're no happier locked up than you are seeing them in those cages."

"You don't figure the chief'll be upset with me?"

"I think he only meant for you to pen them while they were looking for clues." She glanced over her shoulder again. "My guess is that's no longer a consideration."

She said goodbye to Pete, then shoved Buck's leg back onto his side of the floorboard, slid behind the wheel and drove down the driveway to the patrol car. Jared wasn't visible at first, and that was disconcerting. But just as she had about decided to head down in there, he appeared, making his way through the dense brush.

"Looking for a dropped flashlight?" she asked, once he'd climbed up the slope.

"Only making sure we didn't overlook anything last night. Then I ran into Brady Watts down by the creek."

She glanced over his shoulder, although it was impossible to see that far into the vegetation. "I didn't see his truck when we turned off the farm-to-market road."

"He pulled off the side. You can see it once you're closer."

An avid fisherman when he wasn't working, Brady could be seen all over the county, testing his luck at various creeks and lakes. But the fact that he happened to be here the day after Faith's car was found only a few hundred yards away seemed highly coincidental to Michaele.

"Spit it out," Jared said.

"Well, he works at the school, right? It would seem to me that he would be uncomfortable being here. I mean, if Garth feels it's logical to make a connection between Faith and the writing, wouldn't he?"

"He's been out fishing since dawn. He hadn't heard about Faith."

"Oh."

"And I didn't tell him about the writing. Garth and I cleaned it up while he was on the other side of the school."

But he'd been there. He also knew Faith, calling her "Sunshine" when she'd been a student, and asking about her when he'd stop at the station to fill up his ancient pickup.

You really think that sweet old man can spell anything more than his name, let alone be capable of hurting anyone, Ramey?

Ashamed, she squirmed on the increasingly warm vinyl. ''I'm ready to head for the house,'' she told him.

''I'll follow you.''

''It's not necessary.''

''I'm done here. Besides, I want to make sure for myself that no media people are around your place.''

Or anyone else. He didn't say it, but she could see by his expression that the less he came up with clue-wise, the edgier he felt.

It wasn't a smooth run. Coming through the intersection, she saw Jessica Powers standing outside the police station with O. K. Loyal. When the woman flagged them down, Michaele reluctantly pulled over. Jared stopped right behind her.

''Michaele, dear. I'd have been in touch sooner, but I only heard in the last hour.'' Jessica reached into the window and gripped Michaele's wrist. ''How are you coping?''

''Still trying to make sense of things.''

''Is there anything I can do?''

That was Jessica. Michaele had nothing in common with the impeccably put-together woman, but Jessica always made you think that she would stand up lunch with the First Lady herself, if you needed her. ''Thanks,'' she replied, acutely aware of Buck's bloated bulk beside her. ''But I just need to get us home.''

''I've been talking to Loyal.'' Jessica glanced at Jared, who was joining them. His move brought the mayor over, too. ''He hadn't been advised about the incident at the school, Jared. Why not?''

''Are you on the Board of Education now, Jess?'' Jared drawled. ''Or filling a vacated City Council seat I didn't know about?''

Undaunted, Jessica replied, ''I'm speaking on my husband's behalf and those of his students. The monster who slaughtered my sister is not going to take another life.''

''You're playing fast and loose with the facts. Talk like that could get an innocent person hurt.''

''What we want to know is why you don't have even one suspect to interrogate,'' the mayor interjected.

''Because, at the moment, we don't know anything criminal happened.'' Without missing a beat Jared added, ''I thought you were organizing search parties?''

''I am. Things are well under way. I'd just come back to town with Jessica to appeal to you to call in the DPS. They have the experts for this kind of thing, Jared.''

Michaele winced at what Jared couldn't help but see as a vote of no confidence by two of the most influential people in the community.

''Sheriff Cudahy agrees with me that it's too soon to bring in the Texas Department of Public Safety,'' he replied. ''All we need to do is jump the gun, waste their time, and we'll be the joke of the state. That's not to say Detective Box isn't having some dialogue with their Special Crimes Service personnel.''

''He is?'' Loyal looked relieved. ''Well, in that case—''

''If you'd taken a sample of that blood, there wouldn't be any question,'' Jessica snapped.

''We don't know that it was blood, and if it was, whether it was human or what. Who's supposed to pay for that?'' He indicated his sidearm to Loyal. ''You made me and my boys buy our own guns when we got this deal on the Smith and Wesson Sigma .40.''

''Well, how was I to know the town was going to turn into this!'' Loyal replied.

''Into what? You don't know anything yet, so until you do, back off and let us do our job!''

With that, he gestured for Michaele to continue and returned to his vehicle.

She was relieved to get away from there, but not looking forward to being alone with him at the house. Maybe the others hadn't noticed, but she'd seen the change in him, the annoyance shift to cold rage. That wasn't a side of him that she wanted to take on.

At the house, he insisted on slinging Buck over his shoulder and carrying him inside. Her father roused just enough to supplement the silence with epithets before passing out on the couch.

"He'll be okay there for a few hours even if a 757 lands in the back pasture," she said. Hoping she didn't look too obvious, she led the way back into the kitchen.

"Mike," Jared said before she could reach for the screen door. "I know things look bad, but it's all still under control."

Sure, she thought, and she was going to get through one week without being short on cash receipts. "Where are you off to now?" she asked.

"The school. The news has to be out."

While she felt he'd brought some of this on himself, she couldn't help feeling sympathy for him and what he was likely to go through. "If only you'd taken a sample, Jared."

"I did. And now that you know, forget you heard."

She couldn't believe what he was saying, the risk he was taking. "But people are going to think—"

"I don't give a damn. This is like poker. You don't show your hand and then ask if anyone wants to play. It's all maneuvering and bluffing. Even telling you is a risk."

"I won't tell anyone."

"That's what I'm counting on. You do understand what 'anyone' means?"

''Who would I tell?''

His expression lost a bit of its harshness, but his words remained grim. ''You'd be surprised. You're going to be overwhelmed from here on out. People want information. They're going to try to place themselves close to you, suggest relationships that don't exist. And those who do…be careful, Mike. You've always had a good eye for bullshit artists. Don't let a vulnerability take over your common sense.''

''I just want to be left alone.''

''That's a wish that may take a while.''

''How long before you know? The results, I mean.''

''A few days. Sooner, if John's name helps. Try not to tie the two incidents together,'' he said, as she bowed her head. ''I know the temptation's there, but there are things that don't mesh.''

''Like?''

''Faith herself. She has no connection to the school anymore. If she was arbitrarily picked, then why leave the message at the school? And leaving the car at Pete's? Either it was all a big mistake or it was a con.''

''How so?''

''Knowledge. A drifter doesn't know the habits of the people, or who's who in town. Someone chose Pete's farm because they knew him. They knew his habits as well as they knew how wrong it would be for Faith to be on that side of town on a weekday and at that hour.''

Michaele tried to assimilate all that, but it left her mind spinning. ''So if someone in town is behind this…you're thinking Harold?''

''He'd be on top of any investigation list.''

''But he has an alibi.''

''I hope it holds. I hope I'm wrong. About all of it.''

He drew a deep breath. ''I have to go.'' Pausing at the door, he asked, ''You'll stay put?''

Michaele tugged off her hat, slapping it against her thigh before hanging it on the coat tree. ''What if there's a wreck or some other emergency? No.'' He'd been honest with her. So would she. ''What am I supposed to do here, Jared? Listen to Buck snore?''

''You want something to keep you preoccupied? Think about this.''

Before she could catch on to what he had in mind, he slid an arm around her waist and locked his mouth to hers.

It wasn't exactly her first kiss. Jimmy Ficken had wanted to play house with her when they were five, and then there was Steve Bower in the fifth grade, and another Steve—this one a Dunston—in the seventh. But after that...after that her experience had gone the way of the Jamaican bobsled team. Not exactly the kind of foundation to prepare a girl for Jared Long Morgan.

Her breath locked in her chest and the building emotion blended with the pain, sending shock waves through her. So did the feel of his body against hers; it sent final notice of the difference between a boy's hunger and a man's.

Everything she did, she did instinctively. She didn't consciously open her mouth, or answer the thrust of his tongue with her own, or press her hips against his to match the fierce rhythm of his heart and the pulse pounding in her head. But in those moments she learned how some things, while unknown, can still be classified as natural.

By the time she broke free to drag some air into her lungs, she was well on her way to a full-blown anxiety attack.

''Son of a— You think that helps?'' she cried.

As quickly as his passion had exploded, it ebbed. ''That's the pitiful hell of it,'' he muttered, reaching for the door. ''It should have. Guess the joke's on me.''

21

1:10 p.m.

"*M*ayday, *Chief!*"

Having punched the hold button on her phone system, Norma shot Jared a desperate look. "That's number eight in ten minutes. Parents want to know what we're doing about their children's safety, not to mention their own."

Jared ended his call to Cuddy and sat for a moment. Garth's announcement had done it, and things were moving from pressure-cooker tense to explosive, really fast. From now on there would be too many eyes watching, too many probing questions to control the situation as much as he wanted. His access to certain people would diminish, too.

He reached for his hat and headed for the front door. "Tell them I'm unavailable," he said as he passed Norma.

"Where are you going?"

"Fishing."

"Seriously, what do I tell the press when they ask for you?"

"Refer them to Loyal and remind him that we have two bed-and-breakfasts who need business, and the best onion rings in East Texas at Booker's Grill."

"Garth Powers has called twice."

"He played his hand, there's nothing else to say."

"But, Chief..."

He paused at the door. "Norma, darlin', if I don't tell you where I'm going, you don't have to pretend you don't know where I am." Sensing her response, he winked. "No, I don't believe you would. But I'm protecting both of us."

He headed for the car and quickly got himself on the road. Several people attempted to flag him down, but he ignored them. There were things to do now that he and Cuddy had planned their next move.

The Bean residence, not far beyond the high school, was a trailer house on the mostly overgrown acre behind an old metal shop long out of business. Rose Bean's husband had owned the shop, too, but he'd left several years ago for parts unknown. Everything in the area was a study in neglect—worn, damaged by harsh handling and weather, surrounded by overgrown weeds. Trash and discarded appliances had made it no farther than a few feet beyond each building. Thinking of skinny Harold with the responsibility of keeping order, Jared doubted any of it would ever get cleaned up, unless the family sold the place—or there was a massive fire.

He parked by the expanded metal staircase and knocked several times before the front door opened. After a rush of stale air and TV noise came the visual assault of Rose Bean, a neckless mass of a woman with the face of a gargoyle. And to think, he mused, her maiden name had been "Juicy."

"Mrs. Bean." Jared touched the brim of his hat as though responding to a gracious smile, not her angry glare. "Sorry to disturb you, but I need to talk to you for a few minutes."

"What about?"

"Harold."

"He's in class. He's a college student."

"Yes, I know. Mt. Pleasant to be exact. And Wendy's down at the high school, though I believe she should be here shortly."

"Why? Something happened to her?"

Jared raised a hand to stem her immediate shift to anxiety. "No, ma'am. This is about Faith Ramey. You haven't heard the news?"

Rose's eyes narrowed to mere slits in an otherwise puffy, pale face. "Her sister called here yesterday asking for her. But that girl threw away my boy ages ago. Why would he know anything about what she's up to?"

"So you told Michaele Ramey that you didn't know where Faith might be, correct? Or Harold, for that matter?"

"Yeah. But they weren't together. He came home later and explained that much. He had car trouble, which doesn't surprise me considering the piece of junk he's forced to drive. He wouldn't have such problems if his father would've made arrangements for his education. But we ain't got nothing, so my boy does what he can with what he's scraped together for himself."

"I appreciate that, ma'am. The problem is that Faith hasn't shown up." He could tell by the slackness of her facial muscles that she truly hadn't heard. "I'm sorry you had to find out this way."

Rose gripped the wide neckline of her cotton caftan. "Lord have mercy. I didn't take Michaele Ramey seriously when she called. Guess I was still hurt over Faith not dealing Harold a fair hand. 'Course, I know they weren't meant to stay a couple, but that was beside the point, you know?"

"I understand. And it only makes this situation all the more painful and complicated."

"Not that complicated. Not to me. He had car trouble, like I said, and he didn't get home until late. He won't be able to help you with anything about her."

Jared drew a notebook from his pocket. "Do you remember the time when he got in, by any chance?"

"Not to the minute. It was just after a movie on TV. Wait, I'll tell you exactly. It was with Bette Davis, the one where she gets a makeover—and let me tell you, she needs it in that film—but her mama's a controlling witch and almost ruins everything. She dies, though, and Bette helps raise the daughter of her lover. Only they have to hide their feelings because… Well, I forget. But you check the television guide. It's there. Anyway, Harold came in a minute later and explained he'd had that car trouble, like I said. Had to go get a new part at the Mineola Wal-Mart before he could get home. Said a friend stopped to help him. Bless that young man twofold, not that he needs it. Jack Fenton comes from a well-to-do family. But as I said to Harold, it was real Christian of the boy to drive Harold all the way to Mineola to get a new battery and back again. Ain't every day one of those rich folks'll do for you like that."

Jared wrote fast. "Are we talking about the ranching family Fentons?"

Rose nodded. "Their eldest boy. Graduated with Harold at S. C. High, but he was able to take more classes in college, so he come out last summer."

"Understood. And Mr. Fenton drove Harold to…Mineola? From Mt. Pleasant?"

"That's what he said. My boy ain't a liar, Chief. I put the fear of God in him."

"Yes, ma'am. I'm just making sure I have my facts straight."

"He said that the library had just closed and nothing

was open up there. That's why he was so grateful for young Jack coming along. The Fenton boy had been up by Texarkana looking at stock for his family.''

That sounded credible enough, but Jared sensed he had something. If Harold had experienced car trouble in Mt. Pleasant, then why drive all the way to Mineola when there was a Wal-Mart in Mt. Pleasant? Had Mrs. Bean misunderstood? She'd mentioned it twice, though. The Fenton boy would be able to clear up any confusion.

''Harold was at school pretty late, wasn't he, Mrs. Bean?''

''That's what I told him. You can't be too strict with kids these days, but it turns out he'd been at the library, like I said,'' she replied, with a new eagerness to provide information. ''My Harold is going into the Navy as a commissioned officer. We're real proud of him.''

''I'll bet you are, ma'am. Just one more thing—''

''Mama!''

At the urgent cry, Jared turned to see a miniature version of Rose Bean stumbling up the dirt driveway. Jared concluded it was Harold's kid sister, Wendy, and felt a wave of sympathy for the girl who nearly rubbed her blue jeans off her thighs in her attempt to reach the trailer as fast as possible.

''Wendy, sweetie, what're you doing home this early?'' Rose asked.

The young teen paused to eye Jared with a mixture of awe and concern. ''They let us go. Is— Did he show up here, Mama?''

''He who?'' Rose asked. ''What on earth is going on?''

Jared smiled at Wendy. ''Did you have your assembly?''

Her mouth still open, the teen nodded. ''Principal Powers says we're to stay with our families or a responsible adult until further notice.''

"Why?" Rose demanded again. "Will someone tell me what's going on?"

"Everybody at school says Faith Ramey's been kidnapped by the serial killer," Wendy said before Jared could reply. "Principal Powers had just started talking when parents started coming into the auditorium and taking their kids. Guess the kids called 'em on their cellular phones. I wish you would've come for me, Mama.''

"How would I have gotten there? Walk?" Rose turned back to Jared. "What's this about a killer?"

"Some people think another incident is linked to Faith's disappearance." He told her about what had happened at the school.

"Jesus save us. Wendy inside. Get in, damn it." Rose all but shoved the girl past her into the trailer, then glared at Jared anew. "What's wrong with you? Why're you wasting time asking questions about my boy when you should be out tracking that nutcase?"

"Thank you for your time, Mrs. Bean."

"Looking for an easy place to stick the blame, that's what you're doing. Well, I may be a simple woman, but I know my rights, Mr. Lawman. You git, and leave me and mine alone. And don't come back, because I won't talk to you or anybody again without my lawyer!"

Jared knew Rose Bean was bluffing. Not only did she not have an attorney, but she couldn't afford one.

If his hunch played out, however, her boy might need legal help soon.

22

"I need you to look up an address for Fenton Farms," Jared said to Norma over the radio. He'd called as soon he'd left the Beans' place.

"Chief, it's crazy here."

"I imagine it'll get worse before it gets better."

"Principal Powers made an announcement over at the high school—"

"I know, Norma. Any protesters forming outside the station yet?"

"Imagine that's next."

"We'll deal with it then. The Fenton place...it's down a piece from Lake Sawyer, isn't it?"

Norma was a walking almanac as far as town and resident information was concerned. She could practically recite every family tree going back at least three generations, and in some cases more.

"Between the lake and the cemetery, on the east side. Chief, about those calls..."

"Any of them from the mayor?"

"No, he's with the search group out by the lake, so don't be surprised if you run into him while you're over there. You should know, he asked me to ring him if there's any news."

"I'll bet he did. You throw that number in the trash, or

you'll be working in the high school cafeteria until you're legal for social security.''

"Chief!''

"Talk to you as soon as I finish out there.''

He disconnected and drove back toward town. Following Norma's instructions, he found the Fenton ranch just past the lake, and he turned left by a series of white crepe myrtles framing the iron entry gate. Pecan trees lined the driveway leading to the sprawling ranch house. The Fentons were an established, but quiet family in these parts, the type whose lineage carried weight. But they didn't flaunt it as some did, which is why Jared didn't know them except by name.

He found someone he guessed was the patriarch of the family at the front of the barn. There was a considerable amount of banging going on inside, and judging from the sweat staining Jack Sr.'s shirt, Jared figured he'd been doing his share of the labor. Jared decided the man was Jack Sr. because of the way the man eyed his badge without concern, maybe even with a little challenge. Few people could pull that off and appear impressive rather than arrogant.

"Mr. Fenton?''

"That's right.''

"Jared Morgan.''

He didn't know what kept him from using his title, but it proved to be the right thing to do. The man put down the hammer he'd been holding and stepped closer to extend his hand.

"What can I do for you, Chief?''

"Actually, I was wondering if your son was around. I'd like a word with him.''

"About?''

"Verifying someone's story. Your boy's name was used to back up an alibi."

That relaxed the man considerably. "Jack!" he called into the barn. "Come out here."

A moment later, a younger version of the rancher loped toward them. Like his father, he was sweaty and dusty from a hard day's work.

"Sir?"

"This is Chief Morgan. He has something to ask you."

Confusion and concern darkened his brown eyes. Honest eyes, Jared thought, liking the young man instinctively. He decided not to put father or son through any unnecessary unease.

"Do you know Harold Bean?" he asked.

"Who?"

"You two went to school together."

"Oh! 'Stinky' Bean…right. You never wanted to get stuck with the locker next to his. And sometimes we called him 'Wax Bean' because he was always so pale and undernourished looking. Sure. I'd forgotten."

"Forgotten?"

"Well, I haven't seen him in…shoot, a few years, at least."

"My information suggests you saw him as recently as last night."

"No, sir."

"Harold Bean. About five-foot-eleven? Maybe a hundred sixty-five pounds if he has pizza for breakfast, lunch and supper?"

Jack Jr. laughed briefly. "That's the one. But I didn't see him yesterday."

"You didn't give him a ride after he'd had car trouble up in Mt. Pleasant?"

"Couldn't happen. It was my sister's birthday, and I was

here. We had a party for her, and I did the videotaping.''
He turned to his father. ''You didn't tell him?''

''He didn't ask me any of this.''

''I apologize,'' Jared said to the elder Fenton. ''It's faster and cleaner that way. You have the tape, I assume?''

''Shoot, yes. And about a dozen relatives and friends who were there, as well, can back me up. Do you want to see it?''

''If you wouldn't mind. It's just a formality to verify the date and time. I'm assuming your voice is picked up on the audio.''

''It's on there,'' Jack Sr. replied. ''Would you mind telling us what's going on? What's this Bean fellow done, and why'd he mention my son?''

''To be fair, I don't know if he's done anything,'' Jared said. ''But I do know it was important to him to lie to his mother about where he was last night. The problem is that last night Faith Ramey was reported to have disappeared.''

''Faith! She's a doll,'' Jack Jr. said. His expression turned shocked. ''She's missing?''

''That's what it looks like. And naturally, because of her formerly close friendship with Harold Bean, he's at the top of the list of people to question. He said that last night you gave him a lift in Mt. Pleasant, then drove him to the Wal-Mart in Mineola to get his car repaired.''

Jack Jr. shook his head. ''I'm not saying I wouldn't have done it, but, like I said, I was here.''

''He said you'd been up north to buy some new stock for the farm.''

''With the pastures in the condition they are, and the forecast for the rest of the year as grim as it is, we're going to be selling off most of the herd, not adding to it, right, Dad?''

''You got it.''

Jared experienced the rush of having locked onto a strong clue and the disappointment in finding that yet another human was guilty of having feet of clay. "If you'll show me that tape, I'll leave you to your work."

"This way," Jack Sr. said, gesturing to the French doors at the back of the house. "Because when you leave here, I don't want you to have any questions about this."

About twenty minutes later, after viewing the tape and thanking the Fentons, Jared was pulling out of the property. He reached for his radio and called in to the station.

"Good to hear your voice again, Chief," Norma said.

She sounded anticipatory, maybe somewhat more anxious than before. He could only imagine what had gone on since they'd last talked. He doubted, however, that it would be any more dramatic than what was about to happen.

"Put out an APB for Harold Bean," he said.

23

3:22 p.m.

Harold Bean was less than a mile from home when he saw the police car he'd just passed make a sharp *U*-turn. Moments later, its lights and siren came on.

What the hell…?

He glanced at his speedometer. No, he'd been careful not to speed, and he couldn't have committed any other traffic violation—it was a straight road, for crying out loud. This had to be one of those harass-a-young-guy stops to see if something could be stirred up. Unless the cops knew something…

Don't go looking for trouble. You're clean.

Thank goodness. If he hadn't made the stop he had, he would be sweating blood.

He pulled over, then quickly pulled out his wallet and started fishing for his license and proof of insurance.

The cop who stepped out of the patrol car was Sutter— not totally bad news. At least he didn't have the salt-in-the-wound attitude Red Samuels had. He gave the uneasy officer a confused smile.

"Hiya, Officer Sutter. You doing seat belt and insurance checks or something?"

Sutter, his right hand on his unsnapped holster ordered, "Get out of the car."

He smile vanished. "Why? What—"

"Get out of the car! Do it slow and don't try anything stupid."

Holy shit. "But I wasn't speeding."

"Get out. Now!"

The order had Harold quickly shoving open the door and easing out.

"Hands up! Move to the back of the vehicle."

Completely rattled, Harold asked, "Jesus, what for?"

"Lean against the trunk, palms flat. Spread the legs."

"But what for?"

"Do it!"

He did, but nerves got the best of him. "I have a right to be told what this is all about. I wasn't speeding, I have my license and insurance, I wasn't breaking any law." But when instructed, he placed his left hand behind his back, then his right.

The snap of the handcuffs, the tight fit, sent a fight-or-flight impulse surging through him. But a calmer, if faint, inner voice warned him to shut up and sit tight.

He endured the frisk and was escorted to the patrol car. Once they were on their way, Sutter called the station.

"I've got him."

That jarred. This wasn't an accident.

When Harold was escorted to the police station, the humiliation of having people stop in the street and walk out of their stores to gape made him want to hide his face. But there was no protection and inside were more people, staring. Folks he'd known most of his life.

He didn't complain when he was brought to the jail, until he saw the cell they meant to lock him in. He braked hard. "Oh, no. You can't do this."

''Shut up, turd.'' Sutter pushed him forward into the one directly facing the door. Harold was ordered to hold still while the cop removed the cuffs. Then Sutter exited, locking up behind himself.

''Wait!'' Harold cried, realizing the cop meant to leave him there. ''I get to make a phone call!''

''First you talk to the chief.''

''Fine. Take me to him.''

''Wait your turn.''

Harold stared in disbelief as Sutter walked away. What had happened to the laid-back cop who liked drag racing and going to sleep listening to Shania Twain?

The two-cell room was painted an abysmal shade of tick brown. What was next? He sank onto the cot against the brick wall and dropped his head in his hands.

He was still sitting on his cot, a near heart attack and a case of chills later, when the main door opened. Chief Morgan stepped up to his cell and unlocked the door.

''You okay?'' he asked Harold.

''Would you be if you were sitting here?''

''Let's go to my office and talk about it.''

Annoyed though he was, Harold followed, grateful that someone seemed to want to be reasonable. He followed the intimidating man out into the main room. His gaze fell on the automatic on Morgan's hip, but he was also aware of the suspicious stares of Norma and Sutter.

Swallowing, he hurried into the chief's office and lowered himself into the chair Morgan indicated. ''Could I have something to drink?'' he asked.

''This is the way things work,'' Jared replied, closing the door. ''You do something for me, then I do something for you.''

''If I'm under arrest, I should know why, and I should get to make a call. I already told—''

"You're not under arrest."

Harold couldn't stand fast enough.

"Yet."

He dropped back into the chair.

"It all depends," Jared continued, "on how you want to play it, on how long you keep insisting you don't know."

"But I don't." Uncomfortable with Morgan's enigmatic stare, he focused on the files on the chief's desk. Which, he wondered, was about him?

"So where were you going when Sutter found you?"

"Home." Temporarily.

"Rather early, weren't you?"

"I'd finished my exams."

"You were picked up on the road coming from Longview, not Mt. Pleasant."

"I had to run an errand and took a roundabout route. So?"

"What errand?"

"None of your business."

Jared reached for the phone. "In that case, I guess I'd better get Sutter in here."

"It was a—a gift, okay? For my mother."

"Very thoughtful. Is it her birthday?"

"No." Damn, Harold thought, why'd he choose that lame line, of all things?

"Well, I hate to break this to you, but Mother's Day was last Sunday."

"I missed it because I was studying, so I thought I'd do something extra nice for her birthday, which is *next* month, if you must know."

Jared inclined his head. "Okay. I'll buy that—for the moment. Did you find what you were looking for?"

"No. I guess I was more tired than I thought, and I couldn't make up my mind."

"So much for good intentions. Guess things were kind of hectic at the mall, too?"

"Ah…no. Not for a weekday, I mean."

"That may work in our favor."

"How do you mean?"

"I'm guessing that you talked to someone who'll remember you as a customer. You don't have to sweat about an alibi."

Harold didn't like this at all. Sensing he was being set up, he tried to backpedal. "The problem was, I didn't buy anything. I told you."

"Surely you asked a salesclerk to show you, say, a piece of jewelry in a showcase or something like that?"

The room was getting too hot, but Harold didn't dare tug at his collar or make another move that might make him appear guilt-ridden. "No. Sorry."

"That's too bad. I was hoping you could be as helpful as you were about Faith's disappearance, when you explained a guy helped you get that new car battery."

"That's right, I was. So why the hostility now? Does it have to do with Faith?"

"Would that upset you? To hear bad news about her?"

"What kind of question is that? You know it would."

Crossing his arms, Jared leaned against the wall and shrugged. "She dumped you."

"We split up. It was a mutual decision."

"From what I heard, she felt she'd outgrown your puppy-dog crush and that you two no longer had the same goals and outlook on life, but that you continued to tag after her like a lost hound, all but making yourself the laughingstock up at school."

"Bullshit. How many times do I have to say it? We

broke up, but remained friends. Listen, this sucks. What does anything about Faith and me have to do with me being here?''

''A search for motive.''

''Motive for what?'' Harold gripped the arms of the steel chair, waiting for the blow.

Jared only slowly shook his head.

What the hell did that mean? Harold wondered.

''Did I tell you that I visited with your mother earlier today?''

''That explains a lot. She's never liked Faith. Couldn't stand the idea of us as a couple. When we agreed to take a break from each other, she yakked on and on about how that proved Faith was no good. She doesn't think that she's embarrassing me just so she can say she was right all along.''

''We didn't discuss Faith, Harold. We discussed Jack Fenton.''

Harold couldn't react. He couldn't even think.

''See, I had to go to your mother to confirm what you'd said to Michaele Ramey,'' Jared continued. ''The good news is that your story holds. Your mother confirms it. If I can get your receipt for the battery, I could probably end things here.''

''Ah…heck, Chief, I don't know that I kept it.''

''That happens.'' Jared seemed to weigh a few options and then said, ''Guess we can always look at the battery itself.''

They had him. He stood, seeing only one way out. ''I want a clear-cut accusation of some crime, or I'm walking, Chief.''

''Clear-cut I can't do quite yet, as you are well aware,'' Jared replied calmly. ''But this much I do have…Jack Fenton hasn't had any contact with you. Not yesterday, not in years. And if you want to argue the point, hear this—your dean informed me that your classes, unlike Faith's, were over for the semester last *Friday*. In other words, pal, not only was there no *reason* for you to be up in Mt. Pleasant, but I don't believe you were there.''

24

The knock at the door couldn't have been more ill-timed. Jared had wanted to stand there and watch young Harold either wet his britches or prove his stealth by fabricating more expansive lies.

''Chief, it's Cuddy on line one. He says he has to talk to you.''

Had Norma buzzed him? Jared couldn't be sure, and that told him that he was getting a little intense and should take a minute to cool off.

''Okay,'' he called.

Reaching across his desk, he grabbed the telephone receiver. ''Yeah, Sheriff?''

''That sounds formal. You aren't alone?''

''Not at the moment.''

''Then I'll keep this brief. John Box didn't find anything helpful on the girl's purse. Can he come over and have another go at the car?''

''Sure. The place is locked down, so tell him to come here to get the key.''

''How the devil did you manage to get her to do that?''

Jared thought of the last time he had seen Mike, those precious few moments when she'd dropped the barriers before her temper took aim again. ''Hold the praise, I don't expect that to last long.''

"Wish we had some good news for her. Damn, we need a break."

"Hopefully, it's in the works."

"Oh, yeah? Does that remark have anything to do with who you're with right now?"

"You've got it," Jared drawled.

"Are charges pending?"

"Not at the moment, but we're working on it."

"The boyfriend."

"The obvious deduction."

Cuddy sighed. "Something has to turn up soon. John agrees that if something doesn't break soon, we need to call the DPS."

Jared understood, and it wasn't stubborn pride that made him hate the thought; it was the knowledge that Loyal and Jess, and those in their crowd, would see it as his bowing to their dictum. That wouldn't bode well for the next time he had to assert his authority.

"I'll talk to him when he gets here."

"I ran across one of your volunteer search teams," Cuddy added. "They're starting to check wells at abandoned homesteads. Tell them to be careful, for cripe's sake. I know they haven't put in the hours we have yet, but in this heat, fatigue will set in fast. The last thing we need is to have to form a rescue team to pull somebody out. Hell, that'll bring the media from both coasts."

"Sounds as though you need to take a break yourself."

"Aw, my arthritis is acting up. It's gonna finally rain and as much as we need it you know it's just gonna complicate things. Okay, I'm gone. Let me know how things go with the boyfriend."

"You bet."

Jared hung up. He'd been aware of Harold's listening, and finally met the young man's speculative gaze. No, the boy wasn't stupid. Harold knew that at least part of the conversation had been about him. Jared had to make that work in his favor, make it prey on the kid's mind.

"I have to go," he told him. "If you have something to say, now would be the time to tell me."

"There's nothing."

"All right, then let's run through this one more time. When did you last see Faith?"

"Tuesday. Around noon. I was headed for my car, and she was going to hers."

"Did you speak?"

"No."

"Wave?"

"No."

"Why not? You two were still 'friends,' as you yourself put it."

"She was in a hurry. I doubt she ever saw me. She was...preoccupied."

"Going to meet another guy, is that it? And you were jealous. That's why you followed her. She spotted you and pulled over to the side of the road to confront you, tell you to stop. Things got out of hand and your temper got the best of you."

"No!" Harold sat forward, increasingly anxious. "Nothing like that happened!"

"Then what did?"

"I don't know! Nothing. She's fine."

"Which one is it? If you know, you'd better tell us where she is—because until she's back home, you're staying here."

Jared opened the door and called for Sutter. "Lock him back up," he ordered.

"You can't keep me!" Harold cried. "I'm innocent!"

Jared slipped on his hat. "For your sake, I hope so. I'd hate to see what this community would do to you if you're lying."

25

4:09 p.m.

It had been twenty-four hours since Faith's disappearance. With every minute it grew more and more difficult for Michaele to stay put. She'd tried to keep herself busy—washing clothes, cooking food no one would eat, cleaning bathrooms—but aside from the occasional drone of Buck's snoring, she couldn't stand the silence or the horrible scenes her overactive imagination conjured.

Fatigue was getting the best of her. She'd been awake nearly thirty-six hours at this point, and the silence was turning into an enemy. But so was the phone, when it did ring. She'd unplugged all but the kitchen extension, and each time she'd raced from wherever she was, trying to catch it on the first ring. Not for Buck's sake, but in case it was news. The waiting was that awful.

The first few times it was a neighbor or one of Faith's girlfriends asking if there was news and if they could stop by to bring a cake or casserole. Michaele had been touched, but had turned all of them down, including the offers for company. It was a ludicrous thought—a room full of people watching Buck scratch various parts of his anatomy in his sleep. Another call had been from the county paper. She'd referred the reporter to the police and then hung up. Another had been someone calling for a bank credit card. The most recent one, though, had been the most unwelcome.

No one had been there.

Logic told her it was nothing—a wrong number, a disconnect, some sort of mechanical error. But in her imagination she saw Faith frantically dialing, and just as she picked up on her end, the kidnapper clasped a hand over Faith's mouth and dragged her from the room...or Sandy's killer sitting by the phone covered with Faith's blood, smiling as he heard her say, "Hello? *Hello?*"

Ten minutes later, when it happened again, she knew she would either have to pull the plug in the kitchen, too, or get out. She grabbed her keys and wallet and sought escape via the white pickup.

Her first impulse was to join one of the search groups. But when she saw Reverend Dollar in the group walking the road easements at the northernmost edge of town, she quickly detoured before she was spotted, and took a roundabout way back to town. Her gutless reaction embarrassed her, and it was a relief to see Last Writes. Knowing she could refocus on something else there, she pulled into the parking lot; but she was soon less sure about her decision. Dillon had no compunction about closing when business was slow, and from the look of things, the place was empty. Considering how exhausted he'd looked earlier, he might have shut down to catch up on sleep.

She found the front door unlocked. Dillon, however, was nowhere around. Calling his name, she glanced into the New Releases room on her left that had once been someone's living room. She loved this house with its odd-shaped rooms, antique furniture, art deco figurines and lamps, and deep, rich colors. It all came together to create a larger-than-life if moody atmosphere, much like its multifaceted proprietor.

The phone rang and the answering machine immediately picked up. After Dillon's curt instructions to leave a message, a young male voice replied, "Hey, it's me. Listen, I can't talk right now, but a couple of us were out at the east cemetery last night, and we found this spot in the back. Man, it was weird—like an altar, you know, with an honest-to-God pentagram in the middle. I couldn't help thinking that...well, you know that co-ed who's missing? Maybe—"

"What are you doing?"

Michaele started at Dillon's sharp question, but before she could think of something to say, he came the rest of the way down the hall and snatched up the phone behind the front counter.

"Hold on!" he snapped to the caller.

Placing his hand over the mouthpiece, he said to her, "Sorry. This isn't something you need to hear. I'll be right with you."

Michaele dismissed the apology with a shake of her head, but was less sure of his expression; at first so hostile, it quickly softened into a smile of sympathy and chagrin. This was the second time today that his reactions had seemed...off, somehow. Then again, why was she questioning him when *she* was the one with the problem?

She certainly hadn't had to give him space, she realized, turning in the doorway of the Mystery room. He'd not only turned his back to her, but was conducting the rest of his conversation in a voice so low that it was impossible to eavesdrop even if she wanted to.

"I said forget about it!" he suddenly snapped. "Because I didn't invest the time I did in you to see you get lost in that kind of crap. You have Notre Dame to think about. Oh, hell. Later,'' he muttered and slammed down the phone.

Watching him stand there, his shoulders stiff, the energy around him explosive, Michaele decided coming had been a mistake. "I'll come back another time," she said, heading for the door.

"Wait!" Dillon came around the front counter, his smile apologetic. "I'm sorry."

Dressed in one of the infamous black T-shirts and matching jeans that had long had a female tongue wagging, and with his dark features sharpened by shadows due to his own lack of sleep, he looked every bit as mysterious as the merchandise he specialized in. Then he massaged his chest as though he were soothing a deep ache, and she saw the misfit loner so much like herself.

"I'd been out back picking up the trash," he continued. "Some mutt or raccoon got in the cans last night and had stuff spread all over the place. I should have waited until closing, then you wouldn't have heard that." He waved away the excuse. "How are you? Has there been any news?"

She shook her head.

"Damn. I was an ass this morning, Mike. I should never have blown off your concern about Faith."

"Who knows? You may still be right."

"Yeah, which is why you look like you've already done a week in a pressure cooker."

"That's why I'm here. I needed to get out of the house."

"You closed?"

"Chief Morgan insisted." At his sardonic look, Michaele felt herself growing warm. "He did."

"*Chief* Morgan? This is me, okay? Most women can't

even imagine having a guy pant after them the way he does you. Why do you refuse to deal with that?''

Michaele focused on the ancient wood floor, afraid he might see Jared's kiss in her eyes. ''Because like you, I'm just not cut out for a traditional life.''

Arching eyebrows already described by townspeople as ''arrogant,'' Dillon drawled, ''Darlin', I don't think our fearless leader worries about other people's labels. He worries about dying before he gets you.''

''This is not a good time, Dillon.''

He threw back his head and groaned. ''You're right. I'm an insensitive prick. Why do you put up with me?''

''Because you're a friend. You treat me as a person, not a mere female—not less intelligent than you, though I know I am, not unrefined or out of touch, which I definitely am.''

''Stop the pity-party, or I'll send you upstairs to nap until you're in a healthier frame of mind.''

''It's Ch—Jared's fault. He succeeded in getting me out of his way, and now he's ignoring me. It's driving me out of my mind.''

''He's carrying a helluva weight on his shoulders, and on his conscience,'' Dillon replied, serious again. ''Could be he's ashamed because he hasn't found Faith yet, and scared that he won't.''

Michaele closed her eyes. ''God, don't say that.''

''A customer told me they've got several groups looking for her. I should close and join one.''

''I intended to myself, but the one I found was headed by Dollar.''

''What? You have something against my greatest fan?''

''The man makes TV evangelists look legitimate. Besides, he has no right trying to shut you down just because you stock some fantasy and paranormal material.''

"Ah, but you know how fundamentalist minds work—if you read it, you live it. Aren't those types walking proof?"

The sly comment almost won a smile from her. Then her gaze fell on the phone. "Dillon...about that call. Is there really stuff like that going on around here?"

"Look, a couple of kids were out hunting a safe place to drink beer without getting caught by either their parents or the law. I'm not condoning it, but at least they're sticking close to home. Apparently, the one with the lowest tolerance for alcohol imagined a pile of stones as a satanic sign, and a headstone tipped over as an assault on a resting soul. That doesn't make it so."

Nevertheless, his words made Michaele shiver. "But every once in a while there's an incident that starts the speculation all over again," she said. "Like a few pets disappearing, or a cow showing up mutilated and with the blood drained out of it."

"Yeah, and the same people insist individuals like me, who crave their privacy, practice satanic rituals in their attics. Have you personally ever seen any of this so-called 'evidence'?"

"No, but seriously, Dillon, those D&D games some of your kids play?" she said. "What if one or two of the more impressionable individuals take it too seriously?"

"I heard about the incident at the school," Dillon replied. "Let me tell you a story. When I was a kid, I had a teacher whose parents moved here from Germany after the Second World War. Now he was born here, but because he was a little formal and held to some rules a bit more than other teachers with a different upbringing, a few kids painted swastikas on the sidewalk outside his house. Adults don't have the market cornered on cruelty or stupidity, Mike. That's probably what you're looking at—

some dumb yuck about to graduate wanted to create some excitement for his pals. And what's the only really big thing that ever happened in Split Creek? Did he massage two brain cells awake to consider how the Powers or Jared would feel about that? Hell, no. Just as he never would have imagined that Faith wasn't going to make it home from school last night.''

''You sound like Jared.''

''And you're going to drive yourself crazy looking for an inferno where there's only a blown-out match. Give your poor mind a break. Let that one go.''

''But, Dillon—''

''You want a cup of wild berry tea?'' He all but tapped her nose with his index finger. ''That's my signal that I refuse to discuss this further.''

Resigned, she passed on the beverage. ''I'd better get back in case the warden notices I'm not in my cell and threatens to put one of his men at the end of my driveway. There is something you could do for me, though. That Cameo that was at the garage today? I bought it. Would you do me a huge favor and look up the model on the Internet, and see what manuals or books are available about it?''

''Be glad to. I'll print out what I can find for part suppliers, too.''

''Thanks. I don't see myself starting on it yet. There's no telling how long—''

''Not to worry. At least you'll have the information when you're ready for it.'' He followed her to the door. ''Uh…you know what? I'll ask some questions.'' When she eyed him questioningly, he nodded. ''Yeah, about the cemetery and the stuff at the school. Just do me a favor and keep this between you and me, okay?''

Relieved, Michaele nodded. "I appreciate it, Dillon. And you."

As much as their talk helped, once she left Michaele was still too keyed up to return home. Thinking she might stop by the garage to have a soda and maybe do a little paperwork, she pulled into the station.

That's when she saw the back gate open.

26

"Uh-oh."

John Box's soft warning made Jared glance over his shoulder. Michaele was striding toward them carrying a crowbar almost half her size. Equally worthy of caution was the glint in her eye.

"Thanks for keeping me informed, guys."

"You knew this was why we wanted the car here," Jared told her.

"Preferably without me being present."

He stepped between her and Box to allow the detective to keep working, but also to keep their conversation as private as possible. "That's not true, and you know it. What are you doing here, Mike? You should be home resting."

"Half the town is out looking for my sister. Law enforcement people I don't even know are about to start their third shift without a break. You think I can let other people drive themselves to exhaustion while I sit on my butt?"

Jared knew her conscience wouldn't allow that, but hoped there wasn't something else involved. "There hasn't been any trouble with Buck, has there?"

"Despite *The Exorcist* sound effects, he hasn't budged from where you put him. How long have you been here?"

"Long enough to know we collected all the useful samples from the car that we're likely to get."

"Which you told me earlier is virtually zip. So what's the verdict? Did Faith drive the car to Pete's, or did someone wrap themselves completely in plastic wrap before doing it?"

He knew her sarcasm covered a deeper anxiety, and if he was to be totally honest with her, he would have to add to it. "You're forgetting that Faith could have wiped the prints herself to make you think it was done by someone else."

"The question is, would Faith have done something like that? Would she have been in such a psychological state that she saw value in doing that?"

"Trying to earn your own badge?"

"Please. Just broadening my scope enough to imagine she was that vengeful or malicious fried what's left of my working brain cells." For a moment she watched John, who continued with his business as though he were alone. "There isn't anything you need to ask me about? A button, piece of paper with handwriting on it...?"

Jared took her arm and drew her to the other side of the car. There on the ground spread on thick plastic were the contents of what had been in the glove compartment. Aside from the vehicle's papers, most of it was the usual young person's things—cassette tapes, gum and breath mints, a brush with a few lustrous strands of black hair. The toothbrush had raised his interest, but the thing that had Michaele swearing under her breath were the condoms.

"She's almost twenty-one," Jared said, trying to help her make the mental leap.

"She wasn't seeing anyone. I'm not saying I believed she was a virgin, but she *told* me she wasn't seeing anyone."

"They were scrunched in the very back of the glove compartment. She could have forgotten they were there."

"Do they look old to you?"

He didn't bother responding to that. "Did you two talk about birth control?"

"Well, who was going to? Buck?"

Jared couldn't resist. "No," he murmured softly, "it would be an older, more experienced sister."

"Up yours."

Red-faced and seething, she stormed off. He caught up to her only a few yards away.

"Mike, I'm trying to make you realize you're overreacting. What did you expect her to do? Tell you? A six-year age difference is practically a generation considering the pace of life these days. You yourself said you didn't have the kind of relationship that encouraged the sharing of confidences.

"John's going to see if he can pick up a print off them," he said, when she remained silent. "Who knows? Maybe we'll get lucky."

"Is it a common brand? I mean, in town?"

He barely caught the mumble. "Oh, sure, the grocery store carries them, the drugstore, of course. Even the quickie place up the road."

"Keep track of your sources, do you, Morgan?"

"I'm not the kind of man who'd put that responsibility on a woman, and if you're ever seriously interested in an answer to your question, we can talk about it. In the meantime, your point is well taken. Faith may have been involved with a guy who was negligent or lazy—or, like you said, she might not have put that there. We'll keep it in mind."

"Thank you."

Her tone was depressed, her demeanor crushed. He wanted to take her in his arms and reassure her; at the same time, he took comfort from the painful but brief glimpses into what she really felt.

It mattered to her. His sex life mattered. He had no time, no business being pleased, but he was.

"It's getting late. We're about to wind up here. Have you eaten?"

She shook her head. "Not hungry. Besides, I should get back and check on him."

"Where all have you been?"

She shrugged, avoiding his gaze. "Around. I've been thinking, I should go talk to Harold some more. Maybe—"

"Harold's across the street."

"You mean…you've arrested him?"

"He hasn't been formally charged, no. But we are holding him for questioning."

"For how long?"

"Until I have the time to do that."

Jared could tell she didn't much appreciate the parry.

"What do you have on him?" she enunciated slowly.

"Several lies, alibis that don't hold up. Not much more than that at the moment, but it begs the question, why?"

"Harold would never hurt Faith."

"The sad truth is that we rarely know what another human being is capable of in a moment of passion."

"Well, there you go. Harold, passionate? He's twenty going on fifteen."

"I was that age when I had intercourse for the first time." He repressed a smile at her dumbfounded look. "And kids are starting even earlier these days."

"He's still too young for there to be a connection."

"To what?"

She blinked, then glanced away. "Nothing. Just talking to myself."

He didn't buy that for a second. "What's going on, Mike?"

She remained silent, but before he could press for an answer, his car radio sounded. He went to answer Norma's page.

"Chief, we just received word from one of the week-enders out at the lake. Says his cabin has been broken into. There's quite a list of stolen goods."

"What is that, the eighth burglary so far this year?" He pinched the bridge of his nose, thinking what lousy timing for this. And when were people going to realize what a temptation all those empty cabins were and put in some decent alarm systems or better antiburglary devices? "Who would be the easiest to cut loose and send over there?"

"Bruce just pulled in after a few hours making the rounds. He said he'd be happy to go, then he'll stop home for a bite to eat."

"Okay, tell him to go on. You can look for me within the next thirty minutes." Signing off, he said to Michaele. "Where were we?"

"When it rains, it pours. Your people have to be running low on fuel. I'll turn on the pumps for a while."

"Don't change the subject. What do you know that you're not telling me?"

Hands on her hips, she nudged pebbles across the concrete with the toe of her sneaker. "I was only thinking of the message at the school, the possible motive for it."

"You're intent on connecting the two events."

"Maybe I'm thinking they have to be. But if so, Harold would only have been—what?—barely a teenager six years ago."

"I'm not going to like this, am I?"

"Probably not. Because if you can determine he wasn't

capable of having been at the high school in time to have written that message, I don't think there's a fifty-fifty chance that he's guilty. I don't think there's a chance in hell.''

''So you'd be completely comfortable if I let him walk right now?''

She didn't reply.

''You have something to say. Say it. I've been up all night, too. My psychic abilities are waning fast.''

''Let me ask you this. Doesn't what's happened remind you, even vaguely, of the problems that occasionally pop up with cult worship in the area?''

''Oh, hell. This is East Texas. We have as many churches as pine trees. Rumors about that crap keep ministers in business, and for all I know they start them themselves to boost attendance.''

''You've never actually seen any real evidence?''

''Did Garth put that idea in your head? I'll bust his other hand,'' Jared growled in disgust.

''I haven't seen Garth since this morning.''

''Then who did you talk to?''

She didn't answer.

He had a hunch, but he'd pin his badge to his skin before voicing the name. She would only accuse him of being jealous. And be right. What bothered him more was Hancock's motive behind filling her head with bullshit.

''Okay. See?'' He splayed his hands. ''I'm backing off. Whatever's going on in that pretty head of yours, it's your business. But understand this—the longer Faith is missing, the more rumors will spread. *That* one would build a paranoia we don't need, Mike.''

''I wouldn't have said anything if you hadn't pushed.''

''I wouldn't push if you didn't drive me crazy.''

The corner of her mouth twitched. ''That's what they

say about vitamin pills on an empty stomach. You should go home, get yourself something to eat, and get some sleep.''

''Come with me. I'll even let you tuck me in.'' As her gaze fell to his mouth, he sucked in a sharp breath. ''On second thought, maybe I'd tuck you in—beside me.''

''Jared, stop it.''

''Tell me one thing—did you hate it? My kissing you?''

''No, but—''

''Someday I'll do it again when I'm not angry. It'll be better.''

''I liked it fine.''

Her reply was so unexpected that he instinctively reached for her. At the same instant John Box coughed.

''Uh, Chief? Can I talk to you a sec?''

With no small regret, Jared went over to the detective. ''What's up?''

''Clouds are moving in. We're losing daylight faster than usual. I thought I'd bag the contents of the glove compartment and take it with me, and work through it at the station.''

''Let's hope there's a gift in there.''

Jared turned back to Michaele—and found she'd gone.

27

Michaele stood where she'd stood last night at this hour and stared out into the black night. Once she'd gotten Buck upstairs, she'd laid down herself, managed to doze for almost an hour, but then had been harshly wakened by the shrill ring of the telephone. The call had been a wrong number, or someone insisting they had the wrong number. Her suspicion was a sign to her that paranoia was setting in. At any rate it had been enough to make it impossible for her to settle down again; she kept expecting a repeat of the call from before, that eerie voice taunting her.

From upstairs came a series of creeks and groans that told her that her father, for all his attempts to avoid it, was as restless as she was. But she was grateful he didn't come down. She didn't want to have to talk to him, to make up answers to his impossible questions.

Did Faith know what was happening here? With three, they at least had a semblance of a family, dysfunctional or otherwise. With only two…

"Where are you?" she whispered into the darkness.

Was she dead? It was an incredible thought, except those were the kind that came true in her family, as on the night Buck came home and told her that her mother had died. She'd had a cold, for pity's sake. Yes, only in the Ramey family did such insanity occur. She remembered being so dumbfounded, so outraged that she hadn't been able to cry.

She had no tears now, just a heavy dread that made it increasingly hard to breathe, as though she had a tumor growing rapidly inside her.

If someone has to die, why aren't You taking him?

Michaele pressed her hand against her mouth. The question had been so clear, she was convinced she'd said the words aloud.

"I didn't," she whispered into the night. "I didn't mean it that way."

But the protest sounded hollow even to her own ears and, miserable, she closed her eyes and leaned her forehead against the window. That's when she heard a low, guttural sound. An animal's growl?

She looked out, then down into the bushes…and saw the top of a head. A human head.

28

12:01 a.m.

"I have to get out!"

Finally, Jared thought upon hearing Harold Bean's plaintive call. He'd been working in his office since returning from a few hours of rest and a shower at the house. He waved off Curtis's silent query about looking in on the kid and went back there himself. Buddy and Bruce were back on duty and out on patrol.

"You want to talk?" he asked the shaken young man.

"I want out of here. I need to call the house. Don't you realize—?"

"Your mother knows where you are. In fact, she told me to beat the shit out of you if you deserved it, and not to let you go until you confessed all of your sins."

Harold leaped from the cot against the far wall and pressed his face to the bars. "She wouldn't say that!"

"Then you don't know your mama very well. You've embarrassed her. Once we explained what a sniveling little liar you are—"

"I didn't do anything to Faith."

"Then where is she?"

"I don't know!"

"Where were you during the hours you've been lying

about? Give me something you can prove, witnesses who'll testify to it, and you're out of here. It's as simple as that.''

''I can't! There wasn't anyone!''

''Except Faith?''

''No.''

''You had another argument, didn't you? The worst you'd ever had.''

''We never fought. We weren't like that.''

''Did you rape her before you killed her?''

''No-no-no!'' Doubling over, Harold started gagging.

Jared went to the kitchen and brought back a paper cup filled with water. ''Here,'' he said, handing it through the bars.

Harold drank, then crushed the cup in his fist and thumped it against his head over and over. ''Why is this happening to me?''

''Because that's the way things are,'' Jared replied. ''Husbands, boyfriends, lovers—they're always the top suspects because the statistics prove you should be. Talk to me, kid. Tell me why you're different.''

''Because I loved Faith, but I wasn't *in love* with her anymore. Because I was looking forward to graduating and moving on with my life. I'm joining the Navy, you know.''

''Your mother confirmed that. So where were you really last night?''

''Cruisin'.''

The reluctant admission held his interest. ''And?''

''And nothing. I was decompressing from finals. You saw where I live, you saw my mother. Would you want to spend all evening stuck in a trailer with her?''

''Did you get lucky?''

Harold snorted. ''Look at me, man. Girls don't go for geeks like me. That's why I've gotta get into the service.''

"Faith seemed to think you were okay."

"Not in that way. What we shared as kids, it was over. I settled for what time she would give me, but being a year behind her and stuff, I fell farther and farther out of her league. She wasn't hateful about it. It's just who she was."

His pragmatic attitude convinced Jared more than any credible information. "If I let you go, you can't do anything stupid like run away."

"I wouldn't run away. I told you, I'm going into the Navy. Do you think I want to toss away my future?"

"It wouldn't be the first dumb thing you did." Jared leaned back and took the keys that hung outside the room. Then he unlocked the cell.

Harold stared, uncertain. "You mean that's it? I can go."

"That's the idea. But remember—news about you being in for questioning has spread around town, so be careful going home. Tempers and fear are up several notches. You take care not to make any more bad judgment calls."

"Yes, sir."

Jared saw a flash of fear in Harold's eyes, but suffered no guilt for putting it there. Hopefully, the kid had learned a lesson. Hopefully, they wouldn't have to bring him back in. That was the downside to this kind of situation. Until all the facts were in, you just didn't know.

As the front door closed behind Harold, Curtis wheeled around in his chair and gave him a questioning look. He had a hunch it was the calmest response he was likely to get from anyone about his decision.

"We'll see," he said.

The phone buzzed. "Split Creek Police," Curtis began.

Jared was almost at his office when he heard, "Chief! It's Mike. You better get over there, pronto."

29

12:18 a.m.

With Curtis's message from Michaele replaying like a nightmare in his mind, Jared raced like a madman, nearly going into a spin as he turned into her street, and again when he turned into her driveway. He hoped Curtis's alert to Bruce and Buddy would have them following soon.

His headlights picked up nothing around the outside of the house, and it was dark inside except for what appeared to be the stove light Michaele usually left on. Fearing the worst—that the prowler had gotten inside—his throat tightened at the sight of her running from the house toward him.

"Get back inside!" he ordered sharply as he exited the car.

"But—"

"Get in until I tell you it's safe. Move!"

As he spoke, he drew his gun and released the safety, but to his relief she did as ordered, a lithe flash of black in another of her sleep shirts. Thinking of how the Ramey drama could have been compounded, he started checking around the house.

By the time Bruce arrived, Jared had reassured himself

that nothing was under any of the parked vehicles and had made a quick inspection of the back.

"Is she okay?" Bruce asked Jared.

"Seems to be. I haven't talked to her yet. Check the front. I'm going out to the garage and see if anything looks suspicious back there."

Except for a possum who didn't like his halogen flashlight, there was no sign of anything unusual there, and a scan of the open land beyond suggested that if someone had sought escape that way, he'd succeeded.

"Chief!"

Bruce's sharp call brought him running up front. "What've you got?"

The patrolman aimed the beam from his flashlight at the siding of the house.

"Son of a bitch."

"I thought we had our man locked up."

"This isn't him," Jared replied. "But don't ask me what pervert we are dealing with."

Shifting his flashlight to illuminate the ground around the shrubbery, Bruce said, "There's a good footprint, too. I'll go get what we need to collect a semen sample. Don't have anything for the print, though."

"Call Box. I don't want any mistakes with this."

"Will do. Don't worry, Chief, we'll get this clown."

"All we need is a little luck that he's a secretor." Jared knew one of the phenomenas in forensics—in genetics in general—was that up to sixty percent of the population's blood types could be determined from body fluids. The bad news was that the perpetrator was gone, so they didn't have a suspect to match to. "Get the camera out of my trunk and see what pictures you can get, too."

By the time they'd taken the photos and had done the cotton swabbing, putting them in his car for air-drying as protection from the increasing wind, Buddy Eagan pulled in. Following him came a rumble of thunder.

"We can always cover the spot if Box doesn't get here in time," Jared said. "But we can't cover the whole property or the woods." Hoping their luck wouldn't just hold but improve, he sent Buddy and Bruce to do a broader search of the area. Who knew who or what they were dealing with here; the guy could be hiding out in the woods across the street, watching.

Using the momentary break, he went inside to check on Michaele.

She was pacing in the kitchen. Barefoot, with a too-large windbreaker over her sleep shirt, she looked so young and vulnerable that he immediately pulled her into his arms.

Not only didn't she fight him, but she clung to him with an intensity that made his heart ache. Silently thanking heaven that she was safe, he whispered, "That was too close."

"I can't seem to stop shaking."

"Anybody would be."

"Did you get him?"

"No. But we have plenty of evidence that he was here."

"He dropped something?"

"Let's just say there's enough to convict him when we get him. And we will get him. I promise you." Aware of how little time there was before Box's arrival or the weather deteriorated the scene, he said, "Tell me what happened. Where were you?"

"Standing by the front window. I'd been thinking, or rather fighting my thoughts, and that's when I heard something."

"What exactly?"

"At first it sounded like an animal growling, but it was

so close. I looked down into the shrubbery and…that's when I saw him.''

Jared leaned back to study her face. ''Clear enough to identify?''

''No. I didn't have any lights on and only saw the outline of a man's head and shoulders.''

''You're sure? There wasn't anything about the shape, anything he did that reminded you of someone?''

''I'm sorry. It happened so fast, and then my instincts kicked in and…I panicked.''

''Fear is nothing to be ashamed of. It's primal and often a useful defense mechanism.''

''Oh, my self-preservation kicked in, all right. I screamed and ran for the phone in the kitchen like a ten-year-old.''

''You did the right thing. He could have had a gun. If he'd had the time to think about it, and suspected you'd recognized him, he could have silenced you right then and there.'' Or worse yet, she could have been too brave and grabbed something like that crowbar she'd confronted him and John with. He drew her closer as several grim images toyed with his mind.

''About that evidence—what do you have?''

Her words were muffled because he had her face buried against his chest, but there was no pretending he hadn't heard. ''A footprint.''

''That's it?''

Her disappointment would have been amusing if it weren't for what else they did have, and she wouldn't stop until he told her. He didn't want her hearing about it from someone else. ''He masturbated while watching you.''

She immediately pulled free. He let her, understanding the necessary shift her emotions were about to take.

''That—that's sick!''

"You won't get any argument from me."

Her wrinkled-nosed grimace soon turned into a scowl. "Why is this happening to us?"

If he had the answer to that, he'd be on his way to arrest someone. "At least there's one piece of good news—it wasn't Harold."

"True. Sitting in jail definitely gives him an alibi."

"Harold's out, Mike. I released him minutes before you called the station. But," he added before she could respond, "there wouldn't have been time for him to get here. His car is still on the east side of town."

"You cleared him?"

"Not yet. But I also don't have the evidence to keep him. You can't convict a guy for not telling the truth about how he spends his time."

"Why else would he be lying?"

"You'll have to stay tuned for that one."

Michael's tension exhibited itself in the way she tugged at the short hair at her nape. "Does that mean the man who was here was...what? The man who took Faith? Or are we looking at our own homegrown variety of wacko?"

It was a toss-up as to which scenario was more disturbing. Hell, no, he didn't have any illusions about the people that made up his community. Some interesting, disturbing folks lived here. When you had this much freedom and this much creativity, as the saying went, shit happened. But was Mike's visitor someone she dealt with every day, who liked to watch women in order to get his rocks off, or yet another commodity entering the picture?

A flash of lights played across the kitchen window. Good enough reason not to answer her question. "Weather's coming. So's John Box. I have to get outside."

"Go. I'm fine now."

Nevertheless he lingered, glancing toward the stairs. "I can't believe Buck hasn't heard any of this. Why don't you go up and check on him, maybe bring him down. He could keep you company."

"Yeah, right. The fact that you think that tells me you don't have a clue, Morgan. Leave well enough alone."

He left, but only because the next flash was Box pulling in.

"You trying to single-handedly keep me busy?" the detective asked, shaking hands.

"To be honest, I wish it was the SOB's corpse."

John glanced around. "Considering the snake population this year, you may get your wish. Be patient."

"Easy for you to say."

"How is Mike?"

Jared took no offense. He was beginning not to care who knew how strongly he felt about her. Maybe that's what was needed—public disclosure and group momentum on his side.

"Putting up a good front, but hairline fractures are showing," he said.

Box followed Jared to the front of the house. In the distance Griggs and Eagan could be seen reemerging from the woods and heading their way.

John pushed aside the shrubbery a bit more to get a better view of the prints. "What a beaut the left one is. Looks like he pivoted on his right as he was leaving, though. See the slip of the heel and increased depth?"

In truth, Jared hadn't paid that much attention after realizing what they had. "So whoever he is, we're looking at a thirteen—maybe a size fourteen shoe?"

"Emphasis on *shoe*. Formal, not athletic, rubber-soled footwear."

"Cowboy boots?"

"Won't rule 'em out, though this doesn't exactly look like the right kind of heel. In other words, our guy could easily have been wearing a Brooks Brothers suit, and *that* about excludes horny seventeen- or even twenty-year-olds."

Then Harold was doubly safe from being an issue there. For all his size, his feet were average, and he always wore athletic shoes—rather pricey ones, come to think of it, for a guy living on a shoestring—but who was he to judge what people splurged on? He was more interested in who he should be looking at.

They returned to John's vehicle to get what he needed. "That semen sample," John said. "Is it dry enough to be bagged?"

"Doubt it. It's on the passenger side of the front floorboard of my unit when you're ready for it. Listen, about the condoms that were in the Firebird's glove compartment, have you had a chance to check them?"

"There was a print on one, but it was smeared. You seeing a link?"

"Just one more loose thread. When are some of them going to start connecting?"

John glanced around again. "What do you know about where our loverboy went? This isn't exactly Main Street at high noon. If he drove here, he sure would have been conspicuous."

"Mike said she immediately ran out of the room. I don't know that she would have heard anything from the kitchen, especially since she was on the phone. But I'll ask."

"We could try bringing in a couple of dogs to see if we pick up a trail, but I have to tell you, they're all pretty beat from working the parks and roadsides today. So are the handlers." The closest flash of lightning yet made John grimace. "There's that, too. By the time we got them here, any scent would be washed away. Maybe that's in Mike's best interest."

"How do you mean?"

"No way this could be kept quiet. Could Mike handle that added attention on top of everything else she's coping with? For that matter, could you?"

John's meaning suddenly sent a different chill through Jared. He signaled Bruce and Buddy to stop where they were.

"You think this guy was here because of me."

"That hadn't occurred to you—that you're the common denominator?"

"Hell, no. Why should it?"

"I've been thinking about what you told me about what happened at the school. While I agreed with you then that it was probably nothing, while driving over here I started to wonder."

"But my only link to Faith is that she's Mike's sister."

"That's the chink in my theory, but I wouldn't dismiss the idea completely."

"Okay," Jared replied with reluctance. "Let me ask you this—do you think this pig will be back?"

"Probably not tonight. But if that were my house, with my wife in there, she wouldn't spend the rest of the night alone, having to wonder if I was right."

John went back to work, and Jared glanced back at the house. He saw Mike at the living room window, watching them. His mind made up, he called his men to him.

"Anything?" he asked.

"Nothing," Bruce replied.

"Too dark to see," Buddy added. "Vegetation's so thick, you'd need to trip over whatever it was you were looking for to find it."

"Okay, stick close to John and give him whatever help he needs. I have to go back inside."

Mike must have heard him on the stairs because she met him in the kitchen. Without preamble he said, "Pull on some jeans. I'm taking you to my place."

30

Jared's order didn't come as a surprise to Michaele. She'd seen him and John Box conferring and had sensed something was up. This, she concluded, was partly her fault. Her behavior, yet another show of vulnerability, had opened a door from Jared's perspective. Authoritative and confident by nature, it was natural for him to use this as an opportunity to assume control of her, as he had in this situation. Grateful as she was for all he was doing on behalf of her family, it would be a mistake to let him draw conclusions he shouldn't.

"I can't do that," she told him.

"This isn't open for discussion."

"Excuse me?"

"Save the lifted eyebrows routine. You're afraid I plan to jump your bones the minute I get you into my house," he said. "Fantastic fantasy as it is, I think the first time we make love we should have the whole weekend to recover from it, don't you?"

"That's not funny, Jared."

"It wasn't intended to be." He glanced at his watch. "Look, I figure we'll be leaving here within the next half-hour." He locked his gaze with hers again. "Be ready."

"I'll be fine now. You've scared him off."

"Maybe. Hopefully. But for how long?"

Those penetrating gray eyes were getting uncannily

good at undermining her confidence. "If I start running now, I may never stop. Besides, Buck is here."

"Buck isn't in danger. You are. And he's not able to help."

"So give me a gun."

"In a house where there's a drunk? All right, let's try this angle—you need a couple hours of sleep. What's the likelihood of that happening here?"

"It's not going to happen in a strange house in a strange bed, either."

"Will it ease your mind to know it won't be the one I sleep in? You can use the guest room."

To be inundated with his possessions, his smell, his very essence? "I'd rather use one of the cell cots."

"Sold." Before she could protest or point out that she hadn't meant she *would* go, he headed out the door. "Do what you need to do. I'll let you know when we're ready to leave."

"I'm not going, Morgan."

"One way or another, I'm taking you with me."

It was pouring when Mike parked the Cameo at the garage, then dashed across the street to where Jared waited just inside the doorway of the police station. She'd decided to put on her customary uniform for work—denim shirt, jeans and the cleanest baseball cap she could find—because she knew she would be opening for business at first light.

"Don't look as though I'm about to haul you inside for a full body search," Jared drawled, as she wiped rain from her face. He held the inner door open for her.

"Don't *you* be surprised if you trigger more gossip than you can handle. Only two people incarcerated here in twenty-four hours, and one's the missing person's sister? That's almost enough to bring in CNN.''

''You had the option of more privacy at my place.''

''Half the county drives past your house every day. What were you planning on my doing with the Cameo, throwing a bedsheet over it?''

''You forget, you've got everybody convinced you're determined to be a cranky old maid.''

That silenced her, because he was right. She didn't date, and Faith's disappearance was making her more cynical and more apt to crave solitude than ever. Self-conscious, she could barely meet Curtis's speculative gaze, and eagerly accepted Jared's invitation to go on into his office while he had a word with the other cop.

''Take the couch,'' he said when he joined her a moment later. ''Those cell mattresses are as thin as a potato chip.''

''What about you?''

''I had a good nap earlier. Besides, I need to do some computer work.''

She couldn't deny that the weight of the last twenty-four hours was finally bearing down on her, but as he settled at his desk, and she eyed the ancient, leather seat an arm's length from the couch, she doubted if she could make herself close her eyes, let alone sleep, with him so near. Nevertheless, she slipped off her hat and laid it on the seat across from his desk, then curled into a half sitting, half reclining position at one end of the couch.

''Do you always wrap up like a pretzel when you go to bed?''

Michaele half opened her eyes to find him watching her. ''I'm a little chilled from getting wet. I'll be fine once I dry.''

Without commenting, Jared left the room. He returned

just as abruptly with a military-surplus wool blanket, which he patiently wrapped around her, before returning to his seat. "You can breathe again," he said, turning on his monitor.

"You don't have to rub it in."

"You're right. Close your eyes and sleep."

Instead she listened to the almost soothing tapping as his fingers moved over the keyboard. "You're as good as Dillon."

"This is henpecking. Norma's trying to teach me the right way, but I don't practice enough and tend to go back to dueling index fingers."

"Faith wanted a computer, but I wouldn't buy her one."

"You bought her a car."

"Yeah, that's the reason I nixed it. Still, it would have helped her with her schoolwork. I was wrong."

"Life is full of should-haves."

Unable to resist, she asked, "What do you regret not doing? I mean—"

"I know what you mean." He leaned back and gazed up at the ceiling. "Oh, going back to school to get my master's, that kind of thing. This situation is proving to me that if I knew more forensics, criminology, psychology even, I might be doing a better job in finding Faith."

"Well, John Box has more, and he doesn't seem to have any answers yet. Besides, if you had all those credentials you're talking about, you wouldn't be here."

"And if you had any to go with your raw talent, you'd be working for some high-dollar NASCAR team."

Woody used to say that she could be that good one day, when he'd first started teaching her mechanics. Fred Woodson had kept the garage afloat for eight years before that last big falling-out with Buck. He'd dubbed her "a natural," and taught her everything he knew, from ignition systems to calipers, planetary gears to water pumps. But most of all, respect for a piece of machinery that in reality should run three, four, five times longer than Detroit built it to last.

She missed Woody, often wondered what had become of him. No, she couldn't blame him for leaving, but he'd let her down by not staying in touch. Hadn't he told her he'd thought of her as his own daughter?

"When did you see Hancock?"

The unexpected question threw her off guard. "Did I say that?"

"You brought up his name. When a person mentions another person out of the blue, it's because they've recently seen or heard from them."

He didn't need any more credentials, she thought. The man was two-thirds bloodhound and one-third psychic.

"So?"

She sighed and hunkered lower on the couch. "So I stopped there earlier to ask him to look up some stuff for the Cameo. Satisfied?"

"Hardly, because you were evasive about it before. He put that idea about cults in your head, didn't he?"

"No."

"Mike, I know most of what he sells is legit, but some of those games... And that attitude—he's so in-your-face."

"Only when his idea of free enterprise is being challenged. He's been here—what?—six years, and people still expect him to justify his existence in the community."

"Parents have a right to worry about what kind of influence a guy like that has on their kids."

"Don't forget the reverends Dollar and Mooney, who believe he's the Antichrist. So what if he's single, likes to wear black and keeps weird hours? He's as protective of the kids as their parents are,'' Michaele insisted. ''Maybe more. While I was in there, I heard him—''

Brilliant, Ramey. So much for your ability to keep your word.

''Heard what?'' Jared wheeled his chair around to face her. ''Michaele, I'm not going to let you drop this now.''

''If you'd left me at home, I might even be asleep by now,'' she muttered, thoroughly disgusted with herself.

''Only if you'd downed a half-bottle of Buck's booze. Now what does Hancock have to do with your sudden interest in cultist activity around here?''

''He chewed out a kid for letting his imagination go overboard, all right? And he was great. Told him that stuff was garbage and to get his mind on his future. Don't ask me to name names because I won't. The boy's leaving for college soon. It's been handled. Besides, I gave my word to Dillon that I wouldn't tell anyone.''

''Why,'' Jared asked softly, ''would he ask for your secrecy?''

He was intent on making a capital offense out of the smallest thing.

''I'm too beat for this,'' she said, turning her back to him. ''Ask me next time I'm awake.''

Just when she thought he'd let up, he murmured, ''Don't think I won't.''

When Michaele opened her eyes again, it took only the sight of Jared stretched out asleep in his chair to remind her where she was. Despite remembering their last words, she winced in sympathy at what that poor posture was doing to his body. At the same time her gaze was drawn to his strong profile, the tempting darkness of his beard, his mouth softened by sleep…

In self-defense she checked the time. The clock on the opposite wall said 5:20.

Easing her stiff body out from under the blanket, she snatched up her hat and tiptoed out of the office. Norma was already there, although Curtis hadn't relinquished his seat at the front desk yet. Like everyone else, she was putting in extra hours. Michaele supposed it was their conversation, quiet though it was, that had wakened her.

"I forgot to give the chief the message yesterday, because there was so much else going on," Norma said, "but Mrs. Smock is a sweet old thing, and those cats are all she's got now. We shouldn't just ignore her."

"What about Mrs. Smock?" Michaele asked. After the loss of Mr. Smock, Michaele had promised the scatter-brained widow that she would see to it her '78 Ford outlasted her. She checked it regularly, and whenever Mrs. Smock tried to pay her, Mike got a kick out of saying, "But you just did, Mrs. Smock." It tickled her that the old woman then praised her excessively for being so honest.

"Hey," Curtis replied, covering Norma's surprise at finding Michaele there. "Did you get some rest?"

"Must have. I seem to have lost a few hours."

"What happened?"

"Chief still sleeping?" Curtis said, ignoring her.

"Yeah. I imagine his back's going to give him heck when he wakes up, though. He should have let me take one of the cell cots so he could have the couch."

"You want some coffee, hon?" Norma asked, clearly resorting to other means of getting information. "Saw a pretty full pot of that old ruby-red back there when I put away my lunch."

Michaele declined, knowing anything the color of rust remover was more than she could handle this morning. "I need to go wash up and get to it. But about Mrs. Smock…?''

''Her favorite cat is missing,'' Norma said. ''The calico. Considering all the varmints in the area, it's really a surprise that she hasn't lost more of them, but she swears Satan worshippers are at it again. You know Mrs. Smock—she thinks everybody short of the Easter bunny is a heretic. And she's always calling about cars going in and out of the cemetery at night.''

''Buddy's refused to go out there anymore,'' Curtis added. ''You know how Mrs. Smock is, Mike. Once she starts talking, she won't stop. Bruce tries, but she wears him out, too.''

But Michaele was wondering if the old woman wasn't on to something. She didn't dare ask any more questions, though. That would only get back to Jared.

''Guess there hasn't been anything new about Faith?'' she asked. She tried not to look hopeful so that they wouldn't feel obliged to offer another round of sympathy and encouragement.

His lips compressed, Curtis shook his head. ''Except for what went on at your place, the town's been quieter than usual. Got a good rain, though.''

''Is somebody going to tell me—'' Norma began.

''No big deal.'' Wanting to escape before the woman started clucking over her and woke Jared, Mike tugged her hat more firmly on her head and backed toward the door. ''I've gotta go.''

The buzz of whispers followed her. Just as she let the door fall behind her, she heard Norma gasp, ''What's this town coming to?''

31

6:01 a.m.

At the sound of the crash, Jared jerked upright and almost knocked the keyboard off his desk. Recovering it, he noted that Mike was gone and that his body felt as though a sumo wrestler had used him like a stress ball. Rising carefully—the last thing he needed was a strained back—he spotted Red outside his office, wiping his pants. A shattered coffee mug lay at his feet.

"You're more effective than an alarm clock," he said as he stepped into the main room.

"Sorry, Chief. Didn't get as much sleep as I'd hoped. The neighbors came over wanting to talk about the case and what they should do about their kids. Barely got them calmed down, then some gals in Abby's sewing group called for the same reason. Doesn't sound as though y'all had it any less active here, though. How's Mike?"

"Good question. Where is she?"

Norma nodded toward the front door. "Already hard at it."

Sure enough, he saw her in the garage, working under a raised pickup, wrestling with some stubborn nut or something, finally resorting to smacking it with a wrench. What she lacked in strength, she made up for in ingenuity—

outside the garage, too. She sure had managed to avoid his probes about Hancock. But though he admired her resilience and loyalty, he couldn't allow it to keep him from information. One way or another, she was going to have to understand that, and make some choices.

"What's the spin out there?" he asked the group in general, since Jim Sutter was there, too, attacking a bear-claw pastry almost as large as his face.

"You won't like it," Norma replied.

"Changing," Jim added, despite his full mouth.

"Folks've been eager to believe that a stranger is responsible for Faith's disappearance," Red said. "Like last time, they thought it was somebody off one of the freight trains. What's shot holes into that for them was that fiasco at the school. People are hot about that one."

"They don't think it was a kid?"

"Some. Others don't see how their little darlings could be capable of such behavior, but at the same time think a stranger couldn't be in town without somebody having seen him."

Jared had been rubbing his beard, and froze. "I don't think I like where that's going. Have any names come up?"

"The Bean boy for one. No surprise there, though. Also What's-his-name over at the bookstore."

"What reason was given?" Jared asked, careful to be fair despite his own reservations about Hancock.

"He doesn't go to church," Red replied, ticking off items on his fingers, "he never seems to sleep, and he's too damn good-looking to be human—or straight. *That's* from a father who's worried that his boy hangs around the guy too much."

"I'll take that one seriously when someone finds jugs

of blood in his refrigerator or that he's selling porn out of his location." Jared turned to Norma. "Phone calls?"

"Curtis took about thirty messages and I've had seven calls since he left. Twenty-five are about you."

"I can imagine, and every one of 'em has a kid at school, right?"

"Exactly. Six, however, were informant calls. Four against Harold Bean—but one came from his sister, Wendy, so I'm not sure that one counts. One was for poor Mr. Hancock again, and—are you ready for this?—the other was for Garth Powers."

"That makes sense. When in doubt, blame the messenger. What about the other calls?"

"The usual—a domestic problem, a dog bite, another batch of mailboxes bashed in."

"You know what's amazing? In twenty years, these same kids'll be screaming at *their* kids for using too much shampoo and bemoaning the price of stamps. Tell the boys to keep an eye out. What did Bruce come up with at the lake?"

"Not much. He says that it did match the pattern of several other break-ins in the area. It appears it's someone who knows the area pretty well, and the habits of the people. At least this one does the minimum of damage. That's why neighbors often miss noticing anything's wrong."

"This guy is pawning the stuff. Call the sheriff's office," Jared told her. "See if they've got anything going that sounds similar to this. Also DPS. Then contact all the pawnshops to see if they're fencing the goods."

"Will do." Norma cleared her throat. "Um…you know Mrs. Smock out at the east edge of town has been really concerned about her missing cat. Now I know that doesn't sound like much, especially under the circumstances, but—"

The front door swung open and O. K. Loyal strode in.

"Mrs. Smock's cat'll have to wait," Jared said, adding to the mayor, "You want to talk, follow me."

He headed for the men's room, which made Loyal stop in his tracks.

"That's not funny."

"Gotta shave and wash up. You can go pour us some coffee if I'm offending your modesty."

Unhappy but resigned, Loyal disappeared. When Jared reemerged minutes later, the mayor came from the kitchen and handed him his Darth Vader mug.

"You don't want any?" Jared asked, after thanking him.

"Please. I'd like to keep what hair I have left. What I want is an explanation as to why Harold Bean is free to terrorize this community."

"Is he doing that?"

"You know what I mean. Nadine Waters almost hit a utility pole driving home from her shift at the hospital in Tyler, when she saw him walking along the street."

"Where was this?"

"You should know. Down the road by where your people left his car when they arrested him."

"Time?"

"Well, Phil called right after she got home. My clock said twelve-thirty."

"Did you happen to make a tour on your way in and notice if Bean's car is parked at his house?"

"Yes, I looked, and no, I saw nothing."

"And you took all this time to call me? Mrs. Waters's husband is Phil Waters on the City Council, right? If he was concerned for other citizens' safety—and you for that matter—why didn't either of you call me sooner?"

"I told him I'd handle it, but—" Loyal turned a deep shade of red "—I fell asleep. Hey. Don't look at me like that. I'd been out all afternoon doing my part in the search. Guess I drifted off after I hung up.'' He drew himself erect, chest thrust out. ''What's going on, Jared? Is Bean innocent, or do we have a legal technicality that's fouling things up here?''

''I'm not sure.''

''Well, the people want answers.''

''Right now, all I have are possibilities. You can add another problem to your list, though. At the same time I let Bean go, someone was stalking Michaele Ramey.''

''Good God!'' The mayor stood, dumbfounded. ''Is she all right?''

''Yeah. But here's a head-scratcher for you. That means Harold is the only guy in town who *isn't* a suspect, because he couldn't have been there. And we're talking about a guy with real sexual problems, Loyal.'' He told the mayor what had happened.

''That's disgusting. Do you think he's the one who took Faith?''

''I don't know.''

''Must be, them being sisters and all. What are the odds that two people could each target a sister?''

''Interesting point.'' Jared took a sip of his coffee; the ruby-red brew was strong enough to wake up a corpse. ''By the way, did you take that call you mentioned on your home phone or cellular?''

''I told you, I was in bed. Why?''

Jared leaned around the desk and eyed Loyal's boots. ''If necessary, I suppose I can confirm that with the Waters...or your phone company.''

''What are you driving at?''

''The guy who semen-washed the Ramey house was wearing shoes. Not the athletic type.''

''And what does that have to do with— Hell! You think it was *me?* Of all the—''

''Relax. I know it isn't,'' Jared replied calmly. ''Now.''

''Oh, thanks a lot, pal.''

''Just want you to understand what I'm up against. Think. I'm going to need a lot of help from the community, even as I split it apart. Things would go a lot smoother if you stood beside me, help me to keep a rein on tempers and general dissension, instead of adding to the criticism. But first, I had to make absolutely sure you have a rock-solid alibi.''

''But I'm the mayor! I should never have been on the list to begin with.''

''Give me a break. You keep your eyes open. Let me know who the shoe and boot wearers are in town with big feet.''

''Why don't you just have us line up on Main Street and check us for yourself?''

''And then what? Arrest a guy for having big feet? Besides, as fast as gossip moves through this place, he wouldn't wear them.''

Loyal leaned heavily on the desk. ''This is either going to run me out of office or kill me.''

''Think of how Mike's feeling.''

''Yes. Yes, you're right.''

''Are you planning to continue your searches today?''

Loyal bowed his head. ''We all want to, but as you know, not everyone can afford to close their businesses two days in a row. Folks were talking about shifts for today, then resuming a full search tomorrow at noon, once most of the stores close.''

''Nice of you to put your wallets first.''

''People care, Jared, but we don't even know if this is a wild-goose chase.''

"What's that supposed to mean?"

"Someone said—this wasn't me, okay?—someone said that they wondered if Faith didn't just run off. I know y'all are taking that into consideration, but I thought I'd mention it so you know the thought is out there. Also, someone else—actually, a couple of folks—mentioned that they weren't thrilled how some are selling Faith to the news media as a little innocent, and that the police weren't supposed to spend their meager budget being the community's baby-sitter."

"They're not wrong about that. But my people would be out on patrol, anyway, so thus far we aren't really draining the budget."

"You also aren't writing any traffic tickets."

"Ah. They are putting some thought into things, aren't they? The ones commenting about Faith's reputation—did they give any particulars to back up their innuendo?"

"Everybody was big-time hesitant to go on the record, Jared. And Jessica—Mrs. Powers, put a stop to it fairly fast. You would've been proud to hear her. She made all of us ashamed of ourselves. But you know how people are. Rumors flavor everything as fast as salt does. We'll be out there again, though. You can count on us."

"You'll understand if I wait a while before holding my breath."

Visibly unhappy with his response, Loyal drew Jared aside. "If we can't resolve this, we have to move on. I'm not saying today or even this week, but we have the Memorial Day Parade and a fishing tournament in two weeks. It's one of our three biggest moneymakers of the year."

The front door had barely closed behind the mayor when Jared turned to his crew. Interestingly, they were all standing close and not in a hurry to leave, as though they had something to add to the conversation. "Okay," he told them. "If you have something to say, here's your chance. What do any of you know about Faith Ramey's reputation that I don't?"

32

6:47 a.m.

The feeling that he wasn't alone brought Harold Bean awake faster than a cold shower. Opening his eyes, he saw his mother glowering at him through his car's driver's window. It didn't surprise him that she'd spotted him—parking behind the utility shed might have hidden him from the street, but not the trailer—he was amazed that she'd actually come out of her self-made prison, let alone ventured this far across the yard.

She smacked the glass with her fleshy, white fist. "Get out of there. Come out, or I swear I'll take a brick to this window!"

Believing her, he dragged himself upright and eased his sleep-stiff body from the car. "Jeez, Mama, all you have to do is say, 'Good morning.'"

"I'll good-morning you. Where've you been all night?"

"Here."

She cuffed the back of his head.

"Mama!"

"I went to bed at midnight, and you were nowhere around here. Now what the hell's going on?"

"Nothing."

"Don't play me for a fool, boy. The police were here.

The chief himself. Asked me a lot of questions about you and your whereabouts in connection to that Ramey girl. You know how embarrassing that was?''

He hurried to the trailer, hoping his mother would follow before her caterwauling roused the busybodies in the trailers on either side of them. He also had to move for another reason—it was later than he'd intended to sleep. There were things to do.

''I was in jail, okay? They arrested me!''

His mother tugged the door shut behind her. Her huge caftan muted the *click* of the lock, but nothing could camouflage her ominous stare. ''Thank heaven your father is gone. It would kill him to hear this.''

''You sound as though he's dead. Did you get a death certificate that I don't know about?''

His mother turned gray, then a dull purple-red. ''I haven't had my medication yet this morning. You be careful what you say to me.''

''Then shut the fuck up.''

The outburst surprised him, but he also wished he had a camera to capture the shock on her face. She looked like she'd just been gutted. About time, he thought with growing satisfaction. She was long overdue for a reality check.

''How dare you speak to me that way!''

''Yeah, yeah. Tell you what, as soon as I get my stuff, you don't have to listen anymore.''

''Where're you going?''

To kill the morning taste in his mouth, he grabbed a can of diet cola from the refrigerator and popped the tab, then guzzled half of the disgusting stuff. ''You think I'm telling you so you can call the cops?'' He burped. ''No thanks.''

''What's going on, Harold?''

Unable to tolerate more, he left the unfinished soda on the counter and headed for his bedroom. ''It's all coming apart, that's what. My life's closing in on me, thanks to you.''

''What have I done, except to try to raise you right?''

''You've never cared about me,'' he scoffed. ''You used me the same way you use everything and everybody to get your next meal and keep some kind of roof over your head. But you know what? I'm through. I'll be damned if I'm waiting until the rest of the shit hits the fan.''

''What's gotten into you? Does it have to do with Faith Ramey? Don't tell me you're guilty—not after I stood up for you in front of the chief!''

He smirked. ''That's the full scope of your imagination, isn't it, *Mother?* Figure out where the weak link in your chain is and cut it out like a cancer before you lose too much of your Happy Meal.''

''I don't deserve that.''

''Lady, you deserve a lot more.''

She drew herself erect, which in her case meant a minor squaring of very lumpish shoulders. ''I'll pray for your soul.''

''Ha! A welfare hog going to pray for my soul—that's rich. But what can it hurt? Go ahead. At the least, it might fool some in this *morally* upstanding town as to how maternal you are. Who knows, maybe one of the rich ones'll give you their unused hunting camper, so you and the porkette can move out of this dump before it collapses around you.''

Once in his room, he kicked aside a flimsy bedside table, sending the lamp on it flying. Ignoring the crash, he pulled free a loose corner of paneling near the floor. A plastic bag of money slipped to the floor, followed by another.

''Lord, bless me,'' his mother gasped. ''Is that…?''

Her astonishment was a gift in itself. ''Blows your mind, doesn't it? You and Sow Jr. snooped in here all the time,

I'll bet, but it never struck your low-watt imagination to figure out I knew and had worked around that.''

''How much is there?''

''Don't ask. It'll just make you cry.'' He pulled a canvas tote from under the bed and started snatching more bags of money from the wall. As he worked, he recited in a singsong voice, ''One for me, nothing for you. Two for me, nothing for you. Three for me, one for you,'' then flung one bag at her.

His mother deftly caught it, but her look was one of uncertainty. ''Where did it come from? Are you selling drugs?''

''No, I'm a hit man for the Mafia. When they want somebody rubbed out in Split Creek, they call me.''

''Don't ridicule me. I'll go straight to the phone and call Chief Morgan.''

Everything in Harold went quiet. Slowly he looked over his shoulder and said with ominous certainty, ''No. You won't.''

Her lower lip trembled, but she tried to cover her fear. ''W-why the generosity?''

''Call it payment for your silence.''

''I won't break the law for you.''

He ignored that weak protest and tugged out several more packets. Throwing her one more, he shoved his stash into the tote. On top of that he added several pieces of clothing.

''How long are you going to be gone?''

''Now that's a dumb question, even for you.''

''You killed her, didn't you? That's why you have to leave. Dear Jesus, save us.''

''Relax. You're already saved, remember?''

His mother pressed the bags to her chest. ''This is too

much. You're killing me. Make me wish I'd never carried you to term.''

Harold no longer felt the pain that used to come with such pronouncements from her. All he said as he grabbed up the bag and pushed past her was ''You know what? Me, too.''

''Where will you go?'' she called after him. ''The Navy won't take you! Not with a warrant hanging over your head!''

That was his one fear, but one he would worry about later. Maybe there was still a way.

''I'm glad you're going!'' his sister suddenly screeched from the doorway of the bedroom she shared with their mother.

Harold paused and glanced back. ''And you're so ugly you'd make a train take a dirt road.''

It almost felt good driving away.

33

6:47 a.m.

Dillon made the shower water as hot as he could stand it, then let it pound his back until his skin stopped burning and every muscle was numb. Even then he couldn't forget her.

Obsession was a word he'd mocked for years, claiming it was an excuse for weak people to placate their most unhealthy vices. The gods, intent on showing him how great a fool they could turn him into, had sent him *her.* There was no logical explanation for the attraction; they weren't suited in temperament or background, and were opposites in many ways she had yet to see. Nevertheless, it was getting to the point where he all but lost the ability to breathe until he saw her again. Even a glimpse could rejuvenate him.

Doomed, that's what he was. If this was love, he had contracted a fatal dose of it.

He imagined he heard a phone ring. Was it her? Unlikely. She had no phone where he'd left her, unless... Had the truth finally been found out? Not possible. If that were the case, there wouldn't be a call, there'd be a lynching party at the door. Sometimes he almost looked forward to the idea.

His frame of mind didn't improve once the ringing stopped.

Nothing would help until this came to an end. But what would The End mean, if not death? Prison? No way. More likely some redneck would first do what everyone secretly wished him to do—put a bullet between Dillon's legs so he would know the height of pain before another redneck put a bullet between his eyes. Considering how hopeless he was beginning to feel, that might be a relief.

He pressed his forehead against the wall of the shower stall and let the water burn longer.

34

6:47 a.m.

Drawing a deep breath, Garth stepped into the kitchen, where Jessica was busily uncapping a bottle of vitamins to lay one next to his half glass of grapefruit juice.

"Morning, lover." She did a full spin before dancing to the toaster, where she snatched out a crisp raisin bagel. "Margarine or crème-cheese this morning?"

Her cheerfulness and energy depleted what was left of his own, and he backed toward the door. "Uh, margarine. Be back in a sec."

"What's wrong?"

"I forgot something."

His stomach roiling, he hurried to the study, where he grabbed the crystal decanter of brandy on his credenza and took a swallow straight from the bottle. The stuff burned like hell, but it stiffened his spine as nothing had yet this morning. After quickly following that with a spray of mouth refresher from his top drawer, he returned to the kitchen.

"You okay?" Jessica asked, pouring his coffee.

"Sure." He stroked her back, not daring to get too close.

"You tossed and turned all night...once you got to bed."

He took his seat, hoping the heat burning inside him didn't break a sweat on his upper lip and brow. "Sorry, baby. I know the phone rang several times after you went up. Did you get any rest?"

"Don't worry about me. You're the one having to meet deadlines and keep a high profile. All I'm doing is trying to make myself useful around town in the search."

The brandy Garth had swallowed threatened to back up his throat. "It's wonderful of you to rearrange your schedule to do that."

"I feel sorry for Michaele. The burden she's carried all her young life is heavier than ever. She deserves better."

"It's sad."

Jessica set a plate with the bagel in front of him. "And may get worse. Wait until your students start repeating some of what I heard yesterday while out with some of our so-called 'concerned citizens.' I don't want to mention names, but it would appear not everyone considered our Faith to be the dear girl we always thought her."

Garth stared at his food, wondering how he could touch it, let alone try to take a bite without exposing his raw nerves. "Don't tell me. The girl's missing two days and already people are willing to tear into her reputation?"

"Exactly my sentiments. People's memories are so short. Why, remember last Thanksgiving when your entire staff had the flu, arrangements for Homecoming were falling apart faster than you could think, and you didn't have a soul to man the phones, let alone make the media arrangements? Faith was the one who came through, wasn't she, getting some of the alumni together and working around the clock. And she never accepted a moment in the spotlight, did she?"

"No."

"I remember walking in late one afternoon—what was it?—Wednesday, the evening before the game, and she looked like someone had dragged her through a ringer, poor thing. So did you, for that matter, but you oversaw the awards dinner that evening and a halftime celebration the next day that the town will not soon forget. I was so proud when Faith encouraged the school pep squad to surprise you with a cheer in your honor."

Garth was going to throw up. Hoping a sip of coffee would force down the sensation, he reached for his cup.

"I may have bruised a few relationships," Jess continued, "but I'm not going to stand by and listen to anyone say that she was conniving, or worse, a tramp. We're practically in a new century, so what if she flirted occasionally? That's the wonderful thing about youth. And if she yielded to her hormones a few times, is that a crime? She was single, for pity's sake."

Garth almost dropped his cup. "Who's spreading that kind of rumor?"

"Well, that's the painful part. It wasn't just one person. Two people in my group exchanged similar stories—one about catching her when they came home earlier than expected while she was baby-sitting their kids and finding her half naked, the boy seen only as a flash as he ducked out the back door. The other had to retrieve something in the basement of their church, and she found the choir director with his hand up her skirt."

"Not…"

"Hugh? Oh, no, dear me. Not that dear relic. No, it was the one he replaced—Chuck Colbert. Naturally, the level-headed members of the group pointed out that since his wife was in and out of institutions, there were mitigating circumstances."

"What use is any kind of talk like that at a time like this?" Garth snapped.

Jessica massaged his shoulders and kissed him behind his ear. "Sorry, darling. I should have known you'd take it personally on her behalf, just as I did. I'll hush. You eat before everything turns to concrete."

He couldn't if he tried. What she'd said wasn't anything he didn't know, or rather guessed, but he couldn't confess that without her asking how he'd found out. Telling her that would be like opening a spillway that could destroy everything for both of them. He couldn't do that to Jess.

He felt fingers at his temples, before she gently drew his head back against her breasts.

"I hate all this—the mystery, the gossip, you being so torn up with the goings-on at school and with personnel. I want us to go away so you can relax and regroup. Someplace by the ocean, but with a hot tub nearby." She massaged him as she spoke. "We're due a little time off before we slip into a rut."

"It's just this time of year," he said, taking hold of one hand and planting a kiss in her palm. He hoped that she would get the hint and stop with the touching. Sometimes she made him feel as though he were a sofa pillow needing refreshing. "Things will get better once school's out. But you're right, a change of scenery would be good for both of us."

She bent close to kiss him again, her small whimper of pleasure sounding schoolgirlish. "I'll go to the travel agent in Tyler today, and then I'll go to this luscious shop that has the most divine massage oils and soaps."

He summoned a smile. "You'll have me smelling like a floozy."

"Actually, the lotion I have in mind is edible."

Garth closed his eyes, unable to resist imagining the scene. But the head bowed over his lap wasn't Jess's.

He shuddered in torment.

35

7:00 a.m.

Wiping a splatter of oil off her face, Michaele was slow in responding to the car that pulled into the station. When she saw it was Dollar's, she momentarily wished her father were here. Then again, who was she kidding? He wouldn't have rushed out to take care of him, either.

Shoving the rag into her hind pocket, she approached the station wagon, reminding herself that this man was a central part of the volunteers searching for her sister. "Reverend," she said with a nod. "You're up early, considering the long day you put in yesterday."

"Our numbers are fewer this morning, I'm sorry to say, so we want an earlier start. How are you, child? Have you had any rest?"

For once he didn't sound pompous or sneak secretive looks at her body. In fact, he barely made eye contact, and his tone was heavy with concern. The change was gratifying. "I'm okay. Thanks for asking."

Michaele went to start the pump.

"I owe you such an apology," he said, when she returned to see if he wanted her to check under the hood.

"No, you don't." She glanced up and down the street willing another customer to come by, but the town was surprisingly quiet, as though no one wanted to face today. The only difference was the dozens of yellow ribbons on utility poles, street lamps and store doors that had appeared overnight.

"The Good Book reminds us that Satan never sleeps," Dollar went on, "but we have. We've lapsed woefully in our responsibility."

Michaele had never heard him sound this rattled, let alone humble. "Y'all have been really...great."

"We have to do more. *I* need to do more. I realize now I'm being tested."

Here it comes, she thought, more fire-and-brimstone logic. She indicated the ribbons. "Look at that. The side streets are loaded, too, as you've probably seen. And go take a look at the fence in back where the Firebird is parked. People are starting to leave flowers. Between all of you and the police, everything that can be done, is."

She really was moved. At the same time, she had to deal with her own guilt, because as sick as she was about Faith, she hadn't done a damn thing.

"Evil has taken residence in Split Creek. I must overcome it."

Michaele shifted her cap frontward to give herself a moment. "Reverend, I think you need to go back home. Maybe you got a little too much sun yesterday."

"You think I'm sounding unbalanced. I don't mean to frighten you. I would never want to upset you, but has Chief Morgan even shared the news about what happened in the school with you? Those satanic writings?"

"I know about them," she admitted reluctantly.

"And the rest?"

Not sure what he knew, she asked, "What do you mean?"

"There are meetings in remote places, rituals being performed, sacrifices."

"How do you know that? There are rumors, sure. There always are. It's entertaining, like Halloween." She was glad that, as usual, the gas tank clicked off sooner rather than later. She quickly disengaged it and replaced the cap.

When she returned to the driver's window, he grabbed her hand and clutched it close to his chest. "The signs, Michaele. Pay attention. Protect yourself. I lost Faith. I can't lose you."

Jerking free, she lost her balance and backed into the bucket of window wash. The water went everywhere, and she fell hard on the concrete.

"Mike!"

Jared's voice barely cut through her rattled nerves. "Go," she ordered the reverend. "Go on, get out of here before I let him arrest you!"

He went, roaring engine, slipping tires and all, almost taking the oil display at the end of the island in the process. Even Jared's shout was lost in his noisy retreat. Seconds later Jared was crouching beside her.

"Are you hurt?"

"Just wet and humiliated."

"Can't believe he left you like this."

"I told him to."

He helped her to her feet.

"What happened?" he demanded, following her into the garage. "You're hurt."

"You'd limp, too, if you'd landed on your butt at 30 mph. Look, he didn't push me, okay? I just didn't want to listen to any of the junk he was sputtering." Once in the garage, she grabbed a clean grease cloth and rubbed her rear. When she couldn't stand his silence any longer, she whipped around. "Well?"

"I'm waiting for the rest of the story. That wasn't your normal minister-pays-respects-to-anxious-family type of visit."

She made a face. "I should know by now to ignore him, as I usually do. But I felt obligated to be nicer. After all, he is a good part of the motivation behind the community search. Only the man doesn't play with a full deck of cards, you know?"

"What did he say?"

"That he'd failed us. That he'd lost Faith and that I needed to be careful because—what was the line?—'Satan never sleeps.' That kind of thing."

"Could you be more specific?"

"I could, but I won't. It's not your favorite subject." But it was fast becoming a preoccupation of hers.

"Cultists, sacrificial stuff."

"Bingo. Now go away and let me mutter in peace." The rag was soaked, and she tossed it into the collection drum for washing before grabbing up another.

"He *scared* you."

"He *disgusted* me. Wrong, that's past tense. He disgusts me. He grabbed my hand and…I just don't like being touched."

"You like me touching you."

The man was relentless. "Glad you have all the answers."

"Didn't say that, but I am getting fairly certain about that one. It's a nice revelation."

"Well, don't rush to the bank quite yet."

"My, my. If I didn't know any better, I'd guess you woke up on the wrong side of my couch," Jared said.

She started to reply with another zinger, but caught herself, found herself remembering those few moments when she'd first wakened and had studied him while he slept. If she weren't such an emotional disaster, if things had been just a little different, it would have been worth the probable heartbreak to see what happened if she reached for him instead of pushing him away.

As resignation squelched her temper, she abandoned her cleanup attempts and tossed the other rag away, too. "I want this over. This being in psychological limbo about Faith and everything...I can't stand it."

"You have to hang on, Mike. Don't crack on me now."

He was right. She was being weak. How easy had it been for him on this anniversary of losing the woman he'd loved? Had she offered one word of compassion? The fact that she couldn't remember left her feeling like a selfish slug.

"I'm okay. Spleen's vented. I'll be all right." She had to be. There were answers to find, and some of them she would have to find on her own.

Jared's studious gaze made it clear he was making that determination for himself. "You know I have to go talk to him."

"I'm not hurt. Let it go."

"That kind of talk he's spreading isn't good for the community. It triggers more rumors, which inspires pranksters. From the looks of things, we have enough of our own to worry about, without drawing in outsiders. Hancock needs to understand that, too."

Michaele grabbed his forearms. "Please, don't! My word won't be worth spit to him if he finds out I told you."

"Is that the truth, or is something else behind that plea?"

"Believe me or don't, that's your business. This is important to me."

He hesitated, but a faint twinkle began to light his eyes. "You'll owe me."

"Okay."

Clearly he'd expected something other than instant capitulation. "What are you up to?"

Not wanting to behave too suspect, she seasoned her words with a little attitude. "I told you, my word means a lot to me. That's a problem for you?"

He hesitated another moment before angling his head and leaning closer. "Your word means a lot to me, too," he said, his breath tickling her lips. "Don't forget it."

For the rest of the day she was left wondering whether she shivered because she knew that he knew she hadn't been level with him. Or was it because the kiss that followed his warning threatened, too, as much as it tantalized.

36

9:15 p.m.

It seemed to take forever for dark to fall that night. Adding to her impatience was the presence of Buck. He'd shown up just before noon, as sober as a lush could be, but radiating hostility because he'd had to walk into town, since she'd hidden the keys to the trucks back at the house. Once he'd gotten over that, he finally noticed and took delight in seeing the ribbons everywhere, and the people who stopped by to offer words of sympathy and reassurance. After a while, he actually went searching for receptive listeners. Although she knew these bouts of sobriety never lasted long, Michaele couldn't say much for his timing, for when sober, Theodore Carville Ramey talked like nobody's business.

Even the reporter from the Tyler paper, who'd at first been thrilled that Buck had ignored her plea and agreed to an exclusive interview, ultimately had to walk away from the man. Watching Buck follow the woman, asking if she would like to see his collection of animal skulls, did provide some entertainment, though. However, once Michaele had closed up and driven him home, she was sorely tempted to fetch him a bottle of liquor herself, if only to shut him up.

"Loyal tells me he's organizing a group to comb the woods over at Pete's place," Buck had said, as they sat at the kitchen table over the burgers and fries she'd picked up on the way home. "We should go. We haven't done shit, and it don't look good, everybody doing our work for us."

"That's not exactly terrain to be in at night," she'd replied. "All those snakes would be bad enough to deal with in daylight."

"You just don't care," he had mumbled. "You're glad she's gone."

Michaele had seen this coming all day. Buck couldn't be a decent human being for more than a few hours at a stretch; it simply wasn't in his nature. He'd been steeping in his own venom for too many years. However, Mike's own patience was sorely depleted.

"I care, Buck. But there are ways to handle this, and Jared's given us instructions."

"What's he done but drive around looking like a big shot? I told that reporter that somebody ought to take his badge."

"You didn't! God, Buck, how could you? It's not right or fair."

"Who's fair to me? I've lost my wife, my daughter—" he had shot her a glowering look "—you've stolen my business."

"The garage would have been taken from us, the property sold for back taxes if it wasn't for me." She knew better than to argue with him, but her pride wouldn't let her be browbeaten. "You lost interest in the garage even before Mama died. If it wasn't for Woody—"

"Goddamn you, don't you say that name in this house!" Buck had roared. "The stinking thief took food out of my babies' mouths."

"He was no thief. Anything you saw or thought you saw was a result of your being drunk all the time!"

The corners of Buck's mouth had dipped farther. "You. Defending him still. Always following him around like some lost pup, always bragging on him to your ma, 'Woody this' and 'Woody that.' Stupid little bitch, y'never knew all he was doing was priming you to get in your panties, did you?"

Though shaking with rage, she'd risen from the table and walked out of the house. She hadn't gone back in, either; not when she heard him sweep everything on the table to the floor; not when he threw an empty liquor bottle at the door and it shattered; not even when it was safe after she heard him go upstairs. She didn't trust herself.

She waited for dark, wondering where Jared was. There hadn't been any sign of him since mid-afternoon, and considering the dissension and gossip growing in town, she didn't doubt he had his hands full. But if he'd come upon a solid lead, she would have liked to know.

The darker it got, the more she thought she saw things in the woods across the street. Heard things in the tall grass and brush next to her. Was it dark enough to leave? Maybe not quite, but if someone was hanging around here again, she was going.

She took the white truck because it was the quietest. Placing her trusty crowbar beside her on the bench seat, she made the largest circle possible around town to avoid Main Street until she was past the police station, and the Dairy Mart where Buddy liked to park during quiet times and flirt with girls. Along the way she saw that Dillon's van was gone. So was Harold Bean's car when she passed their place down Main.

Farther east, she saw that Mrs. Smock had every light on in and around her little cottage. Michaele didn't blame her, and made herself a mental note to come by tomorrow, if only to visit for a while and get the old woman's mind off her lost pet.

Just beyond the Smock place was the cemetery. It was especially wooded in this part of town, and the graveyard was on a modest hill that eventually plunged into a marshy area—another annex from Big Blackberry Creek. Michaele turned off her headlights as she pulled into the grounds and drove with parking lights only. In a way, it seemed like excessive melodrama, but she wanted her eyes to adjust to the darkness as quickly as possible; also, there was no need to upset Mrs. Smock, if she could avoid it.

She parked at the top of the circular oil-paved drive. Tucking her keys beneath the floor mat, she reached for the crowbar and sturdy halogen flashlight. Dense clouds made it harder to see than usual, but Michaele's vision improved as she checked the outer periphery of the town's oldest cemetery. Some of the most fragile markers showed signs of damage, but that appeared to be a result of age and natural environmental conditions, rather than what Dillon's young patrons were talking about.

Or had she spoken too soon?

Bisecting the grave sites was a dirt path. As she walked down it, she came upon a stone urn that had been knocked off the base of the monument. Next to it, a marble cross lay shattered in three major pieces, but the sound of an approaching vehicle made her shut off her light and crouch. It was only a car on the main road passing by, though, and as soon as it was gone, she rose and went back to her inspection.

The damage to the cross was undoubtedly intentional, but nothing about its condition or that of the toppled urn could be identified as a religious assault. Though disappointed that anyone could sink to such behavior, she was beginning to feel better about what she'd heard. Any wise guy having downed a six-pack of beer was capable of this kind of stupidity.

Just as she was about to return to the car, she saw the path veering off from the newer graves. The overgrown area reminded her about the rest of that mysterious phone call at Dillon's. With an opening barely large enough for a cub-cab pickup to get into, she supposed, this could be where the groundskeeper hid the old flowers once they were removed from graves.

So, go make sure.

Michaele hesitated. All those vine-covered shrubs and trees with thorns made a creepy prospect, not that she expected anyone was in there. But no one knew she was here. If something happened...

Somebody was going to get a crowbar in the crotch.

Woody had taught her a thing or two aside from mechanics. She would be all right, she decided.

She ducked under the draping vines. Her footsteps made no sound on the sandy loam. In fact, except for crickets and tree frogs, this was really a peaceful place.

Beyond the arch-like entrance, she found the interior wasn't quite the cave she'd expected. The trees created a canopy, but not a claustrophobic environment. However, as she directed the beam of her flashlight around, she came to something that did make her heart pound like kodo drums.

There before her was the chest-deep pile of decomposing flowers. To the right was a dilapidated metal shed—no doubt where the lawn mower and such was kept. Leaning against it was a tangle of wire stands, the kind to hold crosses and wreaths. She circled the decomposing pile, looking for what the boy on the phone had alluded to. At the back end, the beam of her light locked on something that made her want to run…at first.

A rubber chicken hung off one of the wire stands. It stood in the center of a circle of stones, where beneath were ashes as though there'd been a fire. Red paint—she hoped it was red paint—crisscrossed it all. In the pattern of a pentagram? She supposed someone could stretch their imagination that far.

But what had her feeling like a fool was the placard around the chicken's neck. It read S.C. rules! This gave Split Creek High School spirit a new meaning, she thought drolly.

Shaking her head, she retraced her steps out, ducking under the vines and ready to return to her car. She was even thinking of how she could tell Mrs. Smock so that the old woman could be reassured somewhat about activity over here—

She heard something snap behind her.

Michaele spun around, the crowbar gripped in readiness.

"I should wring your stubborn neck!"

37

The flashlight swinging toward his skull stopped inches away from his head. But Jared didn't release his viselike hold on Michaele's waist, or his grip on the crowbar.

"Damn it, Jared! I could have hurt you."

"Have you lost your mind?" He didn't know what emotion burned stronger in him, the weakness that came from being relieved that she was safe, or the combustible fury over what risks she'd taken. "What possessed you to come here...alone? You—the one who ridicules horror movies because people do illogical, *dumb-ass* things like going into dark cellars when the light's burned out, or up into an attic when sixteen friends have already been axed up there."

"You don't have to yell," she replied, equally hot. "I'm in your face. I can hear!"

Could she feel, though? Were her breasts aware that his heart was cracking through his sternum? Did that taut tummy understand he was getting hard because he'd had one too many unrealized dreams of being this close to her?

"Fine," he said in a calmer tone. "Now, would you mind lowering that flashlight?"

"What are *you* going to lower?"

His chest shook from restrained laughter. "It's your fault. Deal with it."

She rolled her eyes, but she did lower the thing, and asked, "So, how did you find me?"

"You mean after I went to your house and found you weren't there? I radioed the station to put an APB out on you, and Curtis told me Mrs. Smock had just called to say there was a white pickup pulling into the cemetery. Considering how slippery you were last night and this morning whenever I asked you about your pal and things, it was a short leap toward concluding your independence was rearing it's scary head again. And if you make an off-color crack out of that, I will not be responsible for my actions."

"Drain the adrenaline, Morgan. Truth is, I'm glad you're here. Now I can admit that you were right, and there won't be any witnesses when you tell me 'I told you so.'"

"I wish I had the time to relish this. There's nothing here, is there."

"Oh, there's something…just not what I expected. From what I can tell, the kids were trying to pull Dillon's leg. Well, I don't know about those headstones over there." She clicked on her light and aimed toward his right. "I'm hoping that wasn't their doing. Back in there, though—well, come see."

She led the way under the vines into the tunnel-like opening. Jared couldn't believe she'd come in here by herself. She had far too much courage for his peace of mind.

"A real prize, huh?"

In the beam of light, he saw the sacrificed chicken. He would have been amused, if it weren't for the number of cans and bottles he noticed littering the woods around the cleared area.

"I'm going to have a talk with them about those," he said, indicating the mess with a nod.

Michaele barely spared it a glance. "Wait a minute—talk to them how? You don't know which boys."

"If Mrs. Smock could ID your car, she can describe theirs. Then you can tell me."

"Rat on my customers?"

"You're right. It'd be better to ask Hancock."

Michaele was muttering under her breath as she exited the den of vegetation, and Jared followed, giving her time to stew. It served her right, he thought. He'd experienced seven different kinds of hell imagining the worst had happened to her. But he had his own plan for venting.

Only after they reached her truck, and she tossed the light and crowbar on the front seat, did she spin around ready to challenge him. "You don't mean it, do you? You wouldn't do that to me."

"Glad you figured it out. But I am going to have the guys checking this place more often."

"Thanks."

Instead of answering, he gently nudged her against the side of the truck. "Uh-uh. That's not going to get it."

"Excuse me?"

"Remember when you said you owed me?"

"*You* said that. I…okay, I agreed."

"Works for me." He tugged off her hat and tossed it in with the rest of her stuff, then wrapped his arms around her. "I want to collect."

He let her study him, so she would see there wasn't a trace of teasing left in him. No way was she going to misunderstand this.

"Kiss me," he said, angling his head. "Damn it, for once do it. Kiss me as though you'll go crazy if you don't."

He didn't want to hurt her, but he'd never known a need like this. After the last few days, and what he'd been through driving here, he'd reached some psychological limit. No more keeping his feelings in limbo. No more keeping his hands to himself.

This might not have been the first time he'd felt the raw need for sex, but caring made it hurt worse. From the instant she opened up to him, wrapped her arms around his neck and answered the demanding thrust of his tongue, his whole body reverberated with it. And yet he lifted her to get even closer, pressed her harder against the truck, drove himself deeper into her mouth, trying, trying to reach her very essence, as though that would offer relief. But it only made the hunger worse.

The heat intensified between them. When he rocked his hips against hers, her gasp, the reflexive twitch that had her all but wrapping her legs around him, almost shot him into orbit. How easy it would have been to lay her down here and now on the bench seat of her truck, to bury himself inside her. His imagination was already there.

"Oh, God," he groaned, burying his face against the side of her neck.

She didn't reply, but her shallow breathing and shaky legs—like those of someone who'd just run the mile in a new personal-record time—told him that this wasn't any easier on her.

"So now you know," he murmured, lightly scoring the taut column of her neck with his teeth. There was something about her that drove him, left him swinging like a pendulum, wanting to be alternately tender...and carnivorous.

"I always knew."

And wasn't happy about it. At that note in her voice, he straightened to study her in the dim light.

"Going back to the way it was isn't an option, Sleeping Beauty. Too much has happened."

"That's why I need you not to push."

"Who's pushing? I've been a saint." He hoped his teasing would stop the subtle withdrawal he sensed in her.

"More like a steamroller."

"Just don't overlook how I've tried to soften my approach at critical times." He caressed her lower, slightly swollen, lip with his thumb. "Kissing you may have knocked any future attempts in the warm-fuzzies department out of the picture, though. Kissing you...makes me crazy."

And he did it again, contradicting himself by exhibiting major control, the tip of his tongue only teasing hers; but when he moved his hands to her breasts, he exposed the fact that his intent had been merely to distract her. She perfectly filled his hands, as he knew she would. And even behind the thick denim pockets, he could feel the tightening of her nipples.

"That makes me crazy, too," he murmured. "Your response to me. If I didn't have to get back to the station, I'd take you to my place and take your mind off this hell for a few hours."

Sucking in another steadying breath, she removed his hands, only to press hers to her abdomen. "Talk like that makes my stomach hurt."

"Coming from you, that's almost romantic—except that it's more likely a result of your having neglected to eat today."

"Don't remind me. Even most of dinner was a bust because Buck and I had a humdinger of a fight."

"All the more reason to insist you sleep in my office again."

"I'm going to the house. I need a shower."

"If you're quick, we can stop there first."

"And wake Buck so he can start on me again? No, thanks."

"I'll talk to him."

"You have a penchant for being yes'd to death? His philosophy is 'I am who I am,' and he has no interest in looking at what that is, let alone changing. No, I'll go with you if that's what it takes to keep that from happening." When he didn't budge, she raised her eyebrows. "Haven't you heard your radio? Curtis called you twice already."

"I heard him." He'd parked down on the road below, but the night air carried the sounds clearly. "He can hang on a minute. I've waited a long time for you to stop hissing at me like a bad-tempered kitten. I figure I deserve a moment or two to soothe my wounds."

"First I'm Sleeping Beauty, and now I'm a testy cat?"

"I'm not writing a book. I'll mix my metaphors if I want." He knew what she was dealing with—guilt, that having finally allowed her long-repressed sexuality to surface a little, the timing stunk. "You have nothing to feel guilty about, Mike."

"In a few hours it'll be three days since Faith stormed out of the house."

She didn't have to say more for him to understand, and Jared wanted to give her something to hang on to. It wasn't much; in fact, it could be construed as troubling, but it left a modicum of hope alive. "I got a call from the lab about the sample I took from the school."

"Oh, no. Was it blood?"

"Yes, but not human. Not cat or dog, either. Bovine."

Rather than looking relieved, Michaele frowned. "Someone would have to go through considerable effort to collect enough, wouldn't they?"

True. That's why he'd allowed himself to believe that it had been some water-soluble paint, the mix made to match relatively fresh blood, and to believe it was kids and unrelated to Faith. Now he wasn't so sure.

"Jared? What else haven't you told me?"

"I put out an APB on Harold Bean."

38

10:00 p.m.

Night had always been his friend, but Harold was worried. He'd laid low since leaving home this morning, hiding out in the woods outside Longview until almost sunset. Then he'd quickly made his way to the storage unit he rented on the west side of town. It took only a few minutes to load the car as much as he could, and make the cautious dash to the pawnshop he'd been dealing with. A preliminary phone call had already warned him that Eddy wouldn't take much from him; Eddy was having his own problems with the law.

With two-thirds of his car still filled with hot goods, Harold had finally headed south. Sure, staying due east on I-20 would have gotten him to Louisiana faster, but he figured if anyone had put the word out on him, the DPS would be the first to know, so he took 259, intending to turn east again around Houston. Either way, hiding out in Louisiana for a while until he figured out what his options were seemed the smartest move. Next to the woods of East Texas, Louisiana was a good place to get lost in.

Things had been going well. The only cops he saw were parked at cafés, and when he reached Lufkin he felt confident enough to stop and get something to eat himself.

That proved a mistake. So did believing his mother might keep quiet in the hope that there might be more money coming to her down the road.

As he was pulling out of the burger biggy's parking lot, it happened—fate setting him up like an animal being led to a trophy hunter. He had to stop immediately for a fast-changing traffic light. Just as he breathed a sigh of relief at not broadsiding the car crossing in front of him, a state trooper pulled up behind him. Before the light turned green, the cop flashed him and signaled him to pull to the side of the road.

Seconds, Harold thought. *If only I'd been a half-minute slower or faster out of that fucking parking lot...*

It was past two in the morning when he was returned to Split Creek and put back into the cell he'd inhabited before. By then he'd already lost his dinner, and was alternately contemplating escape or suicide. If his mother had been part of the welcoming committee, he supposed, he might have made a serious attempt at the latter just to avoid having to see her gloating. On the other hand, finding Mike Ramey with Chief Morgan was almost as humiliating.

Buddy was locking him up. It had been Eagan who'd come to fetch him. Morgan didn't waste any time before starting to turn the screws.

"Sorry to interrupt the vacation," Jared drawled over the other cop's shoulder.

Harold shrugged that one away, his attention on Mike. She looked like a kid, all squeaky clean from a shower, her hair still wet and as glossy as a raven's sleek head. However, her eyes were those of an old soul who'd seen too much for one lifetime.

He regretted having to ask, "Has there been any news?"

Not only didn't she answer, but she exchanged odd looks with the chief. That triggered another uneasy feeling.

"Hey, I need to know. Has there been word about Faith?"

"We'll be asking the questions," Morgan replied.

"Harold," Mike said, incredulous. "What have you done?"

The disbelief and disappointment in those knockout eyes made him miss Eagan's redneck jabs at his lack of brilliance as a con. "I don't really feel like talking right now, Mike."

"Tough," Jared snapped. "Because she has as much right to hear this as anyone."

Although Michaele wrapped her arms around her waist, her voice remained calm. Strong. "Could you just tell me why?"

"You mean the burglaries?"

The question clearly threw her. "If...wherever you want to begin."

"Well, let me ask you this—have you seen my mother in, oh, say the last five or six years? No, you haven't. Know why?"

"Fai—I'd heard your mother was an invalid and couldn't easily leave the house."

He wiped hard at the corners of his mouth as he fought down a laugh. "That's good. That's what she likes people to think. What the blivet is, though, is a fake."

"What's a blivet?"

"Ten pounds of shit in a five-pound sack." He knew he was pushing their tolerance, but his rage at his mother had only intensified as a result of this arrest. No one had told him, and he hadn't needed to ask; however, he knew she'd been the one to turn him in. "It's like this—my old man ran off because he couldn't take her anymore. I don't blame him. My only regret is that he didn't take me with him. She worked just long enough to claim an injury and go on disability, but there's not a damn thing wrong with her that a kick in the butt and a two-year fast wouldn't cure. Ask Chief Morgan. He saw her yesterday, didn't you, Chief? Gives new meaning to the word eyeful, huh? As you can imagine, that government check gets spent pretty fast when your idea of entertainment is diet cola, diet snacks and your best friend is Psychics-R-Us.

"Then there's my sister, whose ambition stretches all the way to becoming a chip off the old block. Mike, you know I tried being legit. I did everything from yard work to being stock boy at the grocery store because the night shift paid more, but it was never enough for her. Then came college and the need for a car, tuition… How was I supposed to satisfy her demands, let alone get an education?"

"It wasn't a free ride for Faith, either. I encouraged her to apply for every scholarship she could."

"I applied. You know I did—and got a few. But it was all nickel-and-dime stuff, while tuitions are rising faster than Texas temperatures. It wasn't enough. It's never been enough for her."

"Harold, I sympathize about the situation with your mother," Mike replied, "but you're talking to someone who knows about responsibilities."

Yeah, she did. That's why this was so embarrassing. She made it look matter-of-fact. Oh, he knew otherwise from Faith—if what she'd told him was accurate. But that was the problem. Having been lied to and used for too long by too many, he wasn't sure what he believed anymore.

"You want me to say that I took the easy way out?" He shrugged. "But I never took anything from anybody hurting. If that leaves you still disappointed in me, I'm sorry for that.''

''You let yourself down, not me. My God, you've thrown away your future—that career in the military. You could lose it all.''

''Hey, c'mon. This is bad, but even in Texas they don't give you death by lethal injection for stealing some stuff.''

Once again Mike looked at Morgan.

''Eagan read you your rights, correct?'' the chief asked. He nodded.

''Then I guess I should tell you that you have a right to call an attorney.''

''Whoa. That sounds—'' things were definitely not clicking, and Harold pointed to Mike ''—talk.''

She was pale but the regret in Mike's eyes turned to something harder. ''Don't play this game, Harold. If you really meant what you said about thinking of me as a friend, tell me the truth. What have you done to my sister?''

And he'd thought what he'd felt looking into the rear-view mirror when that trooper pulled behind him was something. This—God Almighty, *this* was the real reason they'd brought him back. ''You think that I'm responsible?''

''The morning after she disappeared, you came to the station, and you didn't act normal. As you pulled away there was that awful thump in your trunk.'' Mike had to wet her lips to get the rest out. ''Was it her?''

Morgan did an interesting double take. It told Harold that she hadn't mentioned the episode to the chief.

''You listen to me,'' he said, anger warring with his fear. ''I told you the truth. It was over between us. As for the trunk—it was a TV. Sure I was concerned. It was hot, and I was fixing to sell it to a guy at school. What was I gonna get for it if it had a crowbar through its screen?''

"Why should I believe you?"

Something about her attitude reminded Harold of something. "You don't really know Faith, do you?"

"Obviously, you think I don't."

"Don't be mad for that. She's the one who fooled you. She likes doing that—conning, teasing. Wanna know your mistake? The way you choose to see her. It's safe—the kid sister, reluctant to grow up because it's easier to let you shoulder all the responsibility in the family. But otherwise, you buy the package—that she's beautiful, smart, *special*. You think that in time, with some distance from here, she'll mature, that her heart's in the right place, and she'll appreciate all you did for her. Well, I've got news for you—forget it.''

Not surprisingly, Mike didn't receive his appraisal well. "That doesn't sound like a guy who supposedly cares about a girl.''

"I care." That was the trouble: he was a fool, too, and would always be a sucker for Faith. "At the same time, I'll always kick myself in the butt for that. It's the truth, Mike. She was dating me and dangling her cherry in front of other guys. I couldn't take it. I preferred being known as a 'pal' to being played as a dumb-ass.''

"I don't deny Faith can be flirty, but that doesn't mean she sleeps around.''

"Considering her taste in men, I don't see how she could avoid it.''

"Meaning…?"

He hesitated, still influenced by those old feelings. On the other hand, it was his neck heading for a noose.

"She likes older guys.''

Michaele relaxed somewhat. "Come on, Harold. It's not

your fault that you look young, but you can't assume that just because things didn't go right for you two that she—''

''I know the difference between having a crush on someone and being determined to find yourself a sugar daddy.''

When Michaele failed to react to that, Morgan said stiffly, ''You thinking of someone in particular?''

''I could be. But look where I'm sitting. I'm not spilling my guts to you for nothing.''

''Is that a hint for a deal? You're in no position, pal.''

He knew that, and that's why sweat had been running down his back since he'd been pulled over. He was getting so dry, he had to keep licking his own lips to keep them from sticking together. But what happened if he shut up now? Would that tick them off? Should he demand an attorney? What public defender were they likely to get for him? Marv Monroe, better known as Mr. Cut 'n' Curl? Five minutes of listening to that windbag, and a jury was likely to bring back the chair and tell the judge to put them both in it.

''Hancock,'' he said, head bowed.

39

Saturday, May 16
3:03 a.m.

Michaele could barely contain herself until she reached the privacy of Jared's office. Fortunately, he sensed it and, after following her in, immediately shut the door.

"Don't worry," she told him. "I'm not going to throw or kick anything."

"I'm grateful. Our budget isn't up for a new pencil sharpener, let alone a new computer. Besides, I don't want to tempt Curtis with gossip too good to keep to himself."

She ignored his attempt at humor. "Just tell me this—did you believe him?"

"You sure you want to ask me that? Unlike you, I'm not a member of the Dillon Hancock Admiration Society."

"Then I'll find out myself."

But as she reached for the doorknob, Jared stretched out his arm to stop her.

"If we demand any more from Harold, I have to allow him access to an attorney—or let him believe we're interested in a deal."

"Forget Harold. I meant to go talk to Dillon."

"It's three in the morning."

"You think I can sleep after hearing this? Could you?"

"One thing I know I won't do is let you go over there by yourself."

"So come with me."

"As simple as that, huh? You know, waking a man in the middle of the night isn't the best way to make him communicative, at least not in the way you want. Besides, if he's running true to form, he may not even be there."

So, he'd noticed, too. Michaele had been thinking about all those mornings when she'd seen Dillon coming in from parts unknown. He'd let her believe his absences were business-related, but what if that wasn't the case?

"I'm going."

She reached again for the doorknob. Jared closed his hand over her wrist.

"Are you forgetting last night's close call?"

"I asked you to come with me."

His sigh sounded more like a growl. "God, I must be nuts."

"No," Michaele replied softly. "You're a good friend. Better than I've wanted to admit."

"Hell. Let's go before you try to put a flea collar on me like some family pet."

On the way out, Jared left instructions with Curtis to notify Cuddy's team that Harold was in custody. He also warned him to keep an eye on the kid, in case he sunk into too deep a depression and attempted something foolish.

Outside everything was still, quiet; the flashing streetlights provided the only sign of activity. There wasn't so much as a breeze to rustle the ribbon on the corner light post, and the heavy silence triggered a deep melancholia in Michaele, despite the compelling presence of the man beside her.

"Tell me what you really think about what Harold said," she said, once they were in the patrol car.

"I wouldn't be going anywhere if I didn't believe Harold's credible. He must have seen or heard something incriminating."

She fastened her seat belt. "Okay, but Dillon? Faith never talked about him or going into his place. Other than for school, she wasn't much of a reader. Her idea of a page-turner was a fashion magazine full of free samples and coupons. As for Dillon, I'd begun to believe that he was…well, you know, not interested in girls."

Jared shot her an incredulous look. "That's a joke, right?"

"I'm not suggesting anything. All I'm saying is that I've never seen him dating anyone."

"You don't date, either. Never in a million years would it cross my mind that—"

"Spare me. It was a prejudicial remark, and I admit it." She focused on what was outside her window, his low drawl having reminded her of the seductive way he'd spoken to her at the cemetery, the desire that his touch had released. For years she'd fought dealing with this side of herself; and yet, suddenly, Jared had only to say a few words and he practically had her pressing her thighs together against the heat building there.

"Will it hurt much if you find out he was involved with Faith?"

Grateful as she was for the interruption, his question wasn't easy to answer. "In a way it would mean he'd been lying to me, wouldn't it?"

"Playing pal and confidant to you, while doing the hot-and-sweaty with your kid sister? Yeah," he muttered, sounding unusually grim. "I guess you could say there's a certain betrayal going on there."

Michaele tried to remember. Had Faith ever shown any unusual smugness at the mention of Dillon? Unfortunately, Michaele couldn't even recall the last time his name had come up in one of their conversations.

When was the last time you had a conversation that wasn't a shouting match?

True. And that underscored how serious things had become between her and her sister: except for the bare essentials, they hadn't talked in some time.

At the corner of Big Blackberry, a streetlight illuminated Dillon's atmospheric two-story, and immediately made it clear that the van wasn't in the driveway. Odd, since, as usual, there was a light on up in Dillon's attic apartment.

"He could have parked it in the garage," Jared said, pulling into the driveway. The garage was separate from the house and at the left rear corner of the property.

"Not likely. He says whenever he parks in there, field mice get into his engine. I've cleaned out a nest or two and replaced some of the wiring in it myself."

"Field mice in this neighborhood? I haven't heard anyone else make that complaint. Why doesn't he just buy a trap or some poison, and be done with it?"

"Maybe because mice multiply as fast as rabbits." He'd barely shut off the engine before she was on her way to the back entrance.

"Will you take it easy, for crying out loud," Jared muttered upon catching up with her. "You don't know what you're dealing with."

Ringing the bell, Michaele took a few steps back to gaze up at a back dormer window. She saw no sign of movement, nor did she hear anything.

"If he's not here, do you suppose you could still get us in?"

"I'm going to pretend you didn't say that."

"He won't be back until about six, if what he said about those business trips is true."

"And what if they're not? What if he's laying low inside?" He took her arm. "Let's go. I don't like all these dark windows."

Actually, they made her uneasy, too. But whether it was because of possible danger or because they looked like accusatory eyes, she couldn't say. One thing she knew for sure, the thought of returning to the station was unbearable.

"Why don't you drop me off at the house?" she told him, as he backed into the street. "It's only another couple of hours until I open. I could use the time by going through Faith's room more thoroughly. It's possible that I missed something from my earlier search."

Jared turned down his radio, muting Bruce's dialogue with Curtis as he patrolled around Lake Sawyer. "Nice going, Ramey. Two genius ideas in a row. Hasn't it struck you that there are too many troubling question marks in all this for me to leave you there? No," he added quickly, as she began to reply, "I don't care whether Buck is sober or not. Besides, you told me she didn't keep a diary or scrapbooks like other girls, and that her room was left as though she expected to come home."

Yes, a new bottle of nail polish in a color she'd wanted to try was on her dresser, a schedule of graduation events on her desk… "But there may be something she hid well. I wasn't a snoop. I didn't want her to feel the way I did with Buck breathing down my neck. If Harold's only partially right, you know what that means, don't you? I gave her too much privacy."

"Stop it!" At the corner of Dogwood, Jared reached over to force her to look at him. "No self-recriminations." He stroked her cheek with his thumb. "If you're that sure you can't sleep, let's go to my place."

She gave him an arched look.

"For breakfast," he intoned. "Yes, I want more, but not any damn quickie. I was thinking about making us both a decent meal for a change. You haven't lived until you've had a Morgan omelette—"

A scream shattered the calm night. A more frantic one followed, and then a third.

"Look!" She pointed between Rena Laurence's house and the Dollar residence, as someone stumbled by in the backyards.

"Stay put! If I don't signal to you that it's all clear in a few minutes, get to the station."

To heck with a few minutes, she thought, as he took off between the two houses. She grabbed for the radio mike.

Just as she got hold of Curtis, she heard yelling. It was too far away to hear what was being said, but Jared's strong voice was unmistakable.

"I'm driving around to the alley," she told Curtis. "You notify Bruce and Buddy."

"No! Hey, Mike, you follow Jared's orders. Mike? Yo, Michaele!"

Ignoring him, she hoisted herself over the shotgun and other equipment to settle into the driver's seat. She would have turned on a siren if she hadn't had a momentary memory lapse as to where it was located. But she did drive around the corner and into the alley. There the headlights illuminated the most incredible scene.

Jared stood over a man lying on the ground, facedown at the back door of the Dollar house. Standing at the door and holding a broom like a weapon was Miriam Dollar. Had the stalker or burglar tried to hide by breaking into her home?

Leaving the car idling and the lights on, Michaele ran

toward the small group. That's when she heard the man on the ground begging.

"Please...*please.* Let me fix my clothes!"

She braked hard.

George Dollar?

40

The commotion was rousing others in the neighborhood, and a number of people were coming out of their houses. As they ventured closer, Jared ordered them to stay in the alley. It was Rena Laurence, however, who kept Michaele's attention, alternately weeping and shouting at the reverend through the screen of her bedroom window.

"Pervert! Monster! To think I believed it a blessing to be living next door to *you.*"

Unbelievable, Michaele thought. The attractive widow owned Rena's, the fashionable boutique next to the flower shop. Poor Jared. He had his hands full.

"Curtis is calling in the others," she said upon reaching him. She cast a wary glance at Mrs. Dollar, then George. "What can I do to help?"

"You don't need to see this. Go do what you can for Mrs. Laurence."

She ran next door. She and Rena Laurence had never had much to do with each other, Rena being a woman who gauged people as to their likelihood of being good customers; however, she let Michaele in, and what followed would have been an earful for anyone. For someone who'd gone through a similar experience only the other night, it was a nightmare revisited.

Dressed in a hunter-green robe worthy of a film star, Rena clutched the satin around her throat and waist, contradicting the warm temperatures. Always a striking woman with deep auburn hair and honey-gold eyes, she looked far less aloof with her face scrubbed free of any trace of makeup and her emotions on edge. Michaele wasn't a spontaneous hugger, but an instinctive sympathy had her urging the woman to talk herself through her emotions.

"I'd woken because it was stifling, so I'd gotten up to get a drink of water," Rena began. "I don't handle air-conditioning well at night, and put off using it as long as possible." She indicated the wrought-iron bars covering her windows. "It seemed perfectly reasonable and safe to open my window, and then I went back to bed. Just as I was beginning to go back to sleep, I heard something...a groaning. I sat up and—"

"Reverend Dollar was by your window?" Michaele prompted.

"Yes. His pants w-were open and he was...I can't even say it."

"That's okay. I have a feeling he paid me a visit last night."

Rena Laurence frowned. "He did this to you? When? Why didn't the police do something about it?"

"Please." The last thing Michaele wanted was for this shrewd businesswoman to get angry with Jared and his people. "They did what they could, but I wasn't able to identify the person. We're so grateful that you could."

"But I didn't. Not at first. I saw a silhouette, that's all. It was only when I heard him speak a moment ago that I realized..." She looked toward the French doors, clearly anxious. "Chief Morgan will lock him up, won't he?"

"Yes." Rena's shocked expression about summed up Michaele's stunned frame of mind. It helped having something to do. She encouraged the attractive widow to come into the kitchen. "Aspirin and a glass of warm milk will make you feel better."

"To hell with that." Rena Laurence retrieved a bottle of Chardonnay from the refrigerator. "Want to join me?"

Michaele shook her head, but didn't blame the upset woman.

While Rena poured, she checked on how things were going outside. Dollar remained on the ground, but Jared had cuffed him. His current priority seemed to be keeping the neighbors from getting too close.

"It must help you to know Mrs. Dollar refused to let the reverend back into the house once she realized why you were screaming," she told Rena.

"Some." The boutique owner took a healthy swallow of her wine. "She wasn't what you'd call a friendly neighbor. Maybe I didn't try as hard as I could have, either, but then I never did like *him.*"

Because she'd felt that herself, Michaele asked, "What was it exactly that bothered you?"

"Oh, not any one thing. It was an overall... Okay, call me a bitch, but he was smarmy, pure and simple."

Michaele nodded. "Yeah. That's the word."

Rena sipped as she studied Michaele. "Do you think she knew what he was?"

She recalled the broom and Miriam Dollar's stony countenance. "They'd been married something like thirty years. She must have suspected something."

"That's what I think, too." Rena finished off her wine, refilled her glass, then froze. "My God. Here I am feeling sorry for myself and I haven't asked how the search is going for your sister."

"Thank you, but there's no real news."

"I'm sorry." Then Rena frowned and tilted her head

toward the scene outside. "Do you suppose he could have something to do with it?"

What a hideous thought. Dollar was a man who sat pre-schoolers on his lap to read them Bible stories during Sunday school class. He supervised a teen council, and was regularly in the homes of the elderly and disabled.

Michaele wanted answers herself, and she wouldn't get them here.

"Do you want to call someone to come stay with you, Mrs. Laurence?"

"No, thank you. I'm fine now, although I don't think I'll go back to bed. You, on the other hand, have to be exhausted."

"In a way. We've been spending every hour either searching or interviewing," Michaele replied. "But it's not as though your mind lets you focus on much else."

"Tell Chief Morgan I'm grateful that you were near," Rena said, walking her toward the door. "And that you caught him."

"The chief may need to speak to you himself."

"If it's to ask me if I plan to file charges, tell him to save himself time. I do and I will."

A strong lady, Michaele thought with admiration as she left.

The scene outside had changed considerably. Bruce's patrol car was parked facing Jared's in the alley, and Buddy's unit was out on the street. While Bruce was urging neighbors back to their homes, Buddy was leading the humiliated, cuffed man to his vehicle.

At first there was no sign of Jared. Then he emerged from the Dollar house.

"You okay?" he asked her.

"As okay as you can be after being spit out from the bottom of a tornado." She glanced over his shoulder and saw Mrs. Dollar at the kitchen window, her Bible held to her chest. She looked as shattered and alone as Rena Laurence had appeared resolute. "Mrs. Laurence wants you to know she'll gladly file charges."

"And will you?"

Michaele exhaled shakily. "I wondered if you would agree with me that he was probably the one who'd been at our house."

"The reverend made it a moot point. As we cuffed him, he asked me to tell you he was sorry."

"Interesting. But what exactly does that mean?"

"Nothing to do with Faith, if that's where your thoughts are headed. Unless the alibis he gave us fall apart, and, from what I gather from Mrs. Dollar, they won't."

"What about Mrs. Dollar? Did she know? Rena asked, too."

"She thought he was having an affair."

"Guess that would have been welcome compared to this." People had retreated—at least to their own yards—but lights remained on at several houses, and she knew sleep was over for many of them tonight This wasn't the kind of thing you easily shrugged off or filed away as another "life's like that" experience. "What's happening to our town, Jared?"

He placed his hand at the base of her neck, and gently squeezed.

Michaele knew the discreet "hug" was an act of consideration, that he was thinking of her because of all the eyes watching them from neighborhood windows. But as they walked back to his car, she wasn't reassured; she worried about why he hadn't answered her question.

41

5:45 a.m.

"Ramey's," Michaele said upon answering the ringing phone.

"Come get me."

Buck. He sounded alert and sober for a change, but also extremely annoyed. "I just opened."

"Well, close for five minutes. I ain't walking into town again."

"It would be good exercise for you, and you could stop by the café and have breakfast."

As he gave her his opinion of her suggestion, she saw the Last Writes van drive through the intersection. Interesting that Dillon hadn't stopped this time, she thought, considering that the nearest fuel after Split Creek was eleven miles down the road and didn't open before six-thirty.

"I've gotta go," she said, hanging up.

Hoping Jared was still in the back of the police station talking to either George Dollar or Harold, she quickly locked the front door and ran to lower the one overhead door she'd already opened. If Jared spotted her, he would put a stop to this fast, or at the least insist on going with her. But this was something she wanted to do on her own.

She didn't turn on the white pickup's lights until she'd turned right on Main. At Big Blackberry she ignored the flashing red light, since she was still the only vehicle on the road, and cut a sharp left. As she had hoped, when she pulled into Dillon's driveway, he was just walking toward the house.

He paused and, upon recognizing her, looked strangely guilty rather than surprised or concerned. That tainted some of the hope she'd let build inside her.

"Successful trip?" Adrenaline made her sound almost breathless.

"Fine. What's—uh, are you okay?"

"I've been better. You missed all the excitement." She didn't like the suspicion and anger that was bubbling to the surface. She'd come because she considered him a friend, and yet, looking at his handsome face composed into a bemused, politely curious mask, she wanted to drive her fist straight into his belly to get a more honest reaction. "First, Reverend Dollar was arrested for—how do I put this delicately?—gratifying himself sexually while peeking in Rena Laurence's bedroom window."

Dillon's disbelief wasn't an act. "You're not serious? Old George…well. Is she going to press charges?"

"We both plan to. He pulled the same thing at my house the other night."

"Holy…why didn't you tell me sooner?"

His concern and indignation were so genuine that she wanted to believe him. She would have, if she hadn't been told what she had. Now, however, she wondered what, if anything, she could believe about him—or anyone.

"At first the consensus was to keep things quiet, hoping that if we did, the perpetrator would be falsely reassured and do it again."

"Uh-huh. 'We' meaning you and your number one admirer?"

She shrugged. "Can't argue with success. Success times two, actually. Harold Bean is in the cell beside Dollar's. You know those lake house burglaries? Seems it was our boy Harold."

"Y'all have been busy little critters."

"It's not as though we have a lot of choice."

He had the grace to look guilty. "What, um, what's Beanie Boy's excuse for doing what he did?"

"Pawning stolen goods apparently pays better than gainful employment."

"Huh. Those must've been some lake houses…" Dillon murmured. At Michaele's reproving look, he shrugged. "Hey, it's late—or early." But he did attempt to show more compassion. "What about Faith? Can he or Dollar be tied to her disappearance, or is Jared still grilling them about her?"

"Interesting that you should bring that up."

His frown deepened. "Something's not right. You're angry with me. Why?"

"You can't guess?"

He made a great show of fatigue—rubbing at his eyes and rolling his shoulders. "Listen, darlin', I've been up virtually all night and I'm in dire need of a pot of caffeine. You want to come in while I get the machine started, and talk?—cool. Otherwise, this had better wait."

"I'm not sure I'll be welcome in there after you hear what I have to say."

Nothing changed in his expression, and yet she felt a wall come up between them. "Okay," he said, the performance suddenly dropped. "It's obvious you came to make some kind of point. Make it."

He wanted it straight and clean? So did she. "I came to give you a chance to clear your name."

"Brave of you to do that without your faithful guard dog. What's the charge?"

"I've been given reason to believe you and Faith had a relationship."

Dillon didn't hesitate a beat. "Whoever has told that is wrong. Note, please, I don't say 'They're lying,' because I'm giving him or her the benefit of the doubt—something that you're obviously not giving me."

"Think again. It could be Jared you're talking to instead of me."

Another wall rose, but he accepted that with a single nod. "Okay, then. My answer is that I haven't seen Faith in…at least a month, and that was when I filled up at the station. You'll remember, because that's when she left that burnt rubber mark on your concrete."

Michaele remembered. She hadn't understood Faith's abrupt decision to leave, and had been furious that she'd almost struck a beverage delivery truck while peeling off into traffic. Could he have been the reason? Was that really the last time Dillon had seen her?

"Do you or do you not know that she had a weakness for older men?"

"If some anonymous finger-pointer says so, and accused me, then it must be the gospel, right?"

Michaele waited.

"Damn it, Mike. Okay, once, *once* a couple of years ago she hung around the store and flirted like crazy. But I never thought anything of it."

"So little that you can still remember it."

"She's your sister. Of course I'd remember it. I still said, *'Hasta la shoo-shoo,* baby.'"

"Why didn't you tell me?"

"I'm a big boy, Mike. I can handle my own headaches. She was testing her power, spreading her wings. It was no big deal."

"Did you sleep with her?"

"No!"

"You never touched her?"

He hesitated, studied the ground, then threw back his head and groaned. "I kissed her. Oh, hell, don't look at me like that. It was a mistake, I admit it, but she was pushing hard. She dared me to do it and then to try to ignore her. Call me stupid, but I did it. And I made my point—ignored her, I mean. Talk about being furious with me… Anyway, that should clear up the mystery as to why she hightailed it out of your place that afternoon. Thankfully, she hasn't been back here since."

Michaele wanted to believe him.

"That's it. I swear."

"On our friendship?"

He pointed his finger at her. "About time you figured that out. I have been a friend to you. If you believe in nothing else, believe in that. Have I hit on you? Have you heard rumors about me and anyone else?"

"That's the conclusion I came to. But you may have a problem convincing Jared."

For a moment he looked about to lose it. He actually spun away and took a few steps, only to return to grip her upper arms. His expression was one of sheer anguish. "Mike, I can't be questioned by him."

"Why?"

"I—" he released her "—I can't tell you."

"Goodbye, Dillon."

"Wait." As she began to leave, he caught her arm again. "Don't go yet."

"I need to open the garage."

''I know, I know, but…ah, God. Mike, I'm dying here.''

''And I'm trying to find my sister!''

Eyes shut, he nodded. When he opened them, they were almost feverishly bright and more bloodshot than before. ''There is someone. But, Mike…she's only a kid.''

''Sometimes I think everyone's a kid compared to you.''

Releasing her, he pressed his hands together, touched them to his lips as though praying that she understand. ''For the first time in my life, I'm in love. Head over heels. Weak from it. Pick a cliché, that's what I've become.''

''You don't sound too happy about it. That's a heckuvan incentive for the rest of us amateurs.''

''It's tough to enjoy it when you're sweating blood that someone will find out, particularly her father.''

His voice trembled with more emotion than she'd ever heard from him. ''Why? Because of the bookstore? Does he belong to one of the congregations trying to shut you down?''

''That, I could deal with. This is worse. She's under age.''

Of all the things he might have said, she hadn't expected this. So many times she'd wondered about the kind of woman he might be attracted to. She'd believed anyone as sharp and intellectually curious, as serious as he was, would want a woman equally mature and brilliant.

''Who is she?'' She wanted to know this young marvel who had achieved what others couldn't.

''Sure—I tell you, you tell Morgan, and Morgan feels obligated to do the right thing and warn her father. The result is the same—I'm fish bait.''

''I can appreciate your concern, Dillon. At the same time, this is a pretty fantastic story, especially under the circumstances. Without something solid…''

She had him. She could see it in the subtle droop of his shoulders.

"Willow Weatherby."

Impossible. Cade Weatherby's only child? Michaele knew the daughter of the successful rancher and businessman. High school senior Willow was a lovely girl, her waist-length fair hair and sweet smile turning heads, and her reputation as class valedictorian making her a father's pride. Of all the females in Split Creek Dillon could have fallen for, Willow was beyond risky. He might as well be putting a gun to his own head.

"These feelings...they're mutual?" she asked.

"Hell, yes. Do you think I'd put us in this predicament if she didn't love me as much as I love her?"

Hopefully not. His protestations and passion seemed real enough. "How do you manage this—I mean meet?"

"We wait until her family's gone to bed. Then she slips out to a cabin on her property, near the creek that her family uses for parties."

"You mean, you don't travel to all these places, the auctions and sales and such that you said you did?"

"Occasionally. Nowhere near as often as you think I do."

If she weren't so naive herself, she might have figured that out. "I must seem pretty dense to you."

"No. You knew something didn't mesh, but you were trying to believe in me. I'm sorry I let you down."

"I think I could slug you except that I know how ripped up you're feeling inside."

He smiled faintly. "I know you do. Did you ever think two supposedly sharp people like us could be so dim about the simplest of things?"

"There's nothing simple about the heart," she replied. "That's the problem."

Exhaling in a rush, she massaged at the spasms in her neck. She'd expected the worst. This was it, in it's own way, and not easily resolved, either.

"So what are you going to do?" he asked her.

"I don't know."

"I need more than that, Mike."

Grimacing, she struggled with her conscience and her principles. "I won't name names," she began, "but I have to talk to Jared. What you need to do is stay away from her. At least for a while."

"Can't. I've tried. We both have—you know her father."

Yes, Cade was a tough character, an ex-oilfield worker who'd been all over the world and had settled down rather late in life with Willow's mom, who was also considerably younger, and quite stunning. Men who broke rules like that didn't tend to be tolerant of others poaching in their territory.

"He intends she go to college at an all-girls' school in the East," Dillon said, as though reading her mind. "She says she'll run away before she does that."

"What does her mother want for her?"

"To marry a future president."

"Nothing like a little pressure," she said wryly. "And Willow? What does she want?"

"She wants to try her hand at filmmaking. Directing."

"Not many opportunities for that here."

"No." Dillon's expression grew even more sober. "But I'm willing to relocate for her."

"I'll miss you."

He smiled. "Well, it's all talk. I'm not gone yet."

Knowing she had to get back, that sooner or later Jared would notice her absence, she took a step backward. "I have to go."

"Mike, about Faith…"

"I know. I'm sorry, too. And for having to pressure you to confide in me. I'll do what I can."

"I know you will."

Neither of them said goodbye, or even good-night, and yet as she drove away, Michaele knew something between them was over. But she'd been dealing with so many blows lately, she just couldn't tell how she felt about that.

42

6:29 a.m.

In the middle of a phone conversation with John Box, Jared had a mental whiteout; it happened the instant Michaele returned across the street to Ramey's. Relief followed, and on its heels a wave of anger that made him turn his back to the window as he tried to keep the emotion out of his voice.

"No, I'm still here, but someone's come in. I appreciate that, John. We'll have our reports to the D.A. at the same time, then. Let me get back to you on the rest, and tell Cuddy I'm grateful for the calls he made up to the school and the stations up there. Me, too. But maybe one of these two characters will get us closer. Talk to you later."

No sooner did he hang up than he was out of his office. But he didn't go back to the cells. Passing Norma with a curt "I'll be back," he exited the building and jogged across the street.

Mike was out of sight. Jared strode through the open front door and found her about to pull the rope to lift the first overhead door in the garage.

"I'd freeze if I were you...unless you don't mind everyone across the street witnessing you getting the butt-chewing of your life."

He expected her to retaliate in kind, to dare him, or better yet to explode into the fiery tirade his overstretched nerves all but craved.

It didn't happen.

"Figured you'd notice," she replied, her tone more resigned than apologetic. "Sorry if I worried you, but I had to leave for a minute."

"Just like that? One minute, you're there—the next, who knows? What if you'd been kidnapped when nobody was looking, or dragged out back and— Where did you go, or need I ask?"

"I doubt it."

Damn straight. And he wanted to wring her pretty neck for that. Not only for taking the risk, but also for messing with his strategy.

"Haven't you learned anything from all that's happened?"

"He's my friend. He owed me the explanation. I owed him a chance to give it."

"The fact that he could be a kidnapper, a *murderer,* never crossed your mind?"

"Yes. No." She shook her head as though still debating her own conclusion. "It's not Dillon you need to be looking for, Jared."

Her calm pronouncement only made him hotter. "Does this verdict come straight from the God hot line, or is this a professional deduction based on your vast experience in law enforcement?"

She lowered her gaze, and it was almost more than he could stand, being shut out. To Jared, it was like a second betrayal. "Heaven help us," he muttered. "He sold you a bill of goods."

"He talked, I listened."

"That's my job."

"When? After you arrested him? He didn't deserve that humiliation."

"And what do I deserve—?"

"At it again, are ya?" Buck's disgruntled observation from the inside doorway caught them both off guard.

Recovering first, Michaele gestured toward the soda machine. "Would you refill that, please? This is a private conversation."

"Not too private, if I could hear you as I reached the pumps," her father replied. "In any case, I got things to do myself."

With that, he retreated to the front desk, leaned over to punch a key on the cash register, and snatched up some money.

"Hey!" Michaele started after him, but Jared stopped her.

"Let him go. What are you going to do, wrestle with him on Main Street? That's the last thing you need to see on the front page of some newspaper."

"Right. Much better to wait until a reporter catches him so drunk that he acts like a dog at a lamppost." She slumped against the corrugated steel siding, her sigh speaking volumes about her soul-deep fatigue. "All right, you wanted your chance—have at it."

"On second thought, why bother? I can see you're not sorry for what you did."

This time she stopped him from leaving. "Wait a minute. I had to see Dillon's face, don't you get it? When I asked him about Faith, I needed to see for myself."

"I heard you the first time. That doesn't make it right— or smart."

And therein lay their problem, he thought. She had been relying on herself for so long, she'd lost the ability to trust with her heart, if she'd ever really learned how in the first place. Oh, she could get there, to a point, intellectually—running to Hancock proved that—but when her heart came into the equation, forget it. Jared had to wonder if he wasn't wasting his time.

"So what did he say?" he asked, fighting the depression that compounded his own fatigue.

"Faith did flirt with him for a while. Needless to say, I wish he'd told me that sooner. But the important thing is that he said he discouraged her, and she got the message. She did, Jared. I've seen her avoid him, but I always thought her attitude was because of me."

"Does he have an alibi for the night she disappeared?"

Michaele hesitated. "Yes."

Jared waited for more. It didn't come. "Well...?"

"Maybe you'd better ask him that yourself."

He planned to, but something wasn't right about her answer. "Why?"

"Because of the rest... He confided something personal to me."

Not trusting himself to continue this conversation, Jared did the only smart thing. He started to leave.

"Jared, please."

Her entreaty was too much. "Save it. You just think about what you said, and then about the people who've been busting their butt for you and your family while ignoring their own families. Then ask yourself what Hancock's done for you lately."

"It's not that simple."

"The hell it's not."

"He's in love."

Furious, Jared retraced his steps, and, as expected, Michaele's eyes widened. She started backing up. At the same instant she bumped into a wall, and he grabbed her, adding a harsh shake for good measure.

"So am I, goddamn it!"

The impulse to do violence was so strong that he abruptly released her. He had to leave, or else risk losing control completely, and so he got out faster than a firefighter smelling gas. Michaele called after him, but he didn't look back. Hell, he didn't even check for traffic as he crossed Main. The way he figured it, a speeding semi would be a blessing in disguise compared to what was going on inside him.

As soon as he returned to his office, he put in a call to Dillon Hancock. All he got was Last Writes's answering machine. He had Norma try every thirty minutes for the rest of the morning, and each time the results were the same.

Around noon he asked Red to go over there and let him know what was going on.

"The place is locked up tight, Chief," the patrolman radioed in. "No sign of Hancock or anybody else here."

43

10:00 p.m.

"Go to bed, Buck."

The only reason Michaele had returned downstairs after showering was to check the doors and turn off some of the lights. She wasn't surprised to find that her father hadn't budged from the kitchen table. Small wonder, considering the half-empty bottle of booze that hadn't been there earlier.

"I'm fine."

Sure he was. More likely, he would break his neck on the stairs trying to reach his room, if he could even remember the house had a second story by the time he was ready for bed. "How about I help you to the couch?" The dinette chair was going to be tough on the back if he passed out and spent the night there.

"Fuck off."

"Good idea." Michaele retraced her steps back to the stairs. "Nothing like some pearls of wisdom from the head of the Ramey family to keep our perspectives clear."

She meant that, too. She'd had it. Attempts at logic, scolding, wheedling…she was emotionally on *E* where he was concerned. What energy she had left had to be directed toward keeping the business going, and finding Faith.

It felt strange to be at the house again; however, with the reverend and Harold both still in jail, she'd concluded it had to be safe to return here—*safe* being a relative term, considering Buck's presence. In this shape, he was as capable of burning the place down as opening the cabinet under the sink and drinking something to finish disintegrating his insides. At any rate, Jared hadn't protested her coming back here. The phone had rung twice, but in both cases it had been a reporter asking for her reaction to the arrests. She'd even called the station to try to talk to Jared, to make peace. The first time he'd had Norma tell her that he was tied up; the second time Curtis had claimed the same thing. But he'd added the disturbing news that Dillon had dropped out of sight. No, the couch in Jared's office was definitely off-limits to her as far as he was concerned. Everything about or near him was.

Settling in bed, Michaele turned off her bed-stand light, but although it felt good to be off her feet after a day that, despite everything, had passed in a sluggish crawl, sleep was impossible. Was Jared having the same problem? Somehow she doubted it.

On her way home, Norma had stopped by for a fill-up and she'd let it slip that Jared had planned to go home tonight, too. After four nights, he'd accepted that he needed more than a thirty-minute catnap at his desk. Michaele knew he'd also lost heart, and that she was responsible.

Regret weighed on her as heavily as did her dread for Faith's safety. Somehow, she thought, rolling onto her side, she had to make him understand how sorry she was. He might listen once he had time to think things over.

But if Dillon had lied…

She rolled onto her back again. God, what a mess.

She continued to toss and turn, but at some point she must have drifted off.

The next thing she knew someone was whispering. The words didn't register, but something tickled her ear. Breath...lips...

Jared, she thought, rousing. He'd changed his mind, he'd come to her. Relief and joy was warmer than the sheet enfolding her. It was him settling behind her, aligning his body to hers, his heat permeating the core of her loneliness. When his hand slid over her hip, the curve of her waist, and upward to cup her breast, sleep's lethargy yielded to languid desire.

"Noreen," he whispered.

Mama's name.

Rancid breath.

Before she could open her mouth to scream, Michaele threw herself out of bed—and immediately slammed into the wall.

Horror, hurt, revulsion...her emotions all raged at once. She gagged, unable to breathe, and her legs had abandoned her entirely.

Dazed and desperate, she scrambled on all fours to the far side of the room.

As she tugged down her tangled sleep shirt, she could barely make out Buck peering back at her through the darkness.

"Norrie...?"

"You bastard. You sick pig... This is my room! *My* room!"

He reached out to her.

Michaele bolted for the door. The only reason she didn't break her neck flying down the stairs was that Buck never had turned off the rest of the lights.

Wanting only to get out and get away, she hunted keys in the kitchen and made a beeline for the white pickup.

The engine missed with her first try. When it did catch, she didn't trust her ability to back up, so she drove around the house, running over a wild rosebush and knocking over the empty birdbath in the process. Only after she made it to the end of the driveway did she think to turn on the headlights.

Navigating the streets was more of an instinctive thing, too. Her psyche under siege, conscious decision-making had shifted into neutral, so she didn't question why she turned north on Dogwood Drive and headed away from the reassuring lights in town. Nor did she think herself insane for flooring the accelerator as though the oil road was a launchpad.

She almost missed Jared's driveway. That's when she understood she was looking for it, and the night erupted with the squeal of abused brakes and tires. Dirt and gravel sprayed every which way as she spun wildly, then again as she floored the accelerator to charge up the driveway. The distance to the house was less than the eighth of a mile of a bracket-racer's run, and stopping in time to avoid his carport and patrol car was as much a challenge as that facing a dragster trying not to run out of track.

By then Jared was already at the back door. Her headlights caught him, automatic in hand, dressed only in jeans, and barely those. So profoundly did he represent safety for her that she couldn't shut off the engine fast enough, and her wobbly legs almost gave again as she launched herself at him.

His response was far more efficient and controlled. He set his gun somewhere inside the doorway and caught her. "What's happened? Are you hurt?"

She didn't want to talk. All she wanted was to absorb— his strength, his solidness...him.

"Mike, what the hell's going on? You're shaking."

"Just don't send me away. Please."

"Send you—" He sighed. "Little fool, you still don't get it, do you?"

Before she could decide whether he expected an answer to that, he was carrying her inside. Where didn't matter, as long as his arms remained tightly around her and she could breathe in that wonderfully reassuring scent of deodorant soap and man. Wrapping her arms around his neck, she buried her face against his shoulder and waited for the world to turn right-side out again.

She'd never been in his house before and didn't look now. All she knew was that it was comfortably dark. He carried her through what she supposed by the sound of his bare feet on linoleum was the kitchen, and then somewhere else before setting her down. It was, she realized, the couch.

"Stay put. I'll be right back. It's okay," he said, as she began to protest. "I have to get your keys and close up your truck before you wear down your battery. I'll only be a second."

No doubt it was no longer, but by the time he returned, setting her keys and his gun on the coffee table, her nerves had begun to betray her again. It must have shown on her face, because, without a word, he sat down beside her and scooped her onto his lap, where she remained curled in a tight fetal ball.

"Take your time." His words were a soft croon, his body gently rocked hers. "You don't have to talk until you're ready—except to answer one question. Do you need a doctor?"

Maybe a shrink. All Rameys did.

She managed a brief shake of her head. "I'm okay. Really."

"I saw you limping."

"Stubbed my toe and bumped my head, I think. No big deal. Getting out was."

Jared didn't think much of her answer; Michaele could tell by the way his breath came out in a harsh rush as though he were fighting for patience he didn't have. That, as much as her initial glimpse of his grim expression and the tension in his body, reiterated how much her well-being mattered to him.

She had to make peace with him, and now that she was regaining control, she would try.

"Jared, I'm so sorry."

"Hey, I'm the one who should apologize. But you scared the hell out of me the way you tore in here."

"I mean about this morning."

"Screw this morning. I overreacted. It's over. You—this—is what bothers me. You got spooked, and don't deny it."

Tucked as she was under his chin, she couldn't see his face, but she could hear the frown in his voice, sense his thoughts churning.

"Yeah, a little. You're going to think I'm a big chicken."

He grunted. "What I think is that you're too damn brave for your own good. And that it's damn late for a drive through the neighborhood if you're not on a wrecker call with a cop waiting at the end of the road."

It was sweet how he tried to ease her into telling him. "Guess I woke you."

"Nope. I was sitting here thinking about you." He touched his lips to the lump at her temple, then grunted again. "Jeez, do you want ice for that?"

"No. Tell me again that you were thinking about me."

"Does it help knowing that?"

More than he knew. It humbled her, and reminded her yet again how lucky she was. Suddenly she understood as never before, and wanted to tell him that, to let him know she wasn't a totally hopeless case. Unfortunately, something a little larger than the Grand Coulee Dam seemed to be stuck in her throat.

"Such heavy thoughts," he murmured. "All you have to do is spit 'em out. What happened, sweetheart?"

"Buck. Buck came to my room."

The rocking stopped.

"I know he didn't realize it. I mean, he—he'd been drinking all day. You know what doctors say about an alcoholic's reasoning," she continued awkwardly. "He thought I was my mother. Called me by her name. But he—I woke and found him in my bed, Jared."

"Ah, no." His arms tightened around her. "Jesus, no."

"It's okay. Like you said, it's over."

"The hell it is," he growled.

She had to make him understand. Sitting up, she looked directly into his tormented eyes. "I told you, I got away."

"You're not just saying that? He didn't…?"

She shook her head.

"Thank God," he whispered, drawing her against him again.

A certain calmness settled over her after that, and they were both silent for a long while. Never could she have imagined knowing such peace simply from being held and feeling the strong, steady beat of his heart under her hand.

"Something still has to be done," Jared said at last.

"What? You can't lock him up, you're running out of jail space as is."

"How can you joke about this?"

"I have to. Besides, it was difficult enough to tell you, do you think I could stand everyone else knowing?"

"Baby, you're not the one who did anything wrong."

"You say. But listen to this—this afternoon a customer passed on what a member of Dollar's church said. The person suggested Rena Laurence must have provoked him into doing what he did by undressing in front of her window or something!"

Jared swore softly. "This whole town is going nuts."

"I'd say we're being very human. It's ironic, but the reverend himself once said that it's common to behave badly—easier, actually—than to own up to our own mistakes."

Jared rubbed his cheek against her hair. "I'd be happy never to have to look at him—the lot of them—again."

She couldn't bear the thought of his growing bitter. Bad enough to be witnessing the disintegration of her already fragmented family; what a tragedy if these horrible events destroyed his faith in a community he'd been so committed to. Even when she'd emotionally held him at arm's length, she'd looked to him as one of the taproots of this town, very much a part of its soul.

"You couldn't leave," she said.

"If it means keeping you safe, damn straight."

Dear God, Michaele thought, what a circle life was at its simplest. The parent became the child; the caregiver became the receiver; the loved, the beloved... She thought she'd come here for comfort? Now she realized she could only find it if she gave in return.

"You should go to bed," she murmured.

"And here I thought I made a pretty good pillow."

"The best." Although her heart was beginning to pound again, she sat up so she could see his face, and he hers. "I meant with me."

Even in the limited light coming from the stove, she saw more emotions than she'd ever before seen flicker across one face—amazement, desire, tenderness... In the end, regret won out.

He lifted one of her hands to his lips and kissed it. "You don't know what you're saying."

"Wrong. I don't want what happened to own one more minute of my thoughts. Or yours."

He wanted to believe; she could see it warring for control inside him. Finally, he slid his hand to the back of her neck and drew her toward him. Just as she was drowning in the bottomless depths of his eyes, her lips tingling with the promise of his, he murmured, "You'd better understand what this means. It's not simply about wanting you. Once this is done, I could never let you back away from me again."

The kiss that followed wasn't just possessive, wasn't only hot; it was so filled with promise that she couldn't hold back the soft sound of anguish that rushed out of her when, too soon, he lifted his head again.

"Okay?"

Such a calm word from a man who'd just kicked down the last walls protecting her heart, and who now watched her with his feelings totally exposed.

"Yes," she replied.

He didn't smile at her almost oath-like solemnity, nor did he look relieved at not having to deal with yet another verbal wrestling match. He simply swept her into his arms and carried her to his bedroom.

44

Sometimes when her life was at its emptiest, Michaele had allowed herself to fantasize about the possibility of this moment. She'd been twenty when the shadowy face above hers had become Jared's—sharply contoured, dark with a day's growth of beard, and his penetrating gray eyes promising...promising. As he lowered her onto the bed, though, daydreams were nothing compared to reality. Reality quite took her breath away.

He surprised her immediately when all he did was hover over her, framing her face between his hands. Was he letting her get used to his considerable weight and size? Giving her a last chance to change her mind?

"What?" she asked.

"You're not nervous."

"I told you the other day, I always knew how it was between us."

"So why did you keep turning me down when I asked you out?"

"It wouldn't have been fair. My family...what we lack in numbers we make up for in high maintenance."

"You don't think I could have helped?"

"It would have seemed too much like pity."

The corner of his mouth twitched. "You obviously have no idea what I was willing to put up with just to get my hands on you."

He took her hand and guided it between them until she covered his erection. Even through his jeans, she could feel his heat.

"Does that feel like pity?"

"Actually, it feels as though maybe I should be nervous. Am I out of my league here, Morgan?"

This time he did laugh. It was a nice sound, tender, relaxed.

"We've got all night to convince you otherwise. Starting—" he shifted his hold to the hem of her shirt and began easing it up "—now."

He'd always made it clear he liked her body. She thought herself okay—for a runt—but as he drew the plain black T-shirt over her head, his slow, thorough gaze made her feel exotic, voluptuous. His touch could only be described as reverential.

"Come here," he murmured. Rolling over, he drew her on top of him, and treating her like butter on corn, rubbed her against him. The languid gliding sent a sizzling excitement radiating from him into her, melting her, the subtle friction of his chest hair caressing her breasts like hundreds of brush strokes. And the way he watched made it even more erotic. His rapt expression only intensified the desire coiling and tightening into an ache deep in her womb, until Michaele ground her hips into his in an instinctive search for relief.

Understanding what she sought, Jared claimed her mouth with his, slipped his hands into her panties, and in a slow synchronized dance of tongues and pelvises he soon burned through her preconceptions about pleasure's limitations.

His low rumbling moan might have been hers, only she was having a hard enough time catching her breath. And inside, she was aching from the liquid heat simmering and increasing in pressure.

"Aren't we still wearing too many clothes?" she whispered. Then she seasoned the taste of his kisses by nibbling at the salty dampness along his neck and shoulder.

"I don't know. Let's see."

Before she realized what he was up to, he shifted one hand to her front. The stealthy invasion of his expert, exploring fingers inside her rushed her to a sharp climax that had her crying out his name, her entire body stiffening— but not completely against the delicious pleasure. This had been a journey she'd wanted to take with him.

"Jared—"

"Shh." He kissed her forehead and then rolled her beneath him again. "Now, we're wearing too many clothes."

With every nerve still humming, Michaele could only lay there and stare as he stripped them both in an astonishing exhibition of grace and speed. He was so much more than her imagination had allowed, his bone structure stronger, his muscles better developed. He was so utterly, perfectly male that when he joined her again, she was already trembling with a new hunger. She couldn't touch him fast enough, couldn't learn his body thoroughly enough. Gripped by a need as fundamental as breathing, she lured and worshipped and seduced by sheer instinct and need rather than experience. All the while he encouraged her with rough whispers and hoarse promises...when he wasn't tasting, nipping and generally driving her crazy.

Although she knew he was trying to give her time to get used to him, to make what was coming as painless as possible, she thought his consideration was bordering on punishment. Her breasts sensitized from his mouth, the ache between her legs unbearable from his probing caresses, she closed her hand around him.

"Please."

He uttered something indecipherable; however, the tension in his feverish, damp body, and the throbbing against her fingers transmitted his meaning clearly. Even so, she had to admire his impressive control as he began easing into her.

Suddenly an unwelcome thought intruded. "Jared?" Her naturally low voice sounded reed thin to her own ears.

"Protection?"

"No."

"No?"

He was watching her again, and now the possessiveness in his eyes matched the passion. "No. I don't want anything between us. Besides, I told you—you're mine now."

"Yes, but—"

"I know you. Come morning, that tidy, pragmatic mind of yours will try to put up barriers again. If it takes getting you pregnant to stop you, so be it."

She opened her mouth to protest, but he stopped her with a kiss as stunning as his other invasion into her body. Physical and mental shock momentarily paralyzed her, then brought a searing pain that went far deeper than any stretching or tearing skin.

Pregnant? Impossible! And... *Oh, God,* so was this.

Michaele moaned into his mouth as the torturous pressure and psychological anguish built, and built. He was ripping her apart emotionally as well as physically, and yet an indescribable need swelled, too. Somewhere between wanting him and wanting to beg him to stop, he began thrusting...and then she learned how being on the losing side of sanity really felt.

A droplet of sweat slipped from him and streaked down the side of her face. It had to be, she reasoned. She didn't cry. She never cried.

"Shhh. It's okay, baby," he rasped, raining kisses over her face. "Oh, God, Mike, don't. I love you. *I love you.*"

With a harsh gasp, he climaxed, and as he did, the rush of liquid heat shooting deep into her triggered her second orgasm. And broke her heart.

45

Sunday, May 17
5:00 a.m.

He woke to thunder first, then the awareness of the sleek but diminutive body tucked against him. Instantly remembering, Jared felt a stirring of arousal, too strong to be believable considering what had transpired during the night. He could have purred in a key to match the rumble of the approaching storm—except for the sudden reminder of what else had occurred. Or rather, what hadn't.

Michaele hadn't spoken to him again. He'd wakened her twice after that first time, unable to ignore the gut-gripping craving to bury himself in her tight little body. And she'd let him. Hell, she'd wanted it as much as he did. But she'd also made him put on one of the condoms she'd found on a trip to the bathroom.

Now, as she woke herself and without comment slipped out of bed to go into the bathroom, he dealt with the cold coil of dread tightening in his belly. He knew he had to get moving himself. Although he was usually off on Sundays, these days at the station nothing was usual about anyone's schedule. Besides, he thought, heading for the other bathroom down the hall, he had to have words with Buck.

Minutes later, all his logic abandoned, Jared strode into the master bath. He found Michaele still as a statue in the shower stall, her face raised to the strong spray. Praying or repenting? he wondered as he slid the clear glass door open.

She spun around. The haunted look in her eyes cut him deeper than any knife could. Her sylph-like body stirred an irascible hunger.

''Give me hell.'' Entering the cubicle, he eased the door closed behind him. ''I can deal with that better than I can the silent treatment. Call me a rat. Tell me that I'm a bully and a jerk, but don't shut me out.''

At first he thought she might ignore him.

''I was thinking,'' she finally said. ''I'll make an appointment Monday to see my doctor and get birth control pills.''

The barely audible, but calm words had him reflexively tightening abdominal muscles as though he'd been gut-punched. ''What if it's too late?'' was all he could manage.

''I can't have a baby, Morgan.''

He always knew what it meant when she started using his last name—she was starting to resurrect those walls she was so fond of. ''Mike...honey, you can't mean that. Okay, so it wouldn't be fair for you to be pregnant right now. I admit I got carried away. It was just so damn good. A dream so long in coming true. But—''

''Never. Do you think I'd ever want a child to go through what I have? To have to call Buck Ramey 'Grampa'?''

As she clenched her teeth and shuddered, Jared enfolded her against him. ''You forgot something—you as the child's mother. A kid couldn't do much better. And as ticked as you are with me at the moment, you know I'll be here for you, come hell or high water. That wasn't just lust talking. I love you, and I'm going to keep saying it until you believe it. Maybe you're not ready to open your heart as much to me, but I know you care, too.''

''You're wrong. I love you. That's why this hurts so much. You deserve more.''

He couldn't believe he'd heard correctly. Tilting back her head, he demanded, ''Say that again.''

''You deserve more.''

''The part before that.''

''I love you.''

He crushed her against his pounding heart and kissed her with everything in his soul. ''Again,'' he demanded abruptly.

''It won't change anything.''

''One miracle at a time. Say it.''

''I love you. I have for a long time.''

''Well, somebody raise a flag.'' And rather than argue about the rest, he shut off the water and carried her to his bed. It was, he decided, the best way to prove his point—that the two of them, their being together, was all that mattered.

The rain came and went. It was almost six by the time Jared and Michaele actually got around to dressing. Actually, *he* got dressed. She muttered about having to drive through town half naked on Sunday while everyone else headed to church. Jared thought that a helluvan improvement over worrying about the odds against their future.

He'd already made it clear that he would be following her to the house to discuss a few hard truths with her father. ''What are you planning to do after you pack?'' he asked her, once again offering her a sip of the instant coffee he'd made. Although the garage was closed Sundays, he knew better than to hope she would stay here, getting some rest and waiting for his return.

"I thought I'd try another chat with a few of Faith's old high school friends. See if any of them agree with Harold. Hopefully, they won't."

"You're still defending her," Jared murmured as she sipped. "I wish she could hear you."

Michaele shrugged away the compliment. "I'm not blaming her for being young or impressionable, merely selfish and lazy."

The use of Faith's name in the present tense didn't slip by Jared, either, and while he admired Mike for it, he worried, too. For more reasons than she knew. "I'm not wild about you being out of my sight, but I guess having you in town will be better than if you said you wanted to go up to Mt. Pleasant."

"That may be my next plan. Don't look at me that way. If I'm no longer Buck's maid and caretaker, there's no excuse for me not to devote that time to helping your people with the search."

"Better that you stay across the street in view of the station and work on—what are you calling her?—Precious." Damn name for a piece of rusting metal, he thought wryly. "Listen, Mike, Cuddy and I are in touch with the sheriff's department up there. Give them and the school administration a chance. Besides, you're not going to find the people you want on a Sunday."

"But everything seems to be going so slowly."

"Not as slow as things would get if we step on toes and invade their jurisdiction."

She made a face. "Politics. Well, what about Dollar? You don't seem to be judging him as much of a suspect as you are Harold."

"That's because it looks like he has confirmable alibis.

I'll be doing some double checking this morning on that, but my hunch is that his problem, while serious enough to ruin him in this town, won't put him on trial for his life.''

''And Dillon? It's so strange that no one's seen or heard from him. Saturday is a busy day for him at the store.''

That's what he'd concluded, too, but Jared didn't want her dwelling on that, let alone depressing herself more than she already was. Putting the empty mug in the sink, he hugged her to his side and walked her toward the door. ''I have an idea. Why don't we meet back here for lunch? I won't be able to stay for too long, but hopefully I'll have more to tell you then.''

''Morgan, you're handling me.''

''And will again as soon as possible.''

Although he'd opened the door for her, she held back— and refused to be lulled by his seductive teasing. ''Look, are you sure about me coming to stay here? Considering what I said about getting pregnant—''

''Which was sensible.'' But Jared did note that she was avoiding the use of the word ''baby'' or ''child,'' which he thought very interesting, and telling.

''I could camp out in the old trailer behind the garage for a while.''

That hot box? He would battle Buck for the couch at her place first. ''I was wrong to pull that on you. Guess my heart overroad my head. Be patient with me?''

She pressed a hand to her stomach. ''I'm definitely being handled.''

Jared smiled as he followed her out and shut the door behind him, but he immediately had to reach out and grab Michaele's shoulders to keep from bumping into her. He realized she had gone stiff—and he saw why.

Sometime during the night, someone had paid them a

visit and left an ugly, unfathomable message across the windshield of her pickup. It was a single word written in some kind of white paint.

Whore!

46

"My God, Jared," Michaele whispered. "Who's doing this? Why?"

The good news was that it wasn't blood. But to see that angry scrawl was chilling—and infuriating.

Jared's hands tightened spasmodically on her arms before he eased her behind him. "Go back into the house, sweetheart."

As he began to hand her his keys, she pushed them back at him. "I'm not going anywhere. Just tell me what to do."

Although he didn't try to force her inside, he didn't reply, either. He was too busy scoping out the area, testing the lock on the shed door at the back of the carport, then he cautiously investigated around back. Finally returning, he pointed to the workbench against the shed. There was a single can of spray paint there.

"One can is missing. I was going to redo the trellis out back."

"Great," she replied, her shock turning to anger. "It'll take me the rest of the morning to get that crap off." She started for the truck again. "Maybe it didn't have a chance to set well before it rained and—hey!"

He literally lifted her and set her back under the carport. "Get behind the shed and stay there until I check out the truck. The rain will have ruined any prints there might have been, but that's the least of my concerns.''

She backed up some, but not all the way as he wanted. She was too fascinated; she watched him circle the vehicle, then circle it again, this time peering through the windows, and once again, practically crawling beneath it.

''You're making me nervous,'' she said. ''What are you looking for, a bomb?''

''Hopefully not, although I didn't expect this, either. But I don't want you to get behind the wheel and find out too late that the brake line has been cut or that someone's put a snake under your seat—that kind of nasty surprise.''

She gaped as he opened the driver's door and started inspecting the interior. ''You know, maybe it was only Buck.''

''Sober before dawn? And how would he know you'd be here instead of at the garage?''

So much for her logic.

''Could've been kids,'' Jared continued upon shutting the cab door. ''Last Halloween, I had more toilet paper in those trees by the road than most people buy in a year. All because I made sure some parents took their son's keys away from him after I'd stopped him twice for speeding in a neighborhood with a lot of kids riding on bikes.''

''I haven't reprimanded any teens. Why pick on me?'' Michaele started toward the truck intending to test how stubborn the paint would be to remove, only to stop in her tracks. ''Oh, jeez. This…this *is* about Faith. This—'' she spun around and saw Jared watching her and understood he already knew what she was going to say ''—this was a message to her because she used to drive this before she got the Trans Am.''

''I was hoping you wouldn't remember that so fast.''

''But she hasn't driven this in months!''

Jared drew her away from the vehicle and into his arms again. "And that's a good clue. It suggests that we're dealing with someone who may not be able to separate the present from the past, or reality from what's going on in his distorted mind. But will you listen to me now when I tell you that you can't wander around without me? You can't trust *anyone.*"

The inflection on that last word made Michaele wary again. "You've heard something. What is it you haven't told me?"

"I didn't want to upset you until we had more information. You already know there's been no sign of Hancock since you two talked yesterday. Well, while you were checking the weather on TV, I called in to the station. Cade Weatherby was on the other line. Willow is missing."

"No."

"It's a duplicate of Faith's disappearance, Mike. Yesterday she told her family she was going to spend the day and night with friends. She'd planned to shop for a graduation party dress, and sleep over. But the Weatherbys had some distant relative get ill, and so they called her friend's this morning to fill her in. The friend was stunned. It appears she hadn't seen Willow. As for the shopping trip, it hadn't been a definite plan."

Michaele swallowed to keep down the little bit of coffee she'd drunk.

"What?" Jared demanded.

"It can't be. He wouldn't have."

"He, who?" Confusion gave way to incredulity. "Hancock's involved with Willow Weatherby?"

As he swore under his breath, Michaele tried to reason things out for herself. It made sense…he'd vanished shortly after they'd talked, and there'd been no sign of him since—or of Willow. But where had they gone?

"They might not know anyone's looking for them."

"Cade Weatherby says his girl would never take off without letting her mother know where she was."

"Well, Dillon says they've been meeting for months. At night. There's a cabin on the Weatherby property." Under the circumstances, there was no way she could continue to keep that secret.

Shaking his head, Jared replied, "I'll pass it on, but she has her mother's Lexus. Believe me, they're not at any cabin, and there's been no sign of her or the car."

"Could they have eloped?"

"Mike, I've met Willow. She's a kid. A pretty serious one for her age, but a kid, nonetheless." Then he pointed at the letters on the windshield. "And Hancock couldn't have done that and planned a legitimate life with her."

"Jared, what if Dillon didn't do that?"

"Christ, Michaele, do you hear what you're saying? Isn't this town coming apart fast enough for you? You need more head cases coming out of the woodwork?"

"Maybe what he's done with Willow isn't ethical, but…he told me she was in love with him, too."

"And a lot of women fell for Ted Bundy."

Michaele had to close her eyes. All the thoughts and images—what she'd known about Dillon, what he had admitted about himself, and what Jared wanted to believe—wouldn't come together into a coherent picture.

"We're putting an APB out on him. If he's responsible for this, he can't have gotten far, and we should get lucky the way we did with Harold. That Last Writes van isn't going to be easy to hide, and that champagne-colored Lexus is an attention-grabber in its own way."

Planting a kiss on the top of her head, Jared directed her toward the truck. "There's no time for recriminations now. We have to move. I need to call the station and report this, and we have to get you to the house and changed. One step at a time, Mike. Let's go."

Minutes later Michaele was in the pickup, followed by Jared in the patrol car. Dreading having to face Buck more than ever, she was glad to know she could leave him to Jared.

When they arrived, the house looked as she supposed she'd left it, all the way down to the kitchen door being open, the lights being on, the bottle sitting on the table beside an empty glass. Buck never let anything go to waste. Everything spoke well enough of how the night had gone—normal for her—and yet, after Jared squeezed her shoulder, he drew his gun. Telling her to stay put, he checked the rest of the downstairs.

Once that was accomplished without incident, he said, "Let me go up first."

Michaele watched, noting how tense and wary he was as he climbed the stairs. He hugged the wall the way they did in police dramas. She wanted to tease him about that, only his tension was beginning to seep into her, and instead she had the strongest urge to call him back, to pull him out of the house.

We're tired, that's all. We need...we need...

At the top he paused; she expected him to turn right, but he didn't. He stepped straight into her room.

Unbelievable, she thought. Had Buck had the gall to spend the night in her bed?

Her stomach roiling, she ran upstairs.

Although she was barefoot, Jared must have heard her. He came out of the room and blocked her path.

"Get out of my way," she demanded, shaking with rage.

"Mike, go back downstairs."

"No. That bastard's not spending another minute in my

bed. He's stained everything else—our lives, our memories...I swear I'll rip the sheets off and burn them myself and this godforsaken house, if I have to!''

"Mike!" Jared shook her hard. "He's dead."

47

7:17 a.m.

There were too damn many people in the house, but not as many as there eventually would be. Jared stood at the top of the stairs and observed the scene below. Michaele right where he'd left her ten minutes ago, expressionless, limp. Sutter beside her, trying to make small talk and failing. The young cop looked miserable. Mike looked as if she were slipping into a black hole and close to self-imploding.

From the room behind him, he heard a window opening. Moments later the door creaked as it was opened, and the town's JP, Sid Simmons, joined him on the landing. Dressed for church, he rubbed at his nose with a linen handkerchief before tucking it back into the pocket of his gray trousers.

"Body's starting to purge. Glad my part's done. These house calls—they make the road accidents almost easier to take. You called in who you need, son?"

"Yeah, the EMS folks are on their way. Appreciate it, Sid. See if you can get Michaele to go sit down in the kitchen or living room, will you? No need for her to see this next part."

"I'll try, but I didn't have any luck on my way up."

The aging town leader gripped Jared's shoulder. "Heard about Cade's girl. Hope this isn't what it sounds like."

"We're all hoping that, Sid."

When Jared failed to offer more, the JP sighed. "Guess I'll see you at the funeral."

Jared watched the longtime elected official ease down the stairs, mindful of his chronic hip problem. Talking to Michaele was something Jared would have done himself, but he knew she would want explanations he couldn't give her yet. The waiting was hacking away at his nerves, too. In fact, it was his closeness to the situation that had compelled John Box to suggest he wait out here.

Finally John emerged, only to pull the door closed behind him. Steeling himself for the worst, but relieved the waiting was over, Jared signaled John to follow him down the hall to get out of sight of Michaele.

"Well?" he demanded in the darker end of the hallway.

"Relax, damn it. You called it. It has all the signs of a heart attack. Once the EMS folks get him to Quitman for the official ruling, they'll release him to whatever funeral home Mike wants. On the downside, that makes things more costly for Mike, but you know the benefit of documenting all the steps if there are questions or comments down the road."

Nodding, Jared finally allowed himself to breathe normally. His gut had told him it would come to this, but experience had demanded he not draw conclusions, and definitely not assume. Actually, he didn't have everything he wanted yet.

"The other good news is that the end must've occurred less than an hour before you got here."

"Yeah, Sid pointed out that things had just started to get ripe in there."

"Even if it had been longer, nothing looks suspicious.

The DA would've been hard-pressed to make any charge stick regardless. Shit, the SOB's a known chronic alcoholic, found in his daughter's bed. Mike's bruised. And everyone knew of Buck's temperament. The weakest defense attorney wouldn't have any problem putting the idea in a jury's head that Faith had probably run away from home because the guy had abused her, too. Mike's untouchable, pal, no matter what happened."

"Nothing happened." Jared wanted that understood. Bad enough that he couldn't keep Sid and the technicians from seeing where Buck was; she shouldn't have to deal with rumors for the rest of her life. John wouldn't spread any, but Jared also wanted him to be sure to shut down any he heard.

"Easy, Chief. I'm on your side."

Jared rubbed at his eyes, the rest from last night already forgotten.

"Sorry about the pickup..." There hadn't been time to clean it off, and John had seen it on his way in. So would everyone else. Jared had briefly told him about what had happened and its possible connection when he'd first come in. "What's your gut say about it?"

"The timing is troubling, I'll give you that. But the intent's even less clear. Worst scenario? You could be looking at increasingly psychotic behavior."

Jared had a momentary flashback image of Sandy, the second before two other cops forced him out of her room that morning six years ago. Brutally repressing the horrific image, he replied, "You heard about Hancock?"

"Yeah. Cuddy said you're discussing whether to bring in a DPS Emergency Management Team or a smaller group of advisory personnel. I know finding Hancock is going to be your number one priority, but I think your notifying the Parks and Wildlife people and specific individuals who have experience in this kind of thing to search deeper into woods and remote areas is a good idea. Before I get to work on dusting the rest of the room just in case, I'd like to go to Faith's room and pick out the clothes the dogs could use to try to pick up her scent.''

''Go ahead. I take it you're going to do the same at the Weatherbys'?''

''Stressful as it will be for them, it's the wise thing to do.''

''I'll do what I can to keep Mike occupied. When you're ready to leave, do me a favor and go by the front door so she doesn't see. Between Faith and now her guilt about Willow, I don't know how she's supposed to plan a damn funeral.''

''There's no one else she could call in to help?''

''She's been the sail, rudder and oars in her family for so long, she hasn't had the time or energy to cultivate closer relationships. You've got your own full plate. Go to it. I'll think of something.''

He descended the stairs, his arrival drawing Jim Sutter's attention.

''Chief, a word?'' Sutter stepped to the other side of the hall with Jared. ''If you're going to be down here for a while, would you mind if I went out and worked on her truck for her? The press has to have picked up this news about Mr. Ramey on the scanner. Figure they'll be here anytime now. It wouldn't be right to put Ms. Mike through questions about the truck, too. As it is, they'll be asking about the Weatherby girl and her possible connection to Faith.''

''Good thinking. There may be paint thinner or a razor blade in the garage. Is Red still outside?''

''Yeah, out by the road. He's not feeling good about this, either, Chief.''

"Bring him up and have him help you as long as he can. But you're going to have to watch the road. You know Bruce and Buddy are doing what they can on the Weatherby situation. As soon as the EMS team arrives, send them in. Oh, and the mayor, I guess."

"He's coming?"

"Who do you think old Simmons will call the minute he gets home? It's all right. It'll save me having to call him for a briefing."

Jim left, and, finally alone for the moment, Jared focused on Michaele. Her demeanor remained the same, no emotion permeating her calm but fragile shell, her face paler than he'd ever seen it, except for the bruise on her left temple. Unhealthy. It might have been easier to watch her sobbing hysterically. A breakdown she could recover from, but something deeper...? He couldn't let himself dwell there; his fear for her would freeze him into inaction.

"Come to the kitchen, honey. We'll make a pot of coffee."

She roused from her trance and immediately began to fidget and fuss. "We don't own a coffeemaker. How many cups do you need right away? God, this house isn't fit for company. I should call the café and—"

"Whoa, stop." In the kitchen Jared locked her in the *V* of the cabinets. "Forget the house. As for the coffee, I was just looking for something to keep you occupied."

"Why? Is there other news? It's about Buck. They think I'm to blame. Jared, I swear all I did was run when he—"

Jared cupped her face with his hands. "It was a heart attack." Once he had her attention, he added softly, "John's confirmed it. He says it looks like it happened only a short while ago."

Michaele pressed a shaking hand against his chest as though needing the contact to keep standing. "All I could think was that people would be suspicious, that they'd accuse you of protecting me. You know how it's getting. The new pastime around here is to jump to conclusions as though they burn calories.''

''Not this time.''

She gripped his wrists as though they were a lifeline. ''Don't let me off the hook yet. When you first came out of that room and told me, I wasn't sorry, I was relieved.''

''That'' room, not *her* room. Hearing that she'd already abandoned psychological claim to where she'd slept her entire life, Jared could only imagine what else she was doing to herself to keep functioning. ''Anyone would be. No one's going to judge you.''

She averted her gaze. ''What needs to be done next?''

Yes, that was easier for her—to be the automaton. Don't think too much, feel even less. But if he let her do that, she could easily shut him out again, and Jared wasn't about to let that happen.

He reached for the phone. ''I'm getting you help. Planning a funeral is tough at any time. You know who would be perfect for this? Jessica.''

''Martha Stewart being unavailable,'' she muttered.

''You're right, Jess is a perfectionist, and has been known to put on airs occasionally. The important thing is, she knows how to get things done. And she can be discreet.''

''I'll give her that. Whenever she would come to the station, she was so discreet, she acted as though Buck were part of the tire display. Don't do this to me, Jared.''

''Don't underestimate yourself. She respects you. More important, you can't do this alone. You need someone to run interference for you when people come by to pay their respects and drop off food. Everything that comes with that.''

"Come where? Here? *I* don't want to be here—why would anyone else come?"

"They'll want to pay their respects to you. They'll come, Mike, because the town's in crisis, too, and this eases the pressure a bit. I'm calling Jessica."

Garth answered the phone. Although somewhat distant at first, when Jared broke the news, he was immediately conciliatory.

"What a blow for Mike. How is she?"

"That's why I called," Jared replied. "I need to ask Jessica for a favor."

She must have been standing close, because she took the phone as though she'd heard his request. "Jared? What's happened? Oh, Lord, Garth's just told me. That poor girl. What can I do?"

"Supervise the whole process. As you can imagine, she's in no shape for this, and having never done it before... Look, I know it's your and Garth's busy time, what with graduation and awards dinners and all—"

"Thank goodness I'm just back from being out of town. Give me a few minutes to change, and I'll be right over. Wait—where do I go?"

"We're at the Ramey's. I mean it, Jess, we're starting at ground zero."

"Tell Michaele not to worry. She has me now."

48

8:10 a.m.

The EMS people were easing the gurney down the steep stairs when Jessica breezed in through the kitchen door. Michaele spotted her first. Dressed in a silk sheath so white it could cause snow blindness, the confident brunette set her clutch purse on the kitchen table and held out her arms to Michaele. Already tall, her high-heel sandals made her tower over almost everyone, and left Michaele feeling like a pygmy. She decided, no way was she going to let the woman sit down on anything in here. Just leaning against the refrigerator would probably incur a dry-cleaning bill.

Yet, as she allowed herself to be hugged, she caught the scent of a fragrance too expensive to be wasted as a sample on the advertising pages of a fashion magazine. Maybe Jessica would leave her feeling like a frump and totally inept, but it would be worth putting up with a little grief to be incubated in that glorious, life-embracing scent, if only for a few moments.

Jessica didn't actually hug the usual way. Clasping Michaele's hands and touching cheeks as though on a state department receiving line, she crooned, "Michaele. Our heartfelt condolences."

"Thank you. It's, um, good of you to do this."

"No, don't feel awkward. Jared was right to call me. Having been in this position several times, I know better than most what you're feeling." Jessica glanced beyond her to inspect the progress of the crew. "Where are they taking him?"

"The hospital, I believe. Some sort of formality. It was a heart attack." She was probably talking too much. Jessica hadn't asked the "how?" question, and why should she? She wasn't here for Buck. "About a funeral home— do you think I should ask them to suggest someplace?"

Jessica wagged her finger and took off for the hallway. "Gentlemen," she said regally, "please inform the staff upon arrival to release the deceased to Ivy and Reece Funeral Home. I'm calling them right now. Jared, a word, please."

Michaele watched him follow Jessica like an obedient Great Dane, but the wink he shot her was anything but subjugating. The reminder—that what Jessica assumed and what Michaele chose to do needn't be the same—helped her feel less like a pollywog on a freeway.

"What do I need to know?" Jessica asked him. "Michaele tells me this is going to be classified as a heart attack, and yet you have half of your department outside."

"Technically, I have everybody on the force somewhere around town virtually around the clock these days, and it doesn't have anything to do with this, Jess."

"Mmm, and that attractive gentleman with all the cases and paraphernalia in the back of his sports utility vehicle...he's the county detective, is he not? I suppose he's only here to help with the spring cleaning? And why is Officer Sutter crawling all over Michaele's truck?"

"No comment." Jared enunciated each word. "And if I hear you're pressing Mike for information, I will personally spank you, and it will not be a turn-on. Understood?"

Although she remained smiling, Jessica narrowed her eyes. "More than you imagine. In fact, I think after we're through at the funeral home, I should take Michaele to our place. Garth and I can provide her with the security she needs, as well as the rest and privacy."

Michaele had just joined them, and before she could protest, Jared said, "Drop her off at the station."

"Jared, really. Something unhealthy is going on here. Any fool can see it."

Michaele wet her lips, her look appealing. "You should at least tell her about the one thing. If she's going to be around me, it's only fair she be warned."

"All right, you're bound to hear about it shortly, anyway. Willow Weatherby is missing," Jared told her. "We have reason to suspect Michaele might be in danger, too. That's why I need you to help her with the service and the reception, and get her back to me. Whatever you do, don't let her out of your sight."

"No reception," Michaele said.

"How dreadful," Jessica replied, ignoring her. "We know the Weatherbys socially. Garth didn't tell me—"

"He wouldn't have heard himself yet." Jared began moving away. "Service and reception only, Jess."

"*No* reception," Michaele repeated.

Both of them looked at her as though she'd just come out of a coma. To her credit, Jessica didn't lose her gracious smile. "Michaele, dear, you don't understand. Things like weddings and funerals are necessary social passages. They bring a community together and help the healing process."

"I've already heard that line. But somehow I can't see you being eager to rub elbows with Buck's bootlegger and his bookie, who are the only two people I can think of who could possibly miss him."

Although the corner of Jared's mouth twitched, he told Michaele, "Jess is right, though." Then to the older woman, he added, "Try to keep it as low-key and brief as you can."

Already unhappy with being overruled in what she thought should be her decision, Michaele stiffened when he leaned over and kissed her on the mouth.

"Hang in there," he murmured. "I'll see you back at the station."

And suddenly the house was as empty and quiet as if a tornado had gutted it of everyone and everything. Jessica's speculative gaze wasn't reassuring, either; after all, she still had to consider Jared as practically family.

All Jessica said, though, was "Well, it would seem I have my orders. I just wish I knew whether to be flattered that he thinks you're safe with me...or offended." With a dismissive wave of her hand, signaling that she didn't want an answer, she collected her purse. "So what do you say we get this done?"

By the time Michaele walked into the station, she was laden with shopping bags and her mind was spinning so fast that her brain felt pureed.

Curtis was manning the front desk and, spotting her, leaped up to grab a slipping sack. "Saw you going into the boutique across the street." He ended up taking them all from her, then set them on his desk and guided her into the chair beside it. "It was real nice of Mrs. Laurence to open for you so you could have privacy shopping for the service."

Michaele couldn't disagree more, but didn't have the energy to answer, let alone to do so politely.

"About Buck..." he began.

Oh, God. "It's okay, Curtis." She knew she sounded

too urgent, almost manic, and struggled to tone herself down a bit. "I appreciate the thought. Has there been any news about Willow? About…anything?"

He glanced toward Jared's office. Michaele looked, too, and saw him on the phone, head bowed, fully concentrating, rubbing and rubbing at his forehead. How could she be angry with the man for abandoning her, when he was trying so hard to fix this insane world?

"Nothing," Curtis replied. "It's downright spooky, if you ask me. Bruce is out talking with the teens around town. He's got the best rapport with them, but he checked in a minute before you got here and he hasn't come up with even the smallest lead."

"What about the car or the van?"

"Red and Buddy are searching for them. Jim's grabbing lunch and handling regular patrol. He'd been out at the Weatherby place, although the ranch is outside city limits. Sheriff Cudahy asked the chief for the favor until he could spare a man to beat off the press out there."

"All you need now is for a 747 to land on Main Street, huh?"

"You're the one overloaded. Can I get you something while you wait? Coffee? A cold drink?"

"It's okay, I'm through," Jared said, coming toward them. He collected her load in one hand; with his other, he helped her to her feet. "Hold the fort, Curtis. If you need me, you know where I am. Be back in an hour."

As the door of the station dropped shut behind them, he asked, "Was it as bad as the expression on your face?"

"Jared, you don't have time for this. Let me make like one of your couch cushions and—"

"The fastest way to run out of gas or to start making mistakes is to deny your body food and rest. I may have to postpone the rest part, but I knew I needed food a half-hour ago when what came out of the paper shredder started to look appetizing.''

He put her purchases in the back seat of his car and settled her in the passenger seat. The sun-heated vinyl actually felt marvelous against her overtired body, and by the time he climbed in beside her, she was half asleep.

''Don't get too comfortable, babe,'' he said, pulling away from the station. ''It'll break my heart to have to wake you in two minutes.''

The blast from the air conditioner was almost an insult, but it did help rouse her. ''I'm okay.''

''Yeah, right. Talk to me. Are you ever going to forgive me for dumping Jess on you?''

''Probably. In eight or ten years or so.''

Jared uttered a low groan. ''I'm sorry, Mike, but I couldn't stay with you, and I knew you needed somebody oblivious to sales pitches and bulldozer tactics.''

''Your former fiancé's sister is the queen of bulldozers. Do you know why her world is such a serene, orderly place?'' Michaele asked drolly. ''It's because the only audible sound there is her voice.''

He swore under his breath. ''I didn't mean for her to make all the decisions, damn it.''

''Well, she did, and I now own a dress I look ridiculous in, shoes I can't walk in...but do you know the worst of it? Gloves.''

''Gloves?''

''To hide my hands.'' Michaele held them up for her own inspection. They were rather nicely shaped, just work-rough and forever stained. ''She said no manicurist alive could perform the kind of miracle it would take to make these presentable by Tuesday, so she insisted I get a pair of gloves. Cripes, it'll be at least ninety!''

Jared took hold of her left hand and brought it to his

lips for a fervent kiss. "I love your hands, especially when they're on me. Was it any better at the funeral home?"

It was humbling the way he kept putting her first. "I'm whining. I hate whiners."

"Understand this. Listening to you helps keep my world sane. So? How was it?"

"It would be cheaper to bury Buck in the white pickup. As it is, I have to sell the thing to pay for the funeral."

"I'll give you the money."

"No, you won't. This is not your problem."

"If it affects you, it is."

Michaele closed her eyes and turned her face to the side window. She knew she was hiding, just as she knew she'd spoken too quickly, too sharply. His gesture was beyond generous; it was additional proof that he'd meant what he'd said about loving her. But how could she make him understand that such gestures felt like chains, imprisoning her and weighing her down when she was already drowning?

The silence stretched between them...pulsated. Nevertheless, Jared didn't speak again until he'd parked the car under the carport.

"It's okay to feel as though you're going crazy," he began quietly. "It's normal to want to strike out at anybody and everybody. I did."

But he had adored Sandy, and that had given him a legitimate explanation, if not an excuse. Michaele couldn't remember a time she'd ever had kindly feelings toward Buck, let alone loved him. As for Faith...God forgive her, but Faith had been fast wearing out what feelings she'd tried to hold on to for her.

"You're exhausted, Mike," Jared said. "Let's go inside. You can lie down, while I make lunch. Even fifteen minutes would help."

She wasn't hungry and she couldn't sleep if she wanted to. But she also didn't want to be alone with her thoughts, so she went. If that was a contradiction, Jared seemed to understand that, too.

Once he set down her bags, he drew her into his arms. ''I have thicker skin and a lot more patience than you're giving me credit for. All I need is time and the chance to prove to you that what we have is worth fighting for. Don't let the past handicap our future.''

No, she didn't want it to. But Faith and Willow might not have a future, and in both cases that might be partly her fault.

What right did she have to be happy if they weren't even alive to try?

49

"Friends, neighbors, brothers and sisters in Jesus…we have come here today not to commend our brethren to the Almighty, but to entreat our forgiving Lord to be lenient and let this poor sinner, Theodore Carville Ramey, join Thee in Thy Kingdom."

Someone coughed. Someone else choked.

Jared was as stunned as anyone to learn Michaele had asked Reverend Isaac Mooney to speak at Buck's graveside service. But as he watched the black preacher sway, gesticulate and articulate about the kingdom of heaven before the all-white assembly, he understood at least a part of her logic. Oblivious to the self-consciousness or outright unease of some of those who'd come, she was thinking that if her atheist and bigoted father was seeing this, he would be spitting mad, and that would give her some sense of justice and satisfaction.

But Mooney was by no means her only gesture of protest. Another that continued to draw sidelong looks from a number of people was that Michaele was wearing denim, not the dress that Jess had pushed her into purchasing. As much as Jared would have liked seeing her in it—especially once he'd peeked in the bags when she was showering—he'd had the pleasure of seeing her in nothing, and that was even better.

"...And woe unto the slackers and the weak in spirit," Mooney droned on, "for they shall be felled by the judgment of the Lord!"

Jess, on the other side of Michaele, sighed deeply, then leaned toward Garth, no doubt to share her opinion of the situation. Jared made out the word "obscene" and "nerve"; then Garth put his arm around her, and Jared suspected the tight hug was a message to keep her peace until this was over.

People continued to shuffle and utter various sounds. To be fair, though, not all of the discontent was because of Mooney and Mike. She'd been right about the heat. It was building to a scorcher, and she'd turned down having a canopy or chairs. "We aren't holding a revival," she'd muttered. As a result, people were uncomfortable—like Pete Fite, who kept taking off his hat and wiping his bald spot with a handkerchief.

What bothered Jared more, however, was seeing that as the sermon went on, Michaele's expression grew more vacant. He recognized what was happening and why. There'd been not so much as an anonymous tip on Faith since Willow's disappearance, and nothing on her. Worse, Hancock's van had been located parked at an apartment complex in Tyler. The cops down there had been great about questioning everyone with a view of the vehicle, but they hadn't turned up anyone who knew the driver's whereabouts, let alone paid attention to when it had been left there. As for the Lexus, it remained a huge question mark.

Jared had hoped that Michaele would at least take some comfort in Harold's being moved to the county jail in Quitman to await arraignment. Also, Dollar had pleaded no-contest and thrown himself on the mercy of the court, and for a probated sentence was admitting himself into a behavioral clinic. But, Jared supposed, much more needed to happen before Michaele would believe the scales were beginning to tip in the other direction.

"...And so it is written, 'ashes to ashes, dust to dust.' Let us pray."

Everyone bowed their heads—everyone except Michaele, who abruptly walked away. Jared immediately followed, but even so didn't catch up with her until they had almost reached his car.

"Do you want me to take you to the hospital?"

"No, I'm fine."

She'd been saying that for days. It was beginning to have the same effect on him as those proverbial fingernails on the chalkboard. "So why do you look ready for a blood transfusion?"

"Just get me to the house, will you? I have a feeling Jessica's ticked enough not to show up, and there's the ice to still put out and the wrapping to take off all that food—"

"Forget the reception. You can't keep up like this." Since Sunday, she and Jessica had been spending a great deal of time together as more plans were fine-tuned, and the house was made presentable for the reception. While the garage remained closed—someone had even put a wreath on one of the gas pumps—people had made an effort to track down Michaele wherever they could to pass on their condolences. For the most part, she'd handled it well—sincerely, if not always politically correctly. But he could see the end was near.

"Too late for second thoughts, Morgan. Besides, you were right. People brought a lot of stuff, and they'll come—including those who want to have another look at

the irreverent daughter, or to lecture me for mocking tra-
dition. If you're lucky and can hang around, maybe someone will criticize you for what is and isn't happening to
their town.''

She said it so calmly, with such fatalism, that he winced.
''It would be a lot easier to watch you cry.'' With that, he
drove her to her house.

An hour later, he knew she'd called the scene accurately.
About half the people who'd come to the service came to
the house. As Jared leaned against the living room door-
jamb watching, Jessica held court, keeping Michaele so
close that she might as well have been a Pekinese on a
short chain. Jess was enjoying herself as woman after
woman came to Michaele, offered polite words of condolences, then, like Ellie Ashley, murmured, ''But, Michaele, dear, the jeans…was that necessary?'' Then there
was Misty Monroe's ''Michaele, you could have borrowed
something, anything from Faith's closet.'' Each time Jess
would make it clear that she wasn't responsible, explaining, ''She had a perfectly divine little dress. But our Michaele is a denim girl at heart and always will be. Personally, I admire her independence.''

Jess, you're gilding your crown as world-class bitch.

It took considerable restraint, but Jared kept his distance
so as not to make a scene, waiting instead for Michaele to
let Jess have it. But her only response was to thank guest
after guest for attending, and for whatever they'd donated
to the reception, then wait for the next hug or criticism.
To Jared, it was like someone taking a whip to themselves,
and he experienced no small guilt for his role in this. And
how the hell could he expect her to have faith in him, faith
in resolving this, if her instincts for self-preservation were
in retreat?

"Glad I could catch you alone for a moment." O. K. Loyal stopped before him, blocking his view. "I've heard Miriam Dollar's put her house on the market. Pineywoods Realty is handling things for her, and she's left for her sister's in Kansas City. Says a lot when your own wife recognizes what a loser you are."

Jared knew what he was driving at. "Nothing would be served by putting him in prison."

"The man's a sexual deviant! There's no telling how many women's privacy he's violated over the years."

"He's a half-baked fruitcake, driven farther over the edge because he can't reconcile his feelings about his faith and his guilt for having a penis."

The mayor grimaced. "Damn, Jared. We're in mixed company."

Jared surveyed the room. "And who here do you think has never heard the word *penis* before?"

"Is that your idea of an appropriate response and capable management? To excuse away serious criminal behavior with late-night TV humor interspersed with psychobabble?"

"I suppose you and your Democrat pals would prefer we outlaw everything, stick everyone behind bars and then declare the country crime-free? All I said was that Dollar appears to be more of a neurotic mess than a dangerous criminal. As for your opinion of my ability to do my job, anytime you want my resignation, say the word."

"Don't get your shorts in a tangle. I'm just voicing some of the concerns people have shared with me. That's part of my job—to let you know what your public is saying."

"Which public would that be, Loyal? Your rancher friends like Weatherby and Fenton? I'm sorry as heck that Fenton's boy's name was linked to Bean, but that was

Harold's doing, and at no time was it suggested young Jack was involved in anything illegal. As for Weatherby, he's scared. He has a right to be, but you know better than to take anything he's saying to heart right now.''

''What is the latest on Hancock? Somebody has to have seen something when he parked his van down in Tyler.''

The Tyler police had suggested to Jared that because of the complex's close proximity to Pounds Field, Hancock might have caught a flight out of the area. Jared had obtained a court order to enter Last Writes late Sunday, and with John Box had sifted through the building, although without success. They had, however, obtained a photo of the entrepreneur, which they were showing around and printing in all the papers, along with Willow's, to try to prompt a sighting call.

''Everybody's doing their be—''

He suddenly realized that Michaele was no longer in his field of vision. A second later he spotted her. She rounded a group of people, and him, to make her way into the kitchen. Judging by the way tension radiated from her and Jess's feline look of satisfaction, he had a hunch his former, almost-sister-in-law had gotten in one unsheathed swat too many.

''Let's step out of the way.''

He retreated to the base of the stairs where he could watch both the living room and the kitchen. Not surprisingly, Loyal saw this as a sign that he wanted to confide something. When proved wrong, the mayor's disappointment had a sting.

''I have to tell you, Jared, if Cade doesn't get his little girl back, or if he gets his hands on Hancock…well, what's left won't register on an aluminum can recycler's scale.''

While Jared understood—hell, if Willow had been his, he would be planning worse for her abductor—his position required a legal response. "If you have any influence with him, you'd do well to remind him that once he breaks the law, he's culpable, too, and we'll go after him no less forcefully than we're going after Hancock."

"But it doesn't look like you're going to get Hancock any more than you're finding those girls," Loyal muttered.

"God save us from TV and instant analysis and justice. Loyal, listen to yourself. Better yet, turn off the talk shows and throw away those *Die Hard* movies you keep running on the VCR in your shop. The real world moves a helluva lot more slowly, and justice isn't won by one guy with a Hollywood budget."

His frown deepened as his attention was drawn to the kitchen. Garth, looking distinguished as ever in a gray summer suit, was hugging Michaele. It was an understandable, even compassionate scene, and yet Jared's inner reaction was wholly negative.

"I thought Cuddy was coming," Loyal grumbled. He was clearly in the mood to get into it about something.

"There was a drowning at Lake Hawkins." Jared continued watching the scene before him. "And right after someone spotted an alligator near the swimming area."

Loyal swore. "There goes the July Fourth crowd. What a year."

Jared offered a guttural agreement, but watched Garth, who was now wholly involved in a lively conversation with Michaele. He couldn't hear what was being said, but his friend was exhibiting far more animation than he'd displayed in some time.

Even as Jared thought that, Garth threw back his head in a hearty laugh. Ooze that charisma, pal, Jared thought. But instead of being amused as he usually was, the hundred-watt charm set his teeth on edge. The only thing that allowed him to stay put was that Michaele, while polite, seemed unimpressed.

"I'd better go call Neil at the marina," Loyal said, beginning to retreat. "If Hawkins suffers, then Lake Sawyer will suffer more, and he was talking about stretching his credit limit to stock up on inventory and take advantage of the holiday crowd. Thanks for the tip."

Jared nodded, more interested that Jessica had detached herself from her own circle and was off to the kitchen. Jess, he mused, had the radar-like instincts of something with four legs.

"Well..." She swished into the kitchen, still fresh in a sophisticated, two-piece, black linen number. "It's clear this is where the party is. Michaele, darling, I bring bad tidings. I think the central air-conditioning is on its last legs."

"Could be, it's a good fifteen years old. Then again, it's hard to cool a house when the doors keep getting opened."

"I must admit, I'm impressed with the turnout myself."

"There would have been more if word had gotten around that beer or something stouter was being served. Even Pete Fite went home after he found out we only had coffee, tea and soda."

"Fortunately, we're not conducting an Irish wake, dear."

"Maybe we should have, considering I haven't seen a tear yet. Music and a few drunks would make all of our restraint less conspicuous."

Garth chuckled, giving her a one-armed hug. "Hon, Michaele was telling me about trying to choose clothes for Buck. She said because he usually wore only overalls or coveralls, the only pants she could find that would fit were cranberry red, and he's wearing the bowling shoes he hadn't put on since his league days."

"Why do you think it was a closed casket service?" Jessica murmured.

"Hey, I think it's great. At a time like this, you need a sense of humor."

"In that case, my darling, maybe you should check and see who else needs a refill of something, because if we're out of cool air, this laugh-fest is over."

"Wait. Listen, Jess, I told Michaele she was welcome to come stay with us, just as you suggested to me the other day." Garth turned to Michaele. "Sorry that I didn't realize what a mausoleum this place was. Jessica's right. With no close neighbors to speak of—"

"I've delivered my spiel, darling," Jessica said. "She said no."

"But I appreciate the offer," Michaele added.

Jessica came to her other side. "Nevertheless, you really should reconsider. We have plenty of room, and you'll have your own private entrance."

"That's really generous of you." Michaele all but squirmed between the two of them. "But there's a great deal to do, and my schedule tends to be pretty strange, even without this stuff going on. Don't forget, I operate a wrecker service, too. You wouldn't care for my odd-hour comings and goings."

Seeing the panic in her eyes, Jared stepped forward. Enough was enough. "Jess, do me a favor," he drawled upon entering the kitchen. "Throw out the company when you get tired of everybody, and lock up the place when you leave."

"Me? Why—?"

Ignoring her, he drew Michaele from between them and led her to the outside door. "And thanks, both of you, for everything," he added over his shoulder.

"Jared!" Jessica cried. "You can't just drag her off like that. She has guests!"

He let the door fall shut behind him and escorted Michaele to his patrol car. When he climbed in beside her, she was lying back in her seat; her eyes were closed, and she was breathing as deeply as a relieved prison escapee who'd just successfully scaled the last wall.

"Thank you, thank you, thank you," she whispered.

"Hell, it's my fault you went through this in the first place. I thought it might help somehow."

"It did. I learned who I don't want to be when I grow up."

Jared smiled ruefully and keyed the ignition. "Jess's problem is that she doesn't have a lot of purpose in her life aside from pushing Garth's career. He should run for political office so she can sink all that energy and need for control into something challenging."

"I'd vote for him no matter where it meant he got transferred."

Pleased, he backed out from between two vehicles, then eased through the maze of parked cars and trucks. "He certainly admires you."

"He likes to test boundaries."

"I'd wondered if you noticed that—the interest in his eyes."

"Morgan, you're the only one who gets turned on by blue jeans and grease stains."

With a skeptical grunt, he turned onto the road. "Do you mind me being a bit jealous?"

"I don't know. It's new territory for me." Her glance was direct, curious. "Were you jealous of him around Sandy?"

The question threw Jared. "Why would you ask that?"

"Well, he flirted with her, didn't he?"

"He was her brother-in-law."

"So? That made it safe." When he didn't answer, Michaele sighed. "You never talk about her. I know all these things about you—how apolitical you try to be, and how traditional you are at your core, how you like cooking and yard work, and how you're well read. But Sandy's influence on you, what you two were like together—it's like a buried vault."

"That part of my life isn't something I like to reminisce over."

"Maybe not the end, but there were happier times. You two dated a few years before you were engaged. You should have some memories that aren't dark or regretful."

The heat made him suddenly reach for the fan lever, and he turned it up full force, directing the refrigerated air more toward him. "She was a sweet kid. In some ways more naive than you ever were."

"I think we're about as different as you can get. That's why it still confounds me that having loved her…well, that you could want me."

Jared didn't want to have this conversation. He knew he owed it to her, to himself, too. Maybe. But she'd call it; that would mean opening doors he'd locked and buried a long time ago. "What difference does it make? I'm a different person now, and—" he shot her an intense look "—I definitely want you."

"I wasn't hinting for a compliment—or for you to try to convince me that your feelings are as strong as they were for her. That wouldn't be fair to either of us."

Jared pulled into his driveway and parked. Shifting in his seat, he once again saw her frown at her small, laborer's hands as though they held the answer to her psychological puzzle. "More to the point," he said, "you don't expect to come first anywhere but in your work."

Her gaze only skimmed his, and she focused on where they were. "Why are we here? You need to get back to the station."

"Yeah. Too damn soon. But not quite yet."

It seemed like forever since Saturday night—or rather Sunday morning. Since then he'd forced himself to keep his hands off her because she'd looked ready to shatter into so many pieces that there might be no putting her back together again. She still did. But this focus on death had been owning her, them, for too long. It was time to embrace life…if only for a brief while.

Michaele finally met his gaze. Without speaking, she opened her door.

50

It was one thing to be bold as brass in the safety of darkness. Daylight chiseled at Michaele's confidence. So had Jessica and some of the others, of course. It took the deep loneliness in Jared's gray eyes, and his corresponding raw need for her, to push her doubts and insecurities aside so she could precede him into his home.

He kept the air conditioner cranked low and the shades drawn; that didn't exactly create the type of environment conducive to potted plants and prisms of sunlight illuminating knickknacks and photographs. But they weren't here to pay attention to the decor; Michaele knew that, as Jared locked up behind them. The truth was in his every movement, a premeditation when he took off his hat and patiently set it on the stand beside the door, then unbuckled his gun belt. Those large capable hands gliding, flexing, stroking…they might as well already have been touching her. In his mind he was.

Mesmerized, she pulled her shirt from her jeans, then tugged at the snaps. The movement, the material's subtle abrasion against her breasts, did what his gaze did—had her imagining, remembering and wondering how long she would have to wait to feel his mouth.

"That's it." He set the gun on the counter.

"What?"

"That's what knocked me out the other night about you…"

Wasting no time, he slid his hands inside her shirt, cupping her breasts, lifting them, and caressing her hard-tipped nipples with his thumbs, sending a sharp needle of pleasure shooting through her body. Before the first ripples subsided, he bent and repeated the tender assault with his mouth.

Michaele let her head fall back, let her eyes drift closed. As he alternately suckled and stroked her, she gave herself up to the potent sensations, until she couldn't contain the shaky moan bubbling up from deep within her.

"…Yeah, that. Your honesty."

Straightening, Jared all but lifted her off her feet to nestle himself in the juncture of her thighs, so she would recognize what these few seconds had done to him, how he was already becoming aroused. Then he claimed her mouth with an equally honest possessiveness.

His kiss made a response impossible, but what could she have said except that the credit was due him. He did this to her. Once their lips met, their so-different bodies aligned, everything magnified into this truth—that together they created something the rest of the world couldn't touch, let alone compete with.

And that was why the kiss quickly went from thorough to wild, because it was all still so new, because time was always their enemy. Besides, even as little as a week ago, they'd believed this might never happen. There was so much emptiness to fill; a dense jungle of darkness to tear through to get to the light they seemed to find only when they were one. So he angled his head one way, she the other, only to switch sides for another tangled, tempest of a kiss. This unspoken communication between lovers was the same mysterious signal that had them attempting to imprint every inch of their bodies on each other, never mind that they were still fully clothed.

As though suddenly becoming aware of that problem, Jared set her on the counter—to free his hands, Michaele realized. That freed hers, too, and they were soon caught in another tangle in their eagerness to expose and explore. More hot, dampening skin was revealed, and their breathing thinned to near-frantic pants that contradicted the cool, still air around them. Finally, she had his shirt off...but her hands caught in her sleeves.

''Better than handcuffs,'' Jared murmured, and proceeded to urge her back on the counter.

A phone book pushed too close to the edge toppled to the floor with a resounding *thud.* As Jared ran a steamy, openmouthed kiss down her torso, Michaele thought her heartbeat had to sound equally loud. But it was his hot breath in her navel, along with the sound of her belt buckle hitting the counter, that had her writhing in a renewed attempt to free herself. She understood what was coming, something they hadn't yet shared; something she didn't know she could bear as his sensual prisoner.

The promise that he would do it regardless was enough to win the freedom of one hand. But he already had her zipper open.

''Jared...bed would be better.''

''Tonight.''

''I'd settle for a carpet burn. Being up here makes me feel as though I'm about to be draped over a bed of lettuce.''

''There's a thought. Should've taken out the salad dressing to get room temperature.''

Despite the teasing light in his eyes, he did scoop her up, and in a smooth move that was testament to his strength and intent, he pivoted and lowered her to the living room carpet. By then she had her other hand free and could help him finish stripping her.

Naked, she rose to her knees and, pushing him onto his back, began removing the rest of his clothes. He helped, neither his gaze nor his hands leaving her. As they caressed and probed, hers explored and incited. And for the moment he allowed it, she spread kisses across the powerful, tanned chest that spoke eloquently of the man who worked as hard at his home as he did for the community. She loved the taste of him, as much as she did his strength and his unexpected gentleness. He cupped the back of her head, as she sipped a droplet of sweat from his belly and let her hand follow the narrow line of dark hair downward, then held him in her hands.

He wasn't wholly gentle, though, when he abruptly rolled her beneath him again. "Someday," he muttered, "we'll have all day and night. A whole week to drive each other crazy. But for now—" he began to slide into her "—sweet heaven, Mike. That's it...take me."

Because this was still new to her, he tried to be slow, and this time his entry was more thrilling than shocking. Soon, however, his kisses and the rhythmic roll of his hips obliterated any lingering discomfort, and the only tension she knew was from a fast-building urgency. Jared added to it by slipping his hand between their bodies and palming her.

"Next time it'll be my mouth here," he whispered, finding her bud. "I'm going to know every inch of you, every taste, every sound you make when you come."

"And then I'll do that to you."

The promise triggered his reflexive spasming inside her, as primal as his next relentless kiss. As much as she wanted it to last, she tightened her vaginal muscles, milking him and relishing the sharp moan that she won from him. With a barely discernable murmur of praise and entreaty, Jared's thrusts became more forceful.

The ride was brief, but perfect, and in the end, as she contracted around him, he poured into her as powerfully as he had their first time together.

It was only after their breathing had stopped being gasps, when he had pressed a kiss to her heart, that Michaele dealt with the knowledge that once again they'd had unprotected sex. She saw a similar awareness light his eyes, and closed hers, unable to address or deny her willing recklessness.

Jared acted as though her silent acceptance was a gift. He buried his face against the side of her feverishly hot throat and whispered, ''I love you.''

51

The van wasn't there. Although Dillon had anticipated the possibility of that, it rattled him nonetheless. Had it been towed or stolen? If towed, by whom—the complex manager, the cops?

He glanced over at the sleeping young woman beside him and decided against waking her. What would be the point?

The point is that it's almost over, and you're about to find out the real price of your folly.

As he sat there, the Lexus idling, someone came to the window in the apartment on the ground floor. One look, and they quickly vanished. A light went on upstairs, and someone else looked out. The woman abruptly grabbed for the phone.

He got the hell out of the parking lot.

What's going on?

Being away these last few days had given him a false sense of confidence. Granted, what he'd done hadn't been the most brilliant move of his life, but it had been right for him. Them. And she'd left a note. So while he'd been careful, nobody could accuse him of being covert. Whatever Cade Weatherby was, he wasn't a Neanderthal, and had Willow's father really wanted to track them down, it wouldn't have required hiring James Bond to do it. Nevertheless, he would bet his last nickel that the woman on the phone had been calling the cops.

Knowing that if he stayed on the Loop they would be spotted for sure, Dillon turned at the next intersection. It took them through a less-than-impressive part of town, and he was glad Willow continued to sleep. The good news was that there was no traffic, and so he risked ignoring one, then another stop sign. But his relief soon turned to deepening concern when he saw a patrol car pass at the intersection ahead at breakneck speed, heading north—exactly where he'd been about to turn.

It doesn't mean he was looking for you. "Yeah, right," he muttered under his breath.

Glancing around, he spotted a newspaper delivery person leaving after filling the machine outside a doughnut shop. Thankful the store was still closed, Dillon pulled in and hurried to get one of the papers. He couldn't say why the urge was so strong—until he saw the story on the bottom of the front page: Hunt Continues For Split Creek Fugitive…Police Suspect Foul Play In Double Abduction Case.

"Shit," he breathed.

Worse yet, there were three photographs—his, Willow's and Faith's.

Not only did they think he was responsible for Faith's disappearance, but that he'd kidnapped Willow, too. How could this happen? He'd explained it all to Michaele. And the Weatherbys had that note.

Hurrying back to the car, he shook Willow awake and handed her the paper. "We've got major trouble."

Although sleepy-eyed, she caught on fast, reading as he shifted into gear and got out of there.

"Oh, my Lord..."

"Tell me you weren't merely trying to appease me when you said you left that note. Tell me you really left it."

Her silence was damning.

"Jesus," he moaned.

"I intended to," she replied urgently. "But you know Daddy would have tried to stop us."

Yeah, this is much better. Now Daddy was just going to feed Dillon his own balls. "Willow, do you realize how bad this is?"

"I'm sorry."

He wasn't listening; he was trying to figure a route north that would avoid any more contact with the authorities. It took a lot of side road detouring, but finally he was across the Loop and heading north again on Highway 14. Taking either of the other two highways would have ensured running into DPS troopers, or at least having to drive through towns. Highway 14 was mostly woods and farmland, at least until they reached Hawkins, but he rarely ran into police in that little community.

As tense as a man about to go before a firing squad, he drove hunched over the steering wheel. Despite the air conditioner running full force, sweat was beginning to pour down his back and his palms were growing so damp that his grip on the steering wheel started to slip, forcing him to wipe them on his jeans every minute or so.

You're real hero material, Hancock.

"Please don't be angry with me," Willow begged.

"The van is gone. I should have known there and then that they were searching for us, but I'd hoped it was just a theft. When we get to your house, I want you to keep your distance from me. In fact, it would be best if you try to get to your mother as soon as possible.''

''You can't go back there. Let's go straight to the police. We'll explain there, and have them escort us home.''

Home? What kind of luck did he have with Cade Weatherby if Willow still thought of the place that way?

As though she heard him, Willow said, ''We talked about this, Dillon. Daddy won't listen to you.''

''And now things are worse than ever,'' he replied. ''My only chance to redeem myself is to face him as a man, ready to take responsibility for my actions.''

''You're reasoning from a logical viewpoint. Dillon, my father doesn't operate that way. He knows only obstructions and solutions. He needs time to get used to things. Once Mother used his favorite putter to kill a coachwhip snake that had gotten into the house through the French doors, and she had to go stay with my Aunt Kendra for the weekend until he cooled down. And when one of the hands—''

''The past doesn't matter,'' Dillon interrupted. ''If we're going to have a prayer of making it, no more secrets, no more lies.''

But her worried expression didn't help his nerves, and by the time he pulled into her family's estate, he was as sick to his stomach as he'd ever been.

No doubt it was the sound of the Lexus that had the front lights of the sprawling mansion going on. Moments later, the door was yanked open, and Cade himself came out. In his hands was a twelve-gauge shotgun.

''Dillon…?'' Willow whispered.

He'd seen Weatherby around town before. Fair like his daughter, tall and trim though muscular, he looked fully capable of keeping his prize Brangus stock in line. He would have no trouble with a bookworm whose favorite muscle was in his head.

Dillon shut off the engine and replied, ''Stay here.''

But Willow didn't listen. She bolted from the vehicle and ran toward her father.

''Willow! No!''

''Daddy, I'm all right. See? I'm fine and everything has been fine. I know you were scared and upset, but it's my fault. Dillon wanted me to leave you a note, but I didn't.''

Cade didn't take his eyes off Dillon, who was hurrying toward them. ''Get in the house, Willow.''

But she saw the two men coming from around the back of the house. ''It's okay, Juan, Miguel,'' she said. ''Everything's under control. You can turn in now.''

''Take her inside!'' Cade roared.

When they exchanged glances and opted to follow orders, Willow quickly retreated to Dillon's side. ''Don't you touch me.''

Of course, they ignored her. But as each took hold of an arm, Dillon went into action. ''Let her go. We don't want any trouble, we just—''

He felt the shift of air and out of the corner of his eye saw Willow's horrified expression, her mouth open to scream—but it was too late. The blinding pain was slicing through the back of his head before he could try to defend himself.

''No!'' Willow screamed. ''Daddy, don't!''

Like a felled tree, Dillon dropped to his knees on the concrete driveway. The sharp blade of pain hadn't finished impaling his body when Cade drove the shotgun into his belly. A third blow came via Cade's boot, which connected with Dillon's ribs, and was followed by a fourth and fifth kick.

''Stop it!'' Sobbing wildly, Willow fought and won her

freedom from the smaller men, only to launch herself at her father. "For God's sake, stop! We're *married!*"

For an instant Cade looked struck himself. Then his face darkened with rage. "You're a baby!"

"No. I can't stay a child just because you want me to. I love him, and you have to accept that. He's my husband. We were married in Mexico Saturday."

The announcement didn't leave the rancher stunned for long. Even as Dillon thought he could overcome the paralyzing pain to help Willow, Cade shrugged off his daughter as though she were nothing more than a chenille throw, and kicked Dillon square in the face.

As Dillon was falling, falling into a pit of white-hot flames, he heard the shotgun blast.

52

2:50 a.m.

When the phone rang, Jared had been asleep at most two hours, having made good his promise to make love to Michaele again, this time in bed. Considering the fact that they hadn't left the station until nearly ten o'clock, they had been looking forward to a few hours' more rest.

Releasing her, he shifted around and gripped the receiver on the third ring.

"Yeah?"

"Sorry for the interruption, Chief, but you may want to get out to the Weatherby place. Dillon Hancock's just showed, and Willow says Cade's in the process of killing him."

"Willow—she's okay?"

"That's what Garrick from the sheriff's office says. He just notified me."

Roused, too, Michaele leaned against his back. "What about Willow?" she whispered.

Jared signaled to her to wait a moment. "Let the sheriff's people know we'll be joining them out there. Notify Buddy and Bruce. I'm on my way."

As soon as he hung up, he shot out of bed and headed for the bathroom. "Willow's back home, and Cade Weatherby's intent on killing Dillon. Do me a favor and resist saying 'I told you so.'''

''Okay, but I am going with you.''

''Wrong! I don't know what I'll be driving into.''

But he could already hear her scrambling around the room, reaching for her clothes.

''Do you think I can stay here and wait?'' she called.

''A man can dream,'' he murmured to himself.

''You know what this means, don't you?'' she continued. ''We misjudged him.''

''Slow down, Mike. We don't know anything yet.''

''Willow's alive. They're together. They were going to see her parents. It's as Dillon told me—they're in love.''

''In which case your pal may end up hoping Weatherby does a thorough job, because what doesn't change is that the kid's underage. If there is anything left of him after Daddy's finished venting, the DA will prosecute, with or without Weatherby's support.''

Two minutes later, they were in the patrol car and racing down Dogwood. Jared didn't use his lights or siren, but he was on the radio with Buddy before he passed the station. Buddy had just arrived and was letting him know Cuddy's deputy Roy Russell was already on the scene, too, and that while things were combustible, they were under control and no one was dead. Yet.

''Hancock's in bad shape, Chief.''

''Shot?''

''He may wish it had come to that. He sure isn't as pretty as he once was. Here comes Griggs.''

When Jared disconnected, he glanced at Michaele, who had heard everything. She might not have had tears for her father, but she looked close to losing it for her friend. ''He brought this on himself, Mike.''

''How much control have you had over your heart?''

If she only knew how bad a case he had for her. There they were heading to a crisis, and all his mind wanted to focus on was how she'd said his name and clung to him only a few short hours ago. This thing between them might be seasoned by lust, but he'd never felt closer to anyone than he did to her; had never felt more complete. That made it too risky to get into an argument over caring now, and so they completed the rest of the trip in silence.

The Weatherby ranch was about a mile beyond the Fenton place. Although the stately mansion built in the style of a plantation house was well back from the street, Jared saw the lights almost instantly through the carefully groomed trees that provided a windbreak as much as they did privacy. As he drove nearer, they saw that there were still only three patrol cars there. No sign yet of the EMS people, but then they were coming all the way from Mineola.

Some unfamiliar faces had joined the group, but like gamblers eager to watch a dog fight and see if their favorite challenger won, they kept a respectable distance. Cade Weatherby was being held back by Buddy Eagan, although Egan was a good half-foot shorter. Jared wasn't surprised, though; his man was the one cop with an attitude big enough to match that of the self-made millionaire. Jared was glad to see calmer, more diplomatic Griggs in possession of the firearm. Roy had planted himself between Weatherby and Hanock and was questioning the rancher. Mrs. Weatherby, looking as pale as her white satin robe and clasping a handful of tissues, seemed torn between offering solace to her daughter and wifely support to her husband.

It wasn't until he and Michaele had made their way between the vehicles that he saw Willow on the ground with Hancock's head in her lap. At the first glimpse of his bloodied face, Mike gasped, but to her credit she quickly recovered and joined the couple. Jared couldn't afford to think about how badly he was hurt. Briefly hoping the blood he coughed up was from mouth injuries and nothing internal, he continued on to the other group.

"How long before the ambulance arrives?" Jared asked Bruce, who was nearest.

"Ten to fifteen more minutes, Chief."

He moved on to the still-seething owner of the ranch. Weatherby was ducking and craning his neck to see around Roy Russell, much like a rabid rottweiler that smelled fresh blood and wanted to finish the kill.

"Gentlemen. Roy, hope you don't mind my stopping by?"

"Glad to have you, Chief. Mr. Weatherby here doesn't seem impressed by us simple working boys. Maybe he'll remember his manners and won't tell you that he can buy and sell a dozen of you like he can us."

Letting the brim of his hat cast his face in shadow, Jared met the rancher's outraged glare. "Mr. Weatherby, there isn't anyone here who doesn't understand what you've been through these last few days. But this would be a good time to take a deep breath and count your blessings. You're one of the fortunate ones. You have your daughter back."

His voice quaking with animosity, Weatherby nodded in the direction of Willow and Hanock. "Does that look like she's back?"

Jared would have ignored the verbal jab, except for the pain he saw in the rancher's eyes. This was a father wounded and unable to conceive the reason this was happening to him. Jared could find something to use in that.

"Okay, things aren't going the way you want or planned. But she's alive, and sometimes we forget that's what counts. As for Mr. Hancock's roll in her absence, all I can say is that the DA will address the matter.''

"Get out of my way, and I'll save him taxpayer dollars.''

"That would only earn you your own court date instead of the one Mr. Hancock may face.''

"What do you mean 'may'? The son of a bitch raped my daughter! She's a minor!''

Roy cleared his throat before quietly informing Jared, "Willow says they were married in Mexico.''

More good news, Jared thought.

"It's illegal,'' Cade Weatherby snapped. "She's still a minor.''

"A few weeks short of eighteen,'' Roy offered under his breath. "She told me she put her hair up to look older and asked a lot of tourist-with-money-to-burn questions. Whoever okayed the license obviously saw a reason to ignore dates.''

The fact that Willow had made her decision willingly, and that Hancock's actions were honorable, could have weight with a U.S. court, but right now Jared didn't know or care about the legalities of the newlywed's marriage. What he wanted was to avoid a murder.

"This isn't going to get resolved tonight, Mr. Weatherby,'' he said. "What you need to do is take Mrs. Weatherby inside.''

"Not without my girl.''

"I'm not yours,'' Willow shouted at him. "And I'm never going to step foot in there again!''

From the expression on her father's face, she might as well have emptied both chambers of that twelve-gauge into him. But with the survival instincts of a dominant ego, he soon roared back, "And I'll see that you get nothing, do you hear? Your car is mine! Your education fund, your inheritance... Gone!''

It was Lizbeth Weatherby who intervened. With a last, longing look at her daughter, she returned to her husband and took hold of his arm. ''Chief Morgan is right. Come inside.''

''I'm not finished saying my piece.''

''You never are. Cade, there's been enough pain. Let's go inside. Tomorrow is soon enough to start working on straightening everything out.''

''There's nothing to straighten out. She has to choose. Him or us.''

''Don't you mean him or *you?*''

The comment hit its mark; however, Weatherby had thicker skin than some. He glared at his daughter. ''You think he's what you want? Wait until you can't go on those vacations you like so much, or have the spending sprees you're used to. Love dies fast for little girls with expensive tastes.''

''Cade!'' Lizbeth Weatherby straightened, the image of wifely censure. ''You may not care if you humiliate yourself in front of all these people, but I would hope that you care about humiliating me. Now come inside. Please.''

Maybe it was the particular words, or the specific tone— something had the right effect on the man. With a covert glance that showed he was beginning to understand the thin line between king and buffoon, he took his wife's arm and led her into the house.

''Just when I think small-town life is getting boring,'' Roy Russell murmured as the front door shut quietly behind the couple.

''I'm pissed I didn't get to drop and cuff him,'' Buddy muttered. ''I could use the practice.''

Jared shot him a droll look before signaling Bruce.

"Make sure the gun's empty and give it to them," he said, indicating the ranch hands. To them he added, "If you're smart, you'll wait until morning before you return it."

The two were more than happy to beat a hasty retreat. As Buddy and Roy speculated about the Weatherby employees' willingness to participate in Cade's Judge-Roy-Bean-type trial, Jared saw the EMS vehicle driving in.

He crouched beside Hancock. "Help's here."

Though Hancock had lost quite a bit of blood, Jared knew that head wounds bled profusely. The EMS crew found only a two-inch gash at the back of Hancock's skull. More serious, they surmised, were the two teeth he'd spit out, and at least one broken rib that might have punctured a lung. Of course, if Willow hadn't ruined her father's aim when he shot...

"I should go with them," Michaele said, as they were loading Hancock into the truck.

Jared vetoed the idea. "It would be better if Willow faced this on her own. They've chosen a tough road for themselves, and cruel as it sounds, it would be best if they realize up front that it's what's between the two of them that counts." Jared watched the driver shut the doors on the ambulance. "Besides, he won't be talking tonight, and I imagine Willow will get a cot in his room. Tomorrow's soon enough for what you have in mind. And when you go, it'll be with me."

Waving to them, the driver climbed in behind the wheel. Michaele was no longer watching, she was looking at Jared.

"Dillon's innocent," she said. "Why are you still angry with him?"

"Because, first of all, there's nothing 'innocent' about the guy, and he would tell you that himself if he could.

And more important, as cold as it may seem to you, I'm not even thinking about Hancock anymore. I'm wholly focused on the questions this still leaves behind—namely, who took Faith and who messed with your truck?''

53

As it turned out, Michaele didn't get to the hospital in Quitman until early evening. A call to the hospital told her that tests and treatment would have made it impossible for Dillon to have visitors, anyway. But the primary reason for the delay was that Cuddy had arranged to have Jared join him for a reassessment meeting with an investigator from the DPS Special Crimes Service. The information the agency had been feeding the Missing Persons Clearinghouse Service in the hope of gaining some new leads or sightings regarding Faith wasn't proving fruitful. What's more, Jared informed her during a check-in call, Willow's return definitely put a different, narrower slant on things. Inevitably, the lack of pattern between the two cases cut the number of state personnel able to assist them, especially since a little boy snatched yesterday outside his home in west Dallas was rife with leads and demanded immediate attention while the evidence trail remained hot.

Michaele spent the day at the station. Despite Jared's suggestion that she remain closed one more day, the re-fueling tanker was due, and as the end of the month approached, vehicle inspections were on the increase. Also, the coming holiday meant more people needed their vehicles serviced for longer trips. All that—seasoned with occasional visits by those who, like Pete Fite, hadn't felt they'd had adequate opportunity to talk to her, as well as those who'd heard about the new Mr. and Mrs. Hancock— justified her decision, and made the time pass fast enough.

She did note, however, that there always seemed to be one of Jared's men hanging around the intersection. That wasn't the norm, and she figured he'd left word that some- one had to keep an eye on her at all times. She appreciated the gesture. That ugly message scrawled on the truck wind- shield somehow unnerved her more now than when Wil- low had been thought abducted. It was always the un- known component that got to you, and Michaele didn't have a clue as to what was going on here.

"So are you going to tell me what the verdict is?" she asked, once she and Jared were driving toward Quitman in his patrol car.

Now that most of the spring flowers had gone to seed, the road department had begun mowing, and the air was lush with the scent of fresh-cut grass. Jared drew a deep breath before rolling up his window and adjusting the air conditioner.

"Why don't we wait until after we deal with Hancock and pick up something for dinner?"

"You mean it's so bad that it doesn't matter if you mess with my appetite?"

"It means that I haven't seen you all day and I've missed you. I'd like nothing more than to park this thing, drag you onto my lap, and kiss you until we've steamed up the windows. But I'll settle for pretending, if only for a few minutes, that we're just your average couple going out for an evening ride."

"In a patrol car, with you and your small riot arsenal, and me and my grease rag." Struggling not to imagine the vivid and appealing scene he'd described, she shifted to tug the forgotten cloth out of her back pocket and toss it to the floor. "Let's face it, Morgan, there's nothing average about us and there never will be."

"I can go for unique...especially once we get home."

Home. The word hit her like the shotgun butt Dillon had been beaten with this morning. Jared picked up on her mood change immediately, testament to how fast their relationship was changing and how close they were becoming.

"What's wrong now? Is it about calling my place our home? I thought you were getting used to it."

"I am. It's just...until you said that, I hadn't realized that if Faith comes back, she'll expect me—things—to go back to the way they were. I don't want that. Buck was nobody's idea of a parent, and that house could have doubled as a professional boxer's training gym. I don't want that link to our unhealthy life-style to continue one day longer than it has to. At the same time, I'm not sure moving me into your place is a healthier solution."

"It works for me."

She shot him a mild look. "It's all so new and fast. We're like a couple on a honeymoon, both of us on our best behavior. You're not thinking that it's *your* house, your parents' dream, and that you've been a bachelor for all of your adult life. I'm going to disrupt all that."

"Bomb away."

His ease with this whole situation grated, and that was unnerving her, too. What was wrong with her emotions? A seesaw was more stable than her mood swings. She didn't care what that article said in that magazine Jessica had sent over about the psychology of loss and becoming an orphan. She wasn't grieving Buck.

She studiously looked out at the countryside. "I'm going to miss the spring flowers this year. They disappeared too fast.''

''Don't do that. If I'm pressuring you somehow that I don't recognize, say so. But I'm not going to apologize for believing you're the missing part of my life.''

''I don't want an apology. I'm just not ready to deal with—there's still too much up in the air about the future.''

Jared didn't respond to that, which spoke volumes about how strongly he disagreed with her, not to mention how disappointed he was.

Unable to bear the weight guilt added to her psyche, she drawled, ''Heavy silences are a definite sign to change the subject. So, tell me—how does Dillon's situation look?''

''Broken nose, more stitches than you want to know about, two teeth knocked out, and a couple of cracked ribs, one of which punctured his lung.''

''I meant legally.''

''Stay tuned. The DA hasn't made his decision yet.''

Willow was helping Dillon get a sip of water when they walked into his hospital room. Had it not been for the girl's blond mane, Michaele and Jared might have passed the room, not recognizing the bandaged, bruised man in the bed. Once they drew closer, his sunken eyes suggested that inside he was feeling every bit as badly as he looked. Michaele attempted a cheery greeting, anyway.

''Up to some company?'' She held out the white teddy bear holding the bouquet of flowers to an exhausted, but smiling, Willow. ''I thought you could hug it until the groom here is available again.''

It was the right thing to say. The girl laughed softly and held it up for her new husband's inspection. Dillon grunted something and, except for a brief glance at Jared, focused on Michaele.

"How's the patient?" she asked.

"'kay."

"The doctors say he can go home in another day or two," Willow announced. "Of course, I'll have to wait longer to be carried over the threshold."

Although Michaele recognized the attempt at humor, she lowered her gaze. They didn't need to see her concerns for their future.

Dillon, however, didn't let her get away with the silence. "Made a mess of things, huh?" he asked, the words mangled by his bruised and swollen mouth.

"If only you had let me know." Michaele sat down on the edge of the bed. "Do you realize what I thought when you vanished? And when Willow was reported missing...I was convinced, like everyone else, that you were also the one we were looking for in connection with Faith's disappearance."

Dillon managed a negative grunt.

"Yes."

"You knew."

"It wouldn't be the first time someone had lied to me, Dillon. And there was reason for me to doubt you. A nasty message was left on my truck, the one Faith used to drive. I thought maybe you believed I'd told Jared about Willow, and you were letting me know how angry you were with me."

"No." He tried to say more, but began to gag and cough. Willow quickly gave him another sip of water. "What'd it say?" he managed at last.

"'Whore.' Nice and concise, huh?"

He grunted again. "Sounds like Buck."

"Yeah. Except that Buck's dead."

Although it was Willow who gasped, Dillon's eyes relayed his shock. Finally, slowly, a grim satisfaction lit his eyes.

"Some justice."

"You have no idea."

"Won't say I'm sorry." But he did cover her clasped hands with his bruised ones. Then his gaze shifted to Jared, and something troubled and troubling darkened his eyes.

Michaele wondered what that was all about. Before she could ask, though, Jared took over the conversation.

"Your mother's worked wonders, Willow. After your father took the DA's call this morning, he didn't give the coercive answers he could have that would have guaranteed an immediate indictment. Have you talked to either of them?"

"No." Although the young girl looked interested, she stuck close to Dillon's other side. "I don't know what you're talking about, Chief Morgan. If my mother stopped my father, it's only to do her own maneuvering to split Dillon and me apart."

"Can you blame her? If what your parents are claiming is true, you've been lying to them for some time."

Dillon started to protest, but Willow touched a hand to his shoulder. "It was the only way for us to see each other. If you don't understand that—" she nodded to Michaele for emphasis "—how could I hope that she would?"

"I understand attraction and desire. Love needs a little more basis to be convincing."

"They don't owe anyone an explanation," Michaele said, not wanting to be a part of this dialogue at all. "It's what they feel for each other that matters, and their willingness to pay for the costs."

"But are they? The court will only see that a man in his thirties took sexual advantage of a young girl almost young enough to be his daughter. Philosophize all you want—in this country that's called statutory rape.''

''That's not the way it was at all!'' Willow cried. ''Dillon did his best to discourage me. I'm the one who pursued this relationship on every level I could. It was six months before he invited me to have a cup of tea.''

Dillon raised his hand, asking for silence. ''My fault,'' he said simply.

''I won't let them think you seduced me like some lecher,'' Willow insisted.

But she was beginning to tear up. With care, Dillon drew her against him. Still, it must have hurt; Michaele could see that by the way he flinched…and the way his gaze burned into Jared's.

''I knew who and what I wanted from the moment she walked into my store.'' It took him a long time to manage that between his swollen lips. ''I didn't have to do the taste-tester thing to figure it out.''

Michaele swung around, but the expression on Jared's face remained a study in blankness.

''For somebody who looks like the remains of a dropped blueberry pie, you talk a lot'' was all he said.

''I can say more.''

''You've made your point. As far as I'm concerned, her parents are your problem. But for what it's worth, I'll tell the DA his time would be better spent prosecuting real criminals.''

Willow's sweet face radiated gratitude. ''Thank you, Chief Morgan.''

To Michaele's amazement, he didn't reply, nor did he tell her he would be waiting for her at the car. He merely walked out.

''Sorry,'' she said, as stunned silence expanded to the point of awkwardness. ''I can't claim to know all that was about, but I do know he's been under a tremendous strain lately."

"Don't worry about it," Dillon said, focusing on Willow's hand—her diamond wedding ring, to be exact. "But maybe it's a good thing for you to see all sides of him before you think about com—" he groaned softly, the talking too much for him "—the future yourself."

"I could say the same thing in his defense." Her attempt at humor failing, Michaele leaned forward and touched his other hand. "You should know something. I've been staying with Jared."

The news visibly disturbed him, but he only said, "I hope it works out for you."

What was going on? She attempted a teasing smile. "That doesn't sound convincing for someone who only weeks ago appeared to be pushing me toward the guy."

"That was when I still believed...believed Faith was pulling a dumb stunt."

A cold weight settled in Michaele's stomach. "What does Faith have to do with this?"

Groaning again, he shifted against the pillows. "Chest is hurting worse. Think I need another shot or something."

"We'd better let him rest," Willow told Michaele. "They warned him against overdoing it."

"But—" Michaele touched her hand to her lips. "Okay. You take care. Both of you." At the door, however, she glanced back. "I am going to ask him, Dillon. And if he doesn't tell me, you're going to have to."

"Just make sure you're ready for the truth."

54

The walk to the car should have been twice the distance for the tension building in Michaele. Jared was ending a call, and he started the engine as soon as she opened the passenger door. Before she had her seat belt fastened, he was backing out of the parking lot and taking Highway 154 back toward Split Creek.

"Are you going to sit there seething the whole way?" he finally asked her.

"I thought I'd give you some time."

"For?"

"Explaining yourself."

"There's nothing to explain."

"That's why the atmosphere in Dillon's room was so friendly, and you left?"

"Hancock and I have never been pals. I said what I had to say and left you to have your visit."

"No, you left because something was going on between you and Dillon, and you didn't want me to find out what it was."

"It has nothing to do with you."

"If it has something to do with Faith, it concerns me."

Jared slipped on his sunglasses. That was telling in itself, since he rarely wore them when he was with her, and as they were driving east and it was well past six, he couldn't need them now, except to hide. Although he remained silent, the straining muscles in his neck gave away his mood; so did the rigidity of his jaw. When minutes passed and he refused to explain himself, Michaele concluded that this wasn't just about a misunderstanding or about simple jealousy of her friendship with Dillon.

And if he couldn't be honest with her now...

"Please drop me off at the garage," she told him.

"What did you forget?"

"Nothing. I need to get the truck."

"Michaele."

"Save the lecture. The last thing I want to hear is you justifying why you can't be honest with me."

"You aren't going to your house."

"Well, I can't stay with you anymore, can I?"

He seemed to think otherwise, because minutes later he pulled into his driveway. Incensed that he thought he could override her decision, Michaele bolted from the car and started heading back to town.

Jared caught her halfway down the driveway. "Damn it, don't be a stubborn little fool."

"*You're* the one hiding something and *I'm* stubborn?"

"All right, I'll tell you, but come inside."

"No, here." She pointed to the ground between them. "Right here, right now. What does Dillon know about you that suddenly has him doubting my being with you?"

Jared had never flattened his lips to a thinner line, and his skin looked too tightly stretched across his cheekbones. But as he removed his glasses and shoved them into his pocket, everything about him spoke of resignation. "It happened a long time ago. He saw something that looked as though it could be something else. I explained things, and everything was fine. But hell, this thing with Faith has everyone doubting everyone. Look at us."

"I don't doubt you, Jared."

"Yet."

"You were upset with me when I found myself torn about keeping a confidence. If this is something like that—"

"You know it's not." He bowed his head, his hat brim momentarily hiding his face, and the only thing that indicated he wasn't as detached as he sounded was his white knuckles as he rested his hands on his hips. "Okay, here it is— Faith came over once."

Prepared for bad news, Michaele still experienced a moment of light-headedness. "I'm assuming you don't mean stopped by for advice on her driving skills or how to get along with me better?"

"She'd been drinking. It was about two years ago."

"And she came to you to turn herself in?" Michaele laughed, the sound brittle—as brittle as her heart was beginning to feel.

"Mike, sweetheart…this isn't necessary."

"Tell me."

He had reached for her and, at her flat response, had let his hands drop to his sides. "Fine, you're a glutton for punishment? She wanted me to take her to bed."

"Out of the clear blue, my sister comes here to make a pass?"

"Maybe she'd begun flirting a little more than she should have when we met around town, but I shrugged it off—it was her age and her testing herself. I didn't see it coming. And I told her that even if she hadn't been soused, I couldn't oblige her because of what I felt about you."

"Ah-ha. And she, not taking no for an answer, had her way with you?"

"She—it wasn't her best moment. She got upset, she got sick. I couldn't very well put her back in her vehicle, and I didn't want you to have to deal with her in that condition, so I made her take a shower and I ran her clothes through the wash. That's when Hancock showed up. He thought the white truck was you, and wanted you to know some books you'd ordered were in. That's when Faith came out of the bathroom in a towel. I'm sure it wasn't an accident.''

Maybe she would get sick, too. So that's why someone had written *Whore!* on the truck's windshield. Obviously Dillon wasn't the only one to have seen the truck there that day. Unless...

''Don't look at me like that. I swear that's all that happened.''

''And Dillon believed you...until Faith vanished.''

Jared grew pale. ''You can't think that *I*...?''

No, her mind rejected the idea. She believed he loved her; but she also believed he would do anything necessary to protect his place in her life. Including lie about what might only have been a moment of bad judgment between him and Faith.

''I need to think,'' she muttered, and started walking again.

Jared stopped her again. ''You can't just wander around town. Believe what you want about me, but there's still a murderer out there. Someone we probably both know.''

''Then drive me to the gas station. I'll start sanding the Cameo. I think better when I'm busy. Curtis is across the street—he can keep an eye on me.''

''You're too upset to work. Look, I won't touch you. Just come inside. I'll make us something to eat, and you can ask me anything, or go to bed and sleep on it. I'll sleep in the other bedroom or on the couch, whatever. Let's work this out.''

She wanted to; it amazed her how much. But her own insecurities refused to erase the image of Faith in the same shower where they'd made love; Faith pressing her naked body against his; Faith hating her so much that she wanted to destroy the dream Michaele hadn't allowed herself to reach for.

''I need some space.''

Once more she started to leave, and this time Jared wasn't as gentle as he drew her back. His expression was formidable. ''So help me, Mike, I'll carry you kicking and screaming to the house if necessary.''

She shook him off. ''You try that, and they'll be finding your teeth in El Paso.''

''And I'm telling you that I can't let you go.''

Just then, a gleaming sedan pulled to a stop at the end of the driveway. Michaele recognized Garth's Cadillac. Since he'd come from the north, she concluded that he'd been out of town himself.

The passenger window rolled down, and he leaned across the seat. ''Hey, you two. Everything okay?''

''Yes,'' Jared said.

''No,'' Michaele countered. She strode to the car. ''Can I have a lift?''

''Michaele!'' Jared warned.

''Sure,'' Garth said, even as she climbed in. His welcoming smile waned when he eyed Jared's stormy face. ''Uh, then again...did I just make a big mistake?''

To Michaele's surprise, Jared backed off.

''Take her to your place. She can't be alone, so don't let her leave and try to go to the garage. Is Jess home? I'll call her and explain myself.''

''Do you mind?'' Michaele ground out. ''I'll make my own decisions.''

''Do it, Garth. I appreciate it.''

Garth nodded and pulled away. ''Whew,'' he said, putting up Michaele's window. ''That's some lover's spat you two must be having.''

More dejected than she wanted to admit, Michaele slumped back in her seat. ''I'm sorry you got dragged into this, but I appreciate the lift. If you'll drop me off as I asked, you'll be rid of me.''

''My dear, you heard Jared. At the least he'd leave his fist imprint on my jaw if I let you go off by yourself. It's okay. Jess mentioned again that she thinks you need someone to take you under her wing and mother you a bit. I think she'd like having someone in the house again, like it was until Sandy moved out on her own. And don't underestimate yourself,'' he added with a wry laugh. ''You'll be as much a positive influence on Jess as she tries to be on you. It's not everyone who can stand up to her and retain her respect.''

Michaele doubted that, and she didn't want to think about having to deal with Jessica's willfulness. But she also knew that if she forced the issue and insisted on going to the station, Garth would only tell Jared, and then she would have him to deal with again. One night, she told herself. Surely after a little rest, by morning she would be thinking more clearly and know what to do.

''Okay, you win,'' she replied.

When he pulled into his driveway moments later, the garage door was lifting and Jessica stood there. She was as impeccably dressed as always, this time in a rose ensemble that only added warmth to her sympathetic smile.

''Jared called and told me everything,'' she said, opening her door for her. ''I think he made the sensible decision sending you to us. Don't worry, dear. This is the best place for you.''

55

8:00 p.m.

"Speaking as someone who gets into trouble the moment he opens a fuse box, I think it's marvelous that you're going to restore that truck. I'm impressed." His dinner plate clean, Garth leaned back in his chair and swirled the last swallow of deep red wine remaining in his glass. "No doubt you can turn a nice profit for something like that."

"I don't plan to sell it." Preferring the lesser of two evils, Michaele chose talking, since the little chicken Alfredo she'd managed to eat, while tasty, weighed like a tire iron in her stomach.

"You're kidding. How many vehicles do you plan to keep over there?"

"Mmm. Good point. I'm planning to sell the white Chevy and—" she moved her dessert spoon between two embroidered flowers on the linen tablecloth "—and once the police release the Firebird, I guess it would be best to sell it if..." Her voice trailed off.

"That was tactless, Mike. I'm sorry."

"No, it's easier when everyone's forthright. In fact, today one of Faith's old classmates who admitted she'd been jealous of her stopped by the station to ask if there was anything she could do. I thought that showed character. As for the search, Jared's people are already returning to their regular schedules because the budget can't carry any more overtime. They're doing what they can, but without any new leads, soon Faith will become another unsolved case.''

Jessica reached over and touched her arm. ''I hate that for you. It was the hardest thing for me to adjust to—the not knowing. You said earlier that Jared had meetings today with the state authorities?''

''Yes, but if something was disclosed or some agreement was reached, he didn't tell me. But it's understandable, I suppose, because they do seem to believe that Faith's abductor is local. So it stands to reason that the more people who know that, the more it compromises their investigation.''

Jessica lifted a hand to her throat. ''Local. That can't be right. What's Jared thinking?''

''It would be a coup for him to be right,'' Garth replied, frowning into his glass. ''Definitely would shut up those who want his resignation because of how he mishandled the school incident.''

Michaele had a compulsive urge to defend Jared, but she held her peace; after all, she didn't know if Jared's critics were right or wrong. ''I do know that Cade Weatherby is backing off his threat to press charges against Dillon,'' she said, hoping to change the subject.

Nodding, Jessica dabbed her linen napkin to her lips. ''That reminds me. I spoke to Lizbeth Weatherby today— Garth, you remember we're both executive board members of the Friends of the Library Council—and she said she's made progress in getting Cade to back off. She reasoned a trial would be more harmful to Willow's reputation, regardless of how much they despise Dillon Hancock. That's one shrewd lady. I'm putting my money on her getting Willow out of this ridiculous liaison and into a more suitable match.''

''Willow and Dillon seem devoted to each other,'' Michaele said.

Jessica's smile was more of a smirk as she began collecting the dishes. ''I'm sorry, but I have no sympathy for predatory males who prey on impressionable girls. On the other hand, any poor dumb thing who believes a man loves her, when his only intent is to get in her panties, deserves what she gets.''

Downing the last of his wine, Garth rose. ''Well, as enjoyable as this was, ladies, I have some work yet to do in my study.''

''But we haven't had dessert yet. I have fresh strawberries and cream.''

''I'd better pass. Maybe a cup of coffee later.''

As he left, Michaele began to rise, too, but Jessica motioned for her to sit.

''Keep eating, dear. You've barely touched your plate.''

''It's wonderful, but really I can't. If you'd wrap it, I'd love to take it for lunch tomorrow.''

''What was I thinking? You do look about ready to drop face first into that plate. Let me take you up to your room.''

''You don't have to do that. I can probably find my way if—''

''Nonsense. You don't know where anything is, and you need something to sleep in. Dear me, what about tomorrow's clothes? I have jeans, but you'd look as though you had three-pound ring weights around your ankles from rolling up the legs that many times.''

''I have a spare set at the garage to change into for

emergencies,'' Michaele said. ''But thanks for the thought.''

''Good. Then let's go up, and I'll find you a nightie or something.''

The Powers home was as gorgeous inside as it was impressive outside. Michaele had never been this close to such elegance and glamour; her self-consciousness kicked in for the umpteenth time as she walked on the plush creamy-white carpeting, even though she'd taken her sneakers off earlier.

The guest room was just an extension of that lushness, the rest of the decor a mix of salmon and white. The white rattan furnishings gave everything a romantic garden-like look. But although all traces of her personal belongings were gone, Michaele couldn't help but think how well this place had suited pretty, feminine Sandy. How was she supposed to sleep here? Her inadequacies alone would torment her, even if she could push aside her heartache over Jared.

''Now all the towels are freshly washed and so are the sheets. The air-conditioning on this side of the house keeps things a little chilly, and I've set out a comforter just in case you're cold-natured. You'll have to forgive me for indulging in the flowers in the bathroom. They're from the sunroom, but I thought you might likc thcm around if you choose a long soak in the tub. And those candles—they're gardenia- and vanilla-scented. Use them, darling, they'll do you good.''

At a loss for words, Michaele hugged herself. ''I feel like I won a trip to a spa. Everything's too pretty to touch.''

''Please,'' Jessica intoned. ''Touch. Use.'' Then she snapped her fingers. ''Gown. One second.''

She left, only to return a moment later with a satin robe

and gown that looked like something from one of those glamorous forties movies Faith loved to watch.

"Th-that's too much," Michaele said, as Jessica set the sexy concoctions on the bed. "Believe me, an old T-shirt or something would suit me fine."

"Dear heart, I don't beat this poor body into shape just so I can hide it in massive lengths of bland cotton." But she chuckled softly and hugged Michaele. "Indulge yourself for once, you deserve it. I want you to feel comfortable here and comfortable with me. Losing my little sister the way I did…I know how you're holding yourself together, trying not to feel too much, to think too much. I found it helps to go ahead and feel, but good things. Fine things." Smiling down at the satin, she stroked it lovingly. "It makes the rest bearable."

They were kind words, and yet Michaele shivered. "Boy, that air-conditioning works, doesn't it?"

"You'll be cozy under the comforter." With a last, satisfied glance around the room, Jessica retreated to the door, where she tapped the combination wall intercom and radio. "If you need anything, don't hesitate to buzz me."

"I'm sure I'll be fine. Better than fine. Thanks for everything, Jessica."

"Sleep well. And don't brood about Jared. Whatever that flare-up was between you—no, I'm not prying—it will work itself out."

"Maybe we weren't meant to be in the first place," Michaele said quietly.

"How strange. That's what Sandy said before—" Jessica shook her head. "No, I'm not going to go there. You dream pleasant dreams."

The door closed. Michaele, however, remained standing there, stunned.

You're exhausted, overwhelmed. You misunderstood.

But she knew she hadn't. So what had Jessica meant about Sandy, and things not working out?

56

Thursday, May 21
7:07 a.m.

"**H**ave a good day," Michaele said, handing the credit card receipt to the stranger who'd stopped for a fuel refill. The man in the crisp white dress shirt and conservative tie smiled and pulled away. A banker or a financial consultant, she decided, and returned to the store to deposit the receipt in the cash register.

She often played that game with customers who were passing through, wondering where they were from and what they did for a living. The guy in the gray Chrysler was definitely about profit margins and low-risk-high-yields; not her type at all, even if he did look rather like Harrison Ford. She was off men again, anyway. They were bad for sleep patterns.

The phone began ringing. Stifling another yawn, Michaele grabbed the receiver.

"Ramey's Garage."

"Mornin', hon'," Norma sang. "You've got a wrecker call. Accident on west Main, right at the city limits. One of our seniors backed out of his driveway without looking and into the path of a semi."

It never ended, Michaele thought, wincing at the image that flashed before her mind's eye. ''Injuries?''

''He's banged up and fairly rattled from what I hear. EMS's ETA is as we speak. By the way, it's Walter Platt.''

''Used to run a vegetable and plant stand. Grew the best tomatoes in East Texas. Shoot. Sorry to hear that. He's a sweetheart. Okay, he drives the Ford pickup, right? I'm on my way.''

That wasn't quite accurate, however. This being her first wrecker call since collecting Faith's vehicle, her first after Buck's death, she was immediately given an abrupt reminder that she definitely operated the business on her own now. That meant extra work as she ran to close the overhead doors, lock up the back, and then lock the store door because no one else was there to watch the place. It was almost five minutes before she pulled the wrecker onto Main and headed west, partly because she'd backtracked, having forgotten to put up a hastily scrawled Wrecker Run—Back in 30 Minutes sign.

She was going to have to think about hiring help. Like wills, bills and everything else coming belatedly to mind these days, this was the tedious, debilitating side of death.

Nevertheless, it wasn't as jarring as the moment she saw, not one, but two police units up ahead, particularly the one marked Chief on the door.

As she saw Jared come around the front of the semi with the truck driver and hand him back his clipboard of registrations and certificates, her heart had a hard encounter with her ribs. She'd seen Jared leaving the station earlier, but at the time she'd merely been relieved to know that at least for a little while she had a break from being watched from his corner office window. It hadn't occurred to her that he would be here; he usually left all but the worst traffic accidents to his men. Then again, he was awfully attentive to the seniors.

It was Jim, though, who acted as intermediary between Walter and the EMS technicians. From the look of things, old Walter wasn't wild about getting in any ambulance. What had Michaele's pulse kicking into overdrive, though, was how that left Jared free. And he was already headed her way.

Sucking in a deep breath, she jumped down from the cab, then tugged her gloves from her back pocket and began pulling them on to have something to do with her hands. The damn things literally itched to reach for him.

"Hi," he said gruffly.

"Morning." She nodded to the pickup with the crushed rear end. "Looks like he's lucky he wasn't going any faster."

"Yeah. You okay?"

"Sure. It took me longer to get here because I had to batten down the hatches, so to speak."

"You know that's not what I meant." Jared exhaled, the sound as shaky as a barn in high wind. "I missed you last night."

No, he wasn't going to cut her any slack whatsoever. "Don't start."

"It's amazing how fast my body got into the habit of having yours to sleep against."

She knew exactly what he meant. Despite enjoying the luxurious bath Jessica had recommended, lying in Sandy's bed, wearing that unbelievable gown that made her look like a stranger to herself, she'd tossed and turned for hours. When she finally did sleep, it was to dream of him.... He'd come into the room as she stood admiring herself in the mirror. Coming up behind her, he'd begun touching her, caressing her breasts, between her legs, everywhere. Then, sliding the spaghetti straps off her shoulders, he'd kissed his way down her body. Just as she'd been about to climax, he'd whispered her name, *"Sandy...Sandy..."* And suddenly there'd been blood everywhere.

That's when she'd wakened, her mouth open to scream. More upsetting, she'd been so wet that she'd thought she'd begun her period. But, of course, she hadn't because that was still a couple of weeks away. Maybe. If she was lucky.

Unable to stop herself, Michaele met his gaze. It was a mistake, because he looked every bit as heartsick as she felt.

"We can't do this," she murmured. "People are going to start noticing in a minute."

"Let them. All I care about is making it right between us."

"Then give me the time I asked for—and the space."

"So you can put up more walls? Get more wrong ideas? How brilliant is that? We need to talk things out."

"What I need to do is to get that poor man's car towed and get back to the garage. I'm sorry." Turning coward, she lowered her gaze to his badge. "But you're asking for more than I can give you right now."

"I know, but I'm asking anyway. *Michaele.* Baby, I'm dying here."

Her throat aching, she met his gaze again and saw he spoke the truth. Her own vision blurred. "Do you think I'm not? Do you think I want to feel this much confusion and pain?"

"Okay." He cupped her cheek with his hand, a move as soothing as it was spontaneous. "Okay." He swallowed hard, his Adam's apple rising and falling with noticeable difficulty. "I'll hang on to that, and to what I see in your eyes."

He backed off then, but she was intensely aware of

him watching her every movement, until they all headed back to town.

It was a relief to close the garage and head back to the Powers's. She wished she were going elsewhere—but Garth was already there, which was a relief, and their warm welcome made her feel a little less of an outsider than she had felt last night.

"Hey, blue eyes." Pausing as he poured Jessica and himself a glass of wine, Garth winked at her. "How did the day go?"

Michaele toed off her shoes by the garage door, ever conscious of Jessica's immaculate housekeeping. "Okay. Glad it's over, though."

"I bet you are." Jessica was preparing a Caesar salad. "Not only did Michaele have to deal with handling the business all by herself," she told her husband, "but there was an accident on the edge of town she had to respond to, as well."

"Don't tell me you're taking up calling to check on her?" Garth asked, amused.

"She thoughtfully brought me a sandwich for lunch on her way to Tyler," Michaele replied. "It was great, Jessica. I really appreciated it."

Garth shook his head as he handed his wife her wine. "Uh-huh. It's as I said, you're already mothering her. Be careful, Mike. Before you know it, she'll try to talk you into putting up ruffled curtains at the garage."

"Stop, you're making me sound hideous," Jessica said. "I am not that bad." She shot Michaele a sly sidelong look. "But I may kidnap her one day and treat her for a makeover in—oh, Lord, I can't believe I used that word. Forgive me, dear."

"It's all right." Actually, she would have been happier

if Jessica hadn't brought attention to the verbal misstep. Sensitivity was one thing; political correctness cheapened compassion.

She must have looked uncomfortable, because Garth came over and placed a gentle hand at the base of her neck. "I know what you said yesterday, but are you sure I can't pour you a glass? You look as though you could use something stronger than water."

"I'm fine, thanks."

"Our friend Jared didn't give you a hard time, did he? He sure looked intense yesterday."

As he spoke, he continued to caress her neck with his thumb, and even Jessica had begun to notice. Uncomfortable with the intimacy because it was also a poignant reminder of how Jared had quickly gotten into the habit of using every excuse to touch her, she stepped over to observe Jessica's progress. "What smells so good?"

"A new veal recipe I've been wanting to try." Jessica beamed brightly at her. "He's right about having you around. It is inspiring me. And I have this marvelous butcher in Tyler who is absolutely divine about getting me anything I want—and he's trustworthy. I particularly like using him when I'm serving beef I need to prepare very rare. You can't be too careful these days. But let's face it, a prime rib isn't a prime rib if the blood isn't flow—"

A sudden crash made them both jump. To Michaele's amazement, Garth stood pale-faced amid a disastrous scene. His suit pants were splattered with wine, and green glass and wine were everywhere.

"Good heavens, darling. Are you all right? What happened?" Stepping gingerly over glass and around the liquid, Jessica took what was left of the bottle out of his hand.

"I don't...know. Sorry, Jess. I meant to set the thing

on the counter and slammed into it, instead. Thank goodness, it wasn't one of your grandparents' glasses.''

''It's not a vintage bottle of wine, either, so don't worry about it. You know, this is proof positive that you need a vacation. Just the two of us. Someplace far enough away to get your mind off Split Creek and your various headaches. Michaele, no, dear, let Garth get that with a broom and dustpan. You might cut yourself. Why don't you go wash up? Dinner will be ready as soon as I finish mixing the dressing.''

Michaele went, and gladly, but the strange vibrations going on in that kitchen stayed with her. No doubt she was letting her imagination get the best of her, she told herself; it had been a simple accident. Surely Garth Powers was allowed to be a klutz once in a while; and the fact that the anniversary of Sandy's death was only days ago probably explained Jessica's behavior, as well.

By the time she returned downstairs, the kitchen was immaculate again and a new bottle of wine had been opened. Listening to Jessica's girlish laughter, Michaele mused that she could have stepped into a scene from *The Stepford Wives*.

They sat down to dinner at the patio table, and that Michaele appreciated. She'd already told Jessica that the back garden was like a postcard photo—perfect blooms, manicured lawns, a fountain in the center providing a soothing background to the cheerful trilling of songbirds. It was as different from her backyard as Jessica's grated fresh Parmesan was to the stuff Buck had insisted she buy in plastic for his spaghetti.

''What's that sad sigh for?'' Jessica asked.

''I was remembering the birdbath I—it's nothing.''

Jessica studied her for a moment longer. ''Poor Michaele. You need a break, too.''

"Well, I'm afraid there's not going to be much time for that."

"No, I don't mean a vacation. I meant a total break from your past. Have you considered moving?"

Even Garth put down his salad fork. "Darling, think what you're saying. Michaele's family has lived here as long as your people."

"You misunderstand me. I'm not being insensitive. It's because I care that I'm telling her what I think." She leaned closer to Michaele. "Sometimes fate uses strange ways to give us another chance. It just struck me that maybe it's offering you one. Think about it. There's nothing to keep you here, now."

"There's Faith."

And Jared.

Jessica blinked once and then went back to her own salad. "You're a noble girl. I admire that about you, too…and worry. Noble people often get hurt."

She thinks Faith's dead.

Jarred, Michaele remained silent, focusing on her plate to avoid seeing the pity in Jessica's eyes. It was the same pity that she was seeing more and more often in other people's faces around town. That, and a subtle frustration. They wanted this over so they could get on with their lives, even if closure meant dealing with another corpse. By holding on to her hope for Faith, and whatever screwy, unorthodox faith she possessed, she wasn't allowing them that.

"You're wrong," she said at last. "I tried to be at first, but I'm not noble at all. I'm finding I'm actually a coward, because if that phone call comes bringing the news that a body has been found, I'm not sure I won't snap. You see, it wouldn't leave me anything to believe in anymore."

Especially if she'd been wrong about Jared, too.

Jessica covered her hand with her own. "Look at me, Michaele. I'm proof you can survive the worst nightmare." Patting Michaele's hand, she smiled brightly. "Enough of this maudlin talk. Let me tell you about the new restaurant they're about to open in Tyler."

A born hostess, Jessica was as good as her word. She kept conversation lighthearted after that, moving on to tell anecdotes about Garth's and her early married days, and then some about Garth's students. The opportunity to sit back and relax was as welcome as the food was delicious, and Michaele actually cleaned her plate for the first time in over a week. She liked seeing this lighter, less deliberate side of Jessica. Encouraged by it, Michaele approached her after dinner with a special request.

"I was wondering if you don't have anything else scheduled, would you do me a favor and come to the house with me? I'm not supposed to go there by myself, and to be honest, I don't want to. But I need to get some clothes. I could pick up what I have at Jared's, but…"

"You don't have to explain. Of course, I'll come with you. Let me tell Garth so he won't worry."

Ten minutes later they were in Jessica's car, following the tangerine-and-lavender sunset. It had been amusing to see her take one look at the white pickup and suggest her car would be more comfortable.

"I really appreciate all your help," Michaele said, as they stopped at the corner of Cedar and Dogwood.

Jessica checked for traffic and made the left turn. "It's my pleasure. You know, there's something else we need to consider, too. We have to empty the refrigerator at your house fairly soon. Not only for obvious reasons, but because there are dishes that need to be returned."

Michaele clapped her hand to her forehead. "I can't believe I let myself forget that."

"You have a lot on your mind. Don't beat yourself up about it. We can tackle it in the evenings. Well, not tomorrow evening, because Garth and I have another of those must-do school dinners, and Saturday we're committed, too, although I'd love to get out of attending that senior's picnic if I can. It's going to be so hot and humid. But you're closed Sunday, right?"

"Yes. Whenever is fine with me. I'll work around your schedule. Heaven knows, I can't recall what belongs to whom." Feeling more and more comfortable with the older woman, she shot Jess a curious glance. "Would you mind if I asked you something personal?"

"Uh-oh. It's not about my weight, is it?"

Michaele smiled. "No. In fact, it may be too painful, so feel free to tell me if that's the case. But last night you said something that...well, that's been troubling me."

"You should have said something sooner. I wouldn't dream—"

"Please, don't apologize. It's just that you began to say something about Sandy, about her feelings. Would it be asking too much for you to finish the thought?"

Jessica drove in silence for several seconds, her expression enigmatic, made more so by her sunglasses. Finally, she said, "I'd hoped you would overlook that slip of the tongue."

"I understand. Forget I asked."

"No, what I mean is...Michaele, to be honest, I don't know the complete story—only what Sandy told me before she died. How strange you should bring this up, though. It's exactly why I said what I did to you earlier. I was remembering that Sandy wanted to leave Split Creek. I wish she had. Then my lovely sister would still be alive."

"But how could she have left?" Michaele asked, incredulous. "She was getting married. Jared's work was here."

Jessica bit at her perfectly painted lips.

"Wasn't she?" Michaele whispered.

With a sigh, Jessica turned onto Cypress. "This has haunted me for years. Michaele...Sandy broke her engagement to Jared the night she died."

It couldn't be. "She loved him."

"Yes, exactly. She loved him. Just as I have to believe he loved her, in his own fashion." As she pulled into the Ramey driveway, Jessica shook her head firmly. "This isn't right. You're beginning your own relationship. What's done is done. Besides, it's what you two share together that counts. He suffered so when we lost her. Even if what she'd confided in me was true, that would have changed him, I'm positive. He's not the same man anymore."

"I'm not sure I understand," Michaele replied. She tried not to think about Faith, and both Dillon and Jared's version of the story, but it was hard not to under the circumstances.

Jessica shut off the car's engine. With studious care, she slipped off her glasses and met Michaele's anxious gaze. "She believed he was having an affair."

57

It was later than Jared expected when he got out of court. The circuit judge, about to leave on vacation, had pressed the DA and defense attorneys to complete their presentation on the child molestation case on which he'd had to testify. The jury had gone in to deliberate when he left the courthouse, but from the looks on their faces, he didn't believe they would be in there long. The slimeball who'd treated his six-year-old stepdaughter like an appendage of his wife was headed for Huntsville, where the inmates would deliver their own brand of justice. Convicts had their own code, and they didn't tolerate child molesters; there were many in law enforcement who were grateful for that.

A day of waiting for the legal gears to grind was taxing at any time; but this one was tacked on to what was proving to be yet another brutal week. He was so emotionally drained that he chose not to stop by the station, but radioed Curtis to let him know he needed to go home for a while. That's why he wasn't sure he should believe his eyes when he pulled into the driveway and saw Michaele's truck there.

NASA didn't have anything to match the internal lift he experienced. He couldn't get inside fast enough.

"Mike!" He burst through the door. "Sweetheart?"

He froze when he spotted her coming out of the bedroom—not to run into his arms, but carrying her clothes. She stopped mid-stride, too.

"Buddy said you were in court." She looked as guilty as a burglar caught in the act.

"I'm done. Never mind that. What's this?" He nodded to her armload.

"I'd hoped to have everything out of here before you got back. I...I was going to leave the key you gave me on the counter."

He believed in the theory that what went up had to come down; he hadn't guessed it could be this kind of torturous, taunting descent, giving him plenty of time to think about how bad the pain was going to be once he crashed. Jared refused to accept that this was his fate.

"You said you just needed some time. I was trying to give you time."

"That was before," she replied.

"Before what?"

He saw her glance toward the door. More than her embarrassment, he disliked the fear in her eyes.

"What the hell's going on, Michaele?"

"Jessica and Garth are waiting for me. I should go."

Good Lord, she was afraid of him. Through the disbelief came the sharp stab of hurt. "What have I done to deserve this? You can't even be honest with me and tell me what's happening?"

"You're the one who hasn't been honest."

"Bull. When?"

She shook her head and started for the door again. "I can't do this."

He blocked her path. Before she could recover, he jerked the clothes from her arms and tossed them on the counter. Then he took hold of her upper arms.

"Jared, you're frightening me."

"And you're scaring the shit out of me. Now tell me what I've supposedly been dishonest about? Is it Faith again? There's nothing else to tell. Nothing happened except in her own childish imagination."

"Is that what you told Sandy, too?"

Whatever new accusation he was expecting, it wasn't that. He'd buried his true feelings about that relationship so deep that he had to release Michaele so she wouldn't feel him quake as a fault line exposed the grave. And still his instinct was to hold on to the considerate story he'd allowed to be built.

"This is nuts. Your sister was still wearing braces when I was with Sandy."

"I'm not talking about Faith. I'm talking about your engagement. About the lies."

He supposed he looked uneasy, but like a child playing with the TV remote control, she was poking at things she didn't understand. The longer he remained silent, the harder she pressed her hands to her stomach.

"My God, it is true. I see it on your face. You were cheating on her."

What the hell...?

"Who have you been talking to?" he demanded. "Jessica? It's her, isn't it?"

"What difference does it make? The point is that the reason they never found Sandy's engagement ring isn't because her killer took it from her. She'd given it back to you!"

"Wrong!" he roared back. He might have willingly protected the past, but he wasn't going to lose his future for it. ''Yes, she talked of breaking things off that night, but not because of anything I had done. *She* was the one who was suddenly nervous and full of doubt. She was the one who wasn't sure who or what she wanted. It was Sandy, Michaele, not me!''

No doubt she'd expected a confession, maybe a denial; the counter-accusation obviously threw her. ''Why would Jessica lie to me?''

''You'll have to ask her that.''

''I'm asking you.''

''I have a better idea—check the house.''

''What? Why?''

''You know. Find it.'' He dragged her to the nearest kitchen drawer and pulled so hard it crashed to the floor. ''Look! Is it there? Wait, how about here?'' He yanked out another, then another. ''Where's the ring, Michaele? Huh? Where's the goddamn ring?''

Finally succeeding in freeing herself, Michaele backed away from him, rubbing her wrist.

He hated knowing he'd probably bruised her; however, the pain of knowing she didn't trust him was eating at him more. ''Thanks for the benefit of the doubt.''

''What did you give me to believe in?'' she cried. ''You're the one who refused to talk about her. She lives on some unapproachable pedestal, as if you felt so guilty about what happened, the only way to make it up to her was to practically beatify her.''

''Yeah, I feel guilty. But not because of anything you're claiming. The question is, can you handle the truth?''

''I asked, didn't I?''

''You asked because you're afraid of what would happen if I stopped talking.''

Although she momentarily closed her eyes, she had the

guts to stay put. ''So maybe I'm not sure I want to know—but I have to hear it. Tell me.''

Jared took a step closer, then another. On the third, her body betrayed her with a slight nervous twitch, but to her credit she didn't make a break for the door. Knowing he had nothing to lose, that he would probably never get this close to her again, he reached out to stroke her cheek, to rub his thumb against her lips…and remembered.

''I live with guilt for all the reasons you imagine, especially for never finding the sick bastard who stole her life just when she had taken her first steps to live with that honesty you and I have been talking so much about. I live with guilt because I should never have given her the ring in the first place,'' he said at last. ''I should have given it to you.''

That was the best of the truth, the only part that should matter to her. The pitiful thing was, not only hadn't it set him free, not only didn't Michaele look thrilled by the admission, but she didn't appear to believe him.

He dropped his hand to his side. His brief laugh was pure self-mockery. ''You don't get it, do you?''

''No.''

''It's been you all along. The day I came to Split Creek and I stopped at the garage to fill up my truck, remember? I was concentrating on reaching for my wallet, expecting to see some guy at my window asking me if I wanted him to check under the hood. Instead, I find a little slip of a thing with eyes that made me glad I was sitting down, because it was over right then and there.''

''You barely looked at me.''

''Not when you could catch me.''

''You called me 'Junior.'''

''Self-defense.''

"And for ages after that, you were usually preoccupied when you came by."

"You've got that right. You scared me to death."

"Right. I was so captivating, it only took you—what?— more than a year after Sandy died before you asked me out."

"At which point you were still barely dry behind the ears and I was pushing thirty fast. Think about it, Michaele. You were how old when we first met? Sixteen. *Sixteen.* I'm not Dillon Hancock, taking what I want just because it's new and untouched. I saw what hell you were in with your family, what dreams you had, if you could ever get out from under your responsibilities. I did the right thing and kept my paws off you."

"Maybe what Dillon did was wrong, but if this is true—"

"It is true."

"Then he was a lot more honest than you were. What about Sandy, Jared? What about her feelings?"

He bowed his head. "You're wrong if you think I didn't care about her. I did. What was there not to like? She was sweet, kind, supportive. In any case, toward the end, as much as we tried, I knew we lacked something. The same something that you and I know is between us.

"Sandy knew, too," he continued. "What I didn't realize until too late was that her reluctance to set a date was her way of trying to tell me she had found it with someone else." *And please God, let that be enough.*

"Did she tell you who it was?" she asked, clearly embarrassed by her curiosity.

"No. That was beside the point. What struck me was how relieved I was to have things out in the open, to be able to admit that in the end, neither of us loved each other as much as we should have. You want to judge me,

Michaele, do it for that. For almost going into the kind of marriage that seventy, almost eighty percent of people have. Convenient. Complacent. A lie.''

She didn't know what to say. He could see it as she tried to take in his words and weigh them against the crap that Jessica had fed her. And truth always weighed more, even when you didn't dump it all on the scale.

For a small eternity after that, Michaele just stood there. She didn't know what to do, or say—he understood that. Most people could shrug off something like this and say, ''So what?'' The ones who lived shallow lives, lives of denial, lives with minimal feeling and inconvenience. Michaele was too sensitive for that. Life had sharpened her to a diamond point.

Her slow exhale was like a last breath. ''You'll want me to go.''

''Who said?'' he asked, as she stepped around him.

As intended, the question stopped her. She waited, and when he remained silent, she whispered, ''What do you want?''

''What I've always wanted.''

A little color returned to her cheeks, but her eyes remained dark with inner turmoil. ''I can't help but wish you had told me this sooner.''

''When, Mike? Out of the clear blue before Faith was missing? You were working too hard at keeping me at arm's length to have any kind of dialogue, let alone this one. The morning after we made love for the first time? Buck died. You're doing well to function on any level at all right now. In fact, I should be kicked in the ass for having given in and taken advantage when you were at your most vulnerable.''

''Let yourself off the hook for that one, Morgan. I seem to remember, I'm the one who did the seducing.''

''You didn't have to work hard to convince me, did you? I wanted you any way I could get you, and the more danger I sensed you were in, the more determined I was to keep you close. And this is the price—doubt, fear, other people who only know their half of a story influencing you.''

Michaele started to press her fingers to his lips, only to see how stained they were from work, She backed off.

Jared caught her hand and kissed her fingertips. ''Tell me.''

''The worst was fearing this—what we've shared— wasn't real.''

''It is.'' He drew her into his arms. ''It is.''

He said it again as he spread kisses over her face, and again before locking his mouth to hers. Everything else he'd felt and hadn't been able to say went into that kiss, and soon she was clinging to him, and they were both shaking from the knowledge of how close they'd come to blowing it.

Lifting her into his arms, he carried her to the bedroom. Along the way, he heard her shoes drop to the floor. But as he laid her across the unmade bed, she made a brief sound of protest.

''My clothes are dirty. They'll ruin the sheets.''

''I don't care.''

Need was driving him. The urgency to make her his once again. She fueled it by attacking the fastenings on his clothes as fast as he was working on hers. He'd just gotten her jeans off, when she released him from his and closed her small fingers around him.

Abandoning any hope of them both getting naked in time, he thrust himself against her hand. ''Ah, Mike…I want you so much.''

Although his conscience reproached him for being too

far ahead of her, when he slipped his fingers inside her to make sure he wouldn't hurt her, he was relieved and grateful to find she wasn't as far behind as he'd feared.

"It's all right. Hurry," she whispered.

When he drove into her, she gasped, but not from pain. Pleasure was a blue flame in her eyes that reached straight to his soul. Pressing his mouth against the side of her neck, he raced them both to release.

It would have suited him to spend the rest of the night that way. But once their heartbeats began to calm, she moaned with regret.

"You should have let me shower first. I'm a mess."

"After spending all day in that musty old courthouse, you think I'm any better?" But his gaze adored her as he lifted himself to his forearms to let the air-conditioned air dry their damp bodies. "Tell you what, though—if you promise to wash my back, I'll let you have half the shower."

"Barely a third, you mean."

He rubbed his nose against hers. "Be really nice to me, and I'll show you how you can be happy with a quarter."

Her laughter could only be described as delighted.

"God, sweetheart…that's the most beautiful sound I've heard in a long, long time."

Her smile growing wobbly, she stroked his chest. "Shower, Morgan, before you turn me into a crybaby."

He eased to her side, allowing her to get up. "I'll be right in. Just let me lock up."

But he did more than that. He picked up the kitchen phone.

When he heard the confident greeting, he replied, "It's Jared, Jessica. Michaele's with me, and this time she's staying."

Then he hung up because it was all he dared let himself say. The rest would have to wait until his first instinct was no longer to wring her neck.

58

Saturday, May 23
3:00 p.m.

When Michaele closed the station on Saturday afternoon, Jared made sure he was there. He wanted to know her plans.

"I know you don't want me over there by myself, but I have to get to the house and empty the refrigerator. I called Jessica this morning—" she rolled her eyes at his frown "—yes, I know you phoned her last night to let her know where I was. But I'm the one they took into their home, and while I agree that she was wrong to say what she did, I don't want any bad blood between us. Besides, she'd reminded me yesterday that I still have some dishes that aren't mine, and she's the only one who knows what's what."

"So she's coming over?"

"Yeah, she said she'd changed her mind about going with Garth to the senior's picnic. She should join me at the house in less than a half-hour. Jared, she's bringing me my things, too."

Not before he set Mrs. Garth Powers straight on a few things, Jared thought. "Promise me you'll lock the door as soon as you get in there?"

She rose on tiptoe and kissed him. "Maybe I should have given Jessica a password, or should I ID her before I let her in?"

He knew she wasn't really taking this lightly and was only trying to tease him out of his grim mood, and he tried to appease her. "Smart-ass. You call that a kiss?"

He loved the way her face gentled. If he'd known confessing how bad a case he'd been carrying for her would have this effect, he might have pulled a Hancock, after all. Then she was wrapping her arms around his neck, and he abandoned the "could haves" and "should haves" entirely. Scooping her against him, he sated a little of the hunger that had been building since he'd seen her this morning. It soon won him a delicious whimper from her, and she wrapped her legs around his waist.

When he finally yielded to common sense and set her back on her feet, her hat was on the floor, her face was flushed, and he was regretting having suggested what he had for tonight.

As though reading his mind, she said, "Let's not go to that restaurant on the lake. I'd settle for peanut butter on crackers if it means we get to be alone."

He owed her much more, a real courtship. Hell, they hadn't had so much as a first date yet. But heaven forgive him, he wanted to be alone with her, too.

"Deal. But I don't want mine on crackers."

"What are you—an all-American white-bread boy?"

"You have an imagination, use it." Kissing the tip of her nose, he forced himself to leave.

His smile vanished the minute he climbed into his patrol car and headed down Main. Last night, as Michaele had slept in his arms, he'd replayed their conversation over and over in his mind. The results were always the same: something wasn't right.

He'd always accepted and admired that Jessica was a strong woman; hell, one of the things that turned him on about Mike was that as adorable as she was, she could be tougher than some guys. But this crap Jess had pulled…it didn't make sense. He wanted to know why she'd done it, and make sure she never tried anything like that again.

As he hoped, there were no guest vehicles in the driveway, and Garth was apparently still over at the picnic. Since the garage was open, no doubt in expectation of Garth's arrival, Jared went through that way and knocked on the inner door.

"Unlocked," she called from inside.

It was as he'd thought. She'd lost a sister, yet she still lived life as though nothing could touch her. All that mattered was making things easy for Garth.

She leaned back from the kitchen counter as he entered. Seeing him, her eyebrows lifted, but her expression didn't change much.

"Have a minute?" he asked.

"I thought you weren't talking to me."

She vanished from his view, and he walked down the short hall to join her in the kitchen. She stood by the sink, stuffing vegetable peelings into the garbage disposal. That explained the motor he'd heard upon entering.

As soon as the grinding stopped, she drawled, "Come to pick up your little girl's things?"

"I thought you were bringing them to her in a few minutes?"

Smiling, Jess wagged a long-bladed knife at him. "She is the right one for you, isn't she? Tells her man everything."

"Yeah. Why do you have a problem with that?"

"Me? If you recall, I'm the one who took the poor thing under my wing. At your request, might I add."

"Only to try to turn her against me."

Her movements as calm as her expression, Jessica scooped the chopped vegetables into a glass bowl. "If Michaele did indeed tell you everything, she must have told you how fond Garth and I are of you. But her conflict with you, whatever it was, made her sensitive to my concern that my sister was having her own doubts about marrying you."

"You're twisting reality and you know it, but that's beside the point. Nobody knew the truth of our last conversation together—except maybe the guy she was screwing on the side."

Jessica stiffened. The jarring effect made her gold hoop earrings tremble slightly. "Do you mind. We are, after all, talking about my sister."

"She was also my fiancée. I think I have the right, just as I have cause to be offended when you suggest to Michaele that I was the one messing around on Sandy. What the hell are you doing, Jess?"

"Protecting my sister's reputation."

"I've been doing that for years. Apparently, you knew that all along, so why cause trouble now?"

Jessica looked up from the chopping block and gazed straight ahead for a moment. "Circumstances change. One has to remain flexible." She glanced over at him. "In effect, she did suggest you two call it off. That much is true, isn't it?"

"Because of her behavior, not mine. Also, unlike your version of the story, I didn't take the ring back that night. What did I want with the damn thing? Whoever murdered her must have stolen it. But what do you plant in Michaele's head? That I took it. Maybe even that I killed her."

"You're getting melodramatic, Jared."

He watched her take a sip of wine. Her hand wasn't quite steady. "So what did Sandy do that night, Jess? Call you after I left?"

"That's right."

"And she didn't tell you that I suggested she sleep on it before she made any major decisions about what she wanted to do?"

"I must say, Jared, I don't know why she blew a good thing. You're incredibly understanding for being the injured party."

"Only because a part of me was relieved. You see, I knew what it was like to be torn myself."

"Ah. Yes, I've long noticed how you look at our little Michaele. I understand that kind of passion. We have that in common, you and I."

"Is that why you tried to destroy what Mike and I have? Because you think I owed it to Sandy?"

Pursing her lips, Jessica took out a long platter bearing a thick salmon fillet. The color perfectly matched her jogging outfit. "It certainly would have made my life easier. Yes, you did let me down there."

What the hell does that mean? "Exactly what are these circumstances you referred to?"

Jessica frowned slightly. "It needn't concern you."

"I think it does, because you know what, Jess? I see reckless behavior here, and I want to know why. You can start by telling me how you found out about me and Sandy."

"I told you, she called me."

"No, she didn't. We tested the redial feature on her phone, and the last number she called was mine."

"Well, maybe I called her—what difference does it make?"

"None." Jared watched her slice the fillet into four portions. "I'm just fascinated with how, despite your effort to make me look like the bad guy, you didn't tell Sandy's biggest secret. Why not, Jess? Why didn't you tell Michaele that Sandy was pregnant?"

"Oh!" She dropped the knife onto the cutting board and grabbed her hand. But instead of running to the sink and washing away the rush of blood, she stood there and stared at him.

"How bad is it?" Jared came around the counter. "It's a bleeder, but it doesn't look too deep. Take this paper towel and—"

His error was in concentrating on her wound. He didn't see the knife until it was too late.

Jessica stabbed him with all her might, driving the blade into his chest up to the hilt. The pain stole his breath and drove him to his knees. At the second blow, he crumpled to the floor.

God help me. I was wrong...so wrong.

"She was not carrying his child," Jessica seethed. "He's mine. Mine! *You* should have claimed the little bastard as your own. Lots of men do. But not you, no, you were too selfish."

Jared struggled to get at his gun, but he was leaning hard against the cabinets and his strength was seeping out of him as fast as the blood was soaking his shirt. He couldn't accept this, though. Michaele was out there, innocent, waiting for Jessica... The horror gave him the will to fight.

Just when he had managed to work his weapon free, Jessica kicked at it and him with her thick-soled jogging shoes. The gun went flying, and his head crashed back into the cabinet.

Michaele.

Jared slumped to the tile floor, unconscious.

59

Michaele shivered. Jared was right, she thought. She shouldn't be here by herself. The place had too many bad memories. She wished Jessica would hurry up and get here; she was already ten minutes late.

"Stay busy," she told herself. It helped keep her mind off the fact that she was alone. Most of all, though, the sooner she finished here, the sooner she could get to Jared.

As Jessica had warned, the bulk of the food left over from the reception was past saving. She had begun feeding the stuff into the garbage disposal before washing the dishes in the twin sink, and was on her third bowl, when she heard a car outside.

"All right," she murmured, relieved. Rising on tiptoe to look out the window, she saw Jessica's car. She set the emptied bowl into the dish drainer, grabbed a towel, and, wiping her hands, went to open the door.

"Hi! Come on in. I was beginning to worry that you'd changed your mind."

"No, merely held up a bit, that's all."

Michaele shut and locked the door behind her. "Uh-oh. Did I interfere with your plans after all, Jessica? Really, I can handle this myself if necessary. If you'll just let me jot down who to bring everything back to..."

"You're sweet, but that won't be necessary."

Jessica put her tote bag on the counter. That's when Michaele saw that she was wearing a thin rubber glove. The inside of the left index finger was bloody. Belatedly, she saw the blood on the woman's coral pink sweat suit. She'd been hiding it by carrying the tote against her chest.

"What have you done to yourself? Let me help. How bad is it?" Michaele reached for her hand to inspect it. "With that much blood, we'd better get you to the hospital. It looks like you need stitches."

"It can wait." Using her right hand, Jessica reached into her pocket and drew out a ring. "Put this on, would you?"

A simple diamond solitaire engagement ring. Michaele looked from it to Jessica's expressionless face, and a sickly knowledge left her legs weak.

"What is this?"

"I'm sorry, dear."

How could she be so calm? Understanding only that she needed to buy herself time, Michaele replied, "For what? Whose ring is it?"

"Please, Michaele. Playing dumb doesn't become you."

"But I honestly don't understand." She took a step backward. "If this is Sandy's ring, why did you tell me what you did yesterday?"

"Because I was trying to save you. You understand that, don't you? I really was. If only you'd broken off with Jared and left town, this wouldn't have to be. But you let Jared win you over again. He doesn't deserve you. He still has secrets, secrets even I wasn't sure he new."

As calmly as she spoke, Jessica drew out a knife from the tote.

Michaele's mouth dropped open. It was wrapped in plastic wrap, the blade already bloody, and she could only wonder, *Whose blood?*

"Put the ring on, Michaele. I don't have a great deal of time."

''No.'' Michaele backed away another step. ''Why would you want me to do that? It won't make any sense.'' *Think, Ramey. Talk.* ''Jared and I aren't engaged. Someone will recognize the ring as being Sandy's.''

Having removed the wrapping, Jessica shoved it back into her tote. ''Yes. That would be good. A link between you two. Jared's collapse after learning that you'd betrayed him, too.''

''But I haven't. I love him.''

''I know you do. It would just be a matter of time before your head was turned, too, though. He can't help it. Everyone wants him.''

Michaele wasn't following this at all, and she was afraid to look around for something to use as a weapon herself for fear of prompting Jessica into attacking. ''Wants who, Jessica? I don't want anyone but Jared.''

Something hardened in the older woman's face. ''Don't lie to me. You and I were going to be good friends, but I could see how once I welcomed you into my home, you were no different from the others. Smiling at him. Touching him. He can't help it. It's not his fault that women misunderstand his compassion as something more.''

Garth? Good grief, she was talking about Garth…and Sandy? Oh, poor Jared. Wait—she'd said *women.*

''Jessica, are you saying that Faith had an affair with Garth?''

Hatred was a frightening mask on Jessica's face. ''She thought she was so clever, so irresistible. I'm ashamed to admit, I enjoyed fooling her into believing I was her friend.'' The cold smile vanished, replaced by sympathy. ''Not like you, Michaele. That's why I need your cooperation, because I don't want this to hurt. You blame Faith. If she'd been a good girl as she should have, I wouldn't have been put in this position, and neither would you.''

Michaele focused on the bloody knife again and tears filled her eyes. Faith was dead. She'd died as Sandy had died. As Michaele would now die.

"No." She sucked air into her lungs. "No, Jessica. Now you listen to me. Jared's due here any minute, and nothing you do to me will protect you from being found out. He'll know."

"You're wrong, because Jared is dead."

60

It seemed to take an hour for him to reach his gun. He was growing weaker by the minute from the loss of blood. And of all the stinking times to leave his f-ing phone in the car, Jared thought. But he hadn't planned to be here long because he hadn't guessed until too late that Jessica had a big problem.

And now she was on her way to Michaele.

Terror kept him moving, crawling inch by inch to the back door.

He heard something. A door slam. Although the pain was excruciating, he aimed at the door. If it was Jessica, he wasn't going to think twice about taking her down. He wasn't even going to ask.

The door opened.

"Jesus Christ!" Garth breathed the instant he spotted him. "Jared…? What happened? Where's Jessica? Jess!"

"Shut up. Help me to my car."

"Where's my wife, Morgan? My God, did you—"

"No, she did me." He coughed and the pain was almost enough to cause him to black out again. Just breathing was becoming an ordeal, and he figured that at the least he was fighting a collapsed lung. He didn't have much time. "Jess killed Sandy, and she's on her way to get Mike. Help me, damn you."

"You're out of your mind! My wife—"

"Knew you were fucking Sandy, asshole! Do I have to spell it out with my blood?"

All the color drained from Garth's face, but he quickly hoisted Jared up. Letting Jared use his body as a crutch, he half dragged, half carried him to the patrol car.

"You have to drive. Get me in there and then drive like hell."

"Where are we going?"

"Michaele's."

He closed his eyes, sick enough to puke. Hell, he wanted to die. Only the thought of Michaele going through this made him fight to hold on.

"Find phone. Dial—" Seeing Garth had located his phone, he told him the memory number programmed in that would connect him to Buddy. The station would be locked up now, and Buddy was the one on call tonight. Then he took the phone back. "Bud? Me. I'm hurt, man. On my way to Mike's house, but may not make it. Get there fast. Jess Powers—Jess Powers is going to kill Mike. Hurry. Get everybody and be careful. She's got a bitch of a knife."

He disconnected and fumbled for the first-aid box. Maybe if he could slow the flow of blood, he could last just long enough.

Garth took the turn onto Main hard. "Sorry," he muttered. "I'm sorry for all of it."

"Floor it and shut up."

"I didn't mean to get involved with Sandy. It just— happened. I was trying to end it when—"

"She was pregnant, you prick."

Garth choked. "I didn't know."

"Like it would have made any difference to you. You didn't give a shit about your wife, our friendship—it's all about you and your zipper, isn't it, pal?"

''But why Mike? I swear, I haven't touched her, Jared.''

''Because you did touch Faith, am I right?''

''It was nothing. Just a fling. She was planning on leaving town soon anyway. She didn't want a commitment any more than I did.''

''Shut the fuck up before I change my mind and shoot you here and now. You've made Jessica so crazy, she thinks if she gets rid of all the competition and witnesses to your indiscretions, you two can still live happily ever after.''

The effort to speak his mind triggered another racking series of coughs that in the end left him gasping for breath.

''Pray, you son of a bitch,'' he wheezed at last, aiming the automatic at Garth. ''Pray I get there in time to save her...'cause if not, you'll never have use for another woman again.''

61

Dead. Jared couldn't be dead. They'd just found each other.

"No," Michaele whispered. "No!"

She grabbed the kitchen chair nearest her and flung it at Jessica. Jess ducked, avoiding the worst of the blow, but her knife was caught in the leg braces and was torn from her hand.

As Jess bent to recover it, Michaele used the opportunity to search for something else. She snatched a platter, intent on hitting her over the head with it, but Jessica's instincts were good and she swung out of the way, sending the thing skimming off her back. And now Jessica was angry.

Michaele ran for the stairs. A third of the way up her right leg was yanked out from under her. Her chin and ribs hit the wood hard, but worse was the razor-like pain in her leg. She knew it was the knife slicing her calf.

She struggled, kicked and fought for a handhold to lift herself out of reach. The stronger of the two, Jessica took hold of her ankle and pulled her down.

"No! Jessica, please! The police will find out. They'll know."

"That Jared found out about you and Garth. He killed you in a jealous rage, and then came after Garth. But only I was home. We fought, but I managed to stop him."

"They won't believe you. It's your knife, Jessica. Jessica, think! There'll—there'll be trace evidence around here. Your hair. Something. I won't let you kill me without a fight. I'll make sure they know.''

''No, the town will be relieved that it's over, all the mysteries resolved. We'll all be so relieved, we'll accept, Michaele. Come down, now. Come down!''

It was beyond bizarre. She sounded like a frustrated schoolteacher.

Jessica made deeper contact with her next blow, which struck Michaele in her thigh. The pain too intense to deny; Michaele screamed and grabbed at her leg. Jessica dragged her down, down, down…

''Jessica, freeze!''

''Jess, for God's sake, stop!''

Having just pulled the knife out of Michaele's leg, Jessica glanced back at the three men in the kitchen doorway. For a moment she stared as though trying to figure out where they'd come from, but then she went limp. ''Garth…?''

Buddy Eagan, his gun aimed, eased up to her and easily plucked the knife from her unresisting grasp. Then he backed away.

''Mike, honey?'' Buddy shot her a quick glance and winced. ''How bad are you hurt? Can you get down the rest of the way by yourself? Ease yourself out of there, hon. I'm gonna cuff her and she won't hurt you any more.''

Relief drained her of everything, including fear of Jessica…until the moment she saw Jared, blood-soaked, near collapse, standing only because of the wall, staring at her the way she stared at him. Mouthing his name, she started down the stairs. As he started sinking to the floor, she tried to run to him, and tumbled the rest of the way.

Ignoring Buddy's epithet and slapping away Garth's

hands as he offered help, she crawled. Just as she reached Jared, Bruce and Red burst in through the kitchen door, but all she focused on was Jared's outstretched hand.

The instant she grabbed it, his head fell forward against his chest.

62

Jared felt better when he gripped Michaele's hand. Although her leg wounds were healing well, there'd been some muscle and tendon damage, and occasionally it still gave, even under her slight weight. His heart didn't need the shock of seeing her toppling off this dock into Lake Sawyer, and his doctor would read him the riot act if he did any more damage to his lungs or anything else by diving in after her.

"Not enjoying the party?" he murmured. Behind them someone had pulled out a guitar and a small group of picnickers were beginning to sing. Children were laughing and screaming on the swing sets and seesaws, and down by the swimming area, others were cavorting in the water. The scent of grilling hot dogs and hamburgers seasoned the early Texas evening, and the sunset, although three or four hours away, was promising to be a beauty because there wasn't a cloud in the sky. This was, ostensibly, the chamber of commerce's Member Appreciation Picnic, but Loyal had admitted that the two of them were everybody's vote as guests of honor.

"I feel like next Thanksgiving's turkey," she muttered. "Everybody's trying to fatten me up."

"Well, you know how folks are—if they can't find the words, they'll love you to death with food." But he understood her inability to take anything at face value. It was the same for him. He doubted either of them would ever take anything for granted again.

The last month had been a stressful one for the entire community. As the news about Jessica had spread, and the truth about Garth and the rest came out, it had left no one unaffected. Garth's quick "voluntary" resignation had been accepted by the Board of Education. Rumor had it that between job-hunting trips and waiting for the results of Jessica's psychological evaluation to be completed to see if she would be able to stand trial for both Sandy's and Faith's murders, he had been in Dallas in the company of a wealthy blond divorcée.

The word from the DA regarding Jessica's tests was that it appeared she would stand trial—and it would be on two counts of murder. While Jessica had been uncooperative in helping to locate Faith's remains, a timber company near where Jared had turned around that first night had been harvesting pine, and a week after Jessica's arrest a dozer found Faith's shallow grave.

The funeral, earlier this week, had been both painful and a relief. Jared had only gotten out of the hospital two days ago, and Michaele had been cussing up a storm over the crutches she'd been forced to use until just days prior to that. The service had been private—the two of them and his men, who'd asked Michaele personally if they could attend. She'd been deeply moved by that; still, she'd saved her tears for when they got home, where she'd collapsed in his arms, sobbing so hard that tears had bled through his tightly shut eyes, too.

She'd been subdued ever since. But then, considering their worry about each other's injuries and their indecision about their future in Split Creek, that was understandable. The town wanted to know their plans, too, and this picnic was Loyal and company's way of asking for a clue—or, hopefully, another chance.

"I hear Dillon and Willow may show up later for the fireworks," she said, leaning her head against his shoulder.

Relieved that he would, indeed, escape prosecution by the DA, Hancock had put Last Writes up for sale and lucked out by quickly finding a buyer. The middle-aged couple had great plans for the store, including a name change, and the community was breathing a second sigh of relief. Just the other day Harold Bean's attorney had won a change of venue moving his trial to Dallas. Now not only would Wood County not be burdened with more debt, its citizens wouldn't be obliged to put one of their own behind bars.

"So the Hancocks are really leaving for California in the morning?"

"Yeah. It's for the best, but I'll still miss Dillon."

Jared kissed the top of her head, which was warm from the sunshine. "Then I'll go out of my way to be nice. Well...nice to Willow and polite to him."

"I have other news."

She sounded so somber, he drew a careful breath to prepare himself. "You don't get to change your mind about marrying me, Mike. I'll turn in my resignation to-morrow, I'll put the house on the market, and you can sign up for classes at the same school Willow's going to attend, or in Topeka, or wherever you want. But you promised."

He'd formally proposed the minute he'd regained con-sciousness, and she had said yes, on the condition there be no engagement ring, and that they wait a month or so.

There had been so much heavy stuff going on, she'd reasoned, and it shouldn't cast a shadow on what should be a day of new beginnings. She was right, of course, but if he couldn't see his ring on her finger in the interim, he wanted the vows and that piece of paper soon, damn it.

"That's right, Morgan, get yourself all wound up and reinjure yourself. I don't mind waiting another month before we can make love."

Groaning over the reminder of the restriction that had been sheer hell, but which would come to an end Monday after his next appointment—if his doc knew what was good for him—Jared lifted her hand to his lips for an impassioned kiss. "Then stop scaring me and tell me what else is up."

"That young guy, the mechanic who called the other day stopped by the station."

Jared held her hand to his heart. He remembered the call—from a nephew of the guy, Woody, who'd taught Michaele about cars. Woody had heard about the family tragedy on the news and had suggested his nephew get in touch.

"And?"

"He's serious. Wants his own place, but he's got a new family and little money."

"Guess you could carry his note. You'd actually sell the station?"

"Do you want to leave Split Creek?"

"Do you?" he asked.

She continued to gaze out at the water. "Pete Fite found a pup half starved in the woods the other day. Cute as anything. It's going to need a home because Pete's got too many dogs as it is."

Jared gently took hold of Michaele's chin and forced her to meet his gaze. "You've never had a dog." She'd once told him that Buck had beaten one to death, and she'd never wanted anything around her father that didn't stand a chance of defending itself.

"But didn't you say something about getting one?"

"Uh-huh. What about the guy?"

"Yeah, well...he'd do better with a partner. At least for a few years. It's tough to attempt any kind of expansion if you're doing everything on your own."

"Exhausting." Jared began to smile.

"Don't laugh at me."

"You want to stay."

"And take the dog?" she asked.

"Maybe even add a cat."

"Umm...whatever comes along."

His heart lurched. Jared drew her completely into his arms. "Look at me, Michaele."

Sure enough, it was there. Her lovely eyes were bright with love, and hope. She might still be too gun-shy to say words like *family* or *baby,* but it was coming. Oh, yeah, he could see it was coming.

"On one condition," he said thickly. "You have to marry me before the dog moves in."

"God, I love you, you big negotiator. I was afraid you were going to ask me to go straight home and throw away my birth control pills before I even find out if they work."

Laughing softly, he kissed her. "I can wait. I can wait."

Because she was right. A lot had been lost, but this was still a good place. A fine place to make a new life.